Bold Piracy

and Adventure

on the High Seas

I was searching her cabin when she opened the door and caught me. I let the mink drop into place and pulled the wardrobe door to. "You shouldn't startle people like that," I said reproachfully. "You should have knocked."

"I should have—" Her mouth tightened; she still wasn't amused. "What were you going to do with that coat?"

"Nothing. I never wear mink, Miss Beresford. It doesn't suit me." I smiled, but she didn't. "I can explain."

"I'm sure you can." She shook her head, then gave me an up-from-under look with those startling green eyes. "I can picture many things, Mr. Carter, but one thing I can't visualize is our worthy chief officer taking off from some deserted island in a ship's lifeboat with my mink in the stern sheets."

"You're right," I admitted. "I wasn't looking for your mink. I am looking for a man. A man who is missing. A man who may be hurt. Or dead."

Fawcett Books
by Alistair MacLean:

ATHABASCA
BEAR ISLAND
THE BLACK SHRIKE
BREAKHEART PASS
CARAVAN TO VACCARES
CIRCUS
FEAR IS THE KEY
FLOODGATE
FORCE 10 FROM NAVARONE
THE GOLDEN GATE
THE GOLDEN RENDEZVOUS
GOODBYE CALIFORNIA
THE GUNS OF NAVARONE
H.M.S. ULYSSES
ICE STATION ZEBRA
NIGHT WITHOUT END
PARTISANS
PUPPET ON A CHAIN
RIVER OF DEATH
SAN ANDREAS
THE SATAN BUG
SEAWITCH
THE SECRET WAYS
SOUTH BY JAVA HEAD
THE WAY TO DUSTY DEATH
WHEN EIGHT BELLS TOLL
WHERE EAGLES DARE

Alistair MacLean

The
Golden
Rendezvous

FAWCETT CREST • NEW YORK

The
Golden
Rendezvous

Chapter 1

MY SHIRT was no longer a shirt but just a limp and sticky rag soaked with sweat. My feet ached from the fierce heat of the steel deck plates. My forehead, under the peaked white cap, ached from the ever-increasing constriction of the leather band that made scalping only a matter of time. My eyes ached from the steely glitter of reflected sunlight from metal, water, and whitewashed harbour buildings. And my throat ached, from pure thirst. I was acutely unhappy.

I was unhappy. The crew was unhappy. The passengers were unhappy. Captain Bullen was unhappy and this last made me doubly unhappy, not because of any tenderness of feeling that I entertained towards the captain, but because when things went wrong with Captain Bullen he invariably took it out of his chief officer. I was his chief officer.

I was bending over the rail, listening to the creak of wire and wood and watching our after jumbo derrick take the strain as it lifted a particularly large crate from the quayside, when a hand touched my arm. Captain Bullen again, I thought drearily; it had been at least half an hour since he'd been around last to talk to me about my short-comings, and then I realised that, whatever the captain's caprices, wearing Chanel No. 5 wasn't one of them. This would be Miss Beresford.

And it was. In addition to the Chanel she was wearing a white silk dress and that quizzical, half-amused smile that made most of the other officers turn mental cartwheels and handsprings but served only to irritate me. I have my weaknesses, but tall, cool, sophisticated, and worldly young women with a slightly malicious sense of humour is not one of them.

"Good afternoon, Mr. First Officer," she said sweetly. She had a soft, musical voice with hardly a hint of superiority or condescension when talking to the lower orders like myself, just enough to show that she had been to the best school and college in the East and I hadn't. "We've been wondering where you were. *You* are not usually an absentee at apéritif time."

"I know, Miss Beresford. I'm sorry." What she said was true enough; what she didn't know was that I turned up for apéritifs with the passengers more or less at the point of a gun. Standing company orders stated that it was as much a part of the ship's officers' duties to entertain the passengers as to sail the ship, and as Captain Bullen loathed all passengers with a fierce and total loathing, he saw to it that most of the entertaining fell to me. I nodded at the big crate now hovering over the hatchway of number four hold, then at the piled-up crates at the quayside. "I'm afraid I have work to do. Four or five hours at least. Can't even manage lunch to-day, far less an apéritif."

"Not Miss Beresford. Susan." It was as if she had heard only my first few words. "How often do I have to ask you?"

Until we reach New York, I said to myself, and even then it will be no use. Aloud I said, smiling, "You mustn't make things difficult for me. Regulations require that we treat all passengers with courtesy, consideration, and respect." And self-respect made me resent the young and unmarried female passengers who regarded me as a source of idle amusement for their all too many idle hours; particularly was this true with rich young idle females—and it was common knowledge that Julius A. Beresford required the full-time services of a whole corps of accountants just to tot up his annual profits. "Especially with respect, Miss Beresford," I finished.

"You're hopeless." She laughed. I was too tiny a pebble to cause even a ripple in her smiling pool of complacency. "And no lunch, you poor man. I thought you were looking pretty glum as I came along." She glanced at the winch driver, then at the seamen manhandling the suspended crate into position on the floor of the hold. "Your men don't seem too pleased at the prospect either. They *are* a morose-looking lot."

I eyed them briefly. They *were* a morose-looking lot.

"Oh, they'll be spelled for food all right. It's just that they have their own private worries. It must be about a hundred and ten down in that hold there, and it's an almost unwritten law that white crews should not work in the afternoons in the tropics. Besides, they're all still brooding darkly over the losses they've suffered. Don't forget that it's less than seventy-two hours since they had that brush with the customs down in Jamaica."

Brush, I thought, was good: in what might very accurately be described as one fell swoop the customs had confiscated from about forty crew members no fewer than twenty-five thousand cigarettes and over two hundred bottles of hard liquor that should have been placed on the ship's bond before arrival in Jamaican waters. That the liquor had not been placed in bond was understandable enough as the crew were expressly forbidden to have any in their quarters in the first place; that not even the cigarettes had been placed in bond had been due to the crew's intention of following their customary practice of smuggling both liquor and tobacco ashore and disposing of them at a handsome profit to Jamaicans more than willing to pay a high price for the luxury of duty-free Kentucky bourbon and American cigarettes. But then, the crew had not been to know that, for the first time in its five years' service on the West Indian run, the S.S. *Campari* was to be searched from stem to stern with a thorough ruthlessness that spared nothing that came in its path, a high and searching wind that swept the ship clean as a whistle. It had been a black day.

And so was this. Even as Miss Beresford was patting me consolingly on the arm and murmuring a few farewell words of sympathy which didn't go any too well with the twinkle in her eyes, I caught sight of Captain Bullen perched on top of the companionway leading down from the main deck. "Glowering" would probably be the most apt term to describe the expression on his face. As he came down the companionway and passed Miss Beresford he made a heroic effort to twist his features into the semblance of a smile and managed to hold it for all of two seconds until he had passed her by, then got back to his glowering again. For a man who is dressed in gleaming whites from top to toe to give the impression of a black approaching thundercloud is no small feat, but Captain Bullen managed it without any trouble. He was a big man, six feet two and very heavily built, with sandy hair and eyebrows, a smooth red face that no amount of sun could ever tan, and a clear blue eye that no amount of whisky could ever dim. He looked at the quayside, the hold, and then at me, all with the same impartial disfavour.

"Well, Mister," he said heavily. "How's it going? Miss Beresford giving you a hand, eh?" When he was in a bad mood, it was invariably "Mister"; in a neutral mood, it was "First"; and when in a good temper—which, to be fair, was most of the time—it was always "Johnny-me-boy." But to-day it was "Mister." I took my guard accordingly and ignored the implied reproof of time-wasting. He would be gruffly apologetic the next day. He always was.

"Not too bad, sir. Bit slow on the dockside." I nodded to where a group of men, some bearded, all wearing denim trousers and vaguely military-looking shirts, were struggling to attach chain slings to a crate that must have been at least eighteen feet in length by six square. "I don't think the Carracio stevedores are accustomed to handling such heavy lifts."

He took a good look.

"They couldn't handle a damned wheelbarrow," he snapped eventually. "Never seen such fumble-handed incompetence in my blasted life. First time in this stinking flea-ridden hellhole"—Carracio was actually one of the cleanest and most picturesquely beautiful ports in the Caribbean—"and I hope to heaven it's the last. Can you manage it by six, Mister?" Six o'clock was an hour past the top of the tide, and we had to clear the harbour-entrance sand bar by then or wait another ten hours.

"I think so, sir," and then, to take his mind off his troubles, and also because I was curious, I asked, "What are in those crates? Motorcars?"

"Motorcars? Are you mad?" His cold blue eye swept over the whitewashed jumble of the little town and the dark green of the steeply rising forested hills behind. "This lot couldn't build a rabbit hutch for export, far less a motorcar. Machinery. So the bills of lading say. Dynamos, generators, refrigerating, air-conditioning, and refining machinery. For New York."

"Do you mean to tell me," I said, carefully, "that the generalissimo, having successfully completed the confiscation of all the American sugar-refining mills, is now dismantling them and selling the machinery back to the Americans? Barefaced theft like that?"

"Petty larceny on the part of the individual is theft," Captain Bullen said morosely. "When governments engage in grand larceny, it's economics. Oh, it'll be all perfectly legal, I've no doubt, but it still doesn't make me feel less of a contraband runner. But if we don't do it, someone else will. And the freight rate's double the normal."

"Which makes the generalissimo and his government pretty desperate for money?"

"What do you think?" Bullen growled. "No one knows how many were killed in the capital and a dozen other towns in Tuesday's hunger riots. Jamaican authorities reckon the number in hundreds. Since they turfed out most foreigners and closed down or confiscated nearly all foreign businesses they haven't been able to earn a penny abroad. The coffers of the revolution are as empty as a drum. Man's completely desperate for money."

He turned away and stood staring over the harbour, big hands wide-spaced on the guardrail, his back ramrod-stiff. He seemed in no hurry to go—and aimless loitering was no part of Captain Bullen's life. He was always in a hurry. I recognised the signs; after three years of sailing with him, it would have been impossible not to. There was something he wanted to say; there was some steam he wanted to blow off, and no better outlet than that tried and trusty relief valve, Chief Officer Carter. Only whenever he wished to blow off steam it was a matter of personal pride with him never to bring up the matter himself. It was no great trick to guess what was troubling him, so I obliged.

I said, conversationally, "The cables we sent to London, sir." They had been sent by the captain himself, but the "we" would spread the load if things had gone wrong, as they almost certainly had. "Any reply to them yet?"

"Just ten minutes ago." He turned round casually as if the matter had really slipped his memory, but the slight purpling tinge in the red face betrayed him, and there was nothing casual about his voice when he went on: "Slapped me down, Mister, that's what they did. Slapped me down. My own company. And the Ministry of Transport. Both of them. Told me to forget about it, said my protests were completely out of order, warned me of the consequences of future lack of co-operation with the appropriate authorities, whatever the hell appropriate authorities might be. Me! My own company! Thirty-five years I've sailed with the Blue Mail Line and now . . . and now . . ." His fists clenched and his voice choked into fuming silence.

"So there was someone bringing very heavy pressure to bear, after all," I murmured.

"There was, Mister, there was." The cold blue eyes were very cold indeed and the big hands opened wide, then closed, tight, till the ivory showed. Bullen was a captain, but he was more than that: he was the Commodore of the Blue Mail fleet, and even the Board of Directors walk softly when the Fleet Commodore is around; at least they don't treat him like an office boy. He went on softly: "If ever I get my hands on Dr. Slingsby Caroline, I'll break his bloody neck."

Captain Bullen would have loved to get his hands on the oddly named Dr. Slingsby Caroline. Tens of thousands of police, government agents, and American servicemen engaged in the hunt for him would also have loved to get their hands on him. So would millions of ordinary citizens if for no other reason than the excellent one that there was a reward of $50,000 for information leading to his capture. But the interest of Captain Bullen and the crew of the *Campari* was even more personal: the missing man was very much the root of all our troubles.

Dr. Slingsby Caroline had vanished, appropriately enough, in South Carolina. He had worked at a U. S. Government's very hush-hush Weapons Research Establishment south of the town of Columbia, an establishment concerned with the evolving, as had only become known in the past week or so, of some sort of small fission weapon for use by either fighter planes or mobile rocket launchers in local tactical nuclear wars. As nuclear weapons went, it was the veriest bagatelle compared to the five megaton monsters already developed by both the United States and Russia, developing barely one-thousandth of the explosive power of those and hardly capable of devastating more than a square mile of territory. Still, with the explosive potential of five thousand tons of T.N.T., it was no toy.

Then, one day—night, to be precise—Dr. Slingsby Caroline had vanished. As he was the Director of the Research Establishment, this was serious enough, but what was even more dismaying was that he had taken the working prototype with him. He had apparently been surprised by two of the night guards at the plant and had killed them both, presumably with a silenced weapon, since no one heard or suspected anything amiss. He had driven through the plant gates about ten o'clock at night at the wheel of his own blue Chevrolet station wagon; the guards at the gate, recognising both the car and their own chief and knowing that he habitually worked until a late hour, had waved him on without a second glance. And that was the last anyone had ever seen of Dr. Caroline or the Twister, as the weapon, for some obscure reason, had been named. But it wasn't the last that was seen of the blue

Chevrolet. That had been discovered abandoned outside the port of Savannah, some nine hours after the crime had been committed, but less than an hour after it had been discovered, which showed pretty smart police work on someone's part.

And it had been just our evil luck that the S.S. *Campari* had called in at Savannah on the afternoon of the day the crime had been committed.

Within an hour of the discovery of the two dead guards in the research establishment, all interstate and foreign air and sea traffic in the southeastern United States had been halted. As from seven o'clock in the morning all planes were grounded until they had been rigorously searched; as from seven o'clock police stopped and examined every truck crossing a state border; and, of course, everything larger than a rowing boat was forbidden to put out to sea. Unfortunately for the authorities in general and us in particular, the S.S. *Campari* had sailed from Savannah at six o'clock that morning. Automatically the *Campari* became very, very "hot," the number one suspect for the getaway.

The first radio call came through at 8:30 A.M. Would Captain Bullen return immediately to Savannah? The captain, no beater about the bush, asked why the hell he should. He was told that it was desperately urgent that he return at once. Not, replied the captain, unless they gave him a very compelling reason indeed. They refused to give him a reason and Captain Bullen refused to return. Deadlock. Then, because they hadn't much option, the federal authorities, who had already taken over from the state, gave him the facts.

Captain Bullen asked for more facts. He asked for a description of the missing scientist and weapon, and he'd soon find out for himself whether or not they were on board. Followed a fifteen-minute delay, no doubt necessary to secure the release of top classified information, then the descriptions were reluctantly given.

There was a curious similarity between the two descriptions. Both the Twister and Dr. Caroline were exactly seventy-five inches in length. Both were very thin, the weapon being only eleven inches in diameter. The doctor weighed 180 pounds, the Twister 280. The Twister was covered in a one-piece sheath of polished anodised aluminium, the doctor in a two-piece grey gabardine. The Twister's head was covered by a grey Pyroceram nose cap, the doctor's by black hair with a telltale lock of grey in the centre.

The orders for the doctor were to identify and apprehend, for the Twister to identify but do not, repeat, *do not* touch. The weapon should be completely stable and safe, and normally it would take one of the only two experts who were as yet sufficiently acquainted with it at least ten minutes to arm it; but no one could guess what effect might have been had upon the Twister's delicate mechanism by the jolting it might have suffered in transit.

Three hours later Captain Bullen was able to report with complete certainty that neither the missing scientist nor weapon was aboard. Intensive would be a poor word to describe that search; every square foot between the chain locker and steering compartment was searched and searched again. Captain Bullen had radioed the federal authorities and then forgotten about it, or would have forgotten about it were it not that twice in the following two nights our radarscope had shown a mysterious vessel, without navigation lights, closing up from astern, then vanishing before dawn. And then we arrived at our most southerly port of call, Kingston, in Jamaica.

And in Kingston the blow had fallen. We had no sooner arrived than the harbour authorities had come on board requesting that a search party from the American destroyer lying almost alongside be allowed to examine the *Campari*. Our friend on the radarscope, without a doubt. The search party, about forty of them, was already lined up on the deck of the destroyer.

They were still there four hours later. Captain Bullen, in a few simple, well-chosen words that had carried far and clear over the sunlit waters of Kingston Harbour, had told the authorities that if the United States Navy proposed, in broad daylight, to board a British Mercantile Marine vessel in a British harbour, then they were welcome to try. They were also welcome, he had added, to suffer, apart from the injuries and the loss of blood they would incur in the process, the very heavy penalties which would be imposed by an international court of maritime law arising from charges ranging from assault, through piracy, to an act of war, which maritime court, Captain Bullen had added pointedly, had its seat, not in Washington, D.C., but in The Hague, Holland.

This stopped them cold. The authorities withdrew to consult with the Americans. Coded cables, we learnt later, were exchanged with Washington and London. Captain Bullen remained adamant. Our passengers, 90 per cent of them Americans, gave him their enthusiastic support. Messages were received from both the company head office and the Ministry of Transport requiring Captain Bullen to co-operate with the United States Navy. Pressure was being brought to bear. Bullen tore the messages up, seized the offer of the local Marconi agent to give the radio equipment an overdue checkup as a heaven-sent excuse to take the wireless officers off watch, and told the quartermaster at the gangway to accept no more messages.

And so it had continued for all of thirty hours. And, because troubles never come singly, it was on the morning following our arrival that the Harrisons and Curtises, related families who occupied the forward two suites on "A" deck, received cables with the shocking news that members of both families had been fatally involved in a car crash and left that afternoon. Black gloom hung heavy over the *Campari*.

Towards evening the deadlock was broken by the skipper of the American destroyer, a diplomatic, courteous, and thoroughly embarrassed commander by the name of Varsi. He had been allowed aboard the *Campari*, been gruffly asked into Bullen's day cabin, accepted a drink, been very apologetic and respectful, and suggested a way out of the dilemma. He said he knew how intolerable it must be for a senior captain to have doubt thrown not only on his ability to carry out a proper search; for his own part of it, he was thoroughly disgusted with the whole assignment.

He had, Commander Varsi had pointed out almost despairingly, to carry out his orders, but how would it be if he and Captain Bullen put their own interpretation on those orders? How would it be if the search were carried out, not by his own men, but by British Customs officials in the regular course of their duty, with his men present solely in the capacity of observers and under the strictest instructions not to touch anything? Captain Bullen, after much outraged humming and hawing, had finally agreed. Not only did this suggestion save face and salvage honour to a certain degree, but he was in an impossible position anyway, and he knew it. Until the search was completed, the Kingston authorities refused medical clearance, and until he had this clearance, it would be impossible to unload the six hundred tons of food and machinery he had for delivery there. And the port officials could also make things very difficult indeed by refusing clearance papers to sail.

And so what seemed like every customs official in Jamaica was routed out and the search began at 9 P.M. It lasted until 2 A.M. the following morning. Captain Bullen fumed as steadily and sulphurously as a volcano about to erupt. The passengers fumed, partly because of having to suffer the indignity of having their cabins so meticulously searched, partly because of being kept out of their beds until the early hours of the morning. And, above all, the crew fumed because, on this occasion, even the normally tolerant customs were forced to take note of the hundreds of bottles of liquor and thousands of cigarettes uncovered by their search.

Nothing else, of course, was found. Apologies were offered and ignored. Medical clearance was given and unloading began: we left Kingston late that night. For all of the following twenty-four hours Captain Bullen had brooded over the recent happenings, then had sent off a couple of cablegrams, one to the head office in London, the other to the Ministry of Transport, telling them what he, Captain Bullen, thought of them. I had seen the cables and they really had been something: not very wise, perhaps, but better than having the threatened apoplectic seizure. And now, it seemed, they in turn had told Captain Bullen what they thought of him. I could understand his feelings about Dr. Slingsby Caroline, who was probably in China by this time.

A high-pitched shout of warning brought us both sharply to the present and what was going on around us. One of the two chain slings round the big crate now poised exactly over the hatchway to number four hold had suddenly come adrift, one end of the crate dropping down through an angle of 60° and bringing up with a jerking jolt that made even the big jumbo derrick shake and quiver with the strain. The chances were good that the crate would now slip through the remaining sling and crash down on to the floor of the hold far below, which is probably what would have happened if two of the crew holding on to a corner guiding rope hadn't been quick-witted enough to throw all their weight on to it and so prevent the crane from tilting over at too steep an angle and sliding free. But even as it was it was still touch and go.

The crate swung back towards the side of the ship, the two men on the guide rope still hanging on desperately. I caught a glimpse of the stevedores on the quayside below, their faces twisted into expressions of frozen panic: in the new people's democracy, where all men were free and equal, the penalty for this sort of carelessness was probably the firing squad; nothing else could have accounted for their otherwise inexplicable genuine terror. The crate began to swing back over the hold. I yelled to the men beneath to run clear and simultaneously gave the signal for emergency lowering. The winchman, fortunately, was as quick-witted as he was experienced, and as the wildly careening crate swung jerkily back to dead centre he lowered away at two or three times the normal speed, braking just seconds before the lowermost corner of the crate crunched and splintered against the floor of the hold. Moments later the entire length of the crate was resting on the bottom.

Captain Bullen fished a handkerchief from his drills, removed his gold-braided cap, and slowly mopped his sandy hair and sweating brow. He appeared to be communing with himself.

"This," he said finally, "is the bloody end. Captain

Bullen in the doghouse. The crew sore as hell. The passengers hopping mad. Two days behind schedule. Searched by the Americans from truck to keelson like a contraband runner. Now probably carrying contraband. No sign of the latest bunch of passengers. Got to clear the harbour bar by six. And now this band of madmen trying to send us to the bottom. A man can stand so much, First, just so much." He replaced his cap. "Shakespeare had something to say about this, First."

"A sea of troubles, sir?"

"No, something else. But apt enough." He sighed. "Get the second officer to relieve you. Third's checking stores. Get the fourth—no, not that blithering nincompoop—get the bo'sun—he talks Spanish like a native anyway—to take over on the shore side. Any objections and that's the last piece of cargo we load. Then you and I are having lunch, First."

"I told Miss Beresford that I wouldn't—"

"If you think," Captain Bullen interrupted heavily, "that I'm going to listen to that bunch jangling their moneybags and bemoaning their hard lot from hors d'oeuvres right through to coffee, you must be out of your mind. We'll have it in my cabin."

And so we had it in his cabin. It was the usual *Campari* meal, something for even the most blasé epicure to dream about, and Captain Bullen, for once and understandably, made an exception to his rule that neither he nor his officers should drink with lunch. By the time the meal was over he was feeling almost human again and once went so far as to call me "Johnny-me-boy." It wouldn't last. But it was all pleasant enough, and it was with reluctance that I finally quit the air-conditioned coolness of the captain's day cabin for the blazing sunshine outside to relieve the second officer.

He smiled widely as I approached number four hold. Tommy Wilson was always smiling. He was a dark, wiry Welshman of middle height, with an infectious grin and an immense zest for life, no matter what came his way. Nothing was too much trouble for Tommy and nothing ever got him down. Nothing, that is, except mathematics: his weakness in that department had already cost him his master's ticket. But he was that rare combination of an outstanding seaman and a tremendous social asset on a passenger ship, and it was for these reasons that Captain Bullen had insisted on having him aboard.

"How's it going?" I asked.

"You can see for yourself." He waved a complacent hand towards the pile of stacked crates on the quayside, now diminished by a good third since I had seen it last. "Speed allied with efficiency. When Wilson is on the job let no man ever—"

"The bo'sun's name is MacDonald, not Wilson," I said.

"So it is." He laughed, glanced down to where the bo'sun, a big, tough, infinitely competent Hebridean Islander was haranguing the bearded stevedores, and shook his head admiringly. "I wish I could understand what he's saying."

"Translation would be superfluous," I said, drily. "I'll take over. Old man wants you to go ashore."

"Ashore?" His face lit up; in two short years the second's shore-going exploits had already passed into the realms of legend. "Let no man ever say that Wilson ignored duty's call. Twenty minutes for a shower, shave and shake out the number ones—"

"The agent's offices are just beyond the dock gates," I interrupted. "You can go as you are. Find out what's happened to our latest passengers. Captain's beginning to worry about them; if they're not here by five o'clock he's sailing without them. Way he's feeling now, he'd just as soon do that. If the agent doesn't know, tell him to find out. Fast."

Wilson left. The sun started westering, but the heat stayed as it was. Thanks to MacDonald's competence and uninhibited command of the Spanish language, the cargo on the quayside steadily and rapidly diminished. Wilson returned to report no sign of our passengers. Their baggage had arrived two days previously and, although only for five people, was enough, Wilson said, to fill a couple of railroad trucks. About the passengers, the agent had been very nervous indeed. They were very important people, señor, very, very important. One of them was the most important man in the whole province of Camafuegos. A jeep had already been dispatched westwards along the coast road to look for them. It sometimes happened, the señor understood, that a car spring would go or a shock absorber snap. When Wilson had innocently inquired if this was because the revolutionary government had no money left to pay for the filling in of the enormous potholes in the roads, the agent had become even more nervous and said indignantly that it was entirely the fault of the inferior metal those perfidious Americanos used in the construction of their vehicles. Wilson said he had left with the impression that Detroit had a special assembly line exclusively devoted to turning out deliberately inferior cars destined solely for this particular corner of the Caribbean.

Wilson went away. The cargo continued to move steadily into number four hold. About four o'clock in the afternoon I heard the sound of the clashing of gears and the asthmatic wheezing of what sounded like a very elderly engine indeed. This, I thought, would be the passengers at last, but no; what clanked into view round the corner of the dock gate was a dilapidated truck with hardly a shred of paint left on the bodywork, white canvas showing on the tyres, and the engine hood removed to reveal what looked, from my elevation, like a solid block of rust. One of the special Detroit jobs probably. On its cracked and splintered platform it carried three medium-sized crates, freshly boxed and metal-banded.

Wrapped in a blue haze from the staccato backfiring of its exhaust, vibrating like a broken tuning fork and rattling in every bolt in its superannuated chassis, the truck trundled heavily across the cobbles and pulled up not five paces from where MacDonald was standing. A little man in white ducks and peaked cap jumped out through the space where the door ought to have been, stood still for a couple of seconds until he got the hang of terra firma again, and then scuttled off in the direction of our gangway. I recognised him as our Carracio agent, the one with the low opinion of Detroit, and wondered what fresh trouble he was bringing with him.

I found out in three minutes flat when Captain Bullen appeared on deck, an anxious-looking agent scurrying along behind him. The captain's blue eyes were snapping; the red complexion was overlaid with puce, but he had the safety valve screwed right down.

"Coffins, Mister," he said tightly. "Coffins, no less."

I suppose there is a quick and clever answer to a conversational gambit like that, but I couldn't find it, so I said politely, "Coffins, sir?"

"Coffins, Mister. Not empty, either. For shipment to New York." He flourished some papers. "Authorizations, shipping notes, everything in order. Including a sealed request signed by no less than the ambassador. Three of them. Two British, one American subject. Killed in the hunger riots."

"The crew won't like it, sir," I said. "Especially the Goanese stewards. You know their superstitions and how——"

"It will be all right, señor," the little man in white broke in hurriedly. Wilson had been right about the nervousness, but there was more to it than that; there was a strange overlay of anxiety that came close to despair. "We have arranged——"

"Shut up!" Captain Bullen said shortly. "No need for the crew to know, Mister. Or the passengers." You could see they were just a careless afterthought. "Coffins are boxed—that's them on the truck there."

"Yes, sir. Killed in the riots. Last week." I paused and went on delicately: "In this heat——"

"Lead-lined, he says. So they can go in the hold Some separate corner, Mister. One of the—um—deceased is a relative of one of the passengers boarding here. Wouldn't do to stack the coffins among the dynamos, I suppose." He sighed heavily. "On top of everything else, we're now in the funeral-undertaking business. Life, First, can hold no more."

"You are accepting this—ah—cargo, sir?"

"But of course, but of course," the little man interrupted

again. "One of them is a cousin of Señor Carreras, who sails with you. Señor Miguel Carreras. Señor Carreras, he is what you say, heartbroken. Señor Carreras is the most important man—"

"Be quiet," Captain Bullen said wearily. He made a gesture with the papers. "Yes, I'm accepting. Note from the ambassador. More pressure. I've had enough of cables flying across the Atlantic. Too much grief. Just an old beaten man, First, just an old beaten man." He stood there for a moment, hands outspread on the guardrail, doing his best to look like an old beaten man and making a singularly unsuccessful job of it, then straightened abruptly as a procession of vehicles turned in through the dock gates and made for the *Campari*. "A pound to a penny, Mister, here comes still more grief."

"Praise be to God," the little agent murmured The tone, no less than the words, was a prayer of thanksgiving. "Señor Carreras himself! Your passengers at last, Captain."

"That's what I said," Bullen growled. "More grief." The little man looked at him in puzzlement, as well as might anyone who didn't understand Bullen's attitude towards the passengers, then turned and hurried off towards the gangway. My attention was diverted for a few moments by another crate swinging aboard, then I heard Captain Bullen saying softly and feelingly, "Like I said, Mister, more grief."

The procession, two big, chauffeur-driven prewar Packards, one towed by a jeep, had just pulled up by the gangway and the passengers were climbing out. Those who could, that was—for very obviously there was one who could not. One of the chauffeurs, dressed in green tropical drills and a bush hat, had opened the boot of his car, pulled out a collapsible hand-propelled wheel chair, and, with the smooth efficiency of experience, had it assembled in ten seconds flat, while the other chauffeur, with the aid of a tall, thin nurse clad in over-all white from her smartly starched cap to the skirt that reached close down to her ankles, tenderly lifted a bent old man from the back seat of the second Packard and set him gently in the wheel chair. The old boy—even at that distance I could see the face creased and trenched with the lines of age, the snowy whiteness of the still plentiful hair—did his best to help them, but his best wasn't very much.

Captain Bullen looked at me. I looked at Captain Bullen. There didn't seem to be any reason to say anything. Nobody in a crew likes having permanent invalids aboard ship: they cause trouble to the ship's doctor who has to look after their health, to the cabin stewards who have to clean their quarters, to the dining-room stewards who have to feed them, and to those members of the deck crew detailed for the duty of moving them around. And when the invalids are elderly and very infirm—and if this one wasn't I sadly missed my guess—there was always the chance of a death at sea, the one thing sailors hate above all else. It was also very bad for the passenger trade But as long as the illness was of neither a contagious nor infectious nature and that a certificate could be produced from the invalid's own doctor to the effect that the invalid was fit for the proposed voyage, there was nothing that could be done about it.

"Well," Captain Bullen said heavily, "I suppose I'd better go and welcome our latest guests aboard. Finish it off as quickly as possible, Mister."

"I'll do that, sir."

Bullen nodded and left. I watched the two chauffeurs slide a couple of poles under the seat of the invalid chair, straighten and carry the chair easily up the sparred foot planks of the gangway. They were followed by the tall angular nurse and she in turn by another nurse, dressed exactly like the first, but shorter and stockier. The old boy was bringing his own medical corps along with him, which meant that he had more money than was good for him or was a hypochondriac or very far through indeed or a combination of any or all of those; on the credit side was the fact that both had that indefinable competent no-nonsense look of the professional nurse which would make the lot of our ship's surgeon, old Dr. Marston, who sometimes had to work a whole hour in one day, all that much easier.

But I was more interested in the last two people to climb out of the Packards.

The first was a man of about my own age and size, but the resemblance stopped there. He looked like a cross between Ramon Novarro and Rudolph Valentino, only handsomer. Tall, broad-shouldered, with deeply tanned, perfectly sculpted Latin features, he had the classical long, thin moustache, strong, even teeth with that in-built neon phosphorescence that seems to shine in any light from high noon till dark, and a darkly gleaming froth of tight black curls on his head; he would have been a lost man if you'd let him loose on the campus of any girls' university. For all that, he looked as far from being a sissy as any man I'd ever met: he had the strong chin, the balanced carriage, the light, springy boxer's step of a man well aware that he can get through this world without any help from a nursemaid. If nothing else, I thought sourly, he would at least take Miss Beresford out of my hair.

The other man was a slightly smaller edition of the first, same features, same teeth, same moustache and hair, only those were greying. He would be about fifty-five. He had about him that indefinable look of authority and assurance which can come from power, money, or a carefully cultivated phoneyness. This, I guessed, would be the Señor Miguel Carreras who inspired such fear in our local Carracio agent. I wondered why.

Ten minutes later the last of our cargo was aboard and all that remained were the three boxed coffins on the back of the old truck. I was watching the bo'sun readying a sling round the first of those when a well-detested voice said behind me:

"This is Mr. Carreras, sir. Captain Bullen sent me."

I turned round and gave Fourth Officer Dexter the look I specially reserved for Fourth Officer Dexter. Dexter was the exception to the rule that the Fleet Commodore always got the best available in the company as far as officers and men were concerned, but that was hardly the old man's fault: there were some men that even a Fleet Commodore has to accept and Dexter was one of them. A personable enough youngster of twenty-one, with fair hair, slightly prominent blue eyes, an excruciatingly genuine public-school accent, and limited intelligence, Dexter was the son—and, unfortunately, heir—of Lord Dexter, Chairman and Managing Director of the Blue Mail. Lord Dexter, who had inherited about ten millions at the age of fifteen and, understandably enough, had never looked back, had the quaint idea that his own son should start from the bottom up and had sent him to sea as a cadet some five years previously. Dexter took a poor view of this arrangement: every man in the ship, from Bullen downwards, took a poor view both of the arrangement and Dexter, but there was nothing we could do about it.

"How do you do, sir?" I accepted Carreras' outstretched hand and took a good look at him. The steady dark eyes, the courteous smile couldn't obscure the fact that there were many more lines about his eyes and mouth at two feet than at fifty; but it also couldn't obscure the compensatory fact that the air of authority and command was now redoubled in force, and I put out of my mind any idea that this air originated in phoneyness; it was the genuine article, and that was that.

"Mr. Carter? My pleasure." The hand was firm, the bow more than a perfunctory nod, the cultured English the product of some Stateside Ivy League college. "I have some interest in the cargo being loaded, and if you would permit—"

"But certainly, Señor Carreras." Carter, that rough-hewn Anglo-Saxon diamond, not to be outdone in Latin courtesy. I waved towards the hatch. "If you would be so kind as to keep to the starboard—the right hand—of the hatch—"

" 'Starboard' will do, Mr. Carter." He smiled. "I have commanded vessels of my own. It was not a life that ever appealed to me." He stood there for a moment, watching MacDonald tightening the sling, while I turned to Dexter, who had made no move to go. Dexter was seldom in a hurry to do anything; he had a remarkably thick skin.

"What are you on now, Fourth?" I enquired.

"Assisting Mr. Cummings."

That meant he was unemployed. Cummings, the purser,

was an extraordinarily competent officer who never required help. He had only one fault, brought on by years of dealing with passengers—he was far too polite. Especially with Dexter. I said, "Those charts we picked up in Kingston. You might get on with the corrections, will you?" Which meant that he would probably land us on a reef off the Great Bahamas in a couple of days' time.

"But Mr. Cummings is expecting—"

"The charts, Dexter."

He looked at me for a long moment, his face slowly darkening, then spun on his heel and left. I let him go three paces, then said, not loudly, "Dexter."

He stopped, then turned slowly.

"The charts, Dexter," I repeated. He stood there for maybe five seconds, eyes locked on mine, then broke his gaze.

"Aye, aye, sir." The accent on the "sir" was faint but unmistakable. He turned again and walked away, and now the flush was round to the back of his neck, his back ramrod stiff. Little I cared; by the time he sat in the chairman's seat I'd have long since quit. I watched him go, then turned to see Carreras looking at me with a slow, still speculation in the steady eyes. He was putting Chief Officer Carter in the balance and weighing him, but whatever figures he came up with he kept to himself, for he turned away without any haste and made his way to the starboard side of number four hold. As he turned, I noticed for the first time the very thin ribbon of black silk stitched across the left lapel of his grey tropical suit. It didn't seem to go any too well with the white rose he wore in his buttonhole, but maybe the two of them together were recognised as a sign of mourning in those parts.

And it seemed very likely, for he stood there perfectly straight, almost at attention, his hands loosely by his sides, as the three crated coffins were hoisted inboard. When the third crate came swinging in over the rail he removed his hat casually, as if to get the benefit of the light breeze that had just sprung up from the north, the direction of the open sea, and then, looking round him almost furtively, lifted his right hand under the cover of the hat held in his left hand and made a quick abbreviated sign of the cross. Even in that heat I could feel the cold cat's-paw of a shiver brush lightly across my shoulders. I don't know why; not even by the furthest stretch of imagination could I visualise that prosaic hatchway giving on number four hold as an open grave. One of my grandmothers was Scots, maybe I was psychic or had the second sight or whatever it was they called it up in the Highlands, or maybe I had just lunched too well.

Whatever might have upset me, it didn't seem to have upset Señor Carreras. He replaced his hat as the last of the crates touched lightly on the floor of the hold, stared down at it for a few seconds, then turned and made his way for-'ard, lifting his hat again and giving me a clear, untroubled smile as he came by. For want of anything better to do, I smiled back at him.

Five minutes later the ancient truck, the two Packards, the jeep, and the last of the stevedores were gone and Mac-Donald was busy supervising the placing of the battens on number four hold. By five o'clock, a whole hour before deadline and exactly on the top of the tide, the S.S. *Campari* was steaming slowly over the bar to the north of the harbour, then northwest into the setting sun, carrying with it its cargo of crates and machinery and dead men, its fuming captain, disgruntled crew, and thoroughly outraged passengers. At five o'clock on that brilliant June evening it was not what one might have called a happy ship.

Chapter 2

[*Tuesday* 8 P.M.–*9.30* P.M.]

BY EIGHT o'clock that night cargo, crates, and coffins were, presumably, just as they had been at five o'clock; but among the living cargo the change for the better, from deep discontent to something closely approaching light-hearted satisfaction, was marked and profound.

There were reasons for this, of course. In Captain Bullen's case—he twice called me "Johnny-me-boy" as he sent me down for dinner—it was because he was clear of what he was pleased to regard as the pestiferous port of Carracio, because he was at sea again, because he was on his bridge again, and because he had thought up an excellent reason for sending me below while he remained on the bridge, thus avoiding the social torture of having to dine with the passengers. In the crew's case it was because the captain had seen fit, partly out of a sense of justice and partly to repay the head office for the indignities they had heaped on him, to award them all many more hours' overtime than they were actually entitled to for their off-duty labours in the past three days. And in the case of the officers and passengers it was simply because there are certain well-defined fundamental laws of human nature

29

and one of them was that it was impossible to be miserable for long aboard the S.S. *Campari.*

As a vessel with no regular ports of call, with only very limited passenger accommodation and capacious cargo holds that were seldom far from full, the S.S *Campari* could properly be classed as a tramp ship and indeed was so classed in the Blue Mail's brochures. But—as the brochures pointed out with a properly delicate restraint in keeping with the presumably refined sensibilities of the extraordinarily well-heeled clientele it was addressing— the S.S. *Campari* was no ordinary tramp ship. Indeed, it was no ordinary ship in any sense at all. It was, as the brochure said simply, quietly, without any pretentiousness and in exactly those words, "a medium-sized cargo vessel offering the most luxurious accommodation and finest cuisine of any ship in the world to-day."

The only thing that prevented all the great passenger shipping companies from the Cunard White Star downwards from suing the Blue Mail for this preposterous statement was the fact that it was perfectly true.

It was the chairman of the Blue Mail, Lord Dexter, who had obviously kept all his brains to himself and refrained from passing any on to his son, our current fourth officer, who had thought it up. It was, as all his competitors who were now exerting themselves strenuously to get into the act admitted, a stroke of pure genius. Lord Dexter concurred.

It had started off simply enough in the early fifties with an earlier Blue Mail vessel, the S.S. *Brandywine.* (For some strange whimsy, explicable only on a psychoanalyst's couch, Lord Dexter, himself a rabid teetotaller, had elected to name his various ships after divers wines and other spirituous liquors.) The *Brandywine* had been one of two Blue Mail vessels engaged on a regular run between New York and various British possessions in the West Indies, and Lord Dexter, eying the luxury cruise liners which plied regularly between New York and the Caribbean and seeing no good reason why he shouldn't elbow his way into this lucrative dollar-earning market, had some extra cabins fitted on the *Brandywine* and advertised them in a few very select American newspapers and magazines, making it quite plain that he was interested only in Top People. Among the attractions offered had been a complete absence of bands, dances, concerts, fancy-dress balls, swimming pools, tombola, deck games, sight-seeing and parties—only a genius could have made such desirable and splendidly resounding virtues out of things he didn't have anyway. All he offered on the positive side was the mystery and romance of a tramp ship which sailed to unknown destinations—this didn't make any alterations to regular schedules; all it meant was that the captain kept the names of the various ports of call to himself until shortly before he arrived there—and the resources and comfort of a telegraph lounge which remained in continuous touch with the New York, London, and Paris stock exchanges.

The initial success of the scheme was fantastic. In stock-exchange parlance, the issue was oversubscribed a hundred times. This was intolerable to Lord Dexter; he was obviously attracting far too many of the not quite Top People, aspiring would-be's on the lower-middle rungs of the ladder who had not yet got past their first few million, people with whom Top People would not care to associate. He doubled his prices. It made no difference. He trebled them and in the process made the gratifying discovery that there were many people in the world who would pay literally almost anything not only to be different and exclusive but to be known to be different and exclusive. Lord Dexter held up the building of his latest ship, the *Campari,* had designed and built into her a dozen of the most luxurious cabin suites ever seen, and sent her to New York, confident that she would soon recoup the outlay of a quarter of a million pounds extra cost incurred through the building of those cabins. As usual, his confidence was not misplaced.

There were imitators, of course, but one might as well have tried to imitate Buckingham Palace, the Grand Canyon, or the Cullinan Diamond. Lord Dexter left them all at the starting gate. He had found his formula and he stuck to it unswervingly: comfort, convenience, quiet, good food, and good company. Where comfort was concerned, the fabulous luxury of the staterooms had to be seen to be believed; convenience, as far as the vast majority of the male passengers was concerned, found its ultimate in the juxtaposition, in the *Campari*'s unique telegraph lounge, of the stock-exchange tickers and one of the most superbly stocked bars in the world. Quiet was achieved by an advanced degree of insulation both in cabin suites and engine room, by imitating the royal yacht *Britannia* inasmuch as that no orders were ever shouted and the deck crew and stewards invariably wore rubber-soled sandals and by eliminating all the bands, parties, games, and dances which lesser cruise passengers believed essential for the enjoyment of shipboard life. The magnificent cuisine had been achieved by luring away, at vast cost and the expense of even more bad feeling, the chefs from one of the biggest embassies in London and one of the finest hotels in Paris; those masters of the culinary world operated on alternate days, and the paradisical results of their efforts to outdo one another was the envious talk of the Western Ocean.

Other shipowners might, perhaps, have succeeded in imitating some or all of those features, although almost certainly to a lesser degree. But Lord Dexter was no ordinary shipowner. He was, as said, a genius, and he showed it in his insistence, above all, on having the right people aboard.

Never a single trip passed but the *Campari* had a Personage on its passenger list, a Personage varying from Notable to World-famous. A special suite was reserved for Personages. Well-known politicians, cabinet ministers, top stars of the stage and screen, the odd famous writer or artist—if he was clean enough and used a razor—and the lower echelons of the English nobility travelled in this suite at vastly reduced prices; royalty, ex-presidents, ex-premiers, ranking dukes and above travelled free. It was said that if all the British peerage on the *Campari*'s waiting list could be accommodated simultaneously, the House of Lords could close its doors. It need hardly be added that there was nothing philanthropic in Lord Dexter's offer of free hospitality: he merely jacked up his prices to the wealthy occupants of the other eleven suites, who would have paid the earth anyway for the privilege of voyaging in such close contact with such exalted company.

After several years on this run our passengers consisted almost entirely of repeaters. Many came as often as three times a year, fair enough indication of the size of their bank roll. By now the passenger list on the *Campari* had become the most exclusive club in the world. Not to put too fine a point on it, Lord Dexter had distilled the aggregate elements of social and financial snobbery and found in its purest quintessence and inexhaustible supply of gold.

I adjusted my napkin and looked over the current gold mine. Five hundred million dollars on the hoof—or on the dove-grey velvet of the armchair seats in that opulent and air-conditioned dining room; perhaps nearer a thousand million dollars, and old man Beresford would account for a good third of it.

Julius Beresford, president and chief stockholder of the Hart-McCormick Mining Federation, sat where he nearly always sat, not only now but on half a dozen previous cruises, at the top right-hand side of the captain's table, next to Captain Bullen himself. He sat there, in the most coveted position in the ship, not because he insisted on it through sheer weight of wealth, but because Captain Bullen himself insisted on it. There are exceptions to every rule, and Julius Beresford was the exception to Bullen's rule that he couldn't abide any passenger, period. Beresford, a tall, thin, relaxed man with tufted black eyebrows, a horseshoe ring of greying hair fringing the sunburnt baldness of his head, and lively hazel eyes twinkling in the lined brown leather of his face, came along only for the peace, comfort, and food: the company of the great left him cold, a fact vastly appreciated by Captain Bullen, who shared his sentiments exactly. Beresford, sitting diagonally across from my table, caught my eye.

"Evening, Mr. Carter." Unlike his daughter, he didn't make me feel that he was conferring an earldom upon me every time he spoke to me. "Splendid to be at sea again, isn't it? And where's our captain to-night?"

"Working, I'm afraid, Mr. Beresford. I have to present his apologies to his table. He couldn't leave the bridge."

"On the bridge?" Mrs. Beresford, seated opposite her husband, twisted round to look at me. "I thought you were usually on watch at this hour, Mr. Carter?"

"I am." I smiled at her. I kept a special sort of smile for Mrs. Beresford in the same way that I kept a special sort of look for young Dexter. Plump, bejewelled, over-dressed, with dyed blonde hair, but still beautiful at fifty, Mrs. Beresford bubbled over with good humour and laughter and kindness, and to the sour remark that it is easy to be that way with 300 million dollars in the bank, I can only observe that, after several years on the millionaires' run, the misery quotient of our wealthy appeared to increase in direct proportion to the bullion in the bank; this was only her first trip, but Mrs. Beresford was already my favourite passenger. I went on: "But there are so many chains of islets, reefs, and coral keys hereabouts that Captain Bullen prefers to see to the navigation himself." I didn't add, as I might have done, that had it been in the middle of the night and all the passengers safely in their beds Captain Bullen would have been in his also, untroubled by any thoughts about his chief officer's competence.

"But I thought a chief officer was fully qualified to run a ship?" Miss Beresford, needling me again, sweet-smiling, the momentarily innocent clear green eyes almost too big for the delicately tanned face. "In case anything went wrong with the captain, I mean. You must hold a master's certificate, mustn't you?"

"I do. I also hold a driver's licence, but you wouldn't catch me driving a bus in the rush hour in downtown Manhattan."

Old man Beresford grinned. His wife smiled. Miss Beresford regarded me thoughtfully for a moment, then bent to examine her hors d'oeuvres, showing the gleaming auburn hair cut in a bouffant style that looked as if it had been achieved with a garden rake and a pair of secateurs but had probably cost a fortune. The man by her side wasn't going to let it go so easily, though. He laid down his fork, raised his thin dark head until he had me more or less sighted along his aquiline nose, and said in his clear high drawling voice, "Oh, come now, Chief Officer. I don't think the comparison is very apt at all."

The "Chief Officer" was to put me in my place. The Duke of Hartwell spent a great deal of his time aboard the *Campari* in putting people in their places, which was pretty ungrateful of him, considering that he was getting it all for free. He had nothing against me personally; it was just that he was publicly lending Miss Beresford his support. Even the very considerable sums of money earned by inveigling the properly respectful lower classes into viewing his stately home at two and six a time were making only a slight dent on the crushing burden of death duties, whereas an alliance with Miss Beresford would solve his difficulties for ever and ever. Things were being complicated for the unfortunate duke by the fact that, though his intellect was bent on Miss Beresford, his attentions and eyes were for the most part on the extravagantly opulent charms—and undeniable beauty—of the platinum-blonde and oft-divorced cinema actress who flanked him on the other side.

"I don't suppose it is, sir," I acknowledged. Captain Bullen refused to address him as "Your Grace," and I'd be damned if I'd do it either. "But the best I could think up on the spur of the moment."

He nodded as though satisfied and returned to attack his hors d'oeuvre. Old Beresford eyed him speculatively, Mrs. Beresford half-smilingly, Miss Harcourt—the cinema actress—admiringly, while Miss Beresford herself just kept on treating us to an uninterrupted view of the auburn bouffant. There's little enough to do during off-duty hours at sea, and watching developments at the captain's table would make a very entertaining pastime indeed. What promised to make it even more entertaining was the very considerable interest being taken in the captain's table by the young man seated at the foot of my own table. One of the passengers who had joined at Carracio.

Tony Carreras—my guess that he was Miguel Carreras' son had been a correct and far from difficult one—was by

any odds the most extraordinarily handsome man who'd
ever passed through the dining-room door of the *Campari*.
In one way this might not have signified much as it takes
many years to amass sufficient cash to sail on the *Campari*
even for a weekend and young men were in a tiny minority
at any time, but nevertheless there was no denying his
impact. Even at close-up range there was none of that
weakness, that almost effeminate regularity of feature so
often found in the faces of many very good-looking men.
He looked for all the world like a slightly Latinate rein-
carnation of a younger Errol Flynn, but harder, tougher,
more enduring. The only flaw, if one could call it flaw,
lay in the eyes. There seemed to be something ever so
slightly wrong with them, as if the pupils were slightly
flattened, giving a hard, bright glitter. Maybe it was just
the lighting at the table. But there was nothing wrong with
them as eyes; he had twenty-twenty vision all right and
was using it all to study the captain's table. Miss Beresford
or Miss Harcourt, I couldn't be sure which; he didn't look
the kind of man who would waste his time studying any
of the others at that table.

The courses came and went. Antoine was on duty in
the kitchen that night, and you could almost reach out and
feel the blissful hush that descended on the company. Vel-
vet-footed Goanese waiters moved soundlessly on the dark
grey pile of the Persian carpet; food appeared and vanished
as if in a dream; an arm always appeared at the precisely
correct moment with the precisely correct wine. But never
for me. I drank soda water. It was in my contract.

The coffee appeared. This was the moment when I had
to earn my money. When Antoine was on duty and on top
of his form, conversation was a desecration and a hallowed
hush of appreciation, an almost cathedral ecstasy, was the
correct form. But about forty minutes of this rapturous
silence was about par for the course. It couldn't and never
did go on. I never yet met a rich man—or woman, for
that matter of it—who didn't list talking, chiefly and pre-
ferably about themselves, as among their favourite occupa-
tions. And the prime targets for their observations was
invariably the officer who sat at the head of the table.

I looked round ours and wondered who would set the ball rolling. Miss Harrbride—her original central-European name was unpronounceable—thin, scrawny, sixtyish, and tough as whalebone, who had made a fortune out of highly expensive and utterly worthless cosmetic preparations which she wisely refrained from using on herself? Mr. Greenstreet, her husband, a gray anonymity of a man with a grey sunken face, who had married her for heaven only knew what reason, for he was a very wealthy man in his own right? Tony Carreras? His father, Miguel Carreras? There should have been a sixth at my table, to replace the Curtis family of three who, along with the Harrisons, had been so hurriedly called home from Kingston, but the old man who had come aboard in his wheel chair was apparently to have his meals served in his cabin during the voyage, with his nurses in attendance. Four men and one woman; it made an ill-balanced table.

Señor Miguel Carreras spoke first.

"The *Campari*'s prices, Mr. Carter, are quite atrocious," he said calmly. He puffed appreciatively at his cigar. "Robbery on the high seas would be a very fitting description. On the other hand, the cuisine is as claimed. You have a chef of divine gifts. It is perhaps not too much to pay for a foretaste of a better world."

This made Señor Carreras very wealthy indeed and was old hat to me. Wealthy men never mentioned money, lest they be thought not to have enough of it. Very wealthy men, on the other hand, to whom money as such no longer mattered, had no such inhibitions. The passengers on the *Campari* complained all the time about the prices. And they kept coming back.

"From all accounts, sir, 'divine' is just about right. Experienced travellers who have stayed in the best hotels on both side of the Atlantic maintain that Antoine has no equal in either Europe or America. Except, perhaps, Henriques."

"Henriques?"

"Our alternate chef. He's on to-morrow."

"Do I detect a certain immodesty, Mr. Carter, in ad-

vancing the claims of the *Campari?*" There was no offence
meant, not with that smile.

"I don't think so, sir. But the next twenty-four hours
will speak for themselves—and Henriques—better than I
can."

"Touché!" He smiled again and reached for the bottle
of Remy Martin—the waiters vanished at coffeetime. "And
the prices?"

"They're terrible," I agreed. I told that to all the passengers and it seemed to please them. "We offer what no other
ship in the world offers, but the prices are still scandalous.
At least a dozen people in this room at this very moment
have told me that—and most of them are here for at least
their third trip."

"You make your point, Mr. Carter." It was Tony Carreras speaking and his voice was as one might have expected—slow, controlled, with a deep resonant timbre.
He looked at his father. "Remember the waiting list at the
Blue Mail's offices?"

"Indeed. We were pretty far down the list—and what
a list. Half the millionaires in Central and South America.
I suppose we may consider ourselves fortunate, Mr. Carter,
in that we were the only ones able to accept at such short
notice after the sudden departure of our predecessors in
Jamaica. But don't forget that to catch the boat we had to
make a hurried four-hundred-mile dash from the capital
to Carracio by air and road. And what roads!"

Señor Carreras obviously didn't share the Carracio
agent's respectful terror of the revolutionary government.
I wondered how a man of Carreras' obviously aristocratic
background had been able to retain his obvious wealth in
the face of the forces of change that had overcome and
completely wiped out the old order—and why, if money
was so desperately short on the island, he was allowed to
convert very large sums of it into dollars to pay for this
cruise, or how and why he had been able to leave the
island at all.

But I kept my wonderings to myself. Instead I said,
"You're still a long way off the record, Señor Carreras.
Last trip we had a family from Santiago and two men from

Beirut, both of whom had flown to New York specially for the round voyage."

"And they can't all be wrong, eh? Don't worry, Mr. Carter, I intend to enjoy myself. Can you give us any idea of our itinerary?"

"That's supposed to be one of the attractions, sir. No set itinerary. Our schedule largely depends on the availability and destination of cargoes. One thing certain, we're going to New York. Most of our passengers boarded there and passengers like to be returned to where they came from." He knew this anyway, knew that we had coffins consigned to New York. "We may stop off at Nassau. Depends how the captain feels—the company gives him a lot of leeway in adjusting local schedules to suit the best needs of the passengers—and the weather reports. This is the hurricane season, Mr. Carreras, or pretty close to it. If the reports are bad Captain Bullen will want all the sea room he can get and give Nassau a bye." I smiled. "Among the other attractions of the S.S. *Campari* is that we do not make our passengers seasick unless it is absolutely essential."

"Considerate, very considerate," Carreras murmured. He looked at me speculatively. "But we'll be making one or two calls on the east coast, I take it?"

"No idea, sir. Normally, yes. Again it's up to the captain, and how the captain behaves depends on a certain Dr. Slingsby Caroline."

"They haven't caught him yet," Miss Harrbride declared in her rough gravelly voice. She scowled with all the fierce patriotism of a first-generation American, looked round the table, and gave us all the impartial benefit of her scowl. "It's incredible, frankly incredible, I still don't believe it. A *thirteenth*-generation American!" I could imagine how unthinkably remote thirteen generations of American ancestors must be to Miss Harrbride; she'd have traded her million-dollar cosmetic empire for even a couple of them. "I was reading all about him in the *Tribune* two days ago. Did you know that the Slingsbys came to the Potomac in 1662, just five years after the Washingtons. Three hundred years! Imagine, American for three hundred years, and now a renegade! A traitor! Thirteen generations!"

"Don't take it too hard, Miss Harrbride," I said encouragingly. "When it comes to skipping with the family silver, Dr. Caroline just doesn't begin to be in the same class as my countrymen. The last Englishman who defected to the Communist world had an ancestor in the *Doomsday Book*. Thirty solid generations. Yet he took off and lit out at the drop of a hat."

"Faugh!" said Miss Harrbride.

"We heard about this character." Tony Carreras, like his father, had had his education in some Ivy League college; he was rather less formal in his attitude towards the English language. "Slingsby Caroline, I mean. Makes very little sense to me. What's he going to do with this weapon —the Twister, they call it, isn't it?—even if he does get it out of the country? Who's going to buy it? I mean, as nuclear devices go it could be ranked almost as a toy: it certainly isn't going to change the balance of world power, no matter who gets his hands on it."

"Tony's right," Miguel Carreras agreed. "Who *is* going to buy it? Besides, there's nothing secret any more about the making of nuclear weapons. If a country has enough wealth and technical resources—so far there are only four in the world—it can build a nuclear weapon any time. If it hasn't, all the plans or working models in the world are useless to them."

"He's going to have an interesting time in hawking the Twister around," Tony Carreras finished. "Especially since from all descriptions you can't get the Twister into a suitcase. But what's this guy got to do with us, Mr. Carter?"

"As long as he is at large every cargo vessel leaving the eastern seaboard gets a pretty thorough going over to make sure that neither he nor the Twister is aboard. Slows up the turn-round of cargo and passenger ships by 100 per cent, which means that the longshoremen are losing stevedoring money pretty fast. They've gone on strike—and the chances are, so many words have been said on both sides, that they'll stay on strike when they do nab Dr. Caroline. If."

"Traitor," said Miss Harrbride. "Thirteen generations!"

"So we stay away from the east coast, eh?" Carreras Senior asked. "Meantime, anyway?"

"As long as possible, sir. But New York is a must. When, I don't know. But if it's still strike-bound, we might go up the St. Lawrence first. Depends."

"Romance, mystery, and adventure." Carreras smiled. "Just like your brochure said." He glanced over my shoulder. "Looks like a visitor for you, Mr. Carter."

I twisted in my seat. It was a visitor for me. Rusty Williams—Rusty, from his shock of flaming hair—was advancing towards me, whites immaculately pressed, uniform cap clasped stiffly under his left arm. Rusty was sixteen, our youngest cadet, desperately shy and very impressionable. Cadets were not normally allowed in the dining room and Rusty's eyes were goggling as they took in the young ladies at the captain's table, but he managed to haul them back to me as he halted by my side with a perceptible click of his heels.

"What is it, Rusty?" Age-old convention said that cadets should always be addressed by their surnames, but everyone called Rusty just that. It seemed impossible not to.

"The captain's compliments, sir. Could he see you on the bridge, please, Mr. Carter?"

"I'll be right up." Rusty turned to leave and I caught the gleam in Susan Beresford's eye, a gleam that generally heralded some crack at my expense. This one predictably would be about my indispensability, about the distraught captain sending for his trusty servant when all was lost, and although I didn't think she was the sort of girl to say it in front of a cadet, I wouldn't have wagered pennies on it, so I rose hastily to my feet, said, "Excuse me, Miss Harrbride, excuse me, gentlemen," and followed Rusty quickly out of the door into the starboard alleyway. He was waiting for me.

"The captain is in his cabin, sir. He'd like to see you there."

"What? You told me—"

"I know, sir. He told me to say that. Mr. Jamieson is

on the bridge"—George Jamieson was our third officer—
"and Captain Bullen is in his cabin. With Mr. Cummings."

I nodded and left. I remembered now that Cummings
hadn't been at his accustomed table as I'd come out, although he'd certainly been there at the beginning of
dinner. The captain's quarters were immediately below the
bridge and I was there in ten seconds. I knocked on the
polished teak door, heard a gruff voice, and went in.

The Blue Mail certainly did its Commodore well. Even
Captain Bullen, no admirer of the sybaritic life, had never
been heard to complain of being pampered. He had a
three-room-and-bathroom suite, done in the best millionaire's taste, and his day cabin, in which I now was, was a
pretty fair guide to the rest—wine-red carpet that sunk
beneath your feet, darkly crimson drapes, gleaming syca-
more panelling, narrow oak beams overhead, oak and
green leather for the chairs and settee. Captain Bullen
looked up at me when I came in. He didn't have any of
the signs of a man enjoying the comforts of home.

"Something wrong, sir?" I asked.

"Sit down." He waved to a chair and sighed. "There's
something wrong all right. Banana-legs Benson is missing.
White reported it ten minutes ago."

Banana-legs Benson sounded like the name of a domes-
ticated anthropoid or, at best, like a professional wrestler
on the small-town circuits, but, in fact, it belonged to our
very suave, polished, and highly accomplished head
steward, Frederick Benson: Benson had the well-deserved
reputation of being a very firm disciplinarian, and it was
one of his disgruntled subordinates who, in the process of
receiving a severe and merited dressing-down, had noticed
the negligible clearance between Benson's knees and re-
christened him as soon as his back was turned. The name
had stuck, chiefly because of its incongruity and utter un-
suitability. White was the assistant chief steward.

I said nothing. Bullen didn't appreciate anyone, especially his officers, indulging in double-takes, exclamations,
or fatuous repetition. Instead I looked at the man seated
across the table from the captain: Howard Cummings.

Cummings, the purser, a small, plump, amiable, and infinitely shrewd Irishman was, next to Bullen, the most important man on the ship. No one questioned that, though Cummings himself gave no sign that this was so. On a passenger ship a good purser is worth his weight in gold and Cummings was a pearl beyond any price. In his three years on the *Campari* friction and trouble among—and complaints from—the passengers had been almost completely unknown. Howard Cummings was a genius in mediation, compromise, the soothing of ruffled feelings, and the handling of people in general. Captain Bullen would as soon have thought of cutting off his right hand as of trying to send Cummings off the ship.

I looked at Cummings for three reasons. He knew everything that went on on the *Campari,* from the secret takeover bids being planned in the telegraph lounge to the heart troubles of the youngest stoker in the boiler room. He was the man ultimately responsible for all the stewards aboard the ship. And, finally, he was a close personal friend of Banana-legs: they had sailed together for ten years, a chief purser and chief steward, on one of the great transatlantic liners, and it had been one of the master strokes in the career of that arch-lurer, Lord Dexter, when he had lured both those men away from their ship and installed them aboard the *Campari.*

Cummings caught my look and shook his dark head.

"Sorry, Johnny, I'm as much in the dark as you. I saw him shortly before dinner, about ten to eight, it would have been, when I was having a noggin with the paying guests." Cummings' noggin came from a special whisky bottle filled only with ginger ale. "We'd White up here just now. He says he saw Benson in cabin suite six, fixing it for the night about eight-twenty—half an hour ago, no, nearer forty minutes now. He expected to see him shortly afterwards because for every night for the past couple of years, whenever the weather was good, Benson and White have had a cigarette together on deck when the passengers were at dinner."

"Regular time?" I interrupted.

"Very. Eight-thirty, near enough, never later than eight thirty-five. But not to-night. At eight-forty White went to look for him in his cabin. No sign of him there. Organized half a dozen stewards for a search and still nothing doing. He sent for me and I came to the captain."

And the captain sent for me, I thought. Send for old trusty Carter when there's dirty work on hand. I looked at Bullen.

"A search, sir?"

"That's it, Mister. Damned nuisance, just one damned thing after another. Quietly, if you can."

"Of course, sir. Can I have Wilson, the bo'sun, some stewards and A.B.s?"

"You can have Lord Dexter and his board of directors just so long as you find Benson," Bullen grunted.

"Yes, sir." I turned to Cummings. "Didn't suffer from any ill-health, did he? Liable to dizziness, faintness, heart attacks, that sort of thing?"

"Flat feet was all." Cummings smiled. He wasn't feeling like smiling. "Had his annual checkup last month from Doc Marston. One hundred per cent. The flat feet are an occupational disease."

I turned back to Captain Bullen.

"Could I have twenty minutes, perhaps half an hour, for a quiet look round, sir, first? With Mr. Cummings. It's a calm, windless night. There's been no word of any shouts, any cries for help, and as there's always a good few of the crew on the lower decks at night the chances are that anything like that would have been heard. And he's not likely to be ill. What I'm getting at is that it's a hundred to one against his being in any trouble where he requires immediate help. If he did require it, he's probably past all help by now. I can't see there's any harm in waiting another twenty minutes before raising the alarm."

"No one's going to raise any alarm, Mister. This is the *Campari.*"

"Yes, sir. But whether it's broadcast over the Tannoy system or whispered in a dark corner, it'll make no difference. If Benson is missing and is going to stay that way it will be all over the ship by midnight to-night. Or earlier."

"Job's comforter," Bullen growled. "All right, Johnny, you, too, Howie, see what you can find."

"Your authority to look anywhere, sir?" I asked.

"Within reason, of course."

"Everywhere?" I insisted. "Or I'm wasting my time. You know that, sir."

"My God! And it's only a couple of days since that Jamaican lot. Remember how our passengers reacted to the customs and American Navy going through their cabins? The board of directors are going to love this." He looked up wearily. "I suppose you *are* referring to the passengers' quarters?"

"We'll do it quietly, sir. They're still at dinner. And Howie here can fix anything that comes up."

"Twenty minutes then. You'll find me on the bridge. Don't tramp on any toes if you can help it."

We left, dropped down to "A" deck, and made a right-left turn into the hundred-foot central passageway between the cabin suites on "A" deck: there were only six of these suites, three on each side. White was about halfway down the passageway, nervously pacing up and down. I beckoned to him and he came walking quickly towards us, a thin, balding character with a permanently pained expression who suffered from the twin disabilities of chronic dyspepsia and over-conscientiousness.

"Got all the passkeys, White?" I asked.

"Yes, sir."

"Fine." I nodded to the first main door on my right, number one suite on the port side. "Open it, will you?"

White looked at Cummings. It was an understood thing at sea that deck officers never, *never* went into the *Campari*'s passenger accommodation except by passenger invitation, and even then only by kind permission of the purser and head steward. But to *burgle* the passenger accommodation . .

"You heard the chief officer." I wondered when I'd previously heard a harsh note in Howie's voice and decided never; he and Banana-legs Benson were pretty good friends. "Open up."

He opened up. I brushed past him, followed by the purser. There was no need to switch on the lights—they were already on; asking the *Campari*'s passengers, at the

prices they were paying, to remember to turn off the lights
would have been a waste of breath and an insult.

There were no bunks in the *Campari*'s cabin suites.
Fourposters, and massive four-posters at that, with concealed and mechanically operated sideboards which could
be quickly raised in bad weather; such was the standard
of modern weather reporting, the latitude allowed Captain
Bullen in avoiding bad weather, and the efficiency of our
Denny-Brown stabilisers that I don't think those sideboards had ever been used. Seasickness was not allowed
aboard the *Campari*.

The suite was composed of a sleeping cabin, an adjacent lounge and bathroom, and beyond the lounge another
cabin. All the plate-glass windows faced out over the port
side. We went through the cabins in a minute, looking beneath beds, examining cupboards, wardrobes, behind
drapes, everywhere. Nothing. We left.

Out in the passageway again I nodded at the suite opposite. Number two.

"This one now," I said to White.

"Sorry, sir. Can't do it. It's the old man and his nurses,
sir. They had three special trays sent up to them—when,
now—let me see; yes, sir, about six-fifteen to-night, and
Mr. Carreras, the gentleman who came aboard to-day. he
gave instructions that they were not to be disturbed till
morning." White was enjoying this. "Very strict instructions, sir."

"Carreras?" I looked at the purser. "What's he got to do
with this, Mr. Cummings?"

"You haven't heard? No, I don't suppose so. Seems like
Mr. Carreras—the father—is the senior partner in one of
the biggest law firms in the country, Cerdan and Carreras.
Mr. Cerdan, founder of the firm, is the old gentleman in
the cabin here. Seems he's been a semi-paralysed cripple
—but a pretty tough old cripple—for the past eight years.
His son and wife—Cerdan Junior being the next senior
partner to Carreras—have had him on their hands all that
time, and I believe the old boy has been a handful and a
half. I understand Carreras offered to take him along pri-
marily to give Cerdan Junior and his wife a break. Car-

reras, naturally, feels responsible for him, so I suppose that's why he left his orders with Benson."

"Doesn't sound like a man at death's door to me " I said. "Nobody's wanting to kill him off, just to ask him a few questions. Or the nurses." White opened his mouth to protest again, but I pushed roughly past him and knocked at the door.

No answer. I waited all of thirty seconds and then knocked again, loudly. White, beside me, was stiff with outrage and disapproval. I ignored him and was lifting my hand to put some real weight on the wood when I heard a movement and suddenly the door opened inwards.

It was the shorter of the two nurses, the plump one, who had answered the door. She had an old-fashioned pull-string linen cap over her head and was clutching with one hand a light woollen wrap that left only the toes of her mules showing. The cabin behind her was only dimly lit, but I could see it held a couple of beds, one of which was rumpled. The free hand with which she rubbed her eyes told the rest of the story.

"My sincere apologies, miss," I said. "I had no idea you were in bed. I'm the chief officer of this ship and this is Mr. Cummings, the purser. Our chief steward is missing and we were wondering if you may have seen or heard anything that might help us."

"Missing?" She clutched the wrap more tightly. "You mean—you mean he's just disappeared?"

"Let's say we can't find him. Can you help us at all?"

"I don't know. I've been asleep. You see," she explained, "we take it in three-hour turns to be by old Mr. Cerdan's bed. It is essential that he is watched all the time. I was trying to get in some sleep before my turn came to relieve Miss Werner."

"I'm sorry," I repeated. "You can't tell us anything then?"

"I'm afraid not."

"Perhaps your friend Miss Werner can?"

"Miss Werner?" She blinked at me. "But Mr. Cerdan is not to be—"

"Please. This might be very serious. One of the crew is

missing, and delay doesn't increase his chances."

"Very well." Like all competent nurses she knew how far she could go and when to make up her mind. "But I must ask you to be very quiet and not to disturb Mr. Cerdan in any way at all."

She didn't say anything about the possibility of Mr. Cerdan disturbing us, but she might have warned us. As we passed through the open door of his cabin he was sitting up in bed, a book on the blankets before him, with a bright overhead bed light illuminating a crimson tasselled nightcap and throwing his face into deep shadow, but a shadow not quite deep enough to hide the hostile gleam under bar-straight tufted eyebrows. The hostile gleam, it seemed to me, was as much a permanent feature of his face as the large beak of a nose that jutted out over a straggling white moustache. The nurse who led the way made to introduce us, but Cerdan waved her to silence with a peremptory hand. Imperious, I thought, was the word for the old boy, not to mention bad-tempered and downright ill-mannered.

"I hope you can explain this damnable outrage, sir." His voice was glacial enough to make a polar bear shiver. "Bursting into my private stateroom without so much as by your leave." He switched his gimlet eyes to Cummings. "You. You there. You had your orders, damn it. Strictest privacy, absolutely. Explain yourself, sir."

"I cannot tell you how sorry I am, Mr. Cerdan," Cummings said smoothly. "Only the most unusual circumstances—"

"Rubbish!" Whatever this old coot was living for, it couldn't have been with the object of outliving his friends; he'd lost his last friend before he'd left the nursery. "Amanda! Get the captain on the phone. At once!"

The tall, thin nurse sitting on the high-backed chair by the bedside made to gather up her knitting—an all but finished pale-blue cardigan—lying on her knees, but I gestured to her to remain where she was.

"No need to tell the captain, Miss Werner. He knows all about it—he sent us here. We have only one small request to make of you and Mr. Cerdan—"

"And I have only one very small request to make of you, sir." His voice cracked into a falsetto, excitement or anger or age or all three of them. "Get the hell out of here!"

I thought about taking a deep breath to calm myself, but even that two or three seconds' delay would only have precipitated another explosion, so I said at once, "Very good, sir. But first I would like to know if either yourself or Miss Werner here heard any strange or unusual sounds inside the past hour or saw anything that struck you as unusual. Our chief steward is missing. So far we have found nothing to explain his disappearance."

"Missing, hah?" Cerdan snorted. "Probably drunk or asleep." Then, as an afterthought: "Or both."

"He is not that sort of man," Cummings said quietly. "Can you help us?"

"I'm sorry, sir." Miss Werner, the nurse, had a low, husky voice. "We heard and saw nothing. Nothing at all that might be of any help. But if there's anything we can do—"

"There's nothing for you to do," Cerdan interrupted harshly, "except your job. We can't help you, gentlemen. Good evening."

Once more outside in the passageway, I let go a long, deep breath that I seemed to have been holding for the past two minutes and turned to Cummings.

"I don't care how much that old battle-axe is paying for his stateroom," I said bitterly. "He's still being undercharged."

"I can see why Mr. and Mrs. Cerdan Junior were glad to have him off their hands for a bit," Cummings conceded. Coming from the normally imperturbable and diplomatic purser, this was the uttermost limit in outright condemnation. He glanced at his watch. "Not getting anywhere, are we? And in another fifteen, twenty minutes the passengers will start drifting back to their cabins. How about if you finish off here while I go below with White?"

"Right. Ten minutes." I took keys from White and started on the remaining four suites while Cummings left for the six on the deck below.

Ten minutes later, having drawn a complete blank in three of the four remaining suites, I found myself in the last of them, the big one on the port side, aft, belonging to Julius Beresford and his family. I searched the cabin belonging to Beresford and his wife—and by this time I was really searching, not just only for Benson, but for any signs that he might have been there—but again a blank. The same in the lounge and bathroom. I moved into a second and smaller cabin—the one belonging to Beresford's daughter. Nothing behind the furniture, nothing behind the drapes, nothing under the four-poster. I moved to the aft bulkhead and slid back the roll doors that turned the entire side of the cabin into one huge wardrobe.

Miss Susan Beresford, I reflected, certainly did herself well in the way of clothes. There must have been about sixty or seventy hangers in that wall cupboard, and if any one hanger was draped with anything that cost less than two or three hundred dollars, I sadly missed my guess. I ploughed my way through the Balenciagas, Diors, and Givenchys, looking behind and beneath. But nothing there.

I closed the roll doors and moved across to a small wardrobe in a corner. It was full of furs, coats, capes, stoles; why anyone should haul that stuff along on a cruise to the Caribbean was completely beyond me. I laid my hand on a particularly fine full-length specimen and was moving it to one side to peer into the darkness behind when I heard a faint click, as of a handle being released, and a voice said:

"It *is* rather a nice mink, isn't it, Mr. Carter? That should be worth two years' salary to you any day."

Chapter 3

[*Tuesday 9.30* P.M.*–10.15* P.M.]

SUSAN BERESFORD was a beauty, all right. A perfectly oval-shaped face, high cheekbones, shining auburn hair, eyebrows two shades darker, and eyes the greenest green you ever saw, she had all the officers on the ship climbing the walls, even the ones she tormented the life out of. All except Carter, that was. A permanent expression of cool amusement does nothing to endear the wearer to me.

Not, just then, that I had any complaint on that ground. She was neither cool nor amused, and that was a fact. Two dull red spots of anger—and was there perhaps a tinge of fear?—touched the tanned cheeks, and if the expression on her face didn't yet indicate the reaction of someone who has just come across a particularly repulsive beetle under a flat stone you could see that it was going to turn into something like that pretty soon; it didn't require any micrometer to measure the curl at the corner of her mouth. I let the mink drop back into place and pulled the wardrobe door to.

"You shouldn't startle people like that," I said reproachfully. "You should have knocked."

"I should have—" Her mouth tightened; she still wasn't

51

amused. "What were you going to do with that coat?"

"Nothing. I never wear mink, Miss Beresford. It doesn't suit me." I smiled, but she didn't. "I can explain "

"I'm sure you can." She was halfway round the edge of the door now, on her way out. "But I think I would rather you made the explanation to my father."

"Suit yourself," I said easily. "But please hurry. What I'm doing is urgent. Use the phone there. Or shall I do it?"

"Leave that phone alone," she said irritably. She sighed, closed the door and leaned against it, and I had to admit that any door, even the expensively panelled ones on the *Campari,* looked twice the door with Susan Beresford draped against it. She shook her head, then gave me an up-from-under look with those startling green eyes. "I can picture many things, Mr. Carter, but one thing I can't visualise is our worthy chief officer taking off for some deserted island in a ship's lifeboat with my mink in the stern sheets." Getting back to normal, I noted with regret. "Besides, why should you? There must be over fifty thousand dollars' worth of jewellery lying loose in that drawer there."

"I missed that," I admitted. "I wasn't looking in drawers. I am looking for a man who is sick or unconscious or worse, and Benson wouldn't fit in any drawer I've ever seen."

"Benson? Our head steward? That nice man?" She came a couple of steps towards me and I was obscurely pleased to see the quick concern in her eyes. "He's missing?"

I told her all I knew myself. That didn't take long. When I was finished, she said, "Well, upon my word! What a to-do about nothing. He could have gone for a stroll round the decks, or a sit-down, or a smoke, yet the first thing you do is to start searching cabins—"

"You don't know Benson, Miss Beresford. He has never in his life left the passenger accommodation before eleven P.M. We couldn't be more concerned if we'd found that the officer of the watch had disappeared from the bridge or the quartermaster had left the wheel. Excuse me a moment." I opened the cabin door to locate the source of voices outside and saw White and another steward some way down the passage. White's eyes lit up as he caught sight of me, then clouded in disapproval when he saw Susan Beresford emerging through the doorway behind me. White's sense of propriety was having a roller-coaster ride that night.

"I was wondering where you were, sir," he said reprovingly. "Mr. Cummings sent me up. No luck down below, I'm afraid, sir. Mr. Cummings is going through our quarters now." He stood still for a moment, then the anxiety came to the foreground and erased the disapproval from his face. "What shall I do now, sir?"

"Nothing. Not personally. You're in charge till we find the chief steward, and the passengers come first, you know that. Detail three stewards to be at the for'ard entrance to the 'A' accommodation in ten minutes' time. One to search the officers' quarters for'ard, another for the officers' quarters aft, the third for the galleys, pantries, storerooms. But wait till I give the word. Miss Beresford, I'd like to use your phone, please."

I didn't wait for permission. I lifted the phone, got the exchange, had them put me through to the bo'sun's cabin, and found I was lucky. He was at home.

"MacDonald? First mate here. Sorry to call you out, Archie, but there's trouble. Benson's missing."

"The chief steward, sir?" There was something infinitely reassuring about that deep, slow voice that had never lost a fraction of its lilting West Highland intonation in twenty years at sea, in the complete lack of surprise or excitement in the tone. MacDonald was never surprised or excited about anything. He was more than my strong right arm; he was deck-side the most important person on the ship. And the most indispensable. "You'll have searched the passengers' and the stewards' quarters then?"

"Yes. Nothing doing. Take some men, on or off watch, doesn't matter, move along the main decks. Lots of the crew usually up there at this time of night. See if any of them saw Benson or saw or heard anything unusual. Maybe he's sick; maybe he fell and hurt himself; for all I know he's overboard."

"And if we've no luck? Another bloody search, sir, I suppose?"

"I'm afraid so. Can you be finished and up here in ten minutes?"

"That will be no trouble, sir."

I hung up, got through to the duty engineer officer, asked him to detain some men to come to the passenger accommodation, make another call to Tommy Wilson, the second officer, then asked to be put through to the captain. While I was waiting, Miss Beresford gave me her smile again, the sweet one with two much malice in it for my liking.

"My, my," she said admiringly. "Aren't we efficient? Phoning here, phoning there, crisp and commanding, General Carter planning his campaign. This is a new chief officer to me."

"A lot of unnecessary fuss," I said apologetically. "Especially for a steward. But he's got a wife and three daughters who think the sun rises and sets on him."

She coloured right up to the roots of her auburn hair, and for a moment I thought she was going to haul off and hit me. Then she spun on her heel, walked across the deep-piled carpet, and stood staring out through a window to the darkness beyond. I'd never realised before that a back could be so expressive of emotion.

Then Captain Bullen was on the phone. His voice was as gruff and brusque as usual, but even the metallic impersonality of the phone couldn't hide the worry.

"Any luck yet, Mister?"

"None at all, sir. I've a search party lined up. Could I start in five minutes?"

There was a pause, then he said, "It has to come to that, I suppose. How long will it take you?"

"Twenty minutes, half an hour."

"You're going to be very quick about it, aren't you?"

"I don't expect him to be hiding from us, sir. Whether he's sick or hurt himself, or had some urgent reason for leaving the passengers' quarters, I expect to find him in some place pretty obvious."

He grunted and said, "Nothing I can do to help?" Half question, half statement.

"No, sir." The sight of the captain searching about the upper deck or peering under lifeboat covers would do nothing to increase the passengers' confidence in the *Campari*.

"Right then, Mister. If you want me, I'll be in the telegraph lounge. I'll try to keep the passengers out of your hair while you're getting on with it." That showed he was worried all right, and badly worried; he'd just as soon have gone into a cage full of Bengal tigers as mingle socially with the passengers.

"Very good, sir." I hung up. Susan Beresford had recrossed the cabin and was standing near, screwing a cigarette into a jade holder about a foot in length. I found the holder vaguely irritating as I found everything about Miss Beresford irritating, not least the way she stood there confidently awaiting a light. I wondered when Miss Beresford had last been reduced to lighting her own cigarettes. Not in years, I supposed, not so long as there was a man within a hundred yards. She got her light, puffed out a lazy cloud of smoke, and said, "A search party, is it? Should be interesting. You can count on me."

"I'm sorry, Miss Beresford." I must say I didn't sound sorry. "Ship's company business. The captain wouldn't like it."

"Nor his first officer, is that it? Don't bother to answer that one." She looked at me consideringly. "But I could be unco-operative too. What would you say if I picked up this phone and told my parents I'd just caught you going through our personal belongings?"

"I should like that, lady. I know your parents. I should like to see you being spanked for behaving like a spoilt child when a man's life may be in danger."

The colour in the high cheekbones was going on and off like a neon light that evening. Now it was on again, she wasn't by a long way as composed and detached as she'd like the world to think. She stubbed out the newly lit cigarette and said quietly, "How would it be if I reported you for insolence?"

"Don't just stand there talking about it. The phone's by your side." When she made no move towards it, I went on: "Quite frankly, lady, you and your kind make me sick. You use your father's great wealth and your privileged position as a passenger on the *Campari* to poke fun, more often than not malicious fun, at members of the crew who are unable to retaliate. They've just got to sit and take it, because they're not like you. They have no money in the bank at all, most of them, but they have families to feed, mothers to support, so they know they have to keep smiling at Miss Beresford when she cracks jokes at their expense or embarrasses or angers them, because if they don't, Miss Beresford and her kind will see to it that they're out of a job."

"Please go on," she said. She had suddenly become very still.

"That's all of it. Misuse of power, even in so small a thing, is contemptible. And then, when anyone dares to retaliate, as I do, you threaten them with dismissal, which is what your threat amounts to. And that's worst than contemptible, it's cowardly."

I turned and made for the door. First I'd look for Benson, then I'd tell Bullen I was quitting. I was getting tired of the *Campari* anyway.

"Mr. Carter."

"Yes?" I turned but kept my hand on the doorknob. The colour mechanism in her cheeks was certainly working overtime; this time she'd gone pale under the tan. She took a couple of steps towards me and put her hand on my arm. Her hand wasn't any too steady.

"I am very, very sorry," she said in a low voice. "I had no idea. Amusement I like, but not malicious amusement. I thought—well, I thought it was harmless, that no one minded. And I would never dream of putting anyone's job in danger."

"Ha!" I said.

"You don't believe me?" Still the same small voice, still the hand on my arm.

"Of course I believe you," I said unconvincingly. And then I looked into her eyes, which was a big mistake and a very dangerous thing to do, for those green eyes, I noticed for the first time, had a curious trick of melting and dissolving that could interfere very seriously with a man's breathing. It was certainly interfering with my breathing. "Of course I believe you," I repeated, and this time the ring of conviction staggered even myself. "You will please forgive my rudeness. But I must hurry, Miss Beresford."

"Can I come with you, please?"

"Oh, damn it all, yes," I said irritably. I'd managed to look away from her eyes and start breathing again. "Come if you want."

At the for'ard end of the passageway, just beyond the entrance to Cerdan's suite, I ran into Carreras Senior. He was smoking a cigar and had that look of contentment and satisfaction that passengers invariably had when Antoine was finished with them.

"Ah, there you are, Mr. Carter," he said. "Wondered why you hadn't returned to our table. What is wrong, if I may ask? There must be at least a dozen of the crew gathered outside the accommodation entrance. I thought regulations forbade—"

"They're waiting for me, sir. Benson—you probably haven't had the chance to meet him since you came aboard; he's our chief steward—is missing. That's a search party outside."

"Missing?" The grey eyebrows went up. "What on earth —well, of course you haven't any idea what has happened to him or you wouldn't be organising this search. Can I help?"

I hesitated, thought of Miss Beresford who had already elbowed her way in, realised I'd now no way of stopping any or all of the passengers from getting into the act if they wanted to, and said, "Thank you, Mr. Carreras. You don't look like a man who would miss very much."

"We come from the same mould, Mr. Carter."

I let this cryptic remark go and hurried outside. A cloudless night, with the sky crowded with the usual impossible number of stars, a soft, warm wind blowing out of the south, a moderate cross swell running, but no match for our Denny-Brown stabilisers that could knock twenty-five degrees off a thirty-degree roll without half trying. A black shape detached itself from a nearby shadowed bulkhead and Archie MacDonald, the bo'sun, came towards me. For all his solid fifteen-stone bulk he was as light on his feet as a dancer.

"Any luck, bo'sun?" I asked.

"No one saw anything; no one heard anything And there were at least a dozen folk on deck tonight, between eight and nine."

"Mr. Wilson there? Ah, there. Mr. Wilson, take the engineroom staff and three A.B.s Main deck and below. You should know where to look by this time," I added bitterly. "MacDonald, you and I will do the upper decks. Port side you, starboard side me. Two seamen and a cadet. Half an hour. Then back here."

I sent one man to examine the boat positions—why Benson should have wished to get into a boat I couldn't even imagine, except that lifeboats have always had a queer attraction for those who wished to hide, although why he should wish to hide I couldn't guess either—and another to scour the superstructure abaft the bridge. I started going through the cabins on the boat deck, charthouse, flag and radar cabins and had Mr. Carreras to help me. Rusty, our youngest apprentice, went aft to work his way for'ard, accompanied by Miss Beresford who had probably guessed, and rightly, that I was in no mood for her company. But Rusty was. He always was. Nothing that Susan Beresford said to or about him made the slightest difference to him. He was her slave and didn't care who knew it. If she'd asked him to jump down the funnel, just for her sake, he'd have considered it an honour. I could just imagine him searching about the upper decks with Susan Beresford by his side, his face the same colour as his flaming shock of hair.

As I stepped out of the radar office I literally bumped into him. He was panting, as if he'd run a long way. and I could see I had been wrong about the colour of his face: in the half-light on the deck it looked grey, like old newspaper.

"Radio office, sir." He gasped out the words and caught my arm, a thing he would never normally have dreamed of doing. "Come quickly, sir. Please."

I was already running. "You found him?"

"No, sir. It's Mr. Brownell." Brownell was our chief wireless operator. "Something seems to have happened to him."

I reached the office in ten seconds, brushed past the pale blur of Susan Beresford standing just outside the door, crossed over the storm sill, and stopped.

Brownell had the overhead rheostat turned down until the room was less than half lit, a fairly common practice among radio operators on duty night watches. He was leaning forward over his table, his head pillowed on his right forearm, so that all I could see was his shoulders, dark hair, and the bald spot that had been the bane of his life. His left hand was outflung, his fingers just brushing the bridge telephone. The transmitting key was sending continuously. I eased the right forearm forward a couple of inches. The transmitting stopped.

I felt for the pulse in the outstretched left wrist. I felt for the pulse in the side of the neck. I turned to Susan Beresford, still standing in the doorway, and said, "Do you have a mirror?" She nodded wordlessly, fumbled in her bag, and handed over a compact, opened, the mirror showing. I turned up the rheostat till the radio cabin was harsh with light, moved Brownell's head slightly, held the mirror near mouth and nostrils for maybe ten seconds, took it away, glanced at it, then handed it back.

"Something's happened to him all right," I said. My voice was steady, unnaturally so. "He's dead. Or I think he's dead. Rusty, get Dr. Marston right away. He's usually in the telegraph lounge this time of night. Tell the captain, if he's there. Not a word to anyone else about this."

Rusty disappeared and another figure appeared to take his place beside Susan Beresford in the doorway. Carreras. He stopped, one foot over the storm sill, and said, "My God! Benson."

"No, Brownell. Wireless officer. I think he's dead." On the off-chance that Bullen hadn't yet gone down to the lounge I reached for the bulkhead phone labelled "Captain's Cabin" and waited for an answer, staring at the dead man sprawled across the table. Middle-aged, cheerful, his only harmless idiosyncrasy being an unusual vanity about his personal appearance that had once even driven him to the length of buying a toupee for his bald spot—public shipboard opinion had forced him to discard it—Brownell was one of the most popular and genuinely liked officers on the ship. Was? Had been. I heard the click of a lifted receiver.

"Captain? Carter here. Could you come down to the wireless office? At once, please."

"Benson?"

"Brownell. Dead, sir, I think."

There was a pause, a click. I hung up, reached for another phone that connected directly to the radio officers' cabins. We had three radio officers and the one with the middle watch, from midnight to 4 A.M., usually skipped dinner in the dining room and made for his bunk instead. A voice answered: "Peters here."

"First mate. Sorry to disturb you, but come up to the radio room right away."

"What's up?"

"You'll find out when you get here."

The overhead light seemed far too bright for a room with a dead man in it. I turned the rheostat and the white glare was replaced by a deep yellow glare. Rusty's face appeared in the doorway. He didn't seem so pale any more, but maybe the subdued light was just being kind to him.

"Surgeon's coming, sir." His breathing was quicker than ever. "Just picking up his bag in the dispensary."

"Thanks. Go and fetch the bo'sun, will you? And no need to kill yourself running, Rusty. There's no great hurry now."

He left, and Susan Beresford said in a low voice, "What's wrong? What—what happened to him?"

"You shouldn't be here, Miss Beresford."

"What happened to him?" she repeated.

"That's for the ship's surgeon to say. Looks to me as if

he just died where he sat. Heart atttack, coronary throm-
bosis, something like that."

She shivered, made no reply. Dead men were no new
thing to me, but the faint icy prickling on the back of my
neck and spine made me feel like shivering myself. The
warm trade wind seemed cooler, much cooler, than it
had a few minutes ago.

Dr. Marston appeared. No running, no haste, even, with
Dr. Marston: a slow measured man with a slow measured
stride. A magnificent mane of white hair, clipped white
moustache, a singularly smooth and unlined complexion
for a man getting so far on in years, steady, clear, keen
blue eyes with a peculiarly penetrating property, here, you
knew instinctively, was a doctor you could trust implicitly,
which only went to show that your instinct should be
taken away from you and locked up in some safe place
where it couldn't do you any harm. Admittedly, even to
look at him made you feel better, and that was all right as
far as it went, but to go further, to put your life in his
hands, say, was a very different and dicey proposition altogether, for there was an even chance that you wouldn't
get it back again. Those piercing blue eyes had not lighted
on the "Lancet" or made any attempt to follow the latest
medical developments since quite a few years prior to the
Second World War. But they didn't have to: he and Lord
Dexter had gone through prep school, public school, and
university together and his job was secure as long as he
could lift a stethescope. And, to be fair to him, when it
came to treating wealthy and hypochondriacal old ladies
he had no equal on the seven seas.

"Well, John," he boomed. With the exception of Captain Bullen, he addressed every officer on the ship by his
first name exactly as a public school headmaster would
have addressed one of his more promising pupils, but a
pupil that needed watching all the same. "What's the
trouble? Beau Brownell taken a turn?"

"Worse than that, I'm afraid, Doctor. Dead."

"Good Lord! Brownell? Dead? Let me see, let me see.
A little more light, if you please, John." He dumped his
bag on the table, fished out his stethescope, sounded

Brownell here and there, took his pulse, and then straight-ened with a sigh. "In the midst of life, John . . . and not recently either. Temperature's high in here, but I should say he's been gone well over an hour."

I could see the dark bulk of Captain Bullen in the doorway now, waiting, listening, saying nothing.

"Heart attack, Doctor?" I ventured. After all, he wasn't all that incompetent, just a quarter of a century out of date.

"Let me see, let me see," he repeated. He turned Brownell's head and looked closely at it. He had to look closely. He was unaware that everyone in the ship knew that, piercing blue eyes or not, he was as shortsighted as a dodo and refused to wear glasses. "Ah, look at this. The tongue, the lips, the eyes, above all the complexion. No doubt about it, no doubt at all. Cerebral haemorrhage. Massive. And at his age. How old, John?"

"Forty-seven, eight. Thereabouts."

"Forty-seven. Just forty-seven." He shook his head. "Gets them younger every day. The stress of modern living."

"And that outstretched hand, Doctor?" I asked. "Reach-ing for the phone. You think—"

"Just confirms my diagnosis, alas. Felt it coming on, tried to call for help, but it was too sudden, too massive. Poor old Beau Brownell." He turned, caught sight of Bullen leaning in the doorway. "Ah, there you are, Cap-tain. A bad business, a bad business."

"A bad business," Bullen agreed heavily. "Miss Beres-ford, you have no right to be here. You're cold and shiver-ing. Go to your cabin at once." When Captain Bullen spoke in that tone, the Beresford millions didn't seem to matter any more. "Dr. Marston will bring you a sedative later."

"And perhaps Mr. Carreras will be so kind—" I began.

"Certainly," Carreras agreed at once. "I will be hon-oured to see the young lady to her cabin." He bowed slightly, offered her his arm; she seemed more than glad to take it, and they disappeared.

Five minutes later all was back to normal in the radio

cabin. Peters had taken the dead man's place; Dr. Marston had returned to his favourite occupation of mingling socially and drinking steadily with our millionaires; the captain had given me his instructions; I'd passed them on to the bo'sun, and Brownell, canvas-wrapped, had been taken for'ard to the carpenter's store.

I stayed in the wireless office for a few minutes, talking to a very shaken Peters, and looked casually at the latest radio message that had come through. All radio messages were written down in duplicate as received, the original for the bridge and the carbon for the daily spiked file.

I lifted the topmost message from the file, but it was nothing very important, just a warning of deteriorating weather far to the southeast of Cuba which might or might not build up to a hurricane. Routine and too far away to bother us. I lifted the blank message pad that lay at Peters' elbow.

"May I have this?"

"Help yourself." He was still too upset even to be curious as to why I wanted it. "Plenty more where that came from."

I left him, walked up and down the deck outside for some time, then made my way to the captain's cabin where I'd been told to report when I was through. He was in his usual seat by the desk with Cummings and the chief engineer sitting on the settee. The presence of McIlroy, a short, stout Tynesider with the facial expression and hair style of Friar Tuck, meant a very worried captain and a council of war. McIlroy's brilliance wasn't confined to reciprocating engines; that plump, laughter-creased face concealed a brain that was probably the shrewdest on the *Campari,* and that included Mr. Julius Beresford, who must have been very shrewd indeed to make his three hundred million dollars or whatever it was.

"Sit down, Mister, sit down," Bullen growled. The "Mister" didn't mean I was in his black books, just another sign that he was worried. "No signs of Benson yet?"

"No sign at all."

"What a bloody trip!" Bullen pushed across a tray with whisky and glasses on it, unaccustomedly openhanded liberality that was just another sign of his worry. "Help yourself, Mister."

"Thank you, sir." I helped myself lavishly—the chance didn't come often—and went on: "What are we going to do about Brownell?"

"What the devil do you mean, 'What are we going to do about Brownell?' He's got no folks to notify, no consent to get about anything. Head Office has been informed. Burial at sea at dawn, before our passengers are up and about. Mustn't spoil their blasted trip, I suppose."

"Wouldn't it be better to take him to Nassau, sir?"

"Nassau?" He stared at me over the rim of his glass, then lowered it carefully to the table. "Just because a man has died, you don't have to go off your blasted rocker, do you?"

"Nassau or some other British territory. Or Miami. Some place where we can get competent authorities, police authorities, to investigate things."

"What things, Johnny?" McIlroy asked. He had his head cocked to one side like a fat and well-stuffed owl.

"Yes, what things?" Bullen's tone was quite different from McIlroy's. "Just because the search party hasn't turned up Benson yet, you—"

"I've called off the search party, sir."

Bullen pushed back his chair till his hands rested on the table at the full stretch of his arms.

"*You've* called off the search party," he said softly. "Who the hell gave you authority to do anything of the kind?"

"No one, sir. But I—"

"*Why* did you do it, Johnny?" McIlroy again, very quietly.

"Because we'll never see Benson again. Not alive, that is. Benson's dead. Benson's been killed."

No one said anything, not for all of ten seconds. The sound of the cool air rushing through the louvres in the overhead trunking seemed abnormally loud. Then Captain Bullen said harshly, "Killed? Benson killed? Are you all right, Mister? What do you mean, killed?"

"Murdered is what I mean."

"Murdered? Murdered?" McIlroy shifted uneasily in his chair. "Have you seen him? Have you any proof? How can you say he was murdered?"

"I haven't seen him. And I haven't any proof. Not a scrap of evidence." I caught a glimpse of the purser sitting there, his hands twisting together and his eyes staring at me, and I remembered that Benson had been his best friend for close on twenty years. "But I *have* proof that Brownell was murdered tonight. And I can tie the two together."

There was an even longer silence.

"You're mad," Bullen said at length with harsh conviction. "So now Brownell's been murdered too. You're mad, Mister, off your bloody trolley. You heard what Dr. Marston said? Massive cerebral haemorrhage. But of course he's only a doctor of forty years' standing. He wouldn't know—"

"How about giving me a chance, sir?" I interrupted. My voice sounded as harsh as his own. "I know he's a doctor. I also know he hasn't very good eyes. But I have. I saw what he missed. I saw a dark smudge on the back of Brownell's uniform collar—and when has anybody on this ship ever seen a mark on any shirt that Brownell ever wore? They didn't call him Beau Brownell for nothing. Somebody had hit him, with something heavy and with tremendous force, on the back of the neck. There was also a faint discolouration under the left ear—I could see it as he lay there. When the bo'sun and I got him down to the carpenter's store we examined him together. There was a corresponding slight bruise under his right ear—and traces of sand under his collar. Someone sandbagged him and then, when he was unconscious, compressed the carotid arteries until he died. Go and see for yourselves."

"Not me," McIlroy murmured. You could see that even his normally monolithic composure had been shaken. "Not me. I believe it—absolutely. It would be too easy to disprove it. I believe it all right—but I still can't accept it."

"But damn it all, Chief!" Bullen's fists were clenched. "The doctor said that—"

"I'm no medical man," McIlroy interrupted. "But I

should imagine the symptoms are pretty much the same in both cases. Can hardly blame old Marston."

Bullen ignored this, gave me the full benefit of his commodore's stare.

"Look, Mister," he said slowly, "you've changed your tune, haven't you? When I was there, you agreed with Dr. Marston. You even put forward the heart-failure idea. You showed no signs—"

"Miss Beresford and Mr. Carreras were there," I interrupted. "I didn't want them to start getting wrong ideas. If word got round the ship—and it would have been bound to—that we suspected murder, then whoever was responsible might have felt themselves forced to act again, and act quickly, to forestall any action we might take. I don't know what they might do, but on the form to date it would have been something damned unpleasant."

"Miss Beresford? Mr. Carreras?" Bullen had stopped clenching his hands, but you could see that it wouldn't take much to make him start up again. "Miss Beresford is above suspicion. But Carreras? And his son? Just aboard to-day—and in most unusual circumstances. It might just tie up."

"It doesn't. I checked. Carreras Senior and Junior had both been in either the telegraph lounge or the dining room for almost two hours before we found Brownell. They're completely in the clear."

"Besides being too obvious," McIlroy agreed. "I think, Captain, it's time we took our hats off to Mr. Carter here. He's been getting round and using his head while all we have been doing is twiddling our thumbs."

"Benson," Captain Bullen said. He didn't show any signs of taking off his hat. "How about Benson? How does he tie up?"

"This way." I slid the empty telegraph book across the table. "I checked the last message that was received and went to the bridge. Routine weather report. Time, 20.07. But later there was another message written on this pad: original, carbon, duplicate. The message is indecipherable —but to people with modern police equipment it would be child's play to find out what was written there. What *is* decipherable is the impression of the last two time figures. Look for yourself. It's quite clear—thirty-three. That means 20.33. A message came through at that moment, a message so urgent in nature that, instead of waiting for the routine bridge messenger collection, Brownell made to phone it through at once. That was why his hand was reaching for the phone when we found him, not because he was feeling ill all of a sudden. And then he was killed. Whoever killed him *had* to kill. Knocking Brownell out and stealing the message would have accomplished nothing, for as soon as he would have come to he would have remembered the contents of the message and immediately sent it to the bridge. It must," I added thoughtfully, "have been a damned important message."

"Benson," Bullen repeated impatiently. "How about Benson?"

"Benson was the victim of a lifetime of habit. Howie here tells us how Benson invariably went out on deck between half-past eight and twenty-five to nine for a smoke while the passengers were at dinner. The radio room is immediately above where he would have been taking his promenade—and the message came through, and Brownell was killed, inside those five minutes. Benson must have seen or heard something unusual and gone to investigate. He might even have caught the murderer in the act. And so Benson had to die too."

"But *why?*" Captain Bullen demanded. He still couldn't believe it all. "Why, why, *why?* Why was he killed? Why was that message so desperately important? The whole damned thing's crazy. And what in God's name was in that message, anyway?"

"That's why we have to go to Nassau to find out, sir."

Bullen looked at me without expression, looked at his drink, evidently decided that he preferred his drink to me —or the ill news I brought with me—and knocked back the contents in a couple of gulps.

McIlroy didn't touch his. He sat there for a whole minute looking at it consideringly, then said, "You haven't missed much, Johnny. But you've missed one thing. The wireless officer on watch—Peters, isn't it? How do you know the same message won't come through again? Maybe it was a message requiring acknowledgement? If it was, and it's not acknowledged, it's pretty certain to come through again. Then what's the guarantee that Peters won't get the same treatment?"

"The bo'sun's the guarantee, Chief. He's sitting in black shadow not ten yards from the wireless office with a mar-line-spike in his hand and Highland murder in his heart. You know MacDonald. Heaven help anyone who goes within a Sunday walk of the wireless office."

Bullen poured himself another small whisky, smiled tiredly, and glanced at his single broad commodore's stripe.

"Mr. Carter, I think you and I should change jackets." It was as far in apology as he could ever go and about twelve hours ahead of par. "Think you'd like this side of my desk?"

"Suit me fine, sir," I agreed. "Especially if you took over entertaining the passengers."

"In that case we'll stay as we are." Another brief smile, no sooner there than vanished. "Who's on the bridge? Jamieson, isn't it? Better take over, First."

"Later, sir, with your permission. There's still the most important thing of all to investigate. But I don't even know how to start."

"Don't tell me there's something else," Bullen said heavily.

"I've had some time to think about this, that's all," I said. "A message came through to our wireless office, a message so important that it had to be intercepted at all costs. But how could anyone possibly know that message was coming through? The only way that message could have come into the *Campari* was through a pair of earphones clamped to Brownell's head, yet someone else was taking down that message at the same instant as Brownell was. Must have been. Brownell had no sooner finished transcribing that message onto his pad than he reached for the phone to get the bridge and he no sooner reached for the phone than he died. There's some other radio receiver aboard the *Campari* tuned into the same wave length, and wherever it is, it's not a hop, skip, and jump from the wireless office, for wherever the eavesdropper was, he got from there to the wireless office in seconds. Problem, find the receiver."

Bullen looked at me. McIlroy looked at me. They both looked at each other. Then McIlroy objected: "But the wireless officer keeps shifting wave lengths. How could anybody know what particular wave length he was on at any one moment?"

"How can anyone know anything?" I asked. I nodded at the message pad on the table. "Until we get that deciphered?"

"The message." Bullen gazed at the pad, abruptly made up his mind. "Nassau it is. Maximum speed, Chief, but slowly, over half an hour, so that no one will notice the step-up in revs. First, the bridge. Get our position." He fetched chart, rules, dividers while I was getting the figures, nodded at me as I hung up. "Lay off the shortest possible course."

It didn't take long. "047 from here to here, sir, approximately 220 miles, then 350."

"Arrival?"

"Maximum speed?"

"Of course."

"Just before midnight to-morrow night."

He reached for a pad, scribbled for a minute, then read out: " 'Port authorities, Nassau. S.S. *Campari*, position such-and-such, arriving 23.30 tomorrow Wednesday. Request police alongside immediate investigation one murdered man, one missing man. Urgent. Bullen, Master.' That should do." He reached for the phone. I touched his arm.

"Whoever has this receiver can monitor outgoing calls just as easily as incoming ones. Then they'll know we're on to them. God only knows what might happen then."

Bullen looked slowly first at me, then at McIlroy, then

at the purser, who hadn't spoken a word since I'd arrived in the cabin, then back at me again. Then he tore the message into tiny shreds and dropped it into the waste-paper basket.

Chapter 4

I DIDN'T get a great deal of investigating done that night. I'd figured out how to start, all right, but the devil of it was I couldn't start till the passengers were up and about in the morning. Nobody likes being turfed out of his bed in the middle of the night, a millionaire least of all.

After having cautiously identified myself to the bo'sun to ensure that I didn't get the back of my head stove in with a marlinespike, I spent a good fifteen minutes in the vicinity of the wireless office, relating its position to other offices and nearby accommodation. The wireless office was on the starboard side, for'ard, immediately above the passengers' "A" deck accommodation—old man Cerdan's suite was directly below—and on the basis of my assumption that the murderer, even if he didn't wait for the last few words of the message to come through, could have had no more than ten seconds to get from wherever the hidden receiver was to the wireless office, then any place within ten seconds' reach of the wireless office automatically came under suspicion.

There were quite a few places within the suspected limits. There was the bridge, flag office, radar office, chart-room, and all the deck officers' and cadets' accommodation. Those could be ruled out at once. There was the dining room, galleys, pantries, officers' lounge, telegraph lounge and, immediately adjacent to the telegraph lounge, another lounge which rejoiced in the name of the drawing room—it having been found necessary to provide an alternative lounge for our millionaires' wives and daughters who weren't all so keen on the alcoholic and ticker-tape attractions of the telegraph lounge as their husbands and fathers were. I spent forty minutes going through those—they were all deserted at that time of night—and if anyone had yet invented a transistor receiver smaller than a matchbox, then I might have missed it; but anything larger, I'd have found it for sure.

That left only the passengers' accommodation, with the cabins on "A" deck, immediately below the wireless office, as the prime suspects. The "B" deck suites, on the next deck below, were not outwith the bounds of possibility; but when I ran a mental eye over the stiff-legged bunch of elderly crocks on "B" deck, I couldn't think of a man among them who could have made it to the wireless office in under ten seconds. And it certainly hadn't been a woman: because whoever had killed Brownell had not only also laid out Benson, but removed him from sight, and Benson weighed a hundred and eighty pounds if he weighed an ounce.

So, "A" or "B" decks. Both of them would have to go through the sieve tomorrow. I prayed for good weather to tempt our passengers out onto the sun decks to give the stewards, in the course of making up beds and cleaning out the cabins, the chance to carry out a thorough search. The customs in Jamaica, of course, had already done this; but they had been looking for a mechanism over six feet in length, not a radio which, in these days of miniaturisation, could easily have been hidden in, say, one of those hefty jewel boxes which were run of the mill among our millionaires' wives.

We were running almost due northeast now, under the same indigo sky ablaze with stars, the *Campari* rolling gently as it sliced along the line of the long, slow swell.

We'd taken almost half an hour to make an eighty-degree change of course so that no night-owl passenger abroad on deck could see the changing direction of our wake, not that those precautions were going to be of any use if any of our passengers had the faintest of stellar navigation or, come to that, the very elementary ability to locate the Pole Star.

I was walking slowly up the boat deck, port side, when I saw Captain Bullen approaching. He lifted his arm, motioned me into the deep shadow cast by one of the ship's lifeboats.

"Thought I would find you here or herabouts," he said softly. He reached under his jacket and pressed something cold and hard into my hand. "I believe you know how to use one of those."

Starlight glinted dully off the blued metal in my hand. A Colt automatic, one of the three kept on a locked chain in a glass cabinet in the captain's sleeping cabin. Captain Bullen was certainly taking things seriously at last.

"I can use it, sir."

"Right. Stick it in your belt or wherever you stick those damned things. Never realised they were so blasted awkward to conceal about your person. And here's a spare magazine. Hope to God we don't have to use them." Which meant the captain had one also.

"The third gun, sir?"

"I don't know." He hesitated. "Wilson, I thought."

"He's a good man. But give it to the bo'sun."

"The bo'sun?" Bullen's voice sharpened, then he remembered the need for secrecy and dropped his voice to a conspiratorial growl. "You know the regulations, Mister. Those guns to be used only in times of war, piracy, or mutiny—and never to be issued to anyone other than an officer."

"The regulations don't concern me half as much as my own neck does, sir. You know MacDonald's record—youngest-ever sergeant-major in the Commandos, a list of decorations as long as your arm. Give it to MacDonald, sir."

"We'll see," he grunted, "we'll see. I've just been to the

carpenter's store. With Doc Marston. First time I've ever seen that old phony shaken to the core. He agrees with you, says there's no doubt Brownell was murdered. You'd think he was up in the dock of the Old Bailey with the alibis he's giving himself. But I think McIlroy was right when he said the symptoms were about the same."

"Well," I said doubtfully, "I hope nothing comes of it, sir."

"What do you mean?"

"You know old Doc Marston as well as I do, sir. The two great loves of his life are Jamaica rum and the desire to give the impression that he's on the inside of everything that goes on. A dangerous combination. Apart from McIlroy, the purser, yourself, and myself, the only person who knows that Brownell didn't die a natural death is the bo'sun, and he'd never talk. Doc Marston is a different proposition altogether."

"Not to worry, my boy," Bullen said with something like relish in his voice. "I told our worthy surgeon that, Lord Dexter's pal or not, if he as much as lifted a glass of rum before we arrived in Nassau, I'd have him on the beach, and for good, within the week."

I tried to imagine anyone telling that venerable and aristocratic doctor anything of the sort: my mind boggled at the very thought. But they hadn't made Bullen company commodore for nothing. I knew he'd done exactly as stated.

"He didn't take off any of Brownell's clothes?" I asked. "His shirt, for instance?"

"No. What does it matter?"

"It's just that it's probable that whoever strangled Brownell had his fingers locked round the back of the neck to give leverage, and I believe that police today can pick up fingerprints from practically any substance, including certain types of clothes. They shouldn't have too much trouble picking up prints from those nice shiny, starched collars that Brownell wore."

"You don't miss much," Bullen said thoughtfully. "Except maybe you've missed your profession. Anything else?"

"Yes. About this burial at sea tomorrow at dawn."

There was a long pause, then he said with the blasphemously weary restraint of a long-suffering man who has already held himself in check far too long, "What bloody burial at dawn? Brownell is our only exhibition for the Nassau police."

"Burial, sir," I repeated. "But not at dawn. About, say, eight o'clock, when a fair number of our passengers will be up and about, having had their morning constitutional. This is what I mean, sir."

I told him what I meant and he listened patiently enough, considering. When I was finished he nodded slowly, two or three times in succession, turned and left me without a word.

I moved out into a lane of light between two lifeboats and glanced at my watch. Twenty-five minutes past eleven. I'd told MacDonald I'd relieve him at midnight. I walked across to the rail and stood there by a life-jacket locker, staring out over the slow shimmering swell of the sea, hands at arms' length on the rail, vainly trying to figure out what could possibly lie behind all that had happened that evening.

When I awoke, it was twenty minutes to one. Not that I was immediately aware of the time when I awoke; I wasn't immediately and clearly aware of anything. It's difficult to be aware of anything when your head is being squeezed between the jaws of a giant vice and your eyes have gone blind, to be aware of anything, that is, except the vice and the blindness. Blindness. My eyes. I was worried about my eyes. I raised a hand and fumbled round for a while and then I found them. They were filled with something hard and encrusted, and when I rubbed the crust came away and there was stickiness beneath. Blood. There was blood in my eyes, blood that was gumming the lids together and making me blind. At least, I hoped vaguely, it was blood that was making me blind.

I rubbed some more blood away with the heel of my hand, and then I could see. Not too well, not the way I was used to seeing; the stars in the sky were not the bright pin points of light to which I was accustomed but just a pale, fuzzy haze seen through a frosted-glass window. I reached out a trembling hand and tried to touch this frosted glass, but it vanished and dissolved as I reached out and what my hand touched was cool and metallic. I strained my eyes wide open and saw that there was indeed no glass there; what I was touching was the lowermost bar of the ship's rail.

I could see better now, at least better than a blind man could. My head was lying in the scuppers, inches away from one of the lifeboat davits. What in God's name was I doing there with my head in the scuppers, inches away from the davits? I managed to get both hands under me and, with a sudden drunken lurch, heaved myself into a semi-sitting position with one elbow still on the deck. A great mistake, a very great mistake, for at once a blinding, agonising pain, that never-recorded pain that must be experienced in the final shattering millisecond of awareness as a plunging guillotine slices through bone, flesh, and muscle before crashing into the block beneath, slashed its paralysing way across head, neck, and shoulders and toppled me back to the deck again. My head must have struck heavily against the iron of the scuppers, but I don't think I even moaned.

Slowly, infinitely slowly, consciousness came back to me. Consciousness of a kind. Where clarity and awareness and speed of recovery were concerned, I was a man chained hand and foot, surfacing from the bottom of a sea of molasses. Something, I dimly realised, was touching my face, my eyes, my mouth: something cold and moist and sweet. Water. Someone was sponging my face with water, gently trying to mop the blood from my eyes. I made to turn my head to see who it was and then I vaguely remembered what had happened last time I moved my head. I raised my right hand instead and touched someone's wrist.

"Take it easy, sir. You just take it easy." The man with the sponge must have had a long arm; he was at least two miles away, but I recognised the voice for all that. Archie MacDonald. "Don't you try moving now. Just you wait a bit. You'll be all right, sir."

"Archie?" We were a real disembodied pair, I thought

fuzzily. I was at least a couple of miles away too. I only hoped we were a couple of miles away in the same direction. "Is that you, Archie?" God knows I didn't doubt it. I just wanted the reassurance of hearing him say so.

"It's myself, sir. Just you leave everything to me." It was the bo'sun all right; he couldn't have used that sentence more than five thousand times in the years I'd known him. "Just you lie still."

I'd no intention of doing anything else. I'd be far gone in years before I'd ever forget the last time I moved, if I lived that long, which didn't seem likely at the moment.

"My neck, Archie." My voice sounded a few hundred yards closer. "I think it's broken."

"Aye, I'm sure it feels that way, sir, but I'm thinking myself maybe it's not as bad as all that. We'll see."

I don't know how long I lay there, maybe two or three minutes, while the bo'sun swabbed the blood away until eventually the stars began to swim into some sort of focus again. Then he slid one arm under my shoulders and under my head and began to lift me, inch by patient inch, into a sitting position.

I waited for the guillotine to fall again, but it didn't. This time it was more like a butcher's meat chopper, but a pretty blunt chopper: several times in a few seconds the *Campari* spun round 360 degrees on its keel, then settled down on course again. 047, I seemed to recall. And this time I didn't lose consciousness.

"What time is it, Archie?" A stupid question to ask, but I wasn't at my very best. And my voice, I was glad to hear, was at last practically next door to me.

He turned my left wrist.

"Twelve forty-five, your watch says, sir. I think you must have been lying here a good hour. You were in the shadow of the boat and no one would have seen you even if they had passed by this way."

I moved my head an experimental inch and winced at the pain of it. Two inches and it would fall off.

"What the hell happened to me, Archie? Some kind of turn or other? I don't remember—"

"Some kind of turn!" His voice was soft and cold. I felt

his fingers touch the back of my neck. "Our friend with the sandbag has been taking a walk again, sir. One of these days," he added thoughtfully, "I'm going to catch him at it."

"Sandbag!" I struggled to my feet, but I'd never have made it without the bo'sun. "The wireless office! Peters!"

"It's young Mr. Jenkins that's on now, sir. He's all right. You said you'd relieve me for the middle watch, and when twenty past twelve came I knew something was wrong. So I just went straight into the wireless office and phoned Captain Bullen."

"The captain?"

"Who else could I phone, sir?" Who else, indeed? Apart from myself the captain was the only deck officer who really knew what had happened, who knew where the bo'sun was concealed and why. MacDonald had his arm round me now, still half supporting me, leading me for'ard to the cross passage that led to the wireless office. "He came at once. He's there now, talking to Mr. Jenkins. Worried stiff—thinks the same thing might have happened to you as happened to Benson. He gave me a present before I came looking for you." He made a movement and I could see the barrel of a pistol that was all but engulfed in his huge hand. "I am hoping that I get a chance to use this, Mr. Carter, and not the butt end, either. I suppose you realise that if you had toppled forward instead of sideways, you'd most likely have fallen over the rail into the sea."

I wondered grimly why they—or he—hadn't, in fact, shoved me over the side but said nothing, just concentrated on reaching the wireless office.

Captain Bullen was waiting there, just outside the door, and the bulge in the pocket of his uniform jacket wasn't caused only by his hand. He came quickly to meet us, probably to get out of earshot of the wireless officer, and his reaction to my condition and story of what had happened was all that anyone could reasonably have wished for. He was just mad clear through. I'd never seen him in such a mood of tightly controlled anger since I'd first met him three years ago. When he'd calmed down a bit, he said, "But why the devil didn't they go the whole hog and throw you overboard while they were at it?"

"They didn't have to, sir," I said wearily. "They didn't want to kill me. Just to get me out of the road."

He peered at me, the cold eyes speculative.

"You talk as if you knew why they coshed you."

"I do. Or I think I do." I rubbed the back of my neck with a gentle hand. I was pretty sure now there weren't any vertebrae broken; it just felt that way. "My own fault. I overlooked the obvious. Come to that, we all overlooked the obvious. Once they'd killed Brownell and we'd deduced, by association, that they'd also killed Benson, I lost all interest in Benson. I just assumed that they'd got rid of him. All I was concerned with, all any of us was concerned with, was to see that there was no further attack made on the wireless office, to try to find out where the receiver was, and to figure what lay behind it all. Benson, we were sure, was dead, and a dead Benson could no longer be of any use to us. So we forgot Benson. Benson belonged to the past."

"Are you trying to tell me that Benson was—or is—still alive?"

"He was dead all right." I felt about ninety, a badly crippled ninety, and the vice round my head wasn't easing off any I could notice. "He was dead, but they hadn't got rid of him. Maybe they hadn't a chance to get rid of him. Maybe they had to wait till it was real good and dark to get rid of him. But they *had* to get rid of him—if we'd found him, we'd have *known* there was a murderer aboard. They probably had him stashed away in some place where we wouldn't have thought of looking for him anyway, lying on top of one of the offices, stuck in a ventilator, behind one of the sundeck benches—it could have been anywhere. And I was either too near where they'd stashed him, so that they couldn't get at him, or they couldn't chuck him overboard as long as I was standing by the rail there. Barring myself, they knew they were safe enough. Going at maximum speed, with a bow wave like we're throwing up right now, no one would have heard anything if they had dropped him into the sea, and on a dark and moonless night like this no one would have seen anything either. So they'd only me to deal with—and they didn't find that any trouble at all," I finished bitterly.

Bullen shook his head. "You never heard a thing? Not the faintest fall of a footstep, not even the swish of a cosh coming through the air?"

"Old flannel-feet must be a pretty dangerous character, sir," I said reflectively. "He didn't make the slightest whisper of sound. I wouldn't have thought it possible. For all I know, I might have taken a fainting turn and struck my head on the davit as I fell. That's what I thought myself—I even suggested it to the bo'sun here. And that's what I'm going to tell anyone who wants to know tomorrow." I grinned and winked at MacDonald, and even the wink hurt. "I'll tell them you've been overworking me, sir, and I collapsed from exhaustion."

"Why tell anyone?" Bullen wasn't amused. "It doesn't show where you have been coshed; that wound is just above the temple and inside the hairline and could be pretty well camouflaged. Agreed?"

"No, sir. *Someone* knows I had an accident—the character responsible for it—and he's going to regard it as damned queer if I make no reference to it at all. But if I do mention it and pass it off as a ladylike swoon, there's an even chance he may accept it, and if he does we're still going to have the advantage of being in the position of knowing there's mayhem and murder aboard, while they will have no suspicion we know anything of the kind."

"Your mind," said Captain Bullen unsympathetically, "is beginning to clear at last."

When I awoke in the morning the already hot sun was streaming in through my uncurtained window. My cabin, immediately abaft the captain's, was on the starboard side, and the sun was coming from for'ard, which meant that we were still steaming northeast. I raised myself on my elbow to have a look at the sea conditions, for the *Campari* had developed a definite if gentle pitching movement, and it was then that I discovered that my neck was rigidly bound in a plaster cast. At least it felt exactly like it. I could move it about an inch to either side and then a pair of clamps took hold. A dull steady ache, but no pain worth mentioning. I tried to force my head beyond the limits of the clamps, but I only tried once. I waited till the cabin stopped swaying round and the red-hot wires in my neck had cooled off to a tolerable temperature, then climbed stiffly out of my bunk. Let them call me stiff-neck Carter if they wanted. That was enough of that lot.

I crossed to the window. Still a cloudless sky with the sun, white, glaring, already high above the horizon, striking a glittering, blinding path across the blueness of the sea. The swell was deeper, longer, heavier than I expected and coming up from the starboard quarter. I wound down the window and there was no wind I could notice, which meant that there was a fair breeze pushing up from astern, but not enough to whiten the smoothly roiled surface of the sea.

I showered, shaved—I'd never before appreciated how difficult it is to shave when the turning motion of your head is limited to an arc of two inches—then examined the wound. Seen in daylight, it looked bad, much worse than it had in the night: above and behind the left temple, it was a two-inch gash, wide and very deep. And it throbbed heavily in a way I didn't much care for. I picked up the phone and asked for Doc Marston. He was still in bed but, yes, he would see me right away, an early-bird Hippocratical willingness that was very much out of character, but maybe his conscience was bothering him about his wrong diagnosis of the previous night. I dressed, put on my hat, adjusted it to a suitably rakish angle till the band just missed the wound, and went down to see him.

Dr. Marston, fresh, rested, and unusually clear of eye—no doubt due to Bullen's warning to lay off the rum—didn't look like a conscience-stricken man who'd tossed and turned the sleepless night long. He didn't seem unduly worried about the fact that we carried aboard a passenger who, if he'd truthfully listed his occupation, would have put down the word "murderer." All he seemed concerned about was the entry in last night's log, and when I told him no entry about Brownell had been made or would be made until we arrived in Nassau, and that when it was made no mention of my name would appear in connection with the diagnosis of Brownell's death, he became positively jovial. He shaved off a few square inches of hair, jabbed in a local anaesthetic, cleaned and sutured the wound, covered it with a sticking-plaster pad, and wished me good morning. He was through for the day.

It was quarter to eight. I dropped down the series of accommodation ladders that led to the fo'c'sle and made my way for'ard to the carpenter's store. The fo'c'sle was unusually crowded for that time of the morning. There must have been close on forty members of the ship's company gathered there, deck staff, engine-room staff, cooks and stewards, all waiting to pay their last respects to Brownell. Nor were these all the spectators. I looked up and saw that the promenade deck, which curved right round the for'ard superstructure of the *Campari*, was dotted with passengers, eleven or twelve in all: not many, but they represented close on the total male passenger complement aboard—I could see no women there—with the exception of old Cerdan and possibly one or two others. Bad news travelled fast, and even for millionaires the chance of seeing a burial at sea didn't come along too often. Right in the middle of them was the Duke of Hartwell, looking nautical as anything in his carefully adjusted Royal Yachting Club cap, silk scarf, and brass-button navy doeskin jacket.

I skirted number one hold and thought grimly that there might indeed be something in the old superstitions: the dead cried out for company, the old salts said, and the dead men loaded only yesterday afternoon and now lying in the bottom of number four hold hadn't been slow to get that company. Two others gone in the space of a few hours, near as a toucher three; only I'd fallen sideways inside of toppling over the rail. I felt those ice-cold fingers on the back of my neck again and shivered, then passed into the comparative gloom of the carpenter's store, right up in the forepeak.

Everything was ready. The bier—a hastily nailed-together platform of boards, seven feet by two—lay on the deck, and the Red Ensign, tied to two corners of the handles at the top of the bier but free at the other end, covered the canvas-swathed mound beneath. Only the bo'sun and the carpenter were there. To look at Mac-Donald you would never have guessed that he hadn't slept the previous night. He had volunteered to remain on guard outside the wireless office until dawn; it had also been his idea that, though the chances of any trouble in daylight were remote, two men should be detailed for holy-stoning the deck outside the wireless office after breakfast, for the entire day if necessary. Meantime the radio office was closed—and heavily padlocked—to allow Peters and Jenkins to attend the funeral of their colleague. There was no difficulty about this: as was common, there was a standard arrangement whereby a bell rang either on the bridge or in the chief wireless operator's cabin whenever a call came through on the distress frequency or on the *Campari's* call sign.

The slight vibration of the *Campari's* engines died away as the engine slowed and the revs dropped until we had just enough speed to give us steerageway in that heavy swell. The captain came down the companionway, carrying a heavy brass-bound Bible under his arm. The heavy steel door in the port hand fo'c'sle side was swung open and back till it secured with a clank in its retaining latch. A long wooden box was slid into position, one end level with the opening in the side of the ship. Then MacDonald and the carpenter, bareheaded, appeared, carrying bier and burden, and laid them on the box.

The service was very brief, very simple. Captain Bullen said a few words about Brownell, about as true as words usually are in those circumstances, led the tattered singing of "Abide with Me," read the burial service, and nodded to the bo'sun. The Royal Navy did this sort of thing better, but we didn't carry any bugles aboard the *Campari*. Mac-Donald lifted the inboard end of the bier; the canvas-swathed mound slid out slowly from beneath the Red Ensign and was gone with only the faintest of splashings to mark its departure. I glanced up at the promenade deck and saw the Duke of Hartwell there, standing stiffly at attention, right arm bent up to his peaked cap in rigid salute.

Even allowing for the natural disadvantages lent him by his face, I had seldom seen a more ludicrous sight. No doubt to the unbiassed observer he was putting up a more fitting show than myself, but I find it hard to be at my reverent best when I know that all I'm committing to the deep is a length of canvas, large quantities of engine-room waste, and a hundred and fifty pounds of rusty chain to give the necessary negative buoyancy.

The door in the ship's side clanged shut; Captain Bullen handed over the Bible to a cadet; the engine revs mounted, and the *Campari* was back in business again. And the first item on the agenda was breakfast.

In my three years aboard the *Campari* I had rarely seen more than half a dozen passengers in the dining saloon for breakfast. Most of them preferred to have it served in their suites or on the private verandahs outside their suites. Barring a few apéritifs followed by Antoine's or Henrique's superb cooking, there was nothing to beat a good funeral to bring out the sociable best in our passengers. There could only have been seven or eight missing altogether.

I had a full complement at my table, except, of course, for the invalid Mr. Cerdan. I should have been on watch, but the captain had decided that, as there was a very able quartermaster on the wheel and no land within seventy miles, young Dexter, who usually stood the watch with me, could stand it alone for the length of breakfast.

No sooner had I pulled in my chair than Miss Harrbride fixed her beady eyes on me.

"What on earth's happened to you, young man?" she demanded.

"To tell you the truth, Miss Harrbride, I don't really know myself."

"You *what?*"

"It's true." I put on my best shamed face. "I was standing up on the boat deck last night and the next thing I knew I was lying in the scuppers with my head cut—I must have struck it against the davit when I fell." I had my story all prepared. "Dr. Marston thinks it was a combination of sunstroke—I was loading cargo most of the day yesterday and I can assure you that the sun *was* very hot—and the fact that, owing to our troubles in Kingston and the delay caused by it, I haven't had very much sleep in the past three days."

"I must say things *do* keep happening aboard the *Campari*," Miguel Carreras said. His face was grave. "One man dead from a heart attack or whatever it was, another missing—they haven't found our chief steward yet, have they?"

"I'm afraid not, sir."

"And now you get yourself banged up. Let's sincerely hope that's the end of it."

"Troubles always happen in threes, sir. I'm sure this is the end of it. We've never before—"

"Young man, let me have a look at you," a peremptory voice demanded from the captain's table. Mrs. Beresford, my favourite passenger. I twisted round in my seat to find that Mrs. Beresford, who normally sat with her back to me, had herself turned completely round in hers. Beyond her the Duke of Hartwell, unlike the previous night, was having no trouble at all in devoting his entire attention to Susan Beresford: the usual counterattraction on his right, in the best traditions of the theatrical world, rarely rose before noon. Mrs. Beresford studied me in silence for the better part of ten seconds.

"You don't look well at all, Mr. Carter," she pronounced finally. "Twisted your neck, didn't you? You didn't have to turn round in your chair to talk to me."

"A little," I admitted. "It's a bit stiff."

"And hurt your back into the bargain," she added triumphantly. "I can tell from the peculiar way you sit."

"It hardly hurts at all," I said bravely. It didn't, in fact, hurt me in the slightest, but I hadn't yet got the hang of carrying a gun in my waistband and the butt kept sticking painfully into my lower ribs.

"Sunstroke, eh?" Her face held genuine concern. "And lack of sleep. You should be in bed. Captain Bullen, I'm afraid you're overworking this young man."

"That's what I keep telling the captain, ma'am," I said, "but he doesn't pay any attention to me."

Captain Bullen smiled briefly and rose to his feet. His eyes, as they roved slowly over the room, held the expression of a man who wanted both attention and quiet: such was the personality of the man that he got it in three seconds flat.

"Ladies and gentlemen," he began. The Duke of Hartwell regarded the tablecloth with that smell-of-bad-fish expression he reserved for tenants wanting a cut in rent and merchant navy captains who forgot to preface public addresses with the words "Your Grace."

"I am most distressed," the captain went on, "as I am sure you are all distressed, by the events of the past twelve hours. That we should lose our chief wireless officer through death by natural causes is, God knows, bad enough, but that our chief steward should vanish the same evening—well, in thirty-six years at sea I have never known anything like it.

"What happened to Chief Steward Benson we cannot say with any certainty, but I can hazard a guess and at the same time issue a warning. There are literally hundreds of cases of men vanishing overboard at night, and I have little doubt but that Benson's death is due to the same reason which probably accounts for 99 per cent of all the other cases. Even on the most experienced sailors the effect of leaning over the rail at night and watching the black water passing below has a weirdly hypnotic effect. I think it's something akin to the vertigo that affects a great number of people, people who are convinced that if they go near, say, the parapet of a high building, some strange force will make them topple over, no matter what their conscious minds may say. Only, with leaning over the rails of a ship, there is no fear. Just a gradual mesmerism. A man just leans further and further over until his centre of gravity is suddenly displaced. And then he is gone."

As an alibi or explanation for Benson's disappearance it was as good as any; as a general statement it was also unfortunately true.

"And so, ladies and gentlemen, I would counsel you all, most strongly, never to approach the ship's rails at night unless you are accompanied by someone else. I would be most grateful if you would all bear that strongly in mind."

I looked round the passengers as far as my stiff neck would allow. They would bear it in mind all right. From now on wild horses wouldn't drag them near the *Campari*'s rails at night.

"But," Bullen went on emphatically, "it will help neither of those unfortunate men and only do ourselves a great disservice if we allow ourselves to brood over those things. I cannot ask you to dismiss those deaths from your minds at once, but I can ask you not to dwell on them. On a ship, as elsewhere, life must go on—especially, I might say, on a ship. You are aboard the *Campari* to enjoy the cruise; we are aboard to help you enjoy it. I would be most grateful if you would give us your every assistance to get shipboard life back to normal as soon as possible."

There was a subdued murmur of agreement, then Julius Beresford, rising from his seat beside the captain, was on his feet.

"Do you mind if I say a few words, sir?" He could have bought the Blue Mail Line without even denting his bank balance, but still he asked permission to speak and called old Bullen "sir."

"Certainly, Mr. Beresford."

"It's just this." Julius Beresford had addressed too many board meetings to be anything other than completely at ease when speaking to people, no matter how many million dollars they represented. "I agree, and agree completely, with everything our captain has said. Captain Bullen has said that he and his crew have a job to do and that that job is to look after the every comfort and convenience of his passengers. Under the rather sad circumstances in which we have to meet this morning, I think that we, the passengers, have also a job to do—to make things as easy as possible for the captain, officers, and crew and to help them to bring things back to normal as soon as possible.

"I'd like to start the ball rolling by asking you all to be my guests for a brief period this evening. To-day, ladies and gentlemen, my wife celebrates her birthday." He smiled down at Mrs. Beresford. "She forgets exactly which one. I cannot invite you to a birthday dinner, for what could I offer you as a special meal that Antoine and Henriques do not give us every night of the week? But Mrs. Beresford and I should be grateful if you would be our guests at a cocktail party this evening. Seven forty-five. In the drawing room. Thank you."

I looked round the table. Miguel Carreras was nodding slightly, as if in grave acceptance and appreciation of Beresford's underlying motives. Miss Harrbride was beaming with pleasure: she doted on the Beresfords, not for their money, but for the fact that they were one of the very oldest American families, with goodness only knew how many generations behind them. Mr. Greenstreet, her husband, studied the tablecloth in his usual intent fashion. And Tony Carreras, more impossibly handsome than ever, leaned back in his chair and regarded Julius Beresford with a slightly amused, speculative interest. Or maybe it was Susan Beresford he was looking at. I was more certain than ever that there was something wrong with Tony Carreras' eyes; it was almost impossible to tell in what direction they were looking. He caught my glance and smiled.

"You'll be there, Mr. Carter?" He had that relaxed, easy-going manner that comes from having a bank account bursting at the seams but none of the usual hint of condescension: Tony Carreras I could get to like.

"Briefly only, I'm afraid. I have to go on watch at eight o'clock this evening." I smiled. "If you're still at it at midnight, I'll join you." Like hell I'd join them: at midnight I'd be showing the Nassau police over the ship. "And I'm afraid you'll have to excuse me now. I have to relieve the officer of the watch."

I made my excuses and left. On the deck I almost bumped into a sandy-haired young seaman, Whitehead, who usually shared my watches on the bridge in his capacity as engine-room telegraphist, lookout, bridge messenger, and coffee maker.

"What are you doing here?" I asked sharply. With young Dexter on watch I wanted as many sharp eyes and quick minds as possible round him: Whitehead had both. "You know you're not to leave the bridge in my absence?"

"Sorry, sir. But Ferguson sent me." Ferguson was the quartermaster on the forenoon watch. "We've missed the last two course alterations and he's getting pretty worried about it." We were bringing round three degrees to the north every fifteen minutes to get on a north by west course, but slowly, so as not to excite anyone.

"Why come and bother me about it?" I said irritably. "Fourth Officer Dexter is perfectly capable of handling those matters." He wasn't, but one of the drawbacks of being a fellow officer of Dexter was that you were forced to lie like fury to maintain an outward appearance of solidarity.

"Yes, sir. But he's not there, Mr. Carter. He left the bridge about twenty minutes ago and he hasn't come back yet."

I pushed violently past Whitehead, knocking him to one side, and made for the bridge at a dead run, three steps at a time up the companionways. Rounding one corner, I caught a glimpse of Whitehead staring up after me with a most peculiar expression on his face. He probably thought I had gone mad.

Chapter 5

FERGUSON, a tall, swarthy, saturnine Cockney with no hair left to speak of, glanced round as I burst through the doorway from the starboard wing of the bridge into the wheelhouse. His face showed his relief.

"Strewth, am I glad to see——"

"Where's the fourth mate?" I demanded.

"Search me, sir. Them course alterations——"

"To hell with the course alterations! Where did he go?"

Ferguson blinked in surprise. He had the same look on his face as Whitehead had had a few seconds ago, the wary bafflement of a man who sees another going off his rocker.

"I don't know, sir. He didn't say."

I reached for the nearest phone, got through to the dining room, asked for Bullen. He came on and I said, "Carter here, sir. Could you come up to the bridge straight-away?"

There was a brief pause, then, "Why?"

"Dexter's missing, sir. He had the watch but he left the bridge twenty minutes ago."

"Left the bridge." Bullen's voice held no inflection, but

90

only because he made it that way. Lord Dexter's son or not, young Dexter was finished on the *Campari* unless he could explain this one away. "Looked for him yet? He could be anywhere."

"That's what I'm afraid of, sir."

The phone clicked and I hung up. Young Whitehead, still looking apprehensive, had just arrived in the cabin. I said, "You'll find the third mate in his cabin. My compliments to him, ask him if he'll take over the bridge for a few minutes. Ferguson?"

"Sir?" The voice was still wary.

"Mr. Dexter said nothing at all when he left?"

"Yes, sir. I heard him say something like, 'Wait a minute, what the hell's going on here?' Or something like that, I can't be sure. Then he said, 'Keep her as she is. Back in a jiffy,' and then he was off."

"That was all?"

"That was all, sir."

"Where was he standing at the time?"

"On the starboard wing, sir. Just outside the door."

"And he went down that side?"

"Yes, sir."

"Where was Whitehead at the time?"

"Out on the port wing, sir." Ferguson's expression and tone showed beyond all doubt that he was vis-à-vis with a loony, but he was playing it cool all the same.

"Didn't cross to see where Mr. Dexter had gone?"

"No, sir." He hesitated. "Well, not right away. But I thought it a bit funny so I asked him to have a look. He couldn't see anything."

"Damn! How long after Mr. Dexter left before he took this look?"

"A minute. Maybe closer on two. Couldn't be sure, sir."

"But whatever Mr. Dexter saw, it was aft?"

"Yes, sir."

I moved out on the wing bridge and looked aft. There was no one to be seen on any of the two decks below. The crew had long finished washing down decks and the passengers were still at breakfast. Nobody there. Nothing of any interest at all to be seen. Even the wireless office was deserted, its door closed and locked. I could see the brass padlock clearly, gleaming and glittering in the morning sun as the *Campari* pitched slowly, gently, through the ever-lengthening swell.

The wireless office! I stood there perfectly rigid for all of three seconds, a candidate, in Ferguson's eyes, for a strait jacket if ever there had been one, then took off down the companionway the same way as I had come up, three steps at a time. Only a smart piece of braking on my part and a surprisingly nimble bit of dodging on the captain's prevented a head-on collision at the foot of the companionway. Bullen put into words the thought that was obviously gaining currency around the bridge.

"Have you gone off your bloody rocker, Mister?"

"The wireless office, sir," I said quickly. "Come on."

I was there in a few seconds, Bullen close behind. I tried the padlock, a heavy-duty, double-action Yale, but it was securely locked.

It was then that I noticed a key sticking out from the bottom of the padlock. I twisted it, first one way, then the other, but it was jammed fast. I tried to pull it out and had the same lack of success. I became aware that Bullen was breathing heavily over my shoulder.

"What the devil's the matter, Mister? What's got into you all of a sudden?"

"One moment, sir." I'd caught sight of Whitehead making his way up to the bridge and beckoned him across. "Get the bo'sun. Tell him to bring a pair of pliers."

"Yes, sir, I'll get the pliers—"

"I said, 'Tell the bo'sun to bring them,' " I said savagely. "Then ask Mr. Peters for the key to this door. Hurry!"

He hurried. You could see he was glad to escape. Bullen said, "Look here, Mister—"

"Dexter left the bridge because he saw something funny going on. So Ferguson said. Where else but here, sir?"

"Why here? Why not—"

"Look at that." I took the padlock in my hand. "That bent key. And everything that's happened has happened because of here."

"The window?"

"No good. I've looked." I led him round the corner to the single square of plate glass. "Night curtains are still drawn."

"Couldn't we smash the damned thing in?"

"What's the point? It's too late now."

Bullen looked at me queerly but said nothing. Half a minute passed in silence. Bullen was getting more worried every second. I wasn't—I was as worried as could be already. Jamieson appeared, on his way to the bridge, caught sight of us, made to come towards us, then carried on as Bullen waved him away. And then the bo'sun was there, carrying a pair of heavy insulated pliers in his hand.

"Open this damned door," Bullen said curtly.

MacDonald tried to remove the key with his fingers, failed, and brought the pliers into use. With the first tug of the pliers the key in the lock snapped cleanly in half.

"Well," Bullen said heavily, "that helps."

MacDonald looked at him, at me, then back at the broken key still held in the jaws of the pliers.

"I didn't even twist it, sir," he said quietly. "And if that's a Yale key," he added with an air of faint distaste, "then I'm an Englishman." He handed over the key for inspection. The break showed the grey, rough, porous composition of some base metal. "Homemade, and not very well made at that, either."

Bullen pocketed the broken key.

"Can you get the other bit out?"

"No, sir. Completely jammed." He fished in his overalls, produced a hacksaw. "Maybe this, sir?"

"Good man."

It took MacDonald three minutes' hard work—the hasp, unlike the padlock, was made of tempered steel—and then the hacksaw was through. He slid out the padlock, then glanced enquiringly at the captain.

"Come in with us," Bullen said. There was sweat on his brow. "See that nobody comes near." He pushed open the door and passed inside; I was on his heels.

We'd found Dexter all right, and we'd found him too late. He had that old-bundle-of-clothes look, that completely relaxed huddled shapelessness that only the dead can achieve; face down, outflung on the corticene flooring, he hardly left standing room for Bullen and myself.

"Shall I get the doctor, sir?" It was MacDonald speaking: he was standing astride the storm sill, and the knuckles of the hand holding the door shone bonily through the tautened skin.

"It's too late for a doctor now, bo'sun," Bullen said stonily. Then his composure broke and he burst out violently: "My God, Mister, where's it all going to end? He's dead—you can see he's dead. What's behind—what murderous fiend—why did they kill him, Mister? Why did they have to kill him? Damn it to hell, why did the fiends have to kill him? He was only a kid—what real harm did young Dexter ever do anybody?" It said much for Bullen at the moment that the thought never even occurred to him that the dead man was the son of the chairman and managing director of the Blue Mail Line. That thought would come later.

"He died for the same reason that Benson died," I said. "He saw too much." I kneeled beside him, examined the back and sides of his neck. No marks there at all. I looked up and said, "Can I turn him over, sir?"

"It can't do any harm now." Bullen's normally ruddy face had lost some colour and the lips were clamped in a thin hard line.

I heaved and pulled for a few seconds and managed to get Dexter more or less turned over, half on his shoulders and half on his back. I didn't waste time checking his breathing or his pulse; when you've been shot three times through the middle of the body the breathing and pulse are things of the past. And Dexter's white uniform shirt, with the three small powder-blackened blood-tinged holes just beneath the breastbone, showed indeed that he had been shot three times: the area covering those holes could have been blotted out by a playing card. Somebody had made very sure indeed. I rose to my feet, looked from the captain to the bo'sun, then said to Bullen, "We can't pass *this* off as a heart attack, sir."

"They shot him three times," Bullen said matter-of-factly.

"We're up against someone in the maniac class, sir." I stared down at Dexter, unable to look away from the face, racked and twisted by his last conscious moment of life, that fleeting moment of tearing agony that had opened the door to death. "Any one of those bullets would have killed him. But whoever killed him killed him three times, someone who likes pressing a trigger, someone who likes seeing bullets thud into a human being, even although that human being is dead already."

"You seem very cool about this, Mister." Bullen was looking at me with a strange look in his eyes.

"Sure I'm cool." I showed Bullen my gun. "Show me the man who did this and I'll give him what he gave Dexter. Exactly the same and to hell with Captain Bullen and the laws of the land. That's how cool I am."

"I'm sorry, Johnny." Then his voice hardened again. "Nobody heard anything. How did nobody hear anything?"

"He had his gun close up to Dexter, maybe jammed right against him. You can see the marks of burnt powder. That would help to deaden the sound. Besides, everything points to this person—or those persons—as being professionals. They would have silencers on their guns."

"I see." Bullen turned to MacDonald. "Could you get Peters here, bo'sun? At once."

"Aye, aye, sir." MacDonald turned to leave, and I said quickly, "Sir, a word before MacDonald goes."

"What is it?" His voice was hard, impatient.

"You're going to send a message?"

"Too right I'm going to send a message. I'm going to ask for a couple of fast patrol boats to be sent out here to meet us. At the speed those gas turbine jobs can go they'll be alongside before noon. And when I tell them I've had three men murdered in twelve hours, they'll come running. I've had enough of playing it smart, First. This fake burial to lull their suspicions this morning, to make them think we've got rid of the only evidence of murder against them. See where it's got us? Another man murdered."

"It's no use, sir. It's too late now."

"What do you mean?"

"He didn't even bother to replace the lid after he left,

sir." I nodded towards the big transmitter-receiver, with its metal lid slightly askew, the securing screws loose. "Maybe he was in a hurry to get away, maybe he just knew there was no point in securing it anyway; we were bound to find it out sooner or later—and sooner rather than later." I lifted the lid and stood to one side to let Bullen look also.

Nothing was ever surer than that no one would ever use that transmitter again. It was littered inside with torn wire, bent metal, smashed condensers and valves. Someone had used a hammer. There was no guesswork about that: the hammer was still lying among the tangled splintered wreckage that was all that was left of the once complicated innards of the transmitter. I replaced the lid.

"There's an emergency set," Bullen said hoarsely. "In the cupboard under the table there. The one with the petrol generator. He'll have missed that."

But the murderer hadn't missed it; he wasn't the type to miss anything. And he certainly hadn't missed with that hammer. If anything, he'd done an even more thorough job on the emergency set than on the main set, and, just for good measure, he'd smashed up the armature of the petrol generator.

"Our friend must have been listening in on his receiver again," MacDonald put in quietly. "So he came out either to stop the message or smash up the sets, so that no more messages could come through. He was lucky; had he been a bit later and the radio officer back on watch, my men would have been holystoning the decks outside and there would have been nothing he would be able to do."

"I don't associate luck with this killer in any way," I said. "He's too damned efficient for that. I don't think any more messages which might have worried him had come through, but he was afraid they might. He *knew* both Peters and Jenkins were off watch at the burial, and he probably checked that the wireless office was locked. So he waited till the coast was clear, came out on deck, unlocked the office, and went inside. And Dexter, unfortunately for himself, saw him going in."

"The key, Mister," Bullen said harshly. "The key. How come?"

"The Marconi man in Kingston who checked the sets, sir. Remember?" He remembered all right: the Marconi man had telephoned the ship, asking if servicing facilities were required, and Bullen had seized on it as a heaven-sent opportunity to close down the radio office and refuse to accept any more embarrassing and infuriating messages from London and New York. "He spent about four hours there. Time to do anything. If he was a Marconi man, I'm the Queen of the May. He had a nice big impressive tool kit with him, but the only tool he used, if you could call it that, was a stick of wax, heated to the right temperature, to take an impression of the Yale—even if he had managed to pinch the Yale and return it unseen it would have been impossible to cut a new one; those special Yales are far too complicated. And my guess is that that was all he did while he was there."

And my guess was completely wrong. But the thought that this fake Marconi man might have employed himself in another way during his stay in the wireless office did not occur to me until many hours later: it was so blindingly obvious that I missed it altogether, although two minutes' constructive thought would have been bound to put me on to it. But hours were to elapse before I got round to the constructive thought, and by that time it was too late. Too late for the *Campari*, too late for for its passengers, and far, far too late for all too many of the crew.

We left young Dexter lying in the wireless office and secured the door with a new padlock. We'd talked for almost five minutes about the problem of where to put him before the simple solution occurred to us: leave him where he was. Nobody was going to use that wireless office any more that day; he was as well there as anywhere till the Nassau police came aboard.

From the wireless office we'd gone straight to the telegraph lounge. The teleprinters in there were coupled to receiver-transmitters on fixed wave lengths to London, Paris, and New York, but could be adapted by men who knew what they were doing, such as Peters and Jenkins, to receive and transmit on practically any wave length. But not even Peters and Jenkins could do anything about the situation we found: there were two big transmitters in the telegraph lounge, cleverly designed to look like cocktail cabinets, and both had received the same treatment as the sets in the wireless office: the exteriors intact, the interiors smashed beyond repair. Somebody had been very busy during the night: the wireless office must have been the last item on his list.

I looked at Bullen.

"With your permission, sir, MacDonald and I will go and have a look at the lifeboats. We might as well waste our time that way as in any other."

He knew what I meant all right and nodded. Captain Bullen was beginning to look slightly hunted. He was the ablest, the most competent master in the Blue Mail; but nothing in his long training and experience had ever been designed to cope with a situation like this.

And so MacDonald and I duly wasted our time. There were three lifeboats equipped with hand-cranked transmitters for emergency use if the *Campari* sank or otherwise had to be abandoned. Or they had been equipped with them. But not any more. The transmitters were gone. No need to waste time or make a racket smashing up sets when all you have to do is to drop them over the side. Our murderous friend hadn't missed a single trick.

When we got back to the captain's cabin, where we had been told to report, there was something in the atmosphere that I didn't like at all. They say you can smell fear. I don't know about that, but you can sense it and you could certainly sense it in that cabin at nine o'clock that morning. The fear, the atmosphere of trapped helplessness, the sense of being completely at the mercy of unknown and infinitely powerful and ruthless forces made for an atmosphere of nervously brittle tension that I could almost reach out and touch.

McIlroy and Cummings were there with the captain and so, too, was our second mate, Tommy Wilson. He had had to be told; the stage had been reached now where every officer would have to be told, so Bullen said, in the interests of their own safety and self-defense. I wasn't so sure. Bullen looked up as we came through the door; his face was grim and still, a thinly opaque mask for the consuming worry that lay beneath.

"Well?"

I shook my head, took a seat; MacDonald remained standing, but Bullen gestured him irritably to a chair. He said, to no one in particular, "I suppose that accounts for all the transmitters on the ship?"

"As far as we know, yes." I went on: "Don't you think we should have White up here, sir?"

"I was about to do that." He reached for the phone, spoke for a moment, hung up, then said roughly, "Well, Mister, you were the man with all the bright ideas last night. Got any this morning?" Just to repeat the words makes them sound harsh and unpleasant, but they were curiously empty of any offence; Bullen didn't know which way to turn and he was grasping at straws.

"None. All we know is that Dexter was killed at eight twenty-six this morning, give or take a minute. No question about that. And at that moment most of our passengers were at breakfast; no question about that either. The only passengers not at breakfast were Miss Harcourt, Mr. Cerdan and his two nurses, Mr. and Mrs. Piper from Miami, and that couple from Venezuela—old Hournos and his wife—and their daughter. Our only suspects, and none of them makes any sense."

"And all of *those* were at dinner last night when Brownell and Benson were killed," McIlroy said thoughtfully, "except the old man and his nurses. Which leaves them as the only suspects, which is not only ridiculous but far too obvious. I think we've already had plenty of proof that whatever the people behind all this are guilty of, being obvious is not one of them. Unless, of course," he added slowly, "some of the passengers are working in collusion with each other."

"Or with the crew," Tommy Wilson murmured.

"What?" Old Bullen gave him the full benefit of his commodore's stare. "What did you say?"

"I said the crew," Wilson repeated clearly. If old Bullen was trying to frighten Tommy Wilson he was wasting his time. "And by the crew I also include the officers. I agree, sir, that I heard—or knew—of those murders for the first time only a few minutes ago, and I admit that I haven't had time to sort out my thoughts. On the other hand, I haven't had the chance to become so involved as all the rest of you are. With all respects, I'm not so deeply lost in the wood that I can't see the trees. You all seem to be convinced that it must be one or more of our passengers responsible—our chief officer here seems to have set this bee firmly in all your bonnets—but if a passenger were in cahoots with one of the crew, then it's quite possible that that member of the crew was detailed to hang round in the vincinity of the wireless office and start laying about him when necessary."

"You said the chief officer was responsible for planting this idea in our minds," Bullen said slowly. "What do you mean by that?"

"No more than I said, sir. I only—" Then the implications of the captain's question struck him. "Good God, sir! Mr. Carter? Do you think I'm crazy?"

"No one thinks you're crazy," McIlroy put in soothingly. Our chief engineer had always regarded Wilson as a bit of a mental bantamweight, but you could see him slowly revising his opinion. "The crew, Tommy. What makes you suspect the crew?"

"Elimination, motive, and opportunity," Wilson said promptly. "We seem to have more or less eliminated the passengers. All with alibis. What are the usual motives?" he asked of no one in particular.

"Revenge, jealousy, gain," said McIlroy. "Those three."

"There you are, then. Take revenge and jealousy. Is it conceivable that any of our passengers should have their knives so deeply stuck in Brownell, Benson, and Dexter as to want to kill them all? Ridiculous. Gain? What could that bunch of bloated plutocrats want with any more lucre?" He looked round slowly. "And what officer or man aboard the *Campari* couldn't do with a little more lucre? I could, for one."

"Opportunity, Tommy," McIlroy prompted him gently. "Opportunity, you said."

"I don't have to go into that," Wilson said. "Engineer and deck crews could be eliminated at once. The engineering side, except for officers at mealtimes, never go anywhere near the passenger and boat decks. The bo'sun's men here are only allowed there in the morning watch, for washing down decks. But"—he looked round him again, even more slowly—"every deck officer, radio officer, radar operator, cook, galley slave, and steward aboard the *Campari* has a perfect right to be within a few yards of the wireless office at any time; no one could question his presence there. Not only that—"

A knock came at the door and Assistant Chief Steward White came in, hat in hand. He was looking acutely unhappy and looked even more so when he saw the extent and composition of the welcoming committee.

"Come in and sit down," Bullen said. He waited till White had done this, then went on: "Where were you between eight and half-past eight this morning, White?"

"This morning. Eight and half-past." White was immediately all stiff outrage. "I was on duty, sir, of course. I—"

"Relax," Bullen said wearily. "No one is accusing you of anything." Then he said, more kindly: "We've all had some very bad news, White. Nothing that concerns you directly, so don't get too apprehensive. You'd better hear it."

Bullen told him, without any trimmings, of the three murders, and the one immediate result was that everyone present could immediately remove White from the list of suspects. He might have been a good actor, but not even an Irving could have turned his colour from a healthy red to a greyish pallor at the touch of a switch, which was what White did. He looked so bad, his breathing got so quick and shallow that I rose hastily and fetched him a glass of water. He swallowed it in a couple of gulps.

"Sorry to upset you, White," Bullen went on. "But you had to know. Now then, between eight and eight-thirty: how many of your passengers had breakfast in their rooms?"

"I don't know, sir, I'm not sure." He shook his head, then went on slowly. "Sorry, sir. I do remember. Mr. Cerdan and his nurses, of course. The Hournos family. Miss Harcourt. Mr. and Mrs. Piper."

"As Mr. Carter said," McIlroy murmured.

"Yes." Bullen nodded. "Now, White, be very careful. Did any of those passengers at any time leave their rooms during this period? At *any* time? Even for a moment?"

"No, sir. Quite definitely not. Not on my deck, anyway. The Hournos are on 'B' deck. But none of the others went in or out of any of the suites, only stewards with trays. I can swear to that, sir. From my cubicle—Mr. Benson's, that is—I can see every door in the passageway."

"That's so," Bullen agreed. He asked for the name of the senior steward on "B" deck, spoke briefly on the phone, then hung up. "All right, White, you can go. But keep your eyes—and ears—open and report to me immediately you come across anything that strikes you as unusual. And don't talk about this to anyone." White rose quickly and left. He seemed glad to go.

"There it is, then," Bullen said heavily. "Everyone—every one of the passengers, that is—in the clear. I'm beginning to think you may have the right of it after all, Mr. Wilson." He looked speculatively at me. "How about it now, Mr. Carter?"

I looked at him, then at Wilson, and said: "Mr. Wilson seems to be the only one of us that makes any sense. What he says is logical, completely plausible, and fits the facts. It's too logical, too plausible. I don't believe it."

"Why not?" Bullen demanded. "Because you can't believe that any crew member of the *Campari* could be bought? Or because it knocks your own pet theories on the head?"

"I can't give you any why's or why not's, sir. It's just a hunch, the way I feel."

Captain Bullen grunted, not a very kindly grunt either, but unexpected support came from the chief engineer.

"I agree with Mr. Carter. We're up against very, very clever people—if it is people." He paused, then said suddenly: "Is the passage money for the Carreras family, father and son, paid in yet?"

"What the devil has that to do with anything?" Bullen demanded.

"Has it been paid?" McIlroy repeated. He was looking at the purser.

"It's been paid," Cummings said quietly. He was still a long way from getting over the shock caused by the murder of his friend Benson.

"In what currency?"

"Traveller's cheques. Drawn on a New York bank."

"Dollars, eh? Now, Captain Bullen, I submit that's very interesting indeed. Paid in dollars. Yet in May of last year the generalissimo made it a penal offence to be in possession of any foreign currency whatsoever. I wonder where our friends got the money from. And why are they permitted to be in possession of it? Instead of lingering in some jungle jail?"

"What are you suggesting, Chief?"

"Nothing," McIlroy confessed. "That's the devil of it. I just don't see how it can tie up with anything. I just submit that it is very curious indeed and that anything curious, in the present circumstances, is worth investigating." He sat silently for a moment, then said idly, "I suppose you know that our generalissimo friend recently received a gift from the other side of the Iron Curtain? A destroyer and a couple of frigates? Trebled his naval strength in one fell swoop. I suppose you know the generalissimo is desperate for money—his regime is coming apart at the seams for lack of it, and that's what lay behind last week's bloody riots. You know that we have a dozen people aboard who could be worth God knows how many millions in ransom money? And that if a frigate suddenly did heave over the horizon and order us to stop—well, how could we send out an SOS with all our transmitters smashed?"

"I have never heard such a ridiculous suggestion in my life," Bullen said heavily. But ridiculous or not, you're thinking about it, Captain Bullen, I said to myself; by heaven, you're thinking about it. "To knock your suggestion on the head straightaway, how could any vessel ever find us? Where to look for us? We changed course last night; we're over a hundred miles away from where they might expect us to be—even if they had any idea where we were going in the first place."

"I could support the chief's arguments in that, sir," I put in. There seemed no point in mentioning that I thought McIlroy's idea as farfetched as did the captain. "Any person with a radio receiver might equally well have a transmitter—and Miguel Carreras himself mentioned to me that he used to command his own ships. Navigation, by sun or stars, would be easy for him. He probably knows our position to within ten miles."

"And those messages that came through on the radio," McIlroy went on. "Message or messages. A message so damned important that two men died, and the possibility that another such message might come through caused a third man to die. What message, Captain, what so tremendously important a message? Warnings: from where, from whom, I don't know. Warnings, Captain Bullen. Knowledge which in our hands would have destroyed some carefully laid plans, and the scope of those plans you can judge from the fact that three men died so that that message should not come through."

Old Bullen was shaken. He tried not to show it, but he was shaken. Badly. And I knew it next moment when he turned to Tommy Wilson.

"On the bridge, Mr. Wilson. Double lookouts. Stay doubled till we get to Nassau." He looked at McIlroy. "If we get to Nassau. Signaller to stand by the Aldis all day. 'I want assistance' flags ready for the yardarm. Radar office: if they take their eyes off the screen for a second I'll have 'em on the beach. No matter how small a blip they see, no matter what distance, report immediately to the bridge."

"We turn towards them for assistance, sir?"

"You blithering idiot," Bullen snarled. "We run for our lives in the opposite direction. Do you want to steam into the waiting guns of a destroyer?" No question but that Bullen was far off balance: the self-contradictory element in his instructions escaped him completely.

"You believe the chief, then, sir?" I asked.

"I don't know what to believe," Bullen growled. "I'm just taking no chances."

When Wilson left I said, "Maybe the chief is right. Maybe Wilson is right too. Both could go together—an armed attack on the *Campari* with certain suborned members of the crew backing up the attackers."

"But you still don't believe it," McIlroy said quietly.

"I'm like the captain. I don't know what to believe. But one thing I do know for certain—the radio receiver that intercepted the message we never got—that's the key to it all."

"And that's the key we're going to find." Bullen heaved himself to his feet. "Chief, I'd be glad if you came with me. We're going to search for this radio personally. First we start in my quarters, then in yours, then we go through the quarters of every member of the crew of the *Campari*. Then we start looking anywhere where it might be cached outside their quarters. You come with us, MacDonald."

The old man was in earnest all right. If that radio was in the crew's quarters, he'd find it. The fact that he'd offered to start the search in his own suite was warranty enough for that.

He went on: "Mr. Carter, I believe it's your watch."

"Yes, sir. But Jamieson could look out for me for an hour. Permission to search the passengers' quarters?"

"Wilson was right about that bee in your bonnet, Mister." Which only went to show how upset Bullen was: normally, where circumstances demanded, he was the most punctilious of men and, in the presence of the bo'sun, he would never have spoken as he had done to Wilson and myself. He glowered at me and walked out.

He hadn't given my permission, but he hadn't refused it either. I glanced at Cummings; he nodded and rose to his feet.

We had luck in the conditions for our search, the purser and I, in that we didn't have to turf anyone out of their cabins: they were completely deserted. Radio reports in the morning watch had spoken of weather conditions deteriorating sharply to the southeast and bulletins had been posted warning of approaching bad weather; the sun decks were crowded with passengers determined to make the most of the blue skies before the weather broke. Even old Cerdan was on deck, flanked by his two watchful nurses, the tall one with a big mesh-string knitting bag and clicking away busily with her needles, the other with a pile of magazines, reading. You had the impression with them, as with all good nurses, that less than half their minds were on what they were doing; without stirring from their chairs they seemed to hover over old Cerdan like a couple of broody hens. I had the feeling that when Cerdan paid nurses to hover he would expect his money's worth. He was in his wheel chair, with a richly embroidered rug over his bony knees. I took a good long look at that rug as I passed by, but I was only wasting my time: so tightly was that rug wrapped round his skinny shanks that he couldn't have concealed a matchbox under it, far less a radio.

With a couple of stewards keeping watch we went through the suites on "A" and "B" decks with meticulous care. I had a bridge megger with me, which was to lend cover to our cover story, if we had to use one, that we were trying to trace an insulation break in a power cable; but no passenger with a guilty mind was going to fall for that one for a moment when he found us in his cabin, so we thought the stewards a good idea.

There should have been no need for any passenger aboard the *Campari* to have a radio. Every passenger's cabin on the ship, with the *Campari*'s usual extravagance, was fitted out with not one but two bulkhead relay receivers, fed from a battery of radios in the telegraph lounge; eight different stations could be brought into circuit simply by pressing the eight pre-selector buttons. This was all explained in the brochure, so normally nobody thought of bringing radios along.

Cummings and I missed nothing. We examined every cupboard, wardrobe, bed, drawer, even my ladies' jewel boxes. Nothing. Nothing anywhere, except in one place: Miss Harcourt's cabin. There was a portable there, but then I had known that there had been one: every night when the weather was fine, Miss Harcourt would wander out on deck, clad in one of her many evening gowns, find a chair, and twiddle around the tuning knob till she found some suitable soft music. Maybe she thought it lent something to the air of enchantment and mystery that should surround a movie queen; maybe she thought it romantic; it could have been, of course, that she just liked soft music. However it was, one thing was certain—Miss Harcourt was not our suspect: not to put too fine a point on it, she just didn't have the intelligence. And, in fairness, despite her pretensions, she was too nice.

I retired, defeated, to the bridge and took over from Jamieson. Almost an hour elapsed before another defeated man came to the bridge; Captain Bullen. He didn't have to tell me he was defeated: it was written on him, in the still, troubled face, the slight sag of the broad shoulders. And a mute headshake from me told him all he needed to know. I made a mental note, in the not unlikely event of Lord Dexter turfing us both out of the Blue Mail, to turn down any suggestions by Captain Bullen that we should go into a detective agency together; there might be faster ways of starving, perhaps, but none more completely certain.

We were on the second leg of our course now, 10 degrees west of north, heading straight for Nassau. Twelve hours and we would be there. My eyes ached from scanning the horizons and skies; even although I knew that there were at least ten others doing the same thing, still my eyes ached. Whether I believed McIlroy's suggestion or not, I certainly behaved as if I did. But the horizon remained clear, completely, miraculously clear, for this was normally a fairly heavily travelled steamer lane. And the loud-speaker from the radar room remained obstinately silent. We had a radar screen on the bridge but rarely troubled to consult it: Walters, the operator on watch, could isolate and identify a blip on the screen long before most of us could even see it.

After maybe half an hour's restless pacing about the bridge, Bullen turned to go. Just at the head of the companionway he hesitated, turned, beckoned me, and walked out to the end of the starboard wing. I followed.

"I've been thinking about Dexter," he said quietly. "What would be the effect—I'm past caring about the passengers now; I'm only worried about the lives of every man and woman aboard—if I announced that Dexter had been murdered?"

"Nothing," I said. "If you can call mass hysteria nothing."

"You don't think the fiends responsible for all this might call it off? Whatever 'it' is?"

"I'm dead certain they wouldn't. As no mention has been made of Dexter yet, no attempt to explain away his absence, they must know *we* know he's dead. They'll know damned well that the officer of the watch can't disappear from the bridge without a hue and cry going up. We'd just be telling them out loud what they already know without being told. You won't scare this bunch off. People don't play as rough as they do unless there's something tremendous at stake."

"That's what I thought myself, Johnny," he said heavily. "That's just what I thought myself." He turned and went below, and I had a sudden foreknowledge of how Bullen would look when he was an old man.

I stayed on the bridge until two o'clock, long past my usual time for relief, but then I'd deprived Jamieson, who had the afternoon watch, of much free time that morning. A tray came up to me from the galley, and for the first time ever I sent an offering by Henriques back untouched. When Jamieson took over the bridge he didn't exchange a word with me except routine remarks about course and speed. From the strained, set expression on his face you would have thought he was carrying the mainmast of the *Campari* over his shoulder. Bullen had been talking to him; he'd probably been talking to all the officers. That would get them all as worried as hell and jittery as a couple of old spinsters lost in the Casbah; I didn't see that it would achieve anything else.

I went to my cabin, closed the door, pulled off shoes and shirt, and lay down on my bunk—no four-posters for the crew of the *Campari*—after adjusting the louvre in the overhead cold-air trunking until the draught was directed on my chest and face. The back of my head ached and ached badly. I adjusted a pillow under it and tried to ease the pain. It still ached, so I let it go and tried to think. Somebody had to think and I didn't see that old Bullen was in any state for it. Neither was I, but I thought all the same. I would have bet my last cent that the enemy—I couldn't think of them as anything else by this time—knew our course, destination, and time of arrival almost as well as we did ourselves. And I knew that they couldn't afford to let us arrive in Nassau that night, not, at least, until they had accomplished what they had set out to acccomplish, whatever that might be. Somebody had to think. Time was terribly short.

By three o'clock I'd got nowhere. I'd worried all round the problem as a terrier worries an old slipper; I'd examined it from every angle; I'd put forward a dozen different solutions, all equally improbable, and turned up a round dozen suspects, all equally impossible. My thinking was getting me nowhere. I sat up, careful of my stiff neck, fished a bottle of whisky from a cupboard, poured a drink, watered it, knocked it back, and then, because it was illegal, helped myself to another. I placed this second on the table by my bunk and lay down again.

The whisky did it. I'll always swear the whisky did it; as a mental lubricant for rusted-up brains it has no parallel. After five more minutes of lying on my back, staring sightlessly up at the cold-air trunking above my head, I suddenly had it. I had it suddenly, completely and all in a moment, and I knew beyond doubt that I had it right. The radio! The receiver on which the message to the wireless office had been intercepted! There had been no radio. God, only a blind man like myself could have missed it; of course there had been no radio. But there had been something else again. I sat bolt upright with a jerk, Archimedes coming out of his bath, and yelped as a hot blade skewered through the back of my neck.

"Are you subject to these attacks often or do you always carry on like this when you are alone?" a solicitous voice enquired from the doorway. Susan Beresford, dressed in a square-necked white silk dress, was standing in the entrance, her expression half amused, half apprehensive.

So complete had been my concentration that I'd never even heard the door open.

"Miss Beresford." I rubbed my aching neck with my right hand. "What are you doing here? You know passengers are not allowed in the officers' quarters?"

"No? I understood my father had been up several times in the past few trips talking to you."

"Your father is not young, female, and unmarried."

"Pfui!" She stepped into the cabin and closed the door behind her. All at once the smile was no longer on her face. "Will *you* talk to me, Mr. Carter?"

"Any time," I said courteously. "But not here. . . ." My voice trailed away. I was changing my mind even as I spoke.

"You see, you're the only person I can talk to," she said.

"Yes." A beautiful girl alone in my cabin and plainly anxious to speak to me and I wasn't even listening to her. I was figuring out something; it did involve Susan Beresford but only incidentally.

"Oh *do* pay attention," she said angrily.

"All right," I said resignedly. "I'm paying."

"You're paying what?" she demanded.

"Attention." I reached for my whisky glass. "Cheers!"

"I thought you were forbidden alcohol on duty?"

"I am. What do you want?"

"I want to know why no one will talk to me." She lifted a hand as I made to speak. "Please don't be facetious. I'm worried. Something's terribly wrong, isn't there? You know I always talk more to the officers than any of the other passengers"—I passed up the pleasure of loosing off a couple of telling shafts—"and now nobody will talk to me. Daddy says I'm imagining it. I'm not. I know I'm not. They won't talk. And not because of me. I know. They're all dead scared about something, going about with tight faces and not looking at anyone but looking at them all the time. Something *is* wrong, isn't there? Terribly, terribly wrong. And Fourth Officer Dexter—he's missing, isn't he?"

"What would be wrong, Miss Beresford?"

"Please." This was something for the books, Susan Beresford pleading with me. She walked across the cabin —with the size of the accommodation old Dexter saw fit to provide for his chief officers that didn't require more than a couple of steps—and stood in front of me. "Tell me the truth. Three men missing in twenty-four hours— don't tell me that's coincidence. And all the officers looking as if they're going to be shot at dawn."

"Don't you think it strange *you're* the only person who seems to have noticed anything unusual? How about all the other passengers?"

"The other passengers!" The tone of her voice didn't say a great deal for the other passengers. "How can they notice anything with all the women either in bed for their afternoon sleep or at the hairdresser's or in the massage room and all the men sitting around in the telegraph lounge like mourners at a funeral just because the stock exchange machines have broken down? And that's another thing. Why *have* those machines broken down? And why is the radio office closed? And why is the *Campari* going so fast? I went right aft just now to listen to the engines and I *know* we've never gone so fast before."

She didn't miss much and that was a fact. I said, "Why come to me?"

"Daddy suggested it." She hesitated, then half smiled. "He said I was imagining things and that for a person suffering from delusions and a hyperactive imagination he could recommend nothing better than a visit to Chief Officer Carter, who doesn't know the meaning of either."

"Your father is wrong."

"Wrong? You do—ah—suffer from delusions?"

"About your imagining things. You aren't." I finished my whisky and got to my feet. "Something is wrong, far wrong, Miss Beresford."

She looked me steadily in the eyes, then said quietly, "Will you tell me what it is? Please?" The cool amusement was now completely absent from both face and voice: a completely different Susan Beresford from the one I'd known, and one I liked very much better than the old one. For the first time, and very late in the day, the thought occurred to me that this might be the real Susan Beresford: when you wear a price ticket marked umpteen million dollars and are travelling in a forest alive with wolves looking for gold and a free meal ticket for life, some sort of shield, some kind of protective device against the wolves, is liable to be very handy indeed, and I had to admit that the air of half-mocking amusement which seldom left her was a most effective deterrent.

"Will you tell me, please?" she repeated. She'd come close to me now; the green eyes had started to melt in that weird way they had, and my breathing was all mixed up again. "I think you could trust me, Mr. Carter."

"Yes." I looked away—it took the last of my will power, but I looked away—and managed to get my breathing working again, in-out, in-out; it wasn't too difficult when you got the hang of it. "I think I could trust you, Miss Beresford. I will tell you. But not right away. If you knew why I say that you wouldn't press me to tell you. Any of the passengers out taking the air or sunbathing?"

"What?" The sudden switch made her blink, but she recovered quickly and gestured to the window. "In this?"

I saw what she meant. The sun had gone, completely, and heavy dark cumulus clouds coming up from the southeast had all but obscured the sky. The sea looked rougher than it had been, but I had the feeling that the temperature would have fallen away. I didn't like the look of the weather. And I could quite understand why none of the passengers would be on deck. That made things awkward. But there was another way.

"I see what you mean. I promise you I'll tell you all you want to know this evening"—that was a pretty elastic time limit—"if you in turn promise you won't tell anyone I've admitted anything is wrong—and if you will do something for me."

"What do you want me to do?"

"This. You know your father is holding some sort of cocktail party for your mother in the drawing room tonight. It's timed for seven forty-five. Get him to advance it to seven-thirty. I want more time before dinner—never mind why now. Use any reason you like, but don't bring me into it. And ask your father to invite old Mr. Cerdan to the party also. Doesn't matter if he has to take his wheel chair and the two nurses along with him. Get him to the party. Your father's a man of considerable powers of persuasion—and I imagine you could persuade your father to do anything. Tell him you feel sorry for the old man, always being left out of things. Tell him anything, only get old man Cerdan to the cocktail party. I can't tell you how vital that is."

She looked at me in slow speculation. She really had the most extraordinary eyes; three weeks she'd been with us and I'd never really noticed them before, eyes of that deep yet translucent green of sea water over sand in the Windward Isles, eyes that melted and shimmered in the same way as when a cat's-paw of wind riffled the surface of the water, eyes that—I dragged my own eyes away. See Carter, old Beresford had said. There's the man for you. No imaginative fancies about him. That's what he thought. I became aware that she was saying quietly, "I'll do it. I promise. I don't know what track you're on, but I know it's the right track."

"What do you mean?" I said slowly.

"That nurse of Mr. Cerdan's. The tall one with the knitting. She can no more knit than fly over the moon. She just sits there, clicking needles, botching every other stitch and getting practically nowhere. I know. Being a millionaire's daughter doesn't mean that you can't be as slick with a pair of knitting needles as the next girl."

"What!" I caught her by the shoulders and stared down at her. "You saw this? You're sure of it?"

"Sure I'm sure."

"Well, now." I was still looking at her, but this time I wasn't seeing the eyes; I was seeing a great number of other things and I didn't like any of them. I said, "This is very interesting. I'll see you later. Be a good girl and get that fixed with your father, will you?" I gave her shoulder an absent-minded pat, turned away, and stared out of the window.

After a few seconds I became aware that she hadn't yet gone. She'd the door opened, one hand on the handle, and was looking at me with a peculiar expression on her face.

"You wouldn't like to give me a toffee apple to suck?" If you can imagine a voice both sweet and bitter at the same moment, then that is how hers was. "Or a ribbon for my pigtails?" With that she banged the door and was gone. The door didn't splinter in any way, but that was only because it was made of steel.

I gazed at the closed door for a moment, then gave up. Any other time I might have devoted some minutes to figuring out the weird and wonderful working of the female brain. But this wasn't just any other time. Whatever it was, this just wasn't any other time. I pulled on shoes, shirt, and jacket, pulled out the Colt from under the mattress, stuck it in my waist belt, and went off in search of the captain.

Chapter 6

AS FAR as attendance went, Mr. Julius Beresford had no grounds for complaint that night: every single passenger on the ship had turned up for his wife's cocktail party and, as far as I could see, every off-duty officer on the *Campari* was there as well. And the party was certainly going splendidly; already, at seven forty-five, practically everyone was already on his or her second drink, and the drinks served up in the drawing room of the *Campari* were never small ones.

Beresford and his wife had been moving round, speaking to each of the guests in rotation, and now it was my turn. I saw them approaching, raised my glass, and said, "Many happy returns, Mrs. Beresford."

"Thank you, young man. Enjoying yourself?"

"Of course. So is everybody. And you should be, most of all."

"Yes." She sounded just the slightest bit doubtful. "I don't know if Julius was right—I mean, it's less than twenty-four hours—"

"If you're thinking about Benson and Brownell, ma'am, you're worrying unnecessarily. You couldn't have done a

115

better thing than arrange this. I'm sure every passenger on the ship is grateful to you for helping to get things back to normal so quickly. I know all the officers are, anyway."

"Just as I told you, my dear." Beresford patted his wife's hand, then looked at me, amusement touching the corners of his eyes. "My wife, like my daughter, seems to have the greatest faith in your judgement, Mr. Carter."

"Yes, sir. I wondered if you could persuade your daughter not to go visiting in the officers' quarters?"

"No," Beresford said regretfully, "it's impossible. Self-willed young lady." He grinned. "I'll bet she didn't even knock."

"She didn't." I looked across the room to where Miss Beresford was giving Tony Carreras the full benefit of her eyes over the rim of a martini glass. They certainly made a striking couple. "She had, with respect, some bee in her bonnet about something being wrong aboard the *Campari*. I think the unfortunate happenings last night must have upset her."

"Naturally. And you managed to remove this—um— bee?"

"I think so, sir."

There was a slight pause, then Mrs. Beresford said impatiently, "Julius, we're just beating about the bush."

"Oh, now, Mary, I don't think—"

"Rubbish," she said briskly. "Young man, do you know one of the principal reasons I came along on this trip? Apart"—she smiled—"from the food? Because my husband asked me to, because he wanted a second opinion— on you. Julius, as you know, has made several trips on your ship. He has, as the saying goes, had an eye on you for a job in his organisation. My husband, I may say, has made his fortune not so much by working himself as by picking the right men to work for him. He's never made a mistake yet. I don't think he's making a mistake now. And you have another very special recommendation."

"Yes, ma'am," I said politely.

"You're the only young man of our acquaintance who doesn't turn himself into a carpet to be trampled on as soon as our daughter appears in sight. A very important qualification, believe me."

"Would you like to work for me, Mr. Carter?" Beresford asked bluntly.

"I think I would, sir."

"Well!" Mrs. Beresford looked at her husband. "That's settled——"

"Will you?" Julius Beresford interrupted.

"No, sir."

"Why not?"

"Because your interests are in steel and oil. I know only the sea and ships. They don't mix. I have no qualifications to work for you, and at my present age I'd be too long in acquiring them. And I couldn't accept a job for which I'd no qualifications."

"Even at double the money? Or three times?"

"I'm grateful for the offer, sir, believe me. I do appreciate it. But there's more to it than money."

"Ah, well." The Beresfords looked at each other. They didn't seem too disturbed over my refusal; there was no reason why they should. "We asked a question, we got an answer. Fair enough." He changed the subject. "What do you think of my feat in getting the old man here tonight?"

"I think it was very thoughtful of you." I glanced across the room to a spot near the door where old Cerdan, sherry glass in hand, was sitting in his wheel chair, with his nurses on a settee by his side. They too had sherry glasses. The old boy seemed to be talking animatedly to the captain. "He must lead a very shut-in life. Much difficulty in persuading him?"

"None at all. He was delighted to come." I filed away this piece of information; my one encounter with Cerdan had left me with the impression that the only thing that would delight him about such an invitation would be the opportunity to give a surly refusal. "If you'll excuse us, Mr. Carter. Hosts' duties to their guests, you know."

"Certainly, sir." I stood to one side, but Mrs. Beresford planted herself in front of me and smiled quizzically.

"Mr. Carter," she said firmly, "you're a very stiff-necked

young man. And please don't for a moment imagine that I'm referring to your accident of last night."

They moved off. I watched them go, thinking all sorts of thoughts, then crossed to the hinged flap that led to the rear of the bar. Whenever I approached that flap I felt it was not a glass I should have in my hand but a machete to help me hack my way through the jungle of flowers, potted shrubs, cacti, and festoons of creepers and hanging plants that transformed the place into the most unlikely looking bar you'd ever seen. The interior designer responsible had gone into rhapsodies about it, but it was all right for him— he didn't have to live with it; all he had to do was to retire nightly to his semi-detached in South London where his wife would have had him out the door if he'd tried on any such nonsense at home. But the passengers seemed to like it.

I made it to the back of the bar without getting scratched too much and said to the barman, "How's it going, Louis?"

"Very well, sir," Louis said stiffly. His bald pate was gleaming with sweat and his hairline moustache twitching nervously. There were irregularities going on and Louis didn't like irregularities. Then he thawed a bit and said, "They seem to be drinking a fair bit more than usual tonight, sir."

"Not half as much as they will later on." I moved to the crystal-laden shelves from where I could see under the back of the bar and said, "You don't look very comfortable to me."

"By God, and I'm not!" And indeed there wasn't much room for the bo'sun to wedge his bulk between the raised deck and the underside of the bar; his knees were up to his chin, but at least he was completely invisible to anyone on the other side of the counter. "Stiff as hell, sir. Never be able to move when the time comes."

"And the smell of all that liquor driving you round the bend," I said sympathetically. I wasn't as cool as I sounded. I had to keep wiping the palms of my hands on the sides of my jacket, but try as I would, I couldn't seem to get them properly dry. I moved over to the counter again. "A double whisky, Louis. A *large* double whisky."

Louis poured the drink and handed it across without a word. I raised it to my lips, lowered it below counter level, and a large hand closed gratefully round it. I said quietly, as if speaking to Louis, "If the captain notices the smell afterwards you can claim it was that careless devil Louis that spilt it over you. I'm taking a walk now, Archie. If everything's O.K., I'll be back in five minutes."

"And if not? If you're wrong?"

"Heaven help me. The old man will feed me to the sharks."

I made my way out from behind the bar and sauntered slowly towards the door. I saw Bullen trying to catch my eye but I ignored him; he was the world's worst actor. I smiled at Susan Beresford and Tony Carreras, nodded civilly enough to old Cerdan, bowed slightly to the two nurses—the thin one, I noticed, had returned to her knitting and she seemed to me to be doing all right—and reached the doorway.

Once outside, I dropped all pretence at sauntering. I reached the entrance to the passengers' accommodation on "A" deck in ten seconds. Halfway down the long central passageway White was sitting in his cubicle. I walked quickly down there, lifted the lid of his desk, and took out the four items lying inside: Colt revolver, torch, screw driver, and master key. I stuffed the Colt into my belt, the torch in one pocket, the screw driver in the other. I looked at White, but he didn't look at me. He was staring down into one corner of his cubicle as if I didn't exist. He had his hands clasped tightly together, like one in prayer. I hoped he was praying for me. Even with his hands locked he couldn't stop them from shaking uncontrollably. I left him without a word and ten seconds later was inside Cerdan's suite with the door locked behind me. On a sudden instinct I switched on my torch and played the beam round the edges of the door. The door was pale blue against a pale-blue bulkhead. Hanging from the top of the bulkhead, dangling down for a couple of inches over the top of the door, was a pale-blue thread. A broken pale-blue thread: to the people who had put it there, an unmistakable calling card that visitors had been there. I wasn't worried about that, but I was worried by the fact that it showed that someone was suspicious, very, very suspicious. This might make things very awkward indeed. Maybe we should have announced Dexter's death.

I passed straight through the nurses' cabin and the lounge into Cerdan's cabin. The curtains were drawn, but I left the lights off: light could show through curtains, and if they were as suspicious as I thought, someone might have wondered why I had left so suddenly and taken a walk outside. I hooded the torch to a small pencil beam and played it over the deckhead. The cold-air trunking ran fore and aft, and the first louvre was directly above Cerdan's bed. I didn't even need the screw driver. I shone the torch through the louvre opening and saw, inside the trunking, something gleaming metallically in the bright spot of light. I reached up two fingers and slowly worked that something metallic down through the louvre. A pair of earphones. I peered into the louvre again. The earphones lead had a plug on the end of it and the plug was fitted into a socket that had been screwed on to the upper wall of the trunking. And the radio office was directly above. I pulled out the plug, rolled the lead round the headphones, and switched off my torch.

White was exactly as I had left him, still vibrating away like a tuning fork. I opened his desk, returned key, screw driver, and torch. The earphones I kept. And the gun.

They were into their third cocktails by the time I returned to the drawing room. I didn't need to count empty bottles to guess that; the laughter, the animated conversation, the increase in the decibel ratio was proof enough. Captain Bullen was still chatting away to Cerdan. The tall nurse was still knitting. Tommy Wilson was over by the bar. I rubbed my cheek and he crushed out the cigarette he was holding. I saw him say something to Miguel and Tony Carreras—at twenty feet, in that racket, it was impossible to hear a word he said—saw Tony Carreras lift a half-amused, half-questioning eyebrow, then all three of them moved towards the bar.

I joined Captain Bullen and Cerdan. Long speeches weren't going to help me here, and only a fool would throw away his life by tipping off people like those.

"Good evening, Mr. Cerdan," I said. I pulled my left hand out from under my jacket and tossed the earphones onto his rug-covered lap. "Recognise them?"

Cerdan's eyes stared wide, then he flung himself forwards and sideways as if to clear his encumbering wheel chair, but old Bullen had been waiting for it and was too quick for him. He hit Cerdan with all the pent-up worry and fury of the past twenty-four hours behind the blow, and Cerdan toppled over the side of his chair and crashed heavily to the carpet.

I didn't see him fall; I only heard the sound of it. I was too busy looking out for myself. The nurse with the sherry glass in her hand, quick as a cat, flung the contents in my face at the same instant as Bullen hit Cerdan. I flung myself sideways to avoid being blinded, and as I fell I saw the tall, thin nurse flinging her knitting to one side and thrusting her hand deep into the string knitting bag.

With my right hand I managed to tug the Colt clear of my belt before I hit the ground and squeezed the trigger twice. It was my right shoulder that hit the carpet first, just as I fired, and I didn't really know where the bullets went, nor, for that one nearly blinding instant of agony as the shock of falling was transmitted to my injured neck, did I care; then my head cleared and I saw that the tall nurse was on her feet. Not only on her feet but raised high on her toes, head and shoulders arched sharply forwards, ivory-knuckled hands pressed deep into her midriff; then she swayed forward, in macabre slow-motion action, and crumpled over the fallen Cerdan. The other nurse hadn't moved from her seat: with Captain Bullen's Colt only six inches from her face, and his finger pretty white on the trigger, she wasn't likely to, either.

The reverberations of my heavy Colt, painful and deafening in their intensity in that confined metal-walled space, faded away into a silence that was deathly in more ways than one, and through that silence came a soft Highland voice saying gently: "If either of you move I will kill you."

Carreras Senior and Junior, who must have had their

backs to the bar, were now turned round halfway towards it, staring at the gun in MacDonald's hand. Miguel Carreras' face was unrecognisable, his expression changed from that of a smooth, urbane, and highly prosperous businessman into something very ugly indeed. His right hand, as he had whirled round, had come to rest on the bar near a cut-glass decanter. Archie MacDonald wasn't wearing any of his medals that night, and Carreras had no means of knowing the long and bloodstained record the bo'sun had behind him, or he would never have tried to hurl that decanter at MacDonald's head. Carreras' reactions were so fast, the movement so unexpected, that against another man he might have made it; against MacDonald he didn't even manage to get the decanter off the counter and a split second later was left staring down at the shattered bloody mess that had been his hand.

For the second time in a few seconds the crashing roar of a heavy gun, this time intermingled with the tinkle of smashed and flying glass, died away and again MacDonald's voice came, almost regretfully: "I should have killed you, but I like reading about those murder trials. We're saving you for the hangman; Mr. Carreras."

I was climbing back to my feet when someone screamed, a harsh, ugly sound that drilled piercingly through the room. Another woman took it up, a sustained shriek like an express, whistle wide open, heading for a level crossing, and the stage seemed all set for mass hysteria.

"Stop that damned screaming," I snarled. "Do you hear? Stop it at once. It's all over now."

The screaming stopped. Silence again, a weird, unnatural silence that was almost as bad as the racket that had gone before. And then Beresford was coming towards me, a bit unsteadily, his lips forming words that didn't come, his face white. I couldn't blame him; in his well-ordered and wealth-cushioned world the entertainments offered his guests couldn't often have ended up with bodies strewn all over the floor.

"You've killed her, Carter," he said at length. His voice was harsh and strained. "You've killed her. I saw it; we all saw it. A—a defenceless woman." He stared at me, and if he had any thought of offering me a job again I couldn't see it in his face. "You murdered her."

"Woman my foot!" I said savagely. I bent down, yanked off the nurse's hat, then ruthlessly ripped away a glued wig to show a black close-croped crew cut. "Attractive, isn't it? The very latest from Paris. And defenceless!" I grabbed her bag, turned it upside down, emptied the contents on the carpet, stooped, and came up with what had originally been a full-length double-barrelled shotgun: the barrels had been sawn off until there was no more than six inches of them left, the wooden stock removed and a roughly made pistol-type grip fitted in its place. "Ever seen one of those before, Mr. Beresford? Native product of your own country, I believe. A whippet or some such name. Fires lead shot, and from the range our nurse friend here intended to use it, it would have blown a hole clear through my middle. Defenceless!" I turned to where Bullen was standing, his gun still trained on the other nurse. "Is that character armed, sir?"

"We'll soon find out," Bullen said grimly. "You carrying a gun, my friend?"

The "nurse" swore at him, two words in basic Anglo-Saxon, in a low, snarling voice. Bullen gave him no warning; he swept up the Colt and struck the barrel heavily across the man's face and temple. He staggered and swayed, out on his feet. I caught him, held him with one hand, while with the other I ripped the dress down the front, pulled out a snub-nosed automatic from a felt holster under the left arm, then let him go. He swayed some more, collapsed on the settee, then rolled to the floor.

"Is—is all this necessary?" Beresford's voice was still hoarse and strained.

"Stand back, everyone," Bullen said authoritatively. "Keep well over to the windows and clear of these two men, our two Carreras friends. They are highly dangerous and might try to jump in among you for cover. MacDonald, that was splendidly done. But next time shoot to kill. That's an order. I accept full responsibility. Dr. Marston, bring the necessary equipment, please, and attend to Carreras' hand." He waited till Marston had left, then turned to Beresford with a wry smile. "Sorry to ruin your party, Mr. Beresford. And all this, I assure you, is highly necessary."

"But—but the violence, the—the killing—"

"They murdered three of my men in twenty-four hours."

"They *what?*"

"Benson, Brownell, and Fourth Officer Dexter. Murdered them. Brownell was strangled; Benson was strangled or shot; Dexter's lying dead in the wireless office with three bullets in his stomach, and God knows how many more men would have died if Chief Officer Carter hadn't got on to them."

I looked round the white, strained, still unbelieving faces; there was no real understanding yet of what the captain was saying; the shock, the fear, the near hysteria left no room for thought in their minds. Of them all, I had to admit that old Beresford had taken it best, to adjust himself to what must have been the incredible spectacle of seeing fellow passengers suddenly gunned down by officers of the *Campari,* to fight his way out of this fog of crazy bewilderment.

"But I mean, Captain, what part can an old cripple like Mr. Cerdan have in all this?"

"According to Mr. Carter, Cerdan isn't old at all—he's just made up to look old. And also, according to Mr. Carter, if Cerdan is a cripple, paralysed from the waist down as he is supposed to be, then you're going to witness a modern miracle of healing just as soon as he recovers consciousness. For all we know, Cerdan is very probably the leader of this bunch of murderers. We don't know."

"But what in God's name is behind it all?" Beresford demanded.

"That's just what we are about to find out," Bullen said tightly. He glanced at Carreras, father and son. "Come here, you two."

They came, MacDonald and Tommy Wilson following. Carreras Senior had a handkerchief wrapped round his shattered hand, trying, not very successfully, to stem the flow of blood, and the eyes that caught mine were wicked with hate; Tony Carreras, on the other hand, seemed calmly unconcerned, even slightly amused. I made a mental note to keep a very close eye indeed on Tony Carreras. He was too calm and relaxed by half.

They halted a few feet away. Bullen said, "Mr. Wilson?"

"Sir?"

"That sawn-off shotgun belonging to our late friend here. Pick it up."

Wilson picked it up.

"Do you think you could use it? And don't point the damned thing at me," he added hastily.

"I think so, sir."

"Cerdan and the so-called nurse. A sharp eye on them. If they come to and try anything . . ." Bullen left the sentence unfinished. "Mr. Carter, Carreras and his son may be armed."

"Yes, sir." I moved round behind Tony Carreras, careful to keep out of the line of fire of both Bullen and MacDonald, caught his jacket by the collar, and jerked it savagely down over shoulders and arms till it reached the level of his elbows.

"You seem to have done this sort of thing before, Mr. Carter," Tony Carreras said easily. He was a cool customer all right, too damned cool for my liking.

"Television," I explained. He was carrying a gun under the left shoulder. He was wearing a specially made shirt with a couple of hemmed slits front and back on the left-hand side so that the chest strap for the holster was concealed under the shirt. Tony Carreras was very thorough in his preparations.

I went over his clothes, but he'd only the one gun. I went through the same routine with Miguel Carreras, who wasn't anywhere near as affable as his son, but maybe his hand was hurting him. He wasn't carrying any gun. And maybe that made Miguel Carreras the boss: maybe he didn't have to carry any gun; maybe he was in a position to order other people to do his killing for him.

"Thank you," Captain Bullen said. "Mr. Carreras, we will be in Nassau in a few hours' time. The police will be aboard by midnight. Do you wish to make a statement now or would you rather make it to the police?"

"My hand is broken." Miguel Carreras' voice was a harsh whisper. "The forefinger is smashed; it will have to be amputated. Someone is going to pay for this."

"I take it that is your answer," Bullen said calmly. "Very well. Bo'sun, four heaving lines, if you please. I want those men trussed like turkeys."

"Aye, aye, sir." The bo'sun took one step forward, then stood stock-still. Through the open doorway had come a flat staccato burst of sound—the unmistakable chattering of a machine gun. It seemed to come from almost directly above, from the bridge. And then all the lights went out.

I think I was the first person to move. I think I was the only person to move. I took a long step forward, hooked my left arm round Tony Carreras' neck, rammed the Colt into the small of his back, and said softly, "Don't even think of trying anything, Carreras."

And then there was silence again. It seemed to go on and on and on, but it probably didn't last more than a few seconds altogether. A woman screamed, a brief choking sound that died away into a moan, and then there was silence once more, a silence that ended abruptly with a violent crashing, splintering, and tinkling as heavy solid metallic objects, operating in almost perfect unison, smashed in the plate-glass windows that gave to the deck outside. At the same instant there came the sharp echoing crash of metal against metal as the door was kicked wide open to smash back against the bulkhead.

"Drop your guns, all of you," Miguel Carreras called in a high clear voice. "Drop them—now! Unless you want a massacre."

The lights came on.

Vaguely outlined against the four smashed windows of the drawing room I could see the blurs of four indistinct heads and shoulders and arms. The blurs I didn't care about; it was what they held in their arms that worried me—the wicked-looking snouts and cylindrical magazines of four submachine guns. A fifth man, dressed in jungle green and wearing a green beret on his head, stood in the doorway, a similar automatic carbine cradled in his hands.

I could see what Carreras meant about dropping our guns. It seemed an excellent idea to me; we had about as much chance as the last ice cream at a children's party. I was already starting to loosen my grip on the gun when, incredulously, I saw Captain Bullen jerk up his Colt on the armed man in the doorway. It was criminal, suicidal folly; either he was acting completely instinctively, without any thought at all, or the bitter chagrin, the killing disappointment after having thought that he had held all the cards in his hands, had been too much for him. I might have known, I thought briefly and wildly, he'd been far too calm and self-controlled, the safety valve screwed down on the bursting boiler.

I tried to shout out a warning, but it was too late; it was far too late. I shoved Tony Carreras violently aside and tried to reach Bullen, to strike down his gun hand, but I was still far too late, a lifetime too late. The heavy Colt was rearing and bucking in Bullen's hand, and the man in the doorway, to whom the ridiculous idea of resistance must have been the very last thought in his head, let the machine gun slide slowly out of lifeless hands and toppled backwards out of sight.

The man outside the window nearest the door had his machine gun lined up on the captain. Bullen, in that second, was the biggest fool in the world, a crazy suicidal maniac, but even so, I couldn't let him be gunned down where he stood. I don't know where my first bullet went, but the second must have struck the machine gun. I saw it jerk violently as if struck aside by a giant hand, and then came a continuous cacophonous drumfire of deafening sound as a third man squeezed the trigger of his machine gun and kept on squeezing it. Something with the power and weight of a plunging pile driver smashed into my left thigh, hurling me back against the bar. My head struck the heavy brass rail at the foot of the counter and the sound of the drumfire died away.

The stink of drifting cordite and the silence of the grave. Even before consciousness came fully back to me, even before I opened my eyes, I was aware of those, of the cordite and the unearthly stillness. I opened my eyes slowly, pushed myself shakily up till I was sitting with my back more or less straight against the bar, and shook my head to try to clear it. I had, understandably enough, forgotten about my stiff neck; the sharp stab of pain did more to clear my head than anything else could have done.

The first thing I was aware of was the passengers. They were all stretched out on the carpet, lying very still. For one heart-stopping moment I thought they were all dead or dying, mown down in swathes by that stuttering machine gun, then I saw Mr. Greenstreet, Miss Harrbride's husband, move his head slightly and look round the drawing room with a cautious and terrified eye. One eye was all I could see. At any other time it would have been very, very funny, but I never felt less like laughing. The passengers, perhaps through wisdom, but more probably through the reflex reaction of instinctive self-preservation, must have flung themselves to the deck the moment the machine gun had opened up and were only now daring to lift their heads. I concluded that I couldn't have been unconscious for more than a few seconds.

I moved my eyes to the right. Carreras and son were standing just where they had been, and Tony Carreras had a gun in his hand now. My gun. Beyond them a huddled group lay sprawling or sitting about the floor. Cerdan, the "nurse" I'd shot, and three others.

Tommy Wilson, the laughing, lovable, happy-go-lucky Tommy Wilson, was dead. He wouldn't have to worry about his mathematics any more.

It didn't need old Doc Marston and his shortsighted peering to tell me that Wilson was dead. He was lying on his back, and it looked to me as if half his chest had been shot away; he must have taken the main brunt of that concentrated burst of machine-gun fire. And Tommy hadn't even lifted his gun.

Archie MacDonald was stretched out on his side, close

to Wilson. He seemed to me to be very still, far, far too still. I couldn't see the front of his body for he was turned away from me; for all I knew machine-gun slugs had torn the life out of him as they had out of Tommy Wilson. But I could see blood all over his face and neck, slowly soaking into the carpet.

Captain Bullen was the one who was sitting. He wasn't dead anyway, but I wouldn't have bet a brass farthing on his chances of staying alive. He was fully conscious, his mouth warped and dragged into an unnatural smile, his face white and twisted with pain. From shoulder almost to the waist his right side was soaked in blood, so soaked that I couldn't see where the bullets had gone home, but I could see bright red bubbles flecking the twisted lips, which meant that he had been shot through the lung.

I looked at the three of them again. Bullen, MacDonald, Wilson. Three better men it would have been hard to find, three better shipmates impossible to find. They had wanted none of this, none of this blood and agony and death; all they had wanted was the chance to do their jobs in peace and quiet and as best they could. Hard-working, companionable, and infinitely decent men, they had sought no violence, thought no violence, so now they lay there dead or dying, MacDonald and Bullen with their wives and families, Tommy Wilson with his fiancée in England and a girl in every port in America and the Caribbean. I looked at them and I felt no sadness or sorrow or anger or shock; I just felt cold and detached and strangely uninvolved in it all. I looked from them to the Carreras family and Cerdan and I made myself a promise, and it was well for me that neither Carreras heard my promise or knew of its irrevocable finality, for they were clever, calculating men and they would have shot me dead as I lay there.

I wasn't feeling any pain at all, but I remembered about the pile driver that had hurled me back against the bar. I looked down at my left leg, and from mid-thigh to well below the knee the trousers were so saturated with blood that there was no trace of white left. The carpet all round my leg was soaked with it. That carpet, I remembered vaguely, had cost over £10,000, and it was certainly taking a terrible beating that night. Lord Dexter would have been furious. I looked at my leg again and fingered the soggy material. Three distinct tears, which meant that I had been shot three times. I supposed the pain would come later. A great deal of blood, far too much blood: I wondered if an artery had been torn.

"Ladies and gentlemen." It was Carreras speaking, and although his hand must have been giving him hell there was no sign of it in his face. The fury, the malevolence I had so recently seen, was only a memory: he was back on balance again, urbane, commanding, in complete control of the situation.

"I regret all this, regret it extremely." He waved his left hand in the direction of Bullen and Wilson, MacDonald and myself. "All so unnecessary, so terribly unnecessary, brought upon Captain Bullen and his men by Captain Bullen's reckless folly." Most of the passengers were on their feet now, and I could see Susan Beresford standing beside her father, staring down at me as if she weren't seeing too well, eyes abnormally large in the pale face. "I regret, too, the distress you have been caused, and to you, Mr. and Mrs. Beresford, I tend my apologies for the ruin of your night's entertainment. Your kindness has been ill-rewarded."

"For God's sake cut out the fancy speeches," I interrupted. My voice didn't sound like mine at all, a harsh, strained croak, a bullfrog with laryngitis. "Get the doctor for Captain Bullen. He's been shot through the lung."

He looked at me speculatively, then at Bullen, then back at me.

"A certain indestructible quality about you, Mr. Carter," he said thoughtfully. He bent over and peered at my blood-stained leg. "Shot three times, your leg must be pretty badly smashed, yet you can observe so tiny a detail as a fleck of blood on Captain Bullen's mouth. You are incapacitated, and I am glad. Had your captain, officers, and crew been composed exclusively of men like yourself, I would never have come within a thousand miles of the

Campari. As for the doctor, he will be here soon. He is tending a man on the bridge."

"Jamieson? Our third officer?"

"Mr. Jamieson is beyond all help," he said curtly. "Like Captain Bullen, he fancied himself as a man cast in a heroic mould; like Captain Bullen, he has paid the price for his stupidity. The man at the wheel was struck in the arm by a stray bullet." He turned to face the passengers. "You need have no further worry about your personal safety. The *Campari* is now completely in my hands and will remain so. However, you form no part of my plans and will be transferred in two or three days to another vessel. Meanwhile you will all eat, live, and sleep in this room: I cannot spare individual guards for each stateroom. Mattresses and blankets will be brought to you. If you co-operate, you can exist in reasonable comfort; you certainly have no more to fear."

"What is the meaning of this damnable outrage, Carreras?" There was a shake in Beresford's voice. "Those desperadoes, those killers, what of them? Who are they? Where in the name of God did they come from? What do you intend to do? You're mad, man, completely mad. Surely you know you can't expect to get off with this?"

"You may use that thought for consolation. Ah, Doctor, there you are." He held out his right hand, swathed in its bloodstained handkerchief. "Have a look at this, will you?"

"Damn you and your hand," Dr. Marston said bitterly. The old boy was trembling; the sight of the dead and dying must have hit him hard, but he was hopping mad for all that. "There are other more seriously injured men here. I must—"

"You may as well realise that I, and I alone, give the orders from now on," Carreras interrupted. "My hand. At once. Ah, Juan." This to a tall, thin, swarthy man who had just entered, a rolled-up chart under his arm. "Give that to Mr. Carter here. That's him, yes. Mr. Carter, Captain Bullen said—and I have been aware of it for many hours—that we are heading for Nassau and are due there in less than four hours. Lay off a course to take us well clear of Nassau, to the east, then out midway between the Great Abaco and Eleuthera islands and so approximately north-northwest into the North Atlantic. My own navigation has become rather rusty, I fear. Mark in the approximate times for course changes."

I took the chart, pencil, parallel rulers, and dividers, and laid the chart on my knee. Carreras said consideringly, "What, no 'Do your own damned navigation' or words to that effect?"

"What's the point?" I said wearily. "You wouldn't hesitate to line up all the passengers and shoot them one by one if I didn't co-operate."

"It's a pleasure to deal with a man who sees and accepts the inevitable." Carreras smiled. "But you greatly overestimate my ruthlessness. Later, Mr. Carter, when we have you fixed up you shall become a permanent installation on the bridge. It is unfortunate, but I suppose you realise that you are the only deck officer left to us?"

"You'll have to get some other installation on the bridge," I said bitterly. "My thighbone is smashed."

"What?" He looked at me narrowly.

"I can feel it grating." I twisted my face up to let him see how I could feel it grating. "Dr. Marston will soon confirm it."

"We can arrive at some other arrangement," Carreras said equably. He winced as Dr. Marston probed at his hand. "The forefinger—it will have to come off?"

"I don't think so. A local anaesthetic, a small operation, and I belive I can save it." Carreras didn't know the danger he was in; if he let old Marston get to work on him he'd probably end up by losing his whole arm. "But it will have to be done in my surgery."

"It's probably time we all went to the surgery. Tony, check engine room, radar room, all men off duty; see that they are all safely under guard. Then take that chart to the bridge and see that the helmsman makes the proper course alterations at the proper time. See that the radar operator is kept under constant supervision and reports the slightest object on his screen: Mr. Carter here is quite capable of laying off a course which would take us smack into the middle of Eleuthera Island. Two men to take Mr. Cerdan to his cabin. Dr. Marston, is it possible to take those men down to your surgery without endangering their lives?" The good Samaritan, all overcome with concern for his fellow men.

"I don't know." Marston finished his temporary bandaging of Carreras' hand and crossed to Bullen. "How do you feel, Captain?"

Bullen looked at him with lack-lustre eyes. He tried to smile but it was no more than an agonised grimace. He tried to speak but no words came, just fresh bubbles of blood at his lips. Marston produced scissors, cut the captain's shirt open, examined him briefly, and said, "We may as well risk it. Two of your men, Mr. Carreras, two strong men. See that his chest is not compressed."

He left Bullen, bent over MacDonald, and straightened almost immediately. "This man can be moved with safety."

"MacDonald!" I said. "The bo'sun. He—he's not dead?"

"He's been hit on the head. Creased, probably concussed, perhaps even the skull fractured, but he'll survive. He seems to have been hit on the knee, too—nothing serious."

I felt as if someone had lifted the Sydney Bridge off my back. The bo'sun had been my friend, my good friend, for too many years now, and, besides, with Archie MacDonald by me all things were possible.

"And Mr. Carter?" Carreras queried.

"Don't you touch my leg," I yelled. "Not until I get an anaesthetic."

"He's probably right," Marston murmured. He peered closely. "Not much blood now—you've been lucky, John. If the main artery had been severed—well, you'd have been gone." He looked at Carreras, his face doubtful. "He could be moved, I think, but with a fractured thighbone the pain will be excruciating."

"Mr. Carter is very tough," Carreras said unsympathetically. It wasn't his thighbone; he'd been a good Samaritan for a whole minute now and the strain had proved too much for him. "Mr. Carter will survive."

Chapter 7

I SURVIVED all right, but no credit for that was due to the handling I received on the way down to the sick bay. The sick bay was on the port side, two decks below the drawing room; on the second companionway one of the two men who were carrying me slipped and fell and I was aware of nothing more until I woke up in bed.

Like every compartment on the *Campari*, the sick bay was fitted out regardless of cost. A large room, twenty feet by sixteen, it had the usual wall-to-wall Persian carpeting and pastel walls decorated with murals depicting water skiing, skin-diving, swimming, and other such sporting activities symbolic of fitness and good health, craftily designed to encourage to get on their feet and out of there with all possible speed any patient unfortunate enough to be confined to any of the three beds. The beds themselves, with their heads close up to the windows in the ship's side, struck a jarring note: they were just plain standard iron hospital beds, the only concession to taste being that they were painted in the same pastel tints as the bulkheads. In the far corner of the room, remote from the door, was old Marston's consulting desk, with a couple of chairs; further along the inner bulkhead, nearer the door, was a flat-topped couch that could be raised for examinations or, if need be, the carrying out of minor operations. Between couch and desk a door led to two smaller compartments, a dispensary and a dentist's surgery. I knew that because I had recently spent three quarters of an hour in that dentist's chair, with Marston attending to a broken tooth; the memory of the experience would stay with me the rest of my days.

The three beds were occupied. Captain Bullen was in the one nearest to the door, the bo'sun next to him, and myself in the corner, opposite Marston's desk, all of us lying on rubber sheets placed over the beds. Marston was bent over the middle bed, examining the bo'sun's knee; beside him, holding a metal tray with bowls, sponges, instruments, and bottles containing some unidentifiable liquids, was Susan Beresford. She looked very pale. I wondered vaguely what she was doing here. Seated on the couch was a young man, badly in need of a shave: he was wearing green trousers, a green sweat-stained epauletted shirt, and green beret. He had his eyes half-closed against the smoke spiralling up from the cigarette stuck in the corner of his mouth and carried an automatic carbine in his hand. I wondered how many men with how many automatic carbines were posted all over the *Campari*. Detailing a man to guard three broken-down crocks like MacDonald, Bullen, and myself showed that Carreras had plenty of men to spare or was excessively cautious. Or maybe both.

"What are you doing here, Miss Beresford?" I asked.

She looked up, startled, and the instruments rattled metallically on the tray in her hands.

"Oh, I *am* glad," she said. She sounded almost as if she meant it. "I thought—I—how do you feel?"

"The way I look. Why are you here?"

"Because I needed her." Doc Marston straightened slowly and rubbed his back. "Dealing with wounds like these—well, I must have a helper. Nurses, John, are usually young and female and there are only two on the

Campari in that category. Miss Beresford and Miss Harcourt."

"I don't see any signs of Miss Harcourt." I tried to visualise the glamorous young actress in the real-life role of Florence Nightingale, but my imagination was in no shape to cope with absurdities like that. I couldn't even see her playing it on the screen.

"She was here," he said curtly. "She fainted."

"That helps. How's the bo'sun?"

"I must ask you not to talk, John," he said severely. "You've lost a great deal of blood and you're very weak. Please conserve your strength."

"How's the bo'sun?" I repeated.

Dr. Marston sighed.

"He'll be all right. That is, he's in no danger. Abnormally thick skull, I should say; that saved him. Concussion, yes, but not fractured, I think. Hard to say without an X-ray. Respiration, pulse, temperature, blood pressure— none of them shows any signs pointing to extensive brain injury. It's his leg I'm worried about."

"His leg?"

"Patella. Kneecap to you. Completely shattered, beyond repair. Tendons sliced, tibia fractured. Leg sawn in half. Must have been hit several times. The damned murderers!"

"Amputation? You don't think—"

"No amputation." He shook his head irritably. "I've removed all the broken pieces I can find. Bones will either have to be fused, so shortening the leg, or a metal plate. Too soon to say. But this I can say: he'll never bend that knee again."

"You're telling me he's crippled? For life?"

"I'm sorry. I know you're very friendly."

"So he's finished with the sea?"

"I'm sorry," Marston repeated. Medical incompetence apart, he was really a pretty decent old buffer. "Your turn now, John."

"Yes." I wasn't looking forward to my turn. I looked at the guard. "Hey, you! Yes, you. Where's Carreras?"

"Señor Carreras." The young man dropped his cigarette on the Persian carpet and ground it out with his heel. Lord

Dexter would have gone off his rocker. "It is not my business to know where Señor Carreras is."

That settled that. He spoke English. I couldn't have cared less at the moment where Carreras was. Marston had his big scissors out, was preparing to slit up my trouser leg.

"Captain Bullen?" I asked. "What chance?"

"I don't know. He's unconscious now." He hesitated. "He was wounded twice. One bullet passed clean through below the shoulder, tearing the pectoral muscle. The other entered the right chest a little lower, breaking a rib, then must have gone through the lung near the apex. The bullet is still lodged inside the body, almost certainly in the vicinity of the shoulder blade. I may decide to operate later to remove it."

"Operate." The thought of old Marston hacking round inside an unconscious Bullen made me feel even paler than I looked. I choked down the next few words I thought of and said, "Operate? You would take the grave chance, you would be willing to risk your lifetime's professional reputation—"

"A man's life is at stake, John," he said solemnly.

"But you might have to penetrate the chest wall. A major operation, Dr. Marston. Without assistant surgeons, without skilled nurses, without a competent anaesthetist, no X-rays, and you might be removing a bullet that's plugging a vital gap in the lung or pleura, or whatever you call it. Besides, the bullet might have been deflected anywhere." I took a deep breath. "Dr. Marston, I cannot say how much I respect and admire you for even thinking of operating in such impossible conditions. But you *will* not run the risk. Doctor, as long as the captain is incapacitated I am in command of the *Campari*—in nominal command, anyway," I added bitterly. "I absolutely forbid you to incur the very heavy responsibility of operating in such adverse conditions. Miss Beresford, you are a witness to that."

"Well, John, you may be right," old Marston said weightily. He was suddenly looking five years younger. "You may indeed be right. But my sense of duty—"

"It does you great credit, Doctor. But think of all those

people who have been carrying a bullet about inside their chests since the First World War and still going strong."

"There's that, of course, there's that." I had rarely seen a man looking so relieved. "We'll give nature a chance, hey?"

"Captain Bullen's as strong as a horse." The old man had at least a fighting chance now; I felt as if I'd just saved a life. I said weakly, "You were right, Doctor. I'm afraid I have been talking too much. Could I have some water, please?"

"Of course, my boy, of course." He brought some, watched me drink it, and said, "That feel better?"

"Thank you." My voice was very faint. I moved my lips several times, as if speaking, but no words came. Marston, alarmed, put his ear close to my mouth to make out what I was trying to say, and I murmured, slowly and distinctly, "My thighbone is not broken, but pretend it is."

He started, eyes reflecting astonishment, opened his mouth to speak, and then closed it again. He wasn't all that slow, the old boy. He nodded slightly and said, "Ready for me to begin?"

He began. Susan Beresford helped him. My leg was a gory sight but looked worse than it was. One bullet had passed directly through the leg, but the other two had just torn superficial gashes on the inside, and it was from those that most of the blood had come. All the while he was working Dr. Marston kept up, for the sake of the guard, a running commentary on the extent and severity of my wounds, and if I hadn't known he was lying fluently he would have made me feel very ill indeed. He certainly must have convinced the guard. When he'd cleaned and bound the wounds, a process I bore with stoic fortitude only because I didn't want to start yelling in front of Susan Beresford, he fixed some splints to my leg and bound those on also. This done, he propped up my leg on a pile of pillows, went into the dispensary and reappeared with a couple of screwed pulleys, a length of wire with a heavy weight attached to the end, and a leather strap. The strap he fitted to my left ankle.

"What's this in aid of?" I demanded.

"I'm the medical officer, please remember," he said curtly. His left eyelid dropped in a slow wink. "Traction, Mr. Carter. You don't want your left leg to be permanently shortened for life?"

"Sorry," I muttered. Maybe I had been misjudging old Marston, just a little. Nothing would ever make me reconsider my opinion of him as a doctor, but he was shrewd enough in other things: the first thing a man like Carreras would have asked was why a man with a broken bone in his thigh was not in traction. Marston screwed the two hooks into holes in the deckhead, passed the wire through, attached the weight to one end and the strap to the other. It didn't feel too uncomfortable. He then picked up the length of trouser leg that had been cut off, checked quickly to see if the guard was watching, splashed some water on it, and then wrung it out on top of my bandages. Even to myself I had to admit that I'd seldom seen a more convincing sight, a patient more completely and thoroughly immobilised.

He finished just in time. He and Susan Beresford were just clearing away when the door opened and Tony Carreras came in. He looked at Bullen, MacDonald, and myself, slowly, consideringly—he wasn't a man who would miss very much—then came to my bedside.

"Good evening, Carter," he said pleasantly. "How are you feeling?"

"Where's that murderous parent of yours?" I asked.

"Murderous parent? You do my father an injustice. Asleep, at the moment, as it happens: his hand was giving him great pain after Marston had finished with it"—I wasn't surprised at that—"so he was given a sleeping draught. The good ship *Campari* is all buttoned up for the night and Captain Tony Carreras in charge. You may all sleep easy. You'll be interested to hear that we've just picked up Nassau on the radarscope—port forty, or some such nautical term—so you weren't playing any funny tricks with that course after all."

I grunted and turned my head away. Carreras walked across to Marston. "How are they, Doctor?"

"How do you expect them to be after your thugs have

riddled them with bullets?" Marston demanded bitterly. "Captain Bullen may live or die, I don't know. MacDonald, the bo'sun, will live, but he'll be a stiff-legged cripple for life. The chief officer has a compound fracture of the femur—the thighbone. Completely shattered. If we don't get him to hospital in a couple of days, he also will be crippled for life; as it is, he'll never be able to walk properly again."

"I am genuinely sorry," Tony Carreras said. He actually sounded as if he meant it. "Killing and crippling good men is an unforgivable waste. Well, almost unforgivable. Some things justify it."

"Your humanity does you credit," I sneered from my pillow.

"We are humane men," he said.

"You've proved that all right." I twisted to look at him. "But you could still show a little consideration for a very sick man."

"Indeed?" He was very good at lifting eyebrows.

"Indeed. Dan'l Boone, here." I nodded towards the sentry with the gun. "You permit your men to smoke on duty?"

"José?" He smiled. "José is an inveterate chain smoker. Take his cigarettes away and he'd probably go on strike. This isn't the Grenadier Guards, you know, Carter. Why the sudden concern?"

"You heard what Dr. Marston said. Captain Bullen. He's in a critical condition with a hole through his lung."

"Ah, I think I understand. You agree, Doctor?"

I held my breath. The chances were that the old boy hadn't even the faintest idea what we were talking about. But again I'd underrated his astuteness.

"For a man with a ruptured lung," he said gravely, "there can be nothing worse than a smoke-laden atmosphere."

"I see. José!" Carreras spoke rapidly in Spanish to the guard, who grinned amiably, got to his feet, and made for the door, picking up a chair en route. The door swung to behind him.

"No discipline." Tony Carreras sighed. "None of this

brisk sentry-go marching and counter-marching like Buckingham Palace, Mr. Carter. A chair tilted against a wall. Our Latin blood, I fear. But, I warn you, none the less effective a guard for all that. I see no harm in his keeping a watch outside; apart from jumping out through one of the windows into the sea below—not that you are in any condition to do that anyway—I can't see what mischief you can get up to." He paused, looked at me consideringly. "You are singularly incurious, Mr. Carter. Far from being in character. Makes one suspicious, you know."

"Curious about what?" I growled. "Nothing to be curious about. How many of those armed thugs do you have aboard the *Campari?*"

"Forty. Not bad, eh? Well, thirty-eight effectives. Captain Bullen killed one and you seriously damaged the hand of another. Where did you learn to shoot like that, Carter?

"Luck. Cerdan recovered yet?"

"Yes," he said briefly. He didn't seem to want to talk about Cerdan.

"He killed Dexter?" I persisted.

"No. Werner, the nurse—the one you killed to-night." For a professed humanitarian, the death of one of his colleagues in crime left him strangely unmoved. "A steward's uniform and a tray of food at face level. Your head steward, White, saw him twice and never suspected, not that he went within thirty feet of White. And it was just Dexter's luck that he saw this steward unlocking the radio room."

"I suppose that same murderous devil got Brownell?"

"And Benson. Benson caught him coming out of the radio room after disposing of Brownell and was shot. Werner was going to dump him straight over the side, but there were people—crew—directly underneath. He dragged him across to the port side. Again crew beneath. So he emptied a lifejacket locker and put Benson inside." Carreras grinned. "And just *your* bad luck that you happened to be standing right beside that locker when we sent Werner up to dispose of the body, just before midnight last night."

"Who dreamed up this scheme of having the false Marconi man in Kingston drill through from the wireless office to the cold-air trunking in Cerdan's room below and buttoning the earphones permanently into the wireless officer's receiving circuit? Cerdan, your old man, or you?"

"My father."

"And the Trojan horse idea. Your father also?"

"He is a brilliant man. Now I know why you were not curious. You knew."

"It wasn't hard to guess," I said wearily. "Not, that is, when it was too late. All our troubles really started in Carracio. And we loaded those huge crates in Carracio. Now I know why the stevedores were so terrified when one of the crates almost slipped from its slings. Now I know why your old man was so damned anxious to inspect the hold—not to pay his respects to the dead men in their coffins, but to see how his men were placed for smashing their way out of the crates. And then they broke out last night and forced the battens of the hatch. How many men in a crate, Carreras?"

"Twenty. Rather uncomfortably jammed, poor fellows. I think they had a rough twenty-four hours."

"Twenty. Two crates. We loaded four of those. What's in the other crates?"

"Machinery, Mr. Carter, just machinery."

"One thing I am really curious about."

"Yes?"

"What's behind all this murderous business? Kidnap? Ransom?"

"I am not at liberty to discuss those things with you." He grinned. "At least, not yet. You remaining here, Miss Beresford, or do you wish me to—ah—escort you up to your parents in the drawing room?"

"Please leave the young lady," Marston said. "I want her to help me keep a twenty-four-hour watch on Captain Bullen. He might have a relapse at any moment."

"As you wish." He bowed to Susan Beresford. "Good night, all."

The door closed. Susan Beresford said, "So *that's* how they came aboard. How in the world did you know?"

"How in the world did I know? You didn't think they

had forty men hidden up inside the funnel, did you? Once we knew it was Carreras and Cerdan, it was obvious. They came aboard at Carracio. So did those huge crates. Two and two, Miss Beresford, have never failed to add up to four." She flushed and gave me a very old-fashioned look, but I ignored it and went on: "You both see what this means, don't you?"

"Let him tell us, Doctor," Miss Beresford said acidly. "He's just dying to tell us."

"It means that there's something very, very big behind it all," I said slowly. "All cargoes, except those in free ports and under certain transshipment conditions, which don't apply here, have to be inspected by customs. Those crates passed the Carracio customs—which means that the customs know what's inside. Probably explains, too, why our Carracio agent was so nervous. But the customs let it pass. Why? Because they had orders to let those crates pass. And who gave them the orders? Their government. And who gave the government its orders? Who but the generalissimo? After all, he *is* the government. The generalissimo," I went on thoughtfully, "is directly behind all this. And we know he's desperate for money. I wonder, I wonder?"

"You wonder what?" Marston asked.

"I don't really know. Tell me, Doctor, have you the facilities for making tea or coffee here?"

"Never yet seen a dispensary that hadn't, my boy."

"What an excellent idea!" Susan Beresford jumped to her feet. "I'd love a cup of tea."

"Coffee."

"Tea."

"Coffee. Humour a sick man. This should be quite an experience for Miss Beresford. Making her own coffee, I mean. You fill the percolator with water—"

"Please stop there." She crossed to my bedside and looked down at me, her face without expression, her eyes very steady. "You have a short memory, Mr. Carter. I told you the night before last that I was sorry—very sorry. Remember?"

"I remember," I acknowledged. "Sorry, Miss Beresford."

"Susan." She smiled. "If you want your coffee, that is."

"Blackmail."

"Oh, for heaven's sake, call her 'Susan' if she wants," Dr. Marston interrupted irritably. "What's the harm?"

"Doctor's orders," I said resignedly. "O.K. Susan, bring the patient his coffee." The circumstances were hardly normal: I could get back to calling her Miss Beresford later on.

Five minutes passed, then she brought the coffee. I looked at the tray and said, "What? Only three cups? There should be four."

"Four?"

"Four. Three for us and one for our friend outside."

"Our friend—you mean the guard?"

"Who else?"

"Have you gone mad, Mr. Carter?"

"Fair's fair," Marston murmured. " 'John' to you."

She looked coldly at him, glared at me, and said icily, "Have you gone mad? Why should I bring that thug coffee. I'll do nothing—"

"Our chief officer *always* has a reason for his actions," Marston said in sharp and surprising support. "Please do as he asks."

She poured a cup of coffee, took it through the outside door, and was back in a few seconds.

"He took it?" I asked.

"Didn't he just. Seems he's had nothing except a little water to drink in the past day or so."

"I can believe it. I should imagine that they weren't too well equipped in the catering line in those crates." I took the cup of coffee she offered me, drained it, and set it down. It tasted just the way coffee ought to taste.

"How was it?" Susan asked.

"Perfect. Any suggestion I made that you didn't even know how to boil water I withdraw unreservedly."

She and Marston looked at each other and then Marston said, "No more thinking or worrying to do to-night, John?"

"Nary a bit. All I want is a good night's sleep."

"And that's why I put a pretty powerful sedative in your coffee." He looked at me consideringly. "Coffee has a remarkable quality of disguising other flavours, hasn't it?"

I knew what he meant and he knew I knew what he meant. I said, "Dr. Marston, I do believe I have been guilty of underestimating you very considerably."

"I believe you have, John," he said jovially. "I believe you have indeed."

I became drowsily aware that my left leg was hurting, not badly, but badly enough to wake me up. Someone was pulling it, giving it a strong, steady tug every few seconds, letting go, then tugging it again. And he kept on talking all the time he was doing it. I wished that that someone, whoever he was, would give it up. The tugging and the talking. Didn't he know I was a sick man?

I opened my eyes. The first thing I saw was the clock on the opposite bulkhead. Ten o'clock. Ten o'clock in the morning, for broad daylight was coming in through uncurtained windows. Dr. Marston had been right about the sedative; "powerful" was hardly the word for it.

Someone was talking, sure enough; old Bullen was babbling away incoherently in a drugged and troubled sleep, but there was no one tugging at my leg. It was the traction weight suspended from the ceiling that was doing the tugging. The *Campari,* in spite of her stabilisers, was rolling through a ten-to-fifteen-degree arc, which meant that there must be a pretty heavy and steep beam sea or swell running. Whenever the ship came to the end of a roll, the suspended pulley, reaching the limit of its pendulum swing, would give a pronounced jerk, a few seconds later another jerk. Now that I was fully awake, it was more painful than I had at first thought. Even if I had had a genuinely fractured femur, that sort of thing wouldn't be doing me any good at all. I looked round to see Dr. Marston and to ask him to remove it.

But the first person who caught my eye was not Dr. Marston but Miguel Carreras. He was standing near the top of my bed; maybe he had been shaking me awake. He was newly shaven, looked fresh and rested, had his neatly bandaged right hand in a sling, and carried some charts under his arm. He gave me a slight smile.

"Good morning, Mr. Carter. How do you feel now?"

I ignored him. Susan Beresford was sitting at the doctor's desk. She looked pretty tired to me and there were dark smudges under the green eyes. I said, "Susan, where's Doc Marston?"

"Susan?" Carreras murmured. "How swiftly contiguity breeds familiarity."

I ignored him again. Susan said, "In the dispensary, asleep. He's been up most of the night."

"Wake him, will you? Tell him I want this damned weight off. It's tearing my leg in two."

She went into the dispensary and Carreras said, "Your attention, Mr. Carter, if you please."

"When I get that weight off," I said surlily. "Not before."

Dr. Marston appeared, rubbing the sleep from his eyes, and started to remove the weight without a word.

"Captain Bullen and the bo'sun?" I asked. "How are they?"

"The captain's holding his own—just." The old boy looked tired and sounded tired. "The bo'sun's recovering fast. Both of them came to early this morning; I gave them sedatives. The longer they sleep, the better."

I nodded, waited till he had lifted me to a sitting position and adjusted my leg, then said curtly, "What do you want, Carreras?"

He unrolled a chart and spread it over my knees. "A little navigational assistance—cross-checking, shall we call it? You will co-operate?"

"I'll co-operate."

"What?" Susan Beresford crossed from the desk and stared down at me. "You—you're going to help this man?"

"You heard me, didn't you? What do you want me to be—a hero?" I nodded at my leg. "Look where being heroic's got me."

"I wouldn't have believed it!" Patches of colour flared

in the pale cheeks. "You. Going to help this—this monster, this murderer."

"If I don't," I said wearily, "he'll like as not start on you. Maybe break a finger at a time or yank out a tooth at a time with Dr. Marston's forceps—and without anaesthetic. I'm not saying he'd like doing it, but he'd do it."

"I'm not afraid of Mr. Carreras," she said defiantly. But she was paler than ever.

"Then it's time you were," I said curtly. "Well, Carreras?"

"You have sailed the North Atlantic, Mr. Carter? Between Europe and America, I mean?"

"Many times."

"Good." He jabbed at the chart. "A vessel leaving the Clyde and sailing for Norfolk, Virginia. I wish you to sketch the course it would take. Any reference books you wish I can have fetched."

"I don't require any." I took his pencil. "North's about round Ireland, so, a slightly flattened great circle route along the westbound summer lane, so, to this point well southeast of Newfoundland. The northward curve looks strange, but that's only because of the projection of the chart: it is the shortest route."

"I believe you. And then?"

"Shortly after that the course diverges from the main west-bound New York lane, approximately here, and comes into Norfolk more or less from the east-northeast." I twisted my head round to try to see out of the surgery door. "What's all that racket? Where's it coming from? Sounds like riveting guns or pneumatic chisels to me."

"Later, later," he said irritably. He unrolled another chart and the irritation vanished from his face. "Splendid, Carter, splendid. Your track coincides almost exactly with the information I have here."

"Why the hell did you ask me—"

"I double-check everything, Mr. Carter. This vessel, now, is due to arrive at Norfolk at exactly ten o'clock at night, on Saturday, in two days' time. Not earlier, not later: exactly ten o'clock. If I wish to meet that vessel at dawn that day, where would the interception point be?"

I kept my questions to myself. "Dawn, in that latitude, at this time, is five o'clock, give or take a few minutes. What speed does this vessel do?"

"Of course. Foolish of me. Ten knots."

"Ten knots. Seventeen hours. One hundred and seventy nautical miles. The interception point would be here."

"Exactly." He'd consulted his own chart again. "Exactly. Most gratifying." He looked at a slip of paper in his hand. "Our present position is 26.52 north, 76.33 west, near enough, anyway. How long would it take us to get to this interception point?"

"What *is* that hammering outside?" I demanded. "What devilry are you up to now, Carreras?"

"Answer my question!" he said sharply.

He held all the cards. I said: "What's our speed just now?"

"Fourteen knots."

"Forty-three hours," I said after a minute. "Just under."

"Forty-three hours," he said slowly. "It's now ten A.M. Thursday and I have to rendezvous at five A.M. on Saturday. My God, that *is* only forty-three hours." The first shadow of worry crossed his face. "What is the maximum speed of the *Campari?*"

"Eighteen knots." I caught a glimpse of Susan's face. She was fast losing all her illusions about Chief Officer Carter.

"Ah! Eighteen?" His face cleared. "And at eighteen knots?"

"At eighteen knots you'll probably tear the stabilisers off and break up the *Campari*," I told him.

He didn't like that. He said, "What do you mean?"

"I mean you've got trouble coming, Carreras. Big trouble." I looked at the window. "I can't see that sea, but I can feel it. An abnormally long deep swell. Ask any fisherman in the Bahamas what that means at this time of the year and he'll tell you. It can mean only one thing, Carreras—tropical storm, pretty certainly a hurricane. The swell is coming from the east, and that's where the heart of the storm lies. Maybe a couple of hundred miles away yet, but it's there. And the swell's getting worse. Have you noticed? It's getting worse because the classic path of a hurricane in these parts is west-northwest, at a speed of ten to fifteen miles an hour. And we're heading north by east. In other words, the hurricane and the *Campari* are on a collision course. Time you started listening to some weather reports, Carreras."

"How long will it take at eighteen knots?" he pressed.

"Thirty-three hours. About. In good weather."

"And the course?"

I laid it off and looked at him. "The same as you have on that chart, undoubtably."

"It is. What wave length for weather reports?"

"No wave length," I said drily. "If there's a hurricane moving in westwards from the Atlantic, every commercial station on the eastern seaboard will be broadcasting practically nothing else."

He moved across to Marston's phone, spoke to the bridge, gave instructions for maximum speed and for listening in to weather reports. When he'd finished, I said, "Eighteen knots? Well, I warned you."

"I must have as much time as possible in hand." He looked down at Bullen who was still rambling on incoherently in his sleep. "What would our captain do in those circumstances?"

"Turn and run in any direction except north. We have our passengers to think of. They don't like getting seasick."

"They're going to be very seasick, I'm afraid. But all in a good cause."

"Yes," I said slowly. I knew now the source of the hammering on deck. "A good cause. For a patriot such as yourself, Carreras, what better cause could there be? The generalissimo's coffers are empty. Not a sou in sight—and his regime is tottering. Only one thing can save the sick man of the Caribbean—a transfusion. A transfusion of gold. This ship that we're going to intercept, Carreras—how many millions in gold bullion is she carrying?"

Marston was back in the surgery now, and he and Susan looked at me, then at each other, and you could see their mutual diagnosis: delayed shock had made me lightheaded. Carreras, I could see, wasn't thinking anything of the kind: his face, like his body, had gone very still.

"You have access to sources of information of which I am completely unaware." His voice was hardly more than a whisper. "What sources, Carter? Quickly!"

"There are no sources, Carreras." I grinned at him. "Should there be?"

"No one plays cat-and-mouse with me." He was still very quiet. "The sources, Carter?"

"Here." I tapped my head. "Only here. This source."

He regarded me for some seconds in cold silence, then nodded fractionally. "I knew it the first time I saw you. There is a—a quality about you. A champion boxer looks a champion boxer even in repose. A dangerous man cannot look anything else but dangerous, even in the most domestic situations, the most harmless surroundings. You have that quality. I have trained myself to recognise such things."

"Hear that?" I said to Susan. "You never even suspected it, hey? Thought I was just like everybody else, didn't you?"

"You are even more astute than I thought, Mr. Carter," Carreras murmured.

"If adding two and two to make an obvious four is what you call being astute, then, sure, I'm astute. My God, if I were astute, I wouldn't be lying here now with a shattered leg." An occasional reminder of my helplessness would do no harm. "The generalissimo needing cash—I should have worked it out long ago."

"Yes?"

"Yes. Shall I tell you why Brownell, our radio officer, was killed?"

"I should be interested."

"Because you had intercepted a message from the Harrisons and Curtises, the two families recalled by cable from Kingston. This message said that the cables had been a hoax, and if we knew it had been a hoax we would have started looking very closely at Messrs. Carreras and Cerdan, the people who had taken their places. The point is that the cables they had received came through *your* capital city, Carreras, which argues post office connivance and, by inference, government knowledge. The government owns the post office.

"Secondly, there is a long waiting list in your country for berths on the *Campari;* you were near the bottom but were mysteriously jumped to the top. You said you were the only people who could take immediate advantage of the two suddenly vacant suites. Poppycock. Somebody in authority—in great authority—said, 'Carreras and Cerdan go to the top.' And no one squawked. I wonder why?

"Thirdly, although there is a waiting list, none of the people on it are your nationals, Carreras. They are not permitted to travel on foreign-owned vessels—and, in addition, find themselves immediately in prison if caught in possession of foreign currency. But *you* were permitted to travel—and you paid in U.S. dollars. You're still with me?"

He nodded. "We had to take the chance of paying in dollars."

"Fourthly, the customs closed their eyes to those crates with your men aboard—and those crates with the cannons. That shows—"

"Cannons?" Marston interrupted. He was looking almost completely dazed. "Cannons?"

"The noise you can hear outside," Carreras said equably. "Mr. Carter will explain by and by. I wish," he went on, almost with regret, "that we were on the same side of the fence. You would have made an incomparable lieutenant, Mr. Carter. You could have named your own price."

"That's just about what Mr. Beresford said to me yesterday," I agreed. "Everybody's offering me jobs these days. The timing of the offers could have been improved."

"Do you mean to tell me," Susan said, "that Daddy offered—"

"Don't panic," I said. "He changed his mind. So, Carreras, there we have it. Government connivance on all sides. And what does the government want? Money. Completely desperate. Paid three hundred and fifty million dollars to Iron Curtain countries in the past year or two for arms. Trouble was, the generalissimo never had three hundred and fifty million dollars in the first place. Now nobody will buy his sugar, trade's practically nonexistent, so how does an honest man raise money? Easy. He steals it."

"Insulting personal remarks we can dispense with."

"Suit yourself. Maybe armed robbery and piracy on the high seas sounds more moral than stealing. I wouldn't know. Anyway, what does he steal? Bonds, stocks, shares, convertible drafts, currency? Not on your life. He only wants something that can never be traced back to him—and the only stuff he can get in sufficient quantity is gold. Your leader, Mr. Carreras," I finished thoughtfully, "must have a very extensive spy network both in Britain and America."

"If one is prepared to lay out sufficient capital on an affair such as this," he said indifferently, "a large spy system is unnecessary. I even have the complete loading plans of the bullion vessel in my cabin. Most men have their price, Mr. Carter."

"I wish someone would try me someday," I said. "Well, there you are. The American government has made no secret recently of its great success in recovering a large proportion of its gold reserves which went to Europe in the past few years. That bullion has to be transported—and part of it, I'll bet my boots, is in this ship we're intercepting. The fact that it is not due to arrive in Norfolk until after dark is interesting enough in itself; what is even more interesting is that Norfolk, in this case, almost certainly means the Hampton Roads Naval Operating Base where the ship can be unloaded with maximum security. And Norfolk, I would say, is the point that offers the shortest overland route to Fort Knox, where the gold will eventually be stored. How much gold, Carreras?"

"One hundred and fifty million dollars," he said calmly. "You have missed very little. And nothing of importance."

One hundred and fifty million dollars. I mentally examined this sum from several different angles, but there didn't seem to be any comment to meet the case, so I asked, "Why did you pick on the *Campari?*"

"I thought you would have guessed that one too. In point of fact we had three other ships under active consideration as well, all ships on the New York-Caribbean run. We have been studying the movements of all four ships for some time. Yours suited best."

"You cut things pretty fine, didn't you? If we had been a couple of days late in arriving in Carracio—"

"There has been a naval vessel, a frigate, standing by and ready to intercept you on a peaceful pretext ever since you left Savannah. I was aboard. But it wasn't necessary." So that explained the vessel we had seen on our radar screens at night after leaving Savannah: not an American warship, as we had thought, but the generalissimo's. "This way was much easier, much more satisfactory."

"And, of course," I said, "you couldn't have used the frigate for this job. Hasn't the cruising range. Hopeless in bad weather. No derricks for heavy trans-shipment lifts. And conspicuous, far too conspicuous. But the *Campari* —who's going to miss the *Campari* if she's only a few days late in arriving at a destination. Only the head office and—"

"The head office is being taken care of," Carreras said. "You don't think we overlooked the obvious, do you? Our own transmitter was brought aboard and is already in circuit. A stream of perfectly satisfactory messages are going out, I assure you."

"So you fixed that. And the *Campari* has the speed to overtake most cargo ships; it's a good large sea boat for practically any weather, has first-class radar for picking up other vessels and jumbo derricks for heavy lifts." I paused and looked at him. "We even have reinforced decks for gun platform both for'ard and on the poop. Most British vessels have had those installed as a matter of course when building. But I warn you that they have to be strengthened from below with angle irons, a couple of days' job in itself. Without them, anything more than a three-inch will buckle and twist the plates beyond repair after even only a couple of shots."

"A couple of shots will be all that we require."

I thought about that last remark. A couple of shots. It didn't make any kind of sense at all. What was Carreras up to?

"What on earth are you both talking about?" Susan asked wearily. "Reinforced steel decks, angle irons—what *is* it all about?"

"Come with me, Miss Beresford, and I shall take pleasure in showing you personally what I mean." Carreras smiled. "Besides, I'm sure your good parents are becoming very anxious about you. I shall see you later, Mr. Carter. Come, Miss Beresford."

She looked at him in doubtful hesitation. I said, "You might as well go, Susan. You never know what luck you'll have. One good shove when he's near the rail and off-balance. Just pick your time."

"Your Anglo-Saxon humour becomes rather wearisome," Carreras said thinly. "One hopes that you will be able to preserve it intact in the days to come."

He left on this suitably sinister note, and Marston looked at me, speculation taking the place of puzzlement in his eyes. "Did Carreras mean what I thought he meant?"

"He did. That's the hammering you've been hearing, the pneumatic drills. There are prepared boltholes in the reinforced sections on the poop and foredeck to accept the base plates of several different sizes of British guns. Carreras' guns probably come from the other side of the Iron Curtain and he has to drill new holes."

"He—he's actually going to fit naval guns."

"He had them in a couple of those crates. Almost certainly stripped down into sections, ready for quick assembly. Don't have to be anything very big—can't be; it's a dockyard job to fit anything of any size. But it will be big enough to stop this ship."

"I don't believe it!" Marston protested. "Holdup on the high seas? Piracy in this day and age? It's ridiculous! It's impossible!"

"You tell that to Carreras. He hasn't a moment's doubt but that it's very, very possible. Neither have I. Can you tell me what's going to stop him?"

"But we've got to stop him, John. We must stop him!"

"Why?"

"Good God! Why? Let a man like that get away with heaven only knows how many million pounds . . ."

"Is that what you're worried about?"

"Of course," Marston snapped. "So would anyone be."

"You're right, of course, Doctor," I agreed. "I'm not at my best to-day." What I could have said was that if he thought about it a bit more, he would become ten times as worried as he was, and not about the money. About half as worried as I was. And I was worried to death and frightened, badly frightened. Carreras was clever, all right, but perhaps a shade less so than he imagined. He made the mistake of letting himself get too involved in conversation, and when a man gets too involved and has anything to hide, he makes the further mistake of either talking too much or not talking enough. Carreras had made the mistake on both counts. But why should he worry about whether he talked too much or not? He couldn't lose. Not now.

Breakfast came. I didn't feel much like eating, but I ate all the same. I had lost far too much blood, and whatever little strength I could recover I was going to need that night. I felt even less like sleep, but for all that I asked Marston for a sedative and he gave it to me. I was going to need all the sleep I could get, too; I wouldn't get much that coming night.

The last sensation I recalled as I dozed off was in my mouth, a queer unnatural dryness that usually comes with overmastering fear. But it wasn't fear, I told myself. It wasn't really fear. Just the effect of the sleeping draught. That's what I told myself.

Chapter 8

[*Thursday 4* P.M.–*10* P.M.]

IT WAS late afternoon when I woke, round four o'clock: still a good four hours short of sunset, but already the surgery lights were on and the sky outside dark, almost, as night. Driving, slanting rain was sheeting down torrentially from the black lowering clouds, and even through closed doors and windows I could hear the high, thin sound, part whine, part whistle, of a gale-force wind howling through the struts and standing rigging.

The *Campari* was taking a hammering. She was still going fast, far, far too fast for the weather conditions, and was smashing her way through high, heavy rolling seas bearing down on her starboard bow. That they weren't mountainous waves, or waves of even an unusual size for a tropical storm, I was quite sure; it was the fact that the *Campari* was battering her way at high speed through quartering seas that seemed to be almost tearing her apart. She was corkscrewing viciously, a movement that applies the maximum possible strain to a ship's hull. With metronomic regularity the *Campari* was crashing, starboard bow first, into a rising sea, lifting bows and rolling over to port as she climbed up the wave, hesitating, then pitching violently for'ard and rolling over to starboard as she slid down the far shoulder of the vanishing wave to thud with a teeth-rattling, jolting violence into the shoulder of the next sea, a shaking, shuddering collision that made the *Campari* vibrate for seconds on end in every plate and rivet throughout her entire length. No doubt but that the Clyde yard that her built her had built her well, but they wouldn't have constructed her on the assumption that she was going to fall into the hands of maniacs. Even steel can come apart.

"Dr. Marston," I said, "try to get Carreras on that phone."

"Hello, awake?" He shook his head. "I've been on to him myself, an hour ago. He's on the bridge and he says he's going to stay there all night, if need be. And he won't reduce speed any further: he's taken her down to fifteen knots already, he says."

"The man's mad. Thank God for the stabilisers. If it weren't for them, we'd be turning somersaults."

"Can they stand up to this sort of thing indefinitely?"

"I should think it highly unlikely. The captain and bo'sun—how are they?"

"The captain's still asleep, still delirious, but breathing easier. Our friend Mr. MacDonald you can ask for yourself."

I twisted in my bed. The bo'sun was indeed awake, grinning at me. Marston said, "Seeing you're both awake, do you mind if I have a kip down in the dispensary for an hour? I could do with it."

He looked as if he could, too, pale and exhausted.

"We'll call you if anything goes wrong." I watched him go, then said to MacDonald, "You like your sleep, don't you?"

"Just naturally idle, Mr. Carter." He smiled. "I was wanting to get up, but the doctor wasn't keen."

"Surprised? You know your kneecap is smashed and it'll be weeks before you can walk properly again." He'd never walk properly again.

"Aye, it's inconvenient. Dr. Marston has been talking

to me about this fellow Carreras and his plans. The man's daft."

"He's all that. But daft or not, what's to stop him?"

"The weather, perhaps. It's pretty nasty outside."

"The weather won't stop him. He's got one of those fanatic one-track minds. But I might have a small try at it myself."

"You?" MacDonald had raised his voice, now lowered it to a murmur. "You! With a smashed thighbone. How in the—"

"It's not broken." I told him of the deception. "I think I can get around on it if I don't have too much climbing to do."

"I see. And the plan, sir?"

I told him. He thought me as daft as Carreras. He did his best to dissuade me, finally accepted the inevitable, and had his own suggestions to make. We were still discussing it in low voices when the sick-bay door opened and a guard showed Susan Beresford in, closed the door, and left.

"Where have you been all day?" I said accusingly.

"I saw the guns." She was pale and tired and seemed to have forgotten that she had been angry with me for cooperating with Carreras. "He's got a big one mounted on the poop and a smaller one on the fo'c'sle. Covered with tarpaulins now. The rest of the day I spent with Mummy and Daddy and the others."

"And how are our passengers?" I enquired. "Hopping mad at being shanghaied, or do they regard it as yet another of the attractions of the *Campari*—a splendid adventure thrown in at no extra charge that they can talk about to the end of their days? I'm sure most of them must be pretty relieved that Carreras is not holding them all to ransom."

"Most of them are not caring one way or another," she said. "They're so seasick they couldn't care if they lived or died. I feel a bit the same way myself, I can tell you."

"You'll get used to it," I said callously. "You'll all get used to it. I want you to do something for me."

"Yes, John." The dutiful murmur in the voice which

was really tiredness, the use of the first name had me glancing sharply across at the bo'sun, but he was busy examining a part of the deckhead that was completely devoid of anything to examine.

"Get permission to go to your cabin. Say you're going for blankets, that you felt too cold here last night. Your father's dinner suit—slip it between the blankets. Not the tropical one, the dark one. For heaven's sake, see you're not observed. Have you any dark-coloured dresses?"

"Dark-coloured dresses?" She frowned. "Why—"

"For pete's sake!" I said in low-voiced exasperation. I could hear the murmur of voices outside. "Answer me!"

"A black cocktail dress . . ."

"Bring it also."

She looked at me steadily. "Would you mind telling me—"

The door opened and Tony Carreras came in, balancing easily on the swaying, dipping deck. He carried a rain-spattered chart under his arm.

"Evening, all." He spoke cheerfully enough, but for all that he looked rather pale. "Carter, a small job from my father. Course positions of the *Fort Ticonderoga* at eight A.M., noon, and four P.M. to-day. Plot them and see if the *Ticonderoga* is on its predicted course."

"*Fort Ticonderoga* being the name of the ship we have to intercept?"

"What else?"

"But—but the positions," I said stupidly. "The course positions of—how the devil do you know? Don't tell me the *Ticonderoga* is actually sending you her positions? Are the—are the radio operators on that ship—"

"My father thinks of everything," Tony Carreras said calmly. "Literally everything. I told you he was a brilliant man. You know we're going to ask the *Ticonderoga* to stand and deliver. Do you think we want it sending out SOSs when we fire a warning shot across its bows? The *Ticonderoga*'s own radio officers had a slight accident before the ship left England and had to be replaced by—ah —more suitable men."

"A slight accident?" Susan said slowly. What with seasickness and emotion, her face was the colour of paper, but she wasn't scared of Carreras any, that I could see. "What kind of accident?"

"A kind that can so easily happen to any of us, Miss Beresford." Tony Carreras was still smiling, but somehow he no longer looked charming and boyish. I couldn't really see any expression on the face at all; all I could see were the curiously flattened eyes. More than ever I was sure that there was something wrong with young Carreras' eyes, and more than ever I was sure that the wrongness lay not in the eyes alone but was symptomatic and indicative of a wrongness that lay much deeper than the eyes. "Nothing serious, I assure you." Meaning that they hadn't been killed more than once. "One of the replacements is not only a radioman but an expert navigator. We saw no reason why we should not take advantage of this fact to keep us informed as to the exact position of the *Ticonderoga*. Every hour, on the hour."

"Your father leaves nothing to chance," I admitted. "Except that he seems to be depending on me as the expert navigator on this ship."

"He didn't know—we weren't to know—that all the other deck officers on the *Campari* were going to be—ah —so foolish. We—both my father and I—dislike killing of any kind." Again the unmistakable ring of sincerity, but I was beginning to wonder if the bell hadn't a crack in it. "My father is also a competent navigator, but unfortunately he has his hands very full at the moment. He happens to be the only professional seaman we have."

"Your other men aren't?"

"Alas, no. But they are perfectly adequate to the task of seeing that professional seamen—your men—do their duties as they should."

This was cheering news. If Carreras persisted in pushing the *Campari* through the storm at this rate, practically everyone who wasn't a professional seaman was going to be feeling very ill indeed. That might help to ease my night's labours.

I said, "What's going to happen to us after you've hijacked this damned bullion?"

"Dump you all on the *Ticonderoga*," he said lazily. "What else?"

"Yes?" I sneered. "So that we can straightaway notify every ship that the *Campari* had—"

"Notify whoever you like," he said placidly. "Think we're crazy? We're abandoning the *Campari* the same morning: another vessel is already standing by. Miguel Carreras *does* thing of everything."

I said nothing and turned my attention to the charts while Susan made her request to be allowed to bring blankets. He smilingly said he would accompany her and they left together. When they returned in five minutes' time I had entered the course positions on the chart and found that the *Fort Ticonderoga* was really on course. I handed the chart to Carreras with that information; he thanked me and left.

Dinner came at eight o'clock. It wasn't much of a meal as *Campari* dinners went; Antoine was never at his best when the elements were against him, but it was fair enough for all that. Susan ate nothing. I suspected that she had been sick more than once but had made no mention of it; millionaire's daughter or not, she was no crybaby and had no self-pity, which was only what I would have expected from the daughter of the Beresfords. I wasn't hungry myself. There was a knot in my stomach that had nothing to do with the motion of the *Campari*, but again on the principle that I was going to need all the strength I could find, I made a good meal. MacDonald ate as if he hadn't seen food for a week. Bullen still slept under sedation, restless against the securing straps that held him to his bed, breathing still distressed, mumbling away continuously to himself.

At nine o'clock Marston said, "Time now for coffee, John?"

"Time for coffee," I agreed. Marston's hands, I noticed, weren't quite steady. After too many years of consuming the better part of a bottle of rum every night, his nerves weren't in any too fit a condition for this sort of thing.

Susan brought in five cups of coffee, one at a time—the

wild pitching of the *Campari,* the jarring, jolting shocks as we crashed down into the troughs, made the carrying of more than one at a time impossible. One for herself, one for MacDonald, one for Marston, one for me—and one for the sentry, the same youngster as had been on guard the previous night. For the four of us, sugar; for the sentry, a spoonful of white powder from Marston's dispensary. Susan took his cup outside.

"How's our friend?" I asked when she returned.

"Almost as green as I am." She tried to smile, but it didn't come off. "Seemed glad to get it."

"Where is he?"

"In the passage. Sitting on the floor, jammed in a corner, gun across his knees."

"How long before that stuff acts, Doctor?"

"If he drinks it all straightaway, maybe twenty minutes. And don't ask me how long the effects will last. People vary so much that I've no idea. Maybe half an hour, maybe three hours. You can never be certain with those things."

"You've done all you can. Except the last thing. Take off those outside bandages and those damned splints, will you?"

He looked nervously at the door. "If someone comes—"

"We've been through all that," I said impatiently. "Even by taking a chance and losing, we'll be no worse off than we were before. Take them off."

Marston fetched a chair to give himself steadier support, sat down, eased the point of his scissors under the bandages holding the splints in place and sliced through them with half a dozen swift, clean cuts. The bandages fell away; the splints came loose, and then the door opened. Half a dozen long strides and Tony Carreras was by my bedside, staring down thoughtfully. He looked even paler than the last time I'd seen him.

"The good healer on the night shift, eh? Having a little patient trouble, Doctor?"

"Trouble?" I said hoarsely. I'd my eyes screwed half shut, lips compressed, fists lying on the coverlet tightly clenched. Carter in agony. I hoped I wasn't overdoing it. "Is your father mad, Carreras?" I closed my eyes completely and stifled—nearly—a moan as the *Campari* lurched forward and down into an abnormally deep trough with a shuddering, jarring impact that all but threw Carreras off his feet. Even through closed doors, even above the eldritch howl of the wind and the lash of the gale-driven rain, the sound of the impact was like gunfire, and not distant gunfire at that. "Does he want to kill us all? Why in God's name can't he slow down?"

"Mr. Carter is in very great pain," Doc Marston said quietly. Whatever his faults as a doctor, he was fast at catching on, and when you looked into those steady, wise blue eyes beneath the magnificent mane of white hair, it was impossible not to believe him. "Agony would be a better word. He has, as you know, a compound fracture of the femur." With delicate fingers he touched the blood-stained bandages that had been concealed by the splints so that Carreras could see just how compound it was. "Every time the ship moves violently the broken ends of the bone grind together. You can imagine what it's like—no, I doubt if you can. I am trying to rearrange and tighten the splints so as to immobilise the leg completely. Difficult job for one man in those conditions. Care to give me a hand?"

Ine one second flat I revised my estimate of Marston's shrewdness. No doubt he's just been trying to allay any suspicions that Carreras might have had, but he couldn't have thought up a worse way. Not, that is, if Carreras offered his help, for the chances were that if he did delay to help he'd find the sentry snoring in the passageway outside when he left.

"Sorry." Beethoven himself never sounded half as sweet as the music of that single word from Carreras. "Can't wait. Captain Carreras making his rounds and all that. That's what Miss Beresford is here for anyway. Failing all else, just shoot him full of morphia." Five seconds later he was gone.

Marston raised an eyebrow.

"Less affable than of yore, John, you would say. A shade lacking in the sympathy he so often professes?"

"He's worried," I said. "He's also a little frightened and perhaps, heaven be praised, even more than a little seasick.

But still very tough for all that. Susan, go and collect the sentry's cup and see if friend Carreras has really gone."

She was back in fifteen seconds.

"He's gone. The coast is clear."

I swung my legs over the side of the bed and stood up. A moment later I had fallen heavily to the floor, my head just missing the iron foot of MacDonald's bed. Four things were responsible for this: the sudden lurch of the deck as the *Campari* had fallen into a trough, the stiffness of both legs, the seeming paralysis of my left leg, and the pain that had gone through my thigh like a flame as soon as my foot had touched the deck.

Hands gripping the bo'sun's bed, I dragged myself to my feet and tried again. Marston had me by the right arm and I needed all the support I could get. I made it to my own bed and sat down heavily. MacDonald's face was expressionless. Susan looked as if she were about to cry. For some obscure reason that made me feel better. I lurched to my feet like an opening jackknife, caught hold of the foot of my own bed, and had another go.

It was no good. I wasn't made of iron. The lurching of the *Campari* I could cope with and the first stiffness was slowly beginning to disappear. Even that frightening weakness in my left leg I could in some measure ignore; I could always hop along. But the pain I couldn't ignore. I wasn't made of iron. I have a nervous system for transmitting pain, just like anyone else's, and mine was operating in top gear at the moment. Even the pain I believe I could have coped with; but every time I set my left foot on the deck, the shooting agony in my left thigh left me dizzy and lightheaded, barely conscious. A few steps on that leg and I just wouldn't be conscious at all. I supposed vaguely it must have had something to do with all the blood I had lost. I sat down again.

"Get back into bed," Marston ordered. "This is madness. You're going to have to lie on your back for at least the next week."

"Good old Tony Carreras," I said. I *was* feeling a bit lightheaded, and that's a fact. "Clever lad, Tony. He'd the right idea. Your hypodermic, Doctor. Painkiller for the thigh. Shoot me full of it. You know, the way a football player with a gammy leg gets an injection before the game."

"No football player ever went out on a field with three bullet holes through his leg," Marston said grimly.

"Don't do it, Dr. Marston," Susan said urgently. *"Please* don't do it. He'll surely kill himself."

"Bo'sun?" Marston queried.

"Give it to him, sir," the bo'sun said quietly. "Mr. Carter knows best."

"Mr. Carter knows best," Susan mimicked furiously. She crossed to the bo'sun and stared down at him. "It's easy for you to lie there and say he knows best. You don't have to go out there and get killed, to be shot down or die from the loss of blood."

"Not me, miss." The bo'sun smiled up at her. "You won't catch me taking risks like that."

"I'm sorry, Mr. MacDonald." She sat down wearily on his bedside. "I'm so ashamed. I know that if your leg wasn't smashed up—but look at him! He can't even stand, far less walk. He'll kill himself, I tell you, kill himself!"

"Perhaps he will. But then he will only be anticipating by about two days, Miss Beresford," MacDonald said quietly. "I know, Mr. Carter knows. We both know that no one on the *Campari* has very long to live—not unless someone can do something. You don't think, Miss Beresford," he went on heavily, "that Mr. Carter is doing this just for the exercise?"

Marston looked at me, face slowly tightening. "You and the bo'sun have been talking? Talking about something I know nothing about?"

"I'll tell you when I come back."

"If you come back." He went to his dispensary, came back with a hypodermic, and injected some pale fluid. "Against all my instincts, this. It'll ease the pain, no doubt about that, but it will also permit you to overstrain your leg and cause permanent damage."

"Not half as permanent as being dead." I hopped across into the dispensary, pulled old man Beresford's suit out from the pile of folded blankets Susan had fetched, and dressed as quickly as my bad leg and the pitching of the *Campari* would allow. I was just turning up the collar and tying the lapels together with a safety pin when Susan came in. She said, abnormally calm, "It suits you very well. Jacket's a bit tight, though."

"It's a damned sight better than parading about the upper deck in the middle of the night wearing a white uniform. Where's this black dress you spoke of?"

"Here." She pulled it out from the bottom blanket.

"Thanks." I looked at the label. Balenciaga. Should make a fair enough mask. I caught the hem of the dress between my hands, glanced at her, saw the nod, and ripped, a dollar a stitch. I tore out a rough square, folded it into a triangle, and tied it round my face, just below the level of my eyes. Another few rips, another square, and I had a knotted cloth covering head and forehead until only my eyes showed. The pale glimmer of my hands I could always conceal.

"Nothing is going to stop you then?" she said steadily.

"I wouldn't say that." I eased a little weight onto my left leg, used my imagination and told myself that it was going numb already. "Lots of things can stop me. Any one of forty-two men, all armed with guns and submachine guns, can stop me. If they see me."

She looked at the ruins of the Balenciaga. "Tear off a piece for me while you're at it."

"For you?" I looked at her. She was as pale as I felt. "What for?"

"I'm coming with you." She gestured at her clothes, the navy blue sweater and slacks. "It wasn't hard to guess what you wanted Daddy's suit for. You don't think I changed into these for nothing?"

"I don't suppose so." I tore off another piece of cloth. "Here you are."

"Well." She stood there with the cloth in her hand. "Well. Just like that, eh?"

"It's what you wanted, isn't it?"

She gave me a slow, old-fashioned up-from-under, shook her head, and tied on the cloth. I hobbled back to the sick bay, Susan following.

"Where's Miss Beresford going?" Marston demanded sharply. "Why is she wearing that hood?"

"She's coming with me," I said. "So she says."

"Going with you? And you'd let her?" He was horrified. "She'll get herself killed."

"It's likely enough," I agreed. Something, probably the anaesthetic, was having a strange effect on my head: I felt enormously detached and very calm. "But, as the bo'sun says, what's a couple of days early? I need another pair of eyes, somebody who can move quickly and lightly to reconnoitre, above all a lookout. Let's have one of your torches, Doctor."

"I object. I strongly protest against—"

"Get him the torch," Susan interrupted.

He stared at her, hesitated, sighed, and turned away. MacDonald beckoned me.

"Sorry I can't be with you, sir, but this is the next best thing." He pressed a seaman's knife into my hand, wide hinged blade on one side, shackle-locking marlinespike on the other; the marline came to a needle point. "If you have to use it, hit upward with the spike, the blade under your hand."

"Take your word for it any time." I hefted the knife, saw Susan staring at it, her eyes wide.

"You—you would use that thing?"

"Stay behind if you like. The torch, Dr. Marston."

I pocketed the flash, kept the knife in my hand, and passed through the surgery door. I didn't let it swing behind me; I knew Susan would be there.

The sentry, sitting wedged into a corner of the passage, was asleep. His automatic carbine was across his knees. It was an awful temptation, but I let it go. A sleeping sentry would call for a few curses and kicks, but a sleeping sentry without his gun would start an all-out search of the ship.

It took me two minutes to climb up two companionways to the level of "A" deck. Nice wide, flat companionways, but it took me two minutes. My left leg was very stiff, very weak, and didn't respond at all to autosuggestion when I kept telling myself it was getting less painful by the minute. Besides, the *Campari* was pitching so violently now that it would have been a full-time job for a fit person to climb upwards without being flung off.

Pitching. The *Campari* was pitching, but with a now even more exaggerated corkscrew motion, great sheets of flying water breaking over the bows and being hurled back against the superstructure. At some hundreds of miles from the centre of a hurricane—and I didn't need any barometers or weather forecasts to tell me what was in the offing—it is the out-spreading swell that indicates the direction of the centre of a hurricane; but closer in, and we were getting far too close for comfort, it is the wind direction that locates the centre. We were heading roughly twenty degrees east of north and the wind blowing from dead ahead. That meant the hurricane was roughly to the east of us, with a little southing, still keeping pace with us, travelling roughly northwest, a more northerly course than was usual, and the *Campari* and the hurricane were on more of a collision course than ever. The strength of the wind I estimated at force eight or nine on the old Beaufort scale: that made the centre of the storm less than a hundred miles away. If Carreras kept on his present course at his present speed, everybody's troubles, his as well as ours, would soon be over.

At the top of the second companionway I stood still for a few moments to steady myself, took Susan's arm for support, then lurched aft in the direction of the drawing room, twenty feet away. I'd hardly started lurching when I stopped. Something was wrong.

Even in my fuzzy state it didn't take long to find out what was wrong. On a normal night at sea the *Campari* was like an illuminated Christmas tree; tonight every deck light was off. Another example of Carreras taking no chances, although this was an unnecessary and exaggerated example. Sure, he didn't want anyone to see him, but in a black gale like this no one could have seen him anyway, even had any vessel been heading on the same course, which was hardly possible, unless its master had taken leave of his senses. But it suited me well enough. We staggered on, making no attempt to be silent. With the shriek of the wind, the thunderous drumming of the torrential rain, and the repeated pistol-shot explosions as the rearing *Campari*'s bows kept smashing into the heavy rolling combers ahead no one could have heard us a couple of feet away.

The smashed windows of the drawing room had been roughly boarded up. Careful not to cut a jugular or put an eye out on one of the jagged splinters of glass, I pressed my face close to the boards and peered through one of the cracks.

The curtains were drawn inside, but with the gale whistling through the gaps between the boards, they were blowing and flapping wildly most of the time. One minute there and I'd seen all I wanted to see and it didn't help me at all. The passengers were all herded together at one end of the room, most of them huddled down on close-packed mattresses, a few sitting with their backs to the bulkhead. A more miserably seasick collection of millionaires I had never seen in my life: their complexions ranged from a faintly greenish shade to a dead-white pallor. They were suffering all right. In one corner I saw some stewards, cooks, and engineer officers, including McIlroy, with Cummings beside him; seaman's branch apart, it looked as if every off-duty man was imprisoned there with the passengers. Carreras was economising on his guards: I could see only two of them, hard-faced, unshaven characters with a Tommy gun apiece. For a moment I had the crazy idea of bursting in the door and rushing them, but only for a moment. Armed with only a clasp knife, and with a top speed of about that of a fairly active tortoise, I wouldn't have got a yard.

Two minutes later we were outside the wireless office. No one had challenged us; no one had seen us; the decks were entirely deserted. It was a night for deserted decks.

The wireless office was in darkness. I pressed one ear to the metal of the door, closed a hand over the other ear to shut out the clamour of the storm, and listened as hard as I could. Nothing. I placed a gentle hand on the knob, turned, and pushed. The door didn't budge a fraction of an inch. I eased my hand off that doorknob with all the wary caution and thistledown delicacy of a man withdrawing the Koh-i-noor from a basket of sleeping cobras.

"What's the matter?" Susan asked. "Is——"

That was as far as she got before my hand closed over her mouth, not gently. We were fifteen feet away from that door before I took my hand away.

"What is it? What is it?" Her low whisper had a shake in it; she didn't know whether to be scared or angry or both.

"The door was locked."

"Why shouldn't it be? Why should they keep watch——"

"The door is locked by a padlock. From the outside. We put a new one there yesterday morning. It's no longer there. Somebody has shut the catch on the inside." I didn't know how much of this she was getting: the roar of the sea, the drumfire of the rain, the wind rushing in from the darkness of the north and playing its high-pitched threnody in the rigging seemed to drown and snatch away the words even as I spoke them. I pulled her into what pitiful shelter was offered by a ventilator, and her next words showed that she had indeed heard and understood most of what I had said.

"They have left a sentry? Just in case anyone tried to break in? How could anyone break in? We're all under guard and lock and key."

"It's as Carreras Junior says—his old man never takes a chance." I hesitated then, because I didn't know what else to say. I went on: "I've no right to do this. But I must. I'm desperate. I want you to be a stalking-horse—help get that character out of there."

"What do you want me to do?"

"Good girl." I squeezed her arm. "Knock at the door. Pull that hood off and show yourself at the window. He'll almost certainly switch on a light or flash a torch, and when he sees it's a girl—well, he'll be astonished but not scared. He'll want to investigate."

"And then you——you——"

"That's it."

"With only a clasp knife." The tremor in her voice was unmistakable. "You're very sure of yourself."

"I'm not sure at all. But if we don't make a move until

we're certain of success we might as well jump over the side now. Ready?"

"What are you going to do? Once you get inside?" She was scared and stalling. Not that I was happy myself.

"Send an SOS on the distress frequency. Warn every vessel within listening range that the *Campari* has been seized by force and is intending to intercept a bullion-carrying vessel at such and such a spot. Within a few hours everyone in North America will know the situation. That'll get action all right."

"Yes." A long pause. "That'll get action. The first action it will get is that Carreras will discover that his guard is missing—and where had you thought of hiding him?"

"In the Atlantic."

She shivered briefly, then said obliquely, "I think perhaps Carreras knows you better than I do . . . The guard's missing. They'll know it must be one of the crew responsible. They'll soon find out that the only guard keeping an eye on the crew who wasn't awake all the time is the boy outside the sick bay." She was silent for a moment, then went on so softly that I could hardly hear her above the storm: "I can just see Carreras ripping those bandages off your leg and finding out that your thigh is not broken. You know what will happen then?"

"It doesn't matter."

"It matters to me." She said the words calmly, matter-of-factly, as if they were of no particular significance. "Another thing. You said everybody would know the setup within a few hours. The two radio operators Carreras has planted on the *Ticonderoga* will know immediately. They will immediately radio the news back to the *Campari* to Carreras."

"After I'm finished in the wireless office no one will ever be able to send or receive on that set again."

"All right. So you'll smash it up. That itself would be enough to let Carreras know what you've done. And you can't smash up every radio receiver on the *Campari*. You can't, for instance, get near the ones in the drawing room. Everybody will know, you say. That means the general-issimo and his government will know also, and then all the stations on the island will do nothing but keep up a non-stop broadcast of the news. Carreras is bound to hear it."

I said nothing. I thought vaguely that I must have lost a great deal of blood. Her mind was working about ten times as quickly and clearly as mine. Not that that made her very smart.

She went on: "You and the bo'sun seem very sure that Carreras won't let us—the passengers and crew—live. Perhaps you think it's because he can't have any witnesses, that whatever advantage the generalissimo gained from getting this money would be offset over and over again by the world-wide reaction against him if the world knew what he had done. Perhaps—"

"Reaction!" I said. "Reaction! He'd find the American and British navies and air forces on his doorstep the following morning, and that would be the end of the generalissimo. Not even Russia would raise a hand to help him; they wouldn't as much as rattle a rocket. Of course he can't afford to let anyone know. He'd be finished."

"In fact, he couldn't even afford to let anyone know he'd made the attempt? So, as soon as Carreras picks up the news of your SOS, he gets rid of all the witnesses—permanently—and sheers off, transships to this other vessel that's waiting and that's that."

I stood there, saying nothing. My mind felt dull and heavy and tired, my body even more so. I tried to tell myself it was just the drug Marston had pumped into me, but it wasn't that; I knew it wasn't that. The sense of defeat is the most powerful opiate of all. I said, hardly knowing what I was saying, "Well, at least we would have saved the gold."

"The gold!" You had to be a millionaire's daughter before you could put all that scorn into your voice when you mentioned the word "gold." "Who cares a fig for all the gold in the world? What's gold compared to your life and my life, my mother's and father's and the lives of everyone on the *Campari?* How much money did Carreras say the *Fort Ticonderoga* was carrying?"

"You heard him. A hundred and fifty million dollars."

"A hundred and fifty million! Daddy could raise that in

a week and still have as much again left."

"Lucky Daddy," I muttered. Lightheaded, that's what I was getting.

"What did you say?"

"Nothing. Nothing. It all seemed such a good idea when MacDonald and I worked it out, Susan."

"I'm sorry." She caught my right hand in both of hers and held it tight. "I'm truly sorry, Johnny."

"Where did you get this 'Johnny' business from?" I mumbled.

"I like it. What's good enough for Captain Bullen— your hands are like ice!" she exclaimed softly. "And you're shivering." Gentle fingers pushed up under my hood. "And your forehead is burning. Running a temperature and fever. You're not well, oh, you're not well. Come on back down to the sick bay, Johnny. Please."

"No."

"Please!"

"Don't nag at me, woman." I pushed myself wearily off the ventilator. "Come on."

"Where are you going?" She was quickly beside me, her arm in mine, and I was glad to hang on.

"Cerdan. Our mysterious friend Mr. Cerdan. Do you realise that we know practically nothing about Mr. Cerdan—except that he seems to be the one who lies back and lets the others do all the work? Carreras and Cerdan —they seem to be the kingpins, and maybe Carreras isn't the boss after all. But I do know this: if I could get a knife sticking into the throat or a gun jabbing into the back of either of those men I would have a big card to play in this game."

"Come on, Johnny," she pleaded. "Come on down below."

"All right, so I'm loopy. But it's still true. If I could shove either of those men into the drawing room ahead of me and threaten the two guards with his death if they didn't drop their guns, I rather think they would. With two machine guns and all the men in there to help, I could do a lot on a night like this. I'm not crazy, Susan, just desperate, like I said."

"You can hardly stand." There was a note of desperation in her voice now.

"That's why you're here. To hold me up. Carreras is out of the question. He'll be on the bridge and that'll be the most heavily guarded place on the ship, because it's the most important place." I winced and shrank back into a corner as a great blue-white jagged streak of forked lightning, almost directly ahead, flickered and stabbed through the black wall of cumulo-nimbus clouds and the driving rain, momentarily illuminating every detail of the *Campari*'s decks in its blinding glare. The curiously flat explosive clap of thunder was muffled, lost in the teeth of the gale.

"That helps," I muttered. "Thunder, lightning, a tropical rainstorm, and moving into the heart of a hurricane. King Lear should have seen this little lot. He'd never have complained of his blasted heath again."

"Macbeth," she said. "That was Macbeth."

"Oh hell," I said. She was getting as nutty as I was. I took her arm, or she took mine, I forget which. "Come on. We're too exposed here."

A minute later we were down on "A" deck, crouched against a bulkhead. I said, "Finesse will get us nowhere. I'm going into the central passageway, straight into Cerdan's cabin. I'll stick my hand in my pocket, pretend I have a gun. Stay at the entrance to the passageway; warn me if anyone comes."

"He's not in," she said. We were standing at the starboard for'ard end of the accommodation, just outside Cerdan's sleeping cabin. "He's not at home. There's no light on."

"The curtains will be drawn," I said impatiently. "The ship's fully darkened. I'll bet Carreras hasn't even got the navigation lights on." We shrank against the bulkhead as another lightning flash reached down from the darkened clouds, seemed almost to dance on the tip of the *Campari*'s mast. "I won't be long."

"Wait!" She held me with both hands. "The curtains aren't drawn. That flash—I could see everything inside the cabin."

"You could see—" For some reason I'd lowered my voice almost to a whisper. "Anyone inside?"

"I couldn't see all the inside. It was just for a second."

I straightened, pressed my face hard against the window, and stared inside. The darkness in the cabin was absolute —absolute, that is, until another forked finger of lightning lit up the entire upperworks of the *Campari* once more. Momentarily I saw my own hooded face and staring eyes reflected back at me in the glass, then exclaimed involuntarily, for I had seen something else again.

"What is it?" Susan demanded huskily. "What's wrong?"

"This is wrong." I fished out Marston's torch, hooded it with my hand, and shone it downwards through the glass.

The bed was up against the bulkhead, almost exactly beneath the window. Cerdan was lying on the bed, clothed and awake, his eyes staring up as if hypnotised by the beam of the torch. Wide eyes, staring eyes. His white hair was not just where his white hair had been; it had slipped back, revealing his own hair beneath. Black hair, jet-black hair, with a startling streak of iron-grey almost exactly in the middle. Black hair with an iron-grey streak? Where had I seen somebody with hair like that? When had I ever heard of somebody with hair like that? All of a sudden I knew it was "when," not "where"; I knew the answer. I switched off the light.

"Cerdan!" There was shock and disbelief and utter lack of comprehension in Susan's voice. "Cerdan! Bound hand and foot and tied to his bed so that he can't move an inch. Cerdan! But—no, no!" She was ready to give up. "Oh, Johnny, what does it all mean?"

"I know what it all means." No question now but that I knew what it all meant and wished to heaven I didn't. I'd only thought I'd been afraid before, the time I'd only been guessing. But the time for guessing was past; oh, my God, it was past. I knew the truth now, and the truth was worse than I had ever dreamed. I fought down the rising panic and said steadily through dry lips, "Have you ever robbed a grave, Susan?"

"Have I ever—" She broke off, and when her voice came again there were tears in it. "We're both worn out,

Johnny. Let's get down below. I want to go back to the sick bay."

"I have news for you, Susan. I'm not mad. But I'm not joking. And I hope to God that grave's not empty." I caught her arm to lead her away, and as I did the lightning flashed again and her eyes were wild and full of fear. I wondered what mine looked like to her.

Chapter 9

[*Thursday 10 P.M.—midnight*]

WHAT WITH the darkness, my bad leg, the intermittent lightning, the wild rearing, wave-top staggering and plunging of the *Campari*, and the need to use the greatest caution all the way, it took us a good fifteen minutes to reach number four hold, far back on the afterdeck. And when we got there, pulled back the tarpaulin, loosened a couple of battens, and peered down into the near-Stygian depths of the hold, I wasn't at all sure that I was glad we had come.

Along with several tools I'd filched an electric lantern from the bo'sun's store on the way there, and though it didn't give off much of a light, it gave off enough to let me see that the floor of the hold was a shambles. I'd secured for sea after leaving Carracio, but I hadn't secured for a near-hurricane, for the excellent reason that whenever the weather was bad the *Campari* had invariably run in the other direction.

But now Carreras had taken us in the wrong direction and he either hadn't bothered or forgotten to secure for the worsening weather conditions. Forgotten, almost certainly; for number four hold presented a threat, to say the least, to the lives of everybody aboard, Carreras and his men included. At least a dozen heavy crates, the weight of one or two of which could be measured in tons, had broken loose and were sliding and lurching across the floor of the hold with every corkscrewing pitch of the *Campari*, alternately crashing into the secured cargo aft or the bulkhead for'ard. My guess was that this wasn't doing the for'ard bulkhead any good, and just let the motion of the *Campari* change from pitching to rolling, especially as we neared the centre of the hurricane, and the massive dead weights of those sliding crates would begin to assault the sides of the ship. Buckled plates, torn rivets, and a leak that couldn't be repaired would be only a matter of time.

To make matters worse, Carreras' men hadn't bothered to remove the broken, splintered sides of the wooden crates in which they and the guns had been slung aboard; they, too, were sliding about the floor with every movement of the ship, being continually smashed and becoming progressively smaller in size as they were crushed between the sliding crates and bulkheads, pillars and fixed cargo. Not the least frightening part of it all was the din, the almost continuous goose-pimpling metallic screech as iron-banded cases slid over steel decks, a high-pitched grating scream that set your teeth on edge, a scream that invariably ended, predictably yet always unexpectedly, in a jarring crash that shook the entire hold as the crates brought up against something solid. And every sound in that echoing, reverberating, emptily cavernous hold was magnified ten times. All in all, the floor of that hold wasn't the place I would have chosen for an afternoon nap.

I gave the electric lantern to Susan, after shining it on a vertical steel ladder tapering down into the depths of the hold.

"Down you go," I said. "For heaven's sake, hang on to that ladder. There's a baffle about three feet high at the bottom of it. Get behind it. You should be safe there."

I watched her climb slowly down, manoeuvred two of the battens back into place over my head—no easy job with one hand—and left them like that. Maybe they would be jarred loose; they might even fall down into the hold.

It was a chance I had to take; they could only be secured from above. And the covering tarpaulin could also only be secured from above. There was nothing I could do about that either. If anyone was crazy enough to be out on deck that night—especially as Carreras had no life lines rigged —the chances were in that blinding storm they wouldn't even notice the flapping corner of the tarpaulin or, if they did, they would only either pass it by or, at the most, secure it. If someone was curious enough to go to the length of pushing back a batten—well, there was no point in worrying about that.

I went down the hatch slowly, awkwardly, painfully— Marston had a higher opinion of his anaesthetics than I had—and joined Susan on the floor behind the baffle. At this level the noise was redoubled, the sight of those head-high behemoths of crates charging across the hold more terrifying than ever. Susan said, "The coffins, where are they?" All I had told her was that I wanted to examine some coffins. I couldn't bring myself to tell her what we might find in them.

"They're boxed. In wooden crates. On the other side of the hold."

"The other side!" She twisted her head, lined up the lantern, and looked at the sliding wreckage and crates screeching and tearing their way across the floor. "The other side! We would—we would be killed before we got halfway there."

"Like enough, but I don't see anything else for it. Hold on a minute, will you?"

"You! With your leg! You can't even hobble. Oh no!" Before I could stop her, she was over the baffle and half running, half staggering across the hold, tripping and stumbling as the ship lurched and her feet caught on broken planks of wood, but always managing to regain balance, to stop suddenly or dodge nimbly as a crate slid her way. She was agile, I had to admit, and quick on her feet, but she was exhausted with seasickness, with bracing herself for the past hours against the constant violent lurching of the *Campari;* she'd never make it.

But make it she did, and I could see her on the other

side, flashing her torch round. My admiration for her spirit was equalled only by my exasperation at her actions. What was she going to do with those boxed coffins when she found them, carry them back across the floor, one under each arm?

But they weren't there, for after she had looked everywhere she shook her head. And then she was coming back and I was shouting out a warning, but the warning stuck in my throat and was only a whisper and she wouldn't have heard it anyway. A plunging, careening crate, propelled by a sudden vicious lurch as the *Campari* plunged headlong into an exceptional trough, caught her back and shoulder and pitched her to the floor, pushing her along before its massive weight as if it were imbued with an almost human—or inhuman—quality of evil and malignance and determined to crush the life out of her against the for'ard bulkhead. And then, in the last second before she would have died, the *Campari* straightened, the crate screeched to a halt less than a yard from the bulkhead, and Susan was lying there between crate and bulkhead, very still. I must have been at least fifteen feet away from her, but I have no recollection of covering the distance from the baffle to where she lay and then back again, but I must have done; for suddenly we were there in a place of safety and she was clinging to me as if I were the last hope left in the world.

"Susan!" My voice was hoarse, a voice belonging to someone else altogether. "Susan, are you hurt?"

She clung even closer. By some miracle she still held the lantern clutched in her right hand. It was round the back of my neck somewhere, but the reflected beam from the ship's side gave enough light to see by. Her mask had been torn off; her face was scratched and bleeding, her hair a bedraggled mess, her clothes soaked and her heart going like a captive bird's. For an incongruous moment an unbidden recollection touched my mind, a recollection of a very cool, very poised, sweetly malicious, pseudo-solicitous young lady asking me about cocktails only two days ago in Carracio, but the vision faded as soon as it had come; the incongruity was too much.

"Susan!" I said urgently. "Are you——"

"I'm not hurt." She gave a long, tremulous sigh that was more shudder than sigh. "I was just too scared to move." She eased her grip a trifle, looked at me with green eyes enormous in the pallor of her face, then buried her face in my shoulder. I thought she was going to choke me.

It didn't last long, fortunately. I felt the grip slowly easing, saw the beam of the lantern shifting, and she was saying in an abnormally matter-of-fact voice: "There they are."

I turned round and there, not ten feet away, they were indeed. Three coffins—Carreras had already removed the cases—and securely stowed between baffle and bulkhead and padded with tarpaulins, so that they could come to no harm. As Tony Carreras kept on repeating, his old man didn't miss much. Dark, shiny coffins with black-braided ropes and brass handles. One of them had an inlet plaque on the lid, copper or brass, I couldn't be sure.

"That saves me some trouble." My voice was almost back to normal. I took the hammer and chisel I'd borrowed from the bo'sun's store and let them drop. "This screw driver will be all I need. We'll find two of those with what's normally inside them. Give me the lantern and stay there. I'll be as quick as I can."

"You'll be quicker if I hold the lantern." Her voice matched my own in steadiness, but the pulse in her throat was going like a trip hammer. "Hurry, please."

I was in no way to argue. I caught the foot of the nearest coffin and pulled it towards me so that I could have room to work. It was jammed. I slid my hand under the end to lift it and suddenly my finger found a hole in the bottom of the coffin. And then another. And a third. A lead-lined coffin with holes bored in the bottom of it. That was curious, to say the least.

When I'd moved it far enough out, I started on the screws. They were brass and very heavy, but so was the screw driver I'd taken from MacDonald's store. And at the back of my mind was the thought that if the knockout drops Dr. Marston had provided for the sentry were in any way as ineffective as the anaesthetic he had given me, then the sentry would be waking up any minute now. If he hadn't already come to. I had that coffin lid off in no time at all.

Beneath the lid was not the satin shroud or silks I would have expected but a filthy old blanket. In the generalissimo's country, perhaps, their customs with coffins were different from ours. I pulled off the blanket and found I was right. Their customs were, on occasion, different. The corpse, in this case, consisted of blocks of amatol —each block was clearly marked with the word, so there was no mistake about it—a primer, a small case of detonators, and a compact square box with wires leading from it, a timing device probably.

Susan was peering over my shoulder. "What's amatol?"

"High explosive. Enough there to blow the *Campari* apart."

She asked nothing else. I replaced the blanket, screwed on the lid, and started on the next coffin. This, too, had holes in the underside, probably to prevent the explosives sweating. I removed the lid, looked at the contents, and replaced the lid. Number two was a duplicate of number one. And then I started on the third one. The one with the plaque. This would be the one. The plaque was heart-shaped and read with impressive simplicity: "Richard Hoskins, Senator." Just that. Senator of what I didn't know. But impressive. Impressive enough to ensure its reverent transportation to the United States. I removed the lid with care, gentleness, and as much respectful reverence as if Richard Hoskins actually were inside, which I knew he wasn't.

Whatever lay inside was covered with a rug. I lifted the rug gingerly; Susan brought the lantern nearer, and there it lay, cushioned in blankets and cotton wool. A polished aluminium cylinder, seventy-five inches in length, eleven inches in diameter, with a whitish Pyroceram nose cap. Just lying there, there was something frightening about it, something unutterably evil; but perhaps that was just because of what was in my own mind.

"What is it?" Susan's voice was so low that she had to

come closer to repeat the words. "Oh, Johnny, what in the world is it?"

"The Twister."

"The—the *what?*"

"The Twister."

"Oh, dear God!" She had it now. "This—this atomic device that was stolen in South Carolina. The Twister." She rose unsteadily to her feet and backed away. "The Twister!"

"It won't bite you," I said. I didn't feel too sure about that either. "The equivalent of five thousand tons of T.N.T. Guaranteed to blast any ship on earth to smithereens, if not actually vaporise. And that's just what Carreras intends to do."

"I—I don't understand." Maybe she was referring to the actual hearing of the words—our talk was continually being punctuated by the screeching of metal and the sounds of wood being crushed and snapped—or to the meaning of what I was saying. "You—when he gets the gold from the *Ticonderoga* and transships it to this vessel he has standing by, he's going to blow up the *Campari* with —with this?"

"There is no ship standing by. There never was. When he's loaded the gold aboard, the kindhearted Miguel Carreras is going to free all the passengers and crew of the *Campari* and let them sail off in the *Fort Ticonderoga*. As a further mark of his sentimentality and kindness he's going to ask that Senator Hoskins here and his two presumably illustrious companions be taken back for burial in their native land. The captain of the *Ticonderoga* would never dream of refusing—and, if it came to the bit, Carreras would make certain that he damned well didn't refuse. See that?" I pointed to a panel near the tail of the Twister.

"Don't touch it!" If you can imagine anyone screaming in a whisper, then that's what she did.

"I wouldn't touch it for all the money in the *Ticonderoga*," I assured her fervently. "I'm even scared to look at the damned thing. Anyway, that panel is almost certainly a timing device which will be preset before the coffin is transshipped. We sail merrily on our way, hell-bent for Norfolk, the Army, Navy, Air Force, F.B.I., and what have you—for Carreras' radio stooges aboard the *Ticonderoga* will make good and certain that the radios will be smashed and we'll have no means of sending a message. Half an hour, an hour after leaving the *Campari*—an hour, at least, I should think; even Carreras wouldn't want to be within miles of an atomic device going up—well, it would be quite a bang."

"He'll never do it—never." The emphatic voice didn't carry the slightest shred of conviction. "The man must be a fiend."

"Grade one," I agreed. "And don't talk rubbish about his not doing it. Why do you think they stole the Twister and made it appear as if Dr. Slingsby Caroline had lit out with it? From the very beginning it was with the one and only purpose of blowing the *Fort Ticonderoga* to kingdom come. So that there would be no possibility of any comeback, everything hinged on the total destruction of the *Ticonderoga* and everyone aboard it, including passengers and crew of the *Campari*. Maybe Carreras' two fake radiomen could have smuggled some explosives aboard—but it would be quite impossible to smuggle enough to ensure complete destruction. Hundreds of tons of high explosives in the magazines of a British battle cruiser blew up in the last war, but still there were survivors. He couldn't sink it by gunfire—a couple of shots from a moderately heavy gun and the *Campari*'s decks would be so buckled that the guns would be useless—and even then there would be bound to be survivors. But with the Twister there will be no chances of survival. None in the world."

"Carreras' men," she said slowly, "they killed the guards in this atomic research establishment?"

"What else? And then forced Dr. Caroline to drive out through the gates with themselves and the Twister in the back. The Twister was probably en route to their island, by air, inside an hour, but someone drove the brake wagon down to Savannah before abandoning it. No doubt to throw suspicion on the *Campari*, which they knew was leaving Savannah that morning. I'm not sure why, but I would take long odds it was because Carreras, knowing the *Campari* was bound for the Caribbean, was reasonably sure that she would be searched at her first port of call, giving him the opportunity to introduce his bogus Marconi man aboard."

While I had been talking I'd been studying two circular dials inset in the panel on the Twister. Now I spread the rug back in position with all the loving care of a father smoothing out the bedcover over his youngest son and started to screw the coffin lid back in position. For a time Susan watched me in silence, then said wonderingly, "Mr. Cerdan. Dr. Caroline. The same person. It *has* to be the same person. I remember now. At the time of the disappearance of the Twister it was mentioned that only one or two people so far know how to arm the Twister."

"He was just as important to their plans as the Twister. Without him, it was useless. Poor old Doc Caroline has had a rough passage, I'm afraid. Not only kidnapped and forced to do as ordered, but knocked about by us also, the only people who could have saved him. Under constant guard by those two thugs disguised as nurses. He bawled me out of his cabin the first time I saw him, but only because he knew that his devoted nurse, sitting beside him with her dear little knitting bag on her lap, had a sawed-off shotgun inside it."

"But—but why the wheel chair? Was it necessary to take such elaborate—"

"Of course it was. They couldn't have him mingling with the passengers, communicating with them. It helped conceal his unusual height. And it also gave them a perfect reason to keep a non-stop watch on incoming radio messages. He came to your father's cocktail party because he was told to—the coup was planned for that evening and it suited Carreras to have his two armed nurses there to help in the takeover. Poor old Caroline. That dive he tried to make from his wheel chair when I showed him the earphones wasn't made with the intention of getting at me at all; he was trying to get at the nurse with the sawed-off shotgun, but Captain Bullen didn't know that, so he laid him out." I tightened the last of the screws and said,

"Don't breathe a word of this back in the sick bay—the old man talks non-stop in his sleep—or anywhere else. Not even to your parents. Come on. That sentry may come to any minute."

"You—you're going to leave that thing here?" She stared at me in disbelief. "You must get rid of it—you must!"

"How? Carry it up a vertical ladder over my shoulder? That thing weighs about three hundred fifty pounds altogether, including the coffin. And what hapens if I *do* get rid of it? Carreras finds out within hours. Whether or not he finds out or guesses who took it doesn't matter: what does matter is that he'll know he can no longer depend on the Twister to get rid of all the inconvenient witnesses on the *Campari*. What then? My guess is that not one member of the crew or passengers will have more than a few hours to live. He would *have* to kill us then—no question of transshipping us to the *Ticonderoga*. As for the *Ticonderoga,* he would have to board it, kill all the crew, and open the sea cocks. That might take hours and would inconvenience him dangerously, might wreck all his plans. But he would have to do it. The point is that getting rid of the Twister is not going to save any lives at all; all it would accomplish is the certain death of all of us."

"What are we going to do?" Her voice was strained and shaky, her face a pale blur in the reflected light. "Oh, Johnny, what are we going to do?"

"I'm going back to bed." Heaven only knew I felt like it. "Then I'll waste my time trying to figure out how to save Dr. Caroline."

"Dr. Caroline? I don't see—why Dr. Caroline?"

"Because he's number one for the high jump, as things stand. Long before the rest of us. Because he's the man who's going to arm the Twister," I said patiently. "Do you think they'll transfer him to the *Ticonderoga* and let him acquaint the captain with the fact that the coffin he's taking back to the States contains not Senator Hoskins but an armed and ticking atom bomb?"

"Where's it all going to end?" There was panic, open panic, in her voice now, a near hysteria. "I can't believe it, I can't *believe* it. It's like some dark nightmare." She had her hands twisted in my lapels, her face buried in my jacket—well, anyway, her old man's jacket—and her voice was muffled. "Oh, Johnny, where's it all going to end?"

"A touching scene, a most touching scene," a mocking voice said from close behind me. "It all ends here and now. This moment."

I whirled round, or at least I tried to whirl round, but I couldn't even do that properly. What with disengaging Susan's grip, the weakness in my leg, and the lurching of the ship, the sudden turn threw me completely off balance and I stumbled and fell against the ship's side. A powerful light switched on, blinding me, and in black silhouette against the light I could see the snub barrel of an automatic.

"On your feet, Carter." There was no mistaking the voice. Tony Carreras, no longer pleasant and affable, but cold, hard, vicious, the real Tony Carreras at last. "I want to see you fall when this slug hits you. Clever-clever Carter. Or so you thought. On your feet, I said! Or you'd rather take it lying there? Suit yourself."

The gun lifted a trifle. The direct no-nonsense type, he didn't believe in fancy farewell speeches. Shoot them and be done with it. I could believe now that he was his father's son. My bad leg was under me and I couldn't get up. I stared into the beam of light, into the black muzzle of the gun. I stopped breathing and tensed myself. Tensing yourself against a .38 fired from a distance of five feet is a great help, but I wasn't feeling very logical at the moment.

"Don't shoot!" Susan screamed. "Don't kill him or we'll all die."

The torch beam wavered, then steadied again. It steadied on me. And the gun hadn't shifted any that I could see. Susan took a couple of steps towards him, but he fended her off, stiff-armed.

"Out of the way, lady." I'd never in my life heard such concentrated venom and malignance. I'd misjudged young Carreras all right. And her words hadn't even begun to register on him, so implacable was his intention. I still wasn't breathing and my mouth was as dry as a kiln.

"The Twister!" Her voice was urgent, compelling, desperate. "He's armed the Twister!"

"What? What are you saying?" This time she had got through. "The Twister? Armed?" The voice malignant as ever, but I thought I detected overtones of fear.

"Yes, Carreras, armed!" I'd never known before how important lubrication of the throat and mouth was to the human voice; a buzzard with tonsillitis had nothing on my croak. "Armed, Carreras, armed!" The repetition was not for emphasis; I couldn't think of anything else to say, how to carry this off, how to exploit the few seconds' grace that Susan had bought for me. I shifted the hand that was propping me up, the one in the black shadow behind me, as if to brace myself against the pitching of the *Campari*. My fingers closed over the handle of the hammer I'd dropped. I wondered bleakly what I was going to do with it. The torch and the gun were as steady as ever.

"You're lying, Carter." The confidence was back in his voice. "God knows how you found out about it, but you're lying: you don't know how to arm it."

That was it: keep him talking, just keep him talking.

"I don't. But Dr. Slingsby Caroline does."

That shook him, literally. The torch wavered. But it didn't waver enough.

"How do you know about Dr. Caroline?" he demanded hoarsely. His voice was almost a shout. "How do you—"

"I was speaking to him to-night," I said calmly.

"Speaking with him! But—but there's a key to arm this. The only key to arm it. And my father has it."

"Dr. Caroline has a spare. In his tobacco pouch. You never thought to look, did you, Carreras?" I sneered.

"You're lying," he repeated mechanically. Then, more strongly: "Lying, I say, Carter! I saw you to-night. I saw you leave the sick bay—my God, do you think I was so stupid as not to get suspicious when I saw the sentry drinking coffee given him by kindhearted Carter?—locked it up, followed you to the radio office and then down to Caroline's cabin. But you never went inside, Carter. I lost you then for a few minutes, I admit. But you never went inside."

"Why didn't you stop us earlier?"

"Because I wanted to find out what you were up to. I found it."

"So he's the person we thought we saw!" I said to Susan. The conviction in my voice astonished even myself. "You poor fool, we noticed something in the shadows and left in a hurry. But we went back, Carreras. Oh yes, we went back. To Dr. Caroline. And we didn't waste any time talking to him either. We had a far smarter idea than that. Miss Beresford wasn't quite accurate. I didn't arm the Twister. Dr. Caroline himself did that." I smiled and shifted my eyes from the beam of the torch to a spot behind and to the right of Carreras. "Tell him, Doctor."

Carreras half turned, cursed viciously, swung back. His mind was fast, his reactions faster; he'd hardly even begun to fall for the old gag. All he'd allowed us was a second of time, and in that brief moment I hadn't even got past tightening my grip on the hammer. And now he was going to kill me.

But he couldn't get his gun lined up. Susan had been waiting for the chance; she sensed that I'd been building up towards the chance. She dropped her lantern and flung herself forward even as Carreras had started to turn and she had only about three feet to go. Now she was clinging desperately to his gun arm, all her weight on it, forcing it down towards the floor. I twisted myself convulsively forward and that two-pound hammer came arcing over my shoulder and flew straight for Carreras' face with all the power, all the hatred and viciousness that was in me.

He saw it coming. His left hand, still gripping the torch, was raised high to smash down on the unprotected nape of Susan's neck. He jerked his head sideways, flung out his left arm in instinctive reaction: the hammer caught him just below the left elbow with tremendous force; his torch went flying through the air, and the hold was plunged into absolute darkness. Where the hammer went I don't know; a heavy crate screeched and rumbled across the floor just at that moment and I never heard it land.

The crate ground to a standstill. In the sudden momentary silence I could hear the sound of struggling, of heavy breathing. I was slow in getting to my feet; my left leg was practically useless, but maybe it only seemed slow to me. Fear, when it is strong enough, has the curious effect of slowing up time. And I was afraid. I was afraid for Susan. Carreras, except as the source of menace to her, didn't exist for me at the moment. Only Susan: he was a big man, a powerful man; he could break her neck with a single wrench, kill her with a single blow.

I heard her cry out, a cry of shock or fear. A moment's silence, a heavy soft thump as of falling bodies, a scream of agony, again from Susan, and then that silence again.

They weren't there. When I reached the spot where they had been struggling, they weren't there. For a second I stood still in that impenetrable darkness, bewildered, then my hand touched the top of the three-foot baffle and I had it: in their wrestling on that crazily careening deck they'd staggered against the baffle and toppled over on to the floor of the hold. I was over that baffle before I had time to think, before I knew what I was doing; the bo'sun's knife was in my hand, the needle-pointed marlinespike open, the locking shackle closed.

I stumbled as the weight came on my left leg, fell to my knees, touched someone's head and hair. Long hair. Susan. I moved away and had just reached my feet again when he came at me. He came at me. He didn't back away, try to keep out of my reach in that darkness. He came at me. That meant he'd lost his gun.

We fell to the floor together, clawing, clubbing, kicking. Once, twice, half a dozen times he caught me on the chest, the side of the body, with sledge-hammer, short-arm jabs that threatened to break my ribs. But I didn't really feel them. He was a strong man, tremendously strong, but even with all his great strength, even had his left arm not been paralysed and useless, he would have found no escape that night.

I grunted with the numbing shock of it and Carreras shrieked out in agony as the hilt of MacDonald's knife jarred solidly home against his breastbone. I wrenched the knife free and struck again. And again. And again. After the fourth blow he didn't cry out any more.

Carreras died hard. He'd stopped hitting me now; his right arm was locked round my neck, and with every blow I struck the throttling pressure of the arm increased. All the convulsive strength of a man dying in agony was brought to bear on exactly that spot where I had been so heavily sandbagged. Pain, crippling pain, red-hot barbed lances of fire shot through my back and head; I thought my neck was going to break. I struck again. And then the knife fell from my hand.

When I came to, the blood was pounding dizzily in my ears, my head felt as if it were going to burst, my lungs were heaving and gasping for air that wouldn't come. I felt as if I were choking, being slowly and surely suffocated.

And then I dimly realised the truth. I *was* being suffocated; the arm of the dead man, by some freak of muscular contraction, was still locked around my neck. I couldn't have been out for long, not for more than a minute. With both hands I grasped his arm by the wrist and managed to tear it free from my neck. For thirty seconds, perhaps longer, I lay there, stretched out on the floor of the hold, my heart pounding, gasping for breath as waves of weakness and dizziness washed over me, while some faraway insistent voice, as desperately urgent as it was distant, kept saying in this remote corner of my mind, you must get up, you must get up.

And then I had it. I was lying on the floor of the hold and those huge crates were still sliding and crashing around with every heave and stagger of the *Campari*. And Susan. She was lying there too.

I pushed myself to my knees, fumbled around in my pocket till I found Marston's pencil flash, and switched it on. It still worked. The beam fell on Carreras and I'd only time to notice that the whole shirt front was soaked with blood before I involuntarily turned the torch away, sick and nauseated.

Susan was lying close in to the baffle, half on her side,

half on her back. Her eyes were open, dull and glazed with shock and pain, but they were open.

"It's finished." I could hardly recognise the voice as mine. "It's all over now." She nodded and tried to smile.

"You can't stay here," I went on. "The other side of the baffle—quick."

I rose to my feet, caught her under the arms, and lifted. She came easily, lightly, then cried out in agony and went limp on me. But I had her before she could fall, braced myself against the ladder, lifted her over the baffle, and laid her down gently on the other side.

In the beam of my torch she lay there on her side, her arms outflung. The left arm, between wrist and elbow, was twisted at an impossible angle. Broken, no doubt of it. Broken. When she and Carreras had toppled over the baffle she must have been underneath: her left arm had taken the combined strain of their falling bodies and the strain had been too much. But there was nothing I could do about it. Not now. I turned my attention to Tony Carreras.

I couldn't leave him there. I knew I couldn't leave him there. When Miguel Carreras found out that his son was missing he'd have the *Campari* searched from end to end. I had to get rid of him, but I couldn't get rid of him in that hold. There was only one place where I could finally, completely and without any fear of rediscovery, put the body of Tony Carreras. In the sea.

Tony Carreras must have weighed at least two hundred pounds; that narrow vertical steel ladder was at least thirty feet high; I was weak from loss of blood and sheer physical exhaustion and I'd only one sound leg, so I never stopped to think about it. If I had, the impossibility of what I had to do would have defeated me even before I had begun.

I hauled him to the ladder, dragged him up to a sitting position against it, hooked my hands under his shoulders and jerked up his dead weight, inch by inch, until his shoulders and hanging head were on a level with my own, stooped quickly, caught him in a fireman's lift, and started climbing.

For the first time that night the pitching, corkscrewing

Campari was my friend. When the ship plunged into a trough, rolling to starboard at the same time, the ladder would incline away from me as much as fifteen degrees and I'd take a couple of quick steps, hang on grimly as the *Campari* rolled back and the ladder swung out above me, wait for the return roll, and then repeat the process. Twice Carreras all but slipped from my shoulder; twice I had to take a quick step down to renew my purchase. I hardly used my left leg at all; my right leg and both arms took all the strain. Above all, my shoulders took the strain. I felt at times as if the muscles would tear, but it wasn't any worse than the pain in my leg, so I kept on going. I kept going till I reached the top. Another half-dozen rungs and I would have had to let him drop for I don't think I could ever have made it.

I heaved him over the hatch coaming, followed, sank down on deck, and waited till my pulse rate dropped down to the low hundreds. After the stench of oil and the close stuffiness of that hold the driving gale-borne rain felt and tasted wonderful. I cupped the torch in my hand—not that there was more than a very remote chance of anyone being round at that hour, in that weather—and went through his pockets till I found a key tagged "Sick Bay." Then I caught him by the collar and started for the side of the ship.

A minute later I was down in the bottom of the hold again. I found Tony Carreras' gun, stuck it in my pocket, and looked at Susan. She was still unconscious, which was the best way to be if I had to carry her up that ladder, and I had. With a broken arm she couldn't have made it alone, and if I waited till she regained consciousness she would be in agony all the way. And she wouldn't have remained conscious long.

After coping with Carreras' dead weight, the task of getting Susan Beresford up on deck seemed almost easy. I laid her carefully on the rain-washed deck, replaced the battens, and tied the tarpaulin back in place. I was just finishing when I sensed rather than heard her stir.

"Don't move," I said quickly. On the upper deck again I had to raise my voice almost to a shout to make myself heard against the bedlam of the storm. "Your forearm's broken."

"Yes." Matter-of-fact, far too matter-of-fact. "Tony Carreras? Did you leave——"

"That's all over. I told you that was all over."

"Where is he?"

"Overboard."

"Overboard?" The tremor was back in her voice and I liked it much better than the abnormal calmness. "How did he——"

"I stabbed him God knows how many times," I said wearily. "Do you think he got up all by himself, climbed the ladder, and jumped—Sorry, Susan. I shouldn't—well, I'm not quite my normal, I guess. Come on. Time old Doc Marston saw that arm."

I made her cradle the broken forearm in her right hand, helped her to her feet, and caught her by the good arm to help steady her on that heaving deck. The blind leading the blind.

When we reached the for'ard break of the well deck I made her sit in the comparative shelter there while I went into the bo'sun's store. It took me only seconds to find what I wanted: two coils of nylon rope which I stuck into a canvas bag, and a short length of thicker manilla. I closed the door, left the bag beside Susan, and staggered across the sliding, treacherous decks to the port side and tied the manilla to one of the guardrail stanchions. I considered knotting the rope, then decided against it. Mac-Donald, whose idea this was, had been confident that no one, in this wild weather, would notice so small a thing as a knot round the base of a stanchion, and even if it were noticed, Carreras' men would not be seamen enough to investigate and pull it in; but anyone peering over the side and seeing the knots might have become very curious indeed. I made the knot round that stanchion very secure indeed, for there was going to depend on it the life of someone who mattered very much to me—myself.

Ten minutes later we were back outside the sick bay. I need not have worried about that sentry. Head bent low over his chest, he was still far away in another world and showed no signs of leaving it. I wondered how he would feel when he came to. Would he suspect he had been drugged—or would he put any unusual symptoms down to a combination of exhaustion and seasickness? I decided I was worrying about nothing; one sure guess I could make, and that was that when the sentry awoke he would tell no one about his sleep. Miguel Carreras struck me as the kind of man who might have a very short way indeed with sentries who slept on duty.

I took out the key I'd found on Tony Carreras and unlocked the door. Marston was at his desk; the bo'sun and Bullen were both sitting up in bed. This was the first time I'd seen Bullen conscious since he'd been shot. He was pale and haggard and obviously in considerable pain, but he didn't look as if he were on his last legs. It took a lot to kill off a man like Bullen.

He gave me a long look that was pretty close to a glare. "Well, Mister, where the hell have you been?" Normally, with those words, it would have come out like a rasp, but his lung wound had softened his rasp to a hoarse whisper. If I'd had the strength to grin, I'd have done just that, but I didn't have the strength; there was hope for the old man yet.

"A minute, sir. Dr. Marston, Miss Beresford has a—"

"I can see, I can see. How in the world did you manage—" Close to us now, he broke off and peered at me with his shortsighted eyes. "I would say, John, that you're in the more immediate need of attention."

"Me? I'm all right."

"Oh, you are, are you?" He took Susan by her good arm and led her into the dispensary. He said, over his shoulder, "Seen yourself in a mirror recently?"

I looked in a mirror. I could see his point. Balenciagas weren't blood-proof. The whole of the left side of my head, face, and neck was covered in blood that had soaked through hood and mask, matted in thick, dark blood that even the rain hadn't been able to remove: the rain, if anything, had made it look worse than it really was. It must all have come from Tony Carreras' bloodstained shirt when I'd carried him up the ladder of number four hold.

"It'll wash off," I said to Bullen and the bo'sun. "It's not mine. That's from Tony Carreras."

"Carreras?" Bullen stared at me, then looked at Mac-Donald. In spite of the evidence in front of his eyes, you could see that he thought I'd gone off my rocker. "What do you mean?"

"I mean what I say. Tony Carreras." I sat heavily on a chair and gazed down vacantly at my soaking clothes. Maybe Captain Bullen wasn't so far wrong: I felt an insane desire to laugh. I knew it was a climbing hysteria that came from weakness, from overexhaustion, from mounting fever, from expending too much emotion in too short a time, and I had to make a physical effort to fight it down. "I killed him to-night down in number four hold."

"You're mad," Bullen said flatly. "You don't know what you're saying."

"Don't I?" I looked at him, then away again. "Ask Susan Beresford."

"Mr. Carter's telling the truth, sir," MacDonald said quietly. "My knife, sir? Did you bring it back?"

I nodded, rose wearily, hobbled across to MacDonald's bed, and handed him the knife. I'd had no chance to clean it. The bo'sun said nothing, just handed it to Bullen, who stared down at it for long, unspeaking moments.

"I'm sorry, my boy," he said at length. His voice was husky. "Damnably sorry. But we've been worried to death."

I grinned faintly. It was an effort even to do that. "So was I, sir, so was I."

"All in your own good time," Bullen said encouragingly.

"I think Mr. Carter should tell us later, sir," MacDonald suggested. "He's got to clean himself up, get those wet clothes off and into bed. If anyone comes—"

"Right, bo'sun, right." You could see that even so little talk was exhausting him. "Better hurry, my boy."

"Yes." I looked vaguely at the bag I'd brought with me. "I've got the ropes there, Archie."

"Let me have them, sir." He took the bag, pulled out the two coils of rope, pulled the pillow from his lower pillowcase, stuffed the ropes inside, and placed them under his top pillow. "Good a place as any, sir. If they really start searching, they're bound to find it anyway. Now if you'd just be dropping this pillow and bag out the window . . ."

I did that, stripped, washed, dried myself as best I could, and climbed into bed, just as Marston came into the bay.

"She'll be all right, John. Simple fracture. All wrapped up and in her blankets and she'll be asleep in a minute. Sedatives, you know."

I nodded. "You did a good job to-night, Doctor. Boy outside is still asleep and I hardly felt a thing in my leg." It was only half a lie and there was no point in hurting his feelings unnecessarily. I glanced down at my leg. "The splints—"

"I'll fix them right away."

He fixed them, not more than half killing me in the process, and while he was doing so I told them what had happened. Or part of what had happened. I told them the encounter with Tony Carreras was the result of an attempt I'd made to spike the gun on the afterdeck; with old Bullen talking away non-stop in his sleep, any mention of the Twister would not have been clever at all.

At the end of it all, after a heavy silence, Bullen said hopelessly, "It's finished. It's all finished. All that work and suffering for nothing. All for nothing."

It wasn't finished; it wasn't going to be finished ever. Not till either Miguel Carreras or myself was finished. If I were a betting man I'd have staked the last cent of my fortune on Carreras.

I didn't say that to them. I told them instead of the simple plan I had in mind, an unlikely plan concerned with taking over the bridge at gun point. But it wasn't half as hopeless and desperate as the plan I really had in mind. The one I'd tell Archie MacDonald about later. Again I couldn't tell the old man, for again the chances were heavy that he would have betrayed it in his half-delirious muttering under sedation. I hadn't even liked to mention Tony Carreras, but the blood had to be explained away.

When I finished, Bullen said in his hoarse whisper, "I'm still the captain of the ship. I will not permit it. Good God, Mister, look at the weather, look at your condition. I will not allow you to throw your life away. I *cannot* permit it."

"Thank you, sir. I know what you mean. But you have to permit it. You must. Because if you don't——"

"What if someone comes into the sick bay when you're not here?" he asked helplessly. He'd accepted the inevitable.

"This." I produced a gun and tossed it to the bo'sun. "This was Tony Carreras'. There are still seven shots in the magazine."

"Thank you, sir," MacDonald said quietly. "I'll be very careful with those shots."

"But yourself, man?" Bullen demanded huskily. "How about yourself?"

"Give me back that knife, Archie," I said.

Chapter 10

[*Friday 9 A.M.–Saturday 1 A.M.*]

I SLEPT that night and slept deeply, as deeply, almost, as Tony Carreras. I had neither sedatives nor sleeping pills; exhaustion was the only drug I needed.

Coming awake next morning was a long, slow climb from the depths of a bottomless pit. I was climbing in the dark, but in the strange way of dreams I wasn't climbing and it wasn't dark; some great beast had me in his jaws and was trying to shake the life out of me. A tiger, but no ordinary tiger. A sabre-toothed tiger, the kind that had passed from the surface of the earth a million years ago. So I kept on climbing in the dark and the sabre-toothed tiger kept on shaking me like a terrier shaking a rat and I knew that my only hope was to reach the light above, but I couldn't see any light. Then, all of a sudden, the light was there, my eyes were open, and Miguel Carreras was bending over me and shaking my shoulder with no gentle hand. I would have preferred the sabre-toothed tiger any day.

Marston stood at the other side of the bed and when he saw I was awake he caught me under the arms and lifted me gently to a sitting position. I did my best to help him but I wasn't concentrating on it; I was concentrating on the lip-biting and eye-closing so that Carreras couldn't miss how far through I was. Marston was protesting.

"He shouldn't be moved, Mr. Carreras. He really shouldn't be moved. He's in constant pain and I repeat that major surgery is essential at the earliest possible moment." It was about forty years too late now, I supposed, for anyone to point out to Marston that he was a born actor. No question in my mind now but that that was what he should have been: the gain to both the Thespian and medical worlds would have been incalculable.

I rubbed the sleep from my eyes and smiled wanly. "Why don't you say it outright, Doctor? Amputation is what you mean."

He looked at me gravely, then went away without saying anything. I looked across at Bullen and MacDonald. Both of them were awake, both of them carefully not looking in my direction. And then I looked at Carreras.

At first glance he looked exactly the same as he had a couple of days ago. At first glance, that was. A second and closer inspection showed the difference: a slight pallor under the tan, a reddening of the eyes, a tightening of the face that had not been there before. He had a chart under his left arm, a slip of paper in his left hand.

"Well," I sneered, "how's the big bold pirate captain this morning?"

"My son is dead," he said dully.

I hadn't expected it to come like this, or so soon, but the very unexpectedness of it helped me to the right reaction, the reaction he would probably expect from me anyway. I stared at him through slightly narrowed eyes and said, "He's *what?*"

"Dead." Miguel Carreras, whatever else he lacked, unquestionably had all the normal instincts of a parent, a father. The very intensity of his restraint showed how badly he had been hit. For a moment I felt genuinely sorry for him. For a very short moment. Then I saw the faces of Wilson and Jamieson and Benson and Brownell and Dexter, the faces of all those dead men, and I wasn't sorry any more.

"Dead?" I repeated. Shocked puzzlement, but not too much shock—it wouldn't be expected of me. "Your son? Dead? How can he be dead? What did he die of?" Almost of its own volition, before I suddenly checked the movement, my hand started reaching for the clasp knife under the pillow. Not that it would have made much difference even if he had seen it—five minutes in the dispensary steriliser had removed the last of the traces of blood.

"I don't know." He shook his head and I felt like cheering; there were no traces of suspicion in his face. "I don't know."

"Dr. Marston," I said. "Surely you—"

"We haven't been able to find him. He has disappeared."

"Disappeared?" It was Captain Bullen making his contribution, and his voice sounded a shade stronger, a little less husky, than it had the previous night. "Vanished? A man just can't vanish aboard a ship like that, Mr. Carreras."

"We spent over two hours searching the ship. My son is not aboard the *Campari*. When did you last see him, Mr. Carter?"

I didn't indulge in guilty starts, sharp upward glances, or anything daft like that. I wondered what his reactions would have been if I'd said: "When I heaved him over the side of the *Campari* last night." Instead I pursed my lips and said, "After dinner last night when he came here. He didn't linger. Said something like: 'Captain Carreras making his rounds,' and left."

"That is correct. I'd sent him to make a tour of inspection. How did he look?"

"Not his usual self. Green. Seasick."

"My son was a poor sailor," Carreras acknowledged. "It is possible—"

"You said he was making rounds," I interrupted. "Of the whole ship? Decks and everything?"

"That is so."

"Did you have life lines rigged on the fore and after decks?"

"No. I had not thought it necessary."

"Well," I said grimly, "there's your possible answer.

Your probable answer. No life lines, nothing to hang on to. Felt ill, ran for the side, a sudden lurch—" I left the sentence hanging.

"It is possible, but not in character. He had an exceptional sense of balance."

"Balance doesn't help much if you slip on a wet deck."

"Quite. I also haven't ruled out the possibility of foul play."

"Foul play?" I stared at him, duly grateful that the gift of telepathy is so very limited. "With all the crew and passengers under guard, lock and key, how is foul play possible? Unless," I added thoughtfully, "there's a nigger in your own woodpile."

"I have not yet completed my investigations." The voice was cold; the subject was closed, and Miguel Carreras was back in business again. Bereavement wouldn't crush this man. However much he might inwardly mourn his son, it wouldn't in the slightest detract from his efficiency or his ruthless determination to carry out exactly the plans he had made. It wasn't, for instance, going to make the slightest difference to his plans to send us all into orbit the following day. Signs of humanity there might be, but the abiding fundamental in Carreras' character was an utter, an all-excluding fanaticism that was all the more dangerous in that it lay so deeply hidden beneath the smooth urbanity of the surface.

"The chart, Carter." He handed it across to me along with a paper giving a list of fixes. "Let me know if the *Fort Ticonderoga* is on course. And if she is running on time. We can later calculate our time of interception if and when I get a fix this morning."

"You'll get a fix," Bullen assured him huskily. "They say the devil is good to his own, Carreras, and he's been good to you. You're running out of the hurricane and you'll have clear patches of sky by noon. Rain later in the evening, but first clearing."

"You are sure, Captain Bullen? You are sure we are running out of the hurricane?"

"I'm sure. Or, rather, the hurricane is running away from us." Old Bullen was an authority on hurricanes and would lecture on his pet subject at the drop of a hat, even to Carreras, even when a hoarse whisper was all the voice he could summon. "Neither wind nor sea have moderated very much"—and they certainly hadn't—"but what matters is the direction of the wind. It's from the northwest now, which means that the hurricane lies to the northeast of us. It passed us by to the east, on our starboard hand, sometime during the night, moving northwards, then suddenly swung northeast. Quite often when a hurricane reaches the northern limits of its latitude and then is caught up by the westerlies it can remain stationary at its point of recurvature for twelve or twenty-four hours—which would have meant that you would have had to sail through it. But you had the luck: it recurved and moved to the east almost without a break." Bullen lay back, close to exhaustion. Even so little had been too much for him.

"You can tell all this just lying in your bed there?" Carreras demanded.

Bullen gave him the commodore's look he would have given any cadet who dared question his knowledge and ignored him.

"The weather is going to moderate?" Carreras persisted.

"That's obvious, isn't it?"

Carreras nodded slowly. Making his rendezvous in time and being able to transship the gold had been his two great worries, and now both of them were gone. He turned abruptly, walked out of the sick bay.

Bullen cleared his throat and said formally, in his strained whisper, "Congratulations, Mr. Carter. You are the most fluent liar I've ever known."

MacDonald just grinned.

The forenoon, the afternoon came and went. The sun duly appeared, as Bullen had prophesied, and later disappeared, also as he had prophesied. The sea moderated, although not much, not enough, I guessed, to alleviate the sufferings of our passengers, and the wind stayed where it was, out of the northwest. Bullen, under sedation, slept nearly all day, once again relapsing into his incoherent mumblings—none of them, I was relieved to note, were about Tony Carreras—while MacDonald and I talked or slept. But we didn't sleep before I told him what I hoped to do that night when—or if—I managed to get loose on the upper deck.

Susan I hardly saw that day. She made her appearance after breakfast with her arm in plaster and in a sling. There was no danger of this arousing any suspicion, even in a mind like Carreras'; the story was to be that she had gone to sleep in a chair, been flung out of it during the storm, and sprained her wrist. Such accidents were so commonplace in heavy weather that no one would think to raise an eyebrow. About ten o'clock in the morning she asked to be allowed to join her parents in the drawing room and stayed there all day.

Fifteen minutes after noon Carreras appeared again. If his investigations into possible foul play connected with his son's death had made any progress, he made no mention of it; he did not even refer to the disappearance again. He had the inevitable chart—two of them this time— with him and the noon position of the *Campari*. Seemingly he'd managed to get a good fix from the sun.

"Our position, our speed, their position, their speed, and our respective courses. Do we intercept at the point marked *X*?"

"I suppose you've already worked it out for yourself?"

"I have."

"We don't intercept," I said after a few minutes. "At our present speed we should arrive at your rendezvous in between eleven and eleven and a half hours. Say midnight. Five hours ahead of schedule."

"Thank you, Mr. Carter. My own conclusion exactly. The five-hour wait for the *Ticonderoga* won't take long in passing."

I felt a queer sensation in my middle; the phrase about a person's heart sinking may not be physiologically accurate but it described the feeling accurately. This would ruin everything, completely destroy what little chance my plan ever had of succeeding. But I knew the consternation did not show in my face.

"Planning on arriving there at midnight and hanging round till the fly walks into your parlour?" I shrugged. "Well, you're the man who's making the decisions."

"What do you mean by that?" he asked sharply.

"Nothing much," I said indifferently. "It's just that I would have thought that you would want your crew at the maximum stage of efficiency for transshipping the gold when we met the *Fort Ticonderoga.*"

"So?"

"So there's still going to be a heavy sea running in twelve hours' time. When we stop at the rendezvous, the *Campari* is going to lie in the trough of the seas and, in the elegant phrase of our times, roll her guts out. I don't know how many of that crowd of landlubbers you have along with you were seasick last night, but I'll bet there will be twice as many to-night. And don't think our stabilisers are going to save you—they depend upon the factor of the ship's speed for their effect."

"A well-taken point," he agreed calmly. "I shall reduce speed, aim at being there about four A.M." He looked at me with sudden speculation. "Remarkably co-operative, full of helpful suggestions. Curiously out of the estimate I had formed of your character."

"Which only goes to show how wrong your estimate is, my friend. Common sense and self-interest explain it. I want to get into a proper hospital as soon as possible— the prospect of going through life with one leg doesn't appeal. The sooner I see passengers, crew, and myself transferred aboard the *Ticonderoga* the happier I'll be. Only a fool kicks against the pricks; I know a *fait accompli* when I see one. You *are* going to transfer us all aboard the *Ticonderoga,* aren't you, Carreras?"

"I shall have no further use for any member of the *Campari's* crew, far less for the passengers." He smiled thinly. "Captain Teach and Blackbeard are not my ideals, Mr. Carter. I should like to be remembered as a humane pirate. You have my word that all of you will be transferred in safety and unharmed." The last sentence had the ring of truth and sincerity, because it was true and sincere. It was the truth, but it wasn't, of course, the whole truth:

he'd left out the bit about our being blown out of existence half an hour later.

About seven o'clock in the evening Susan Beresford returned and Marston left, under guard, to dispense pills and soothing words to the passengers in the drawing room, many of whom were, after twenty-four hours of continuously heavy weather, understandably not feeling at their best.

Susan looked tired and pale—no doubt the emotional and physical suffering of the previous night together with the pain from her broken arm accounted for that—but I had to admit for the first time, in an unbiassed fashion, that she also looked very lovely. I'd never before realised that auburn hair and green eyes were a combination that couldn't be matched, but possibly this was because I'd never before seen an auburn-haired girl with green eyes.

She was also tense, nervous, and jumpy as a cat. Unlike old Doc Marston and myself, she'd never have made it in the Method school.

She came softly to my bedside—Bullen was still under sedation and MacDonald either asleep or dozing—and sat down on a chair. After I'd asked her how she was and how the passengers were, and she'd asked me how I was and I'd told her and she hadn't believed me, she said suddenly, "Johnny, if everything goes all right will you get another ship?"

"I don't follow."

"Well," she said impatiently, "if the *Campari*'s blown up and we get away or if we're saved some other way, will you—"

"I see. I suppose I would. Blue Mail has plenty of ships and I'm supposed to be the senior chief officer."

"You'll like that? Getting back to sea again?"

This was a crazy conversation, but she was only whistling in the dark. I said, "I don't think I'll be back to sea again somehow."

"Giving in?"

"Giving up. A different thing altogether. I don't want to spend the rest of my life catering to the whims of wealthy passengers. I don't include the Beresford family, father, mother—or daughter."

She smiled at this, going into the weird routine of melting the green in her eyes, the kind of smile that could have a very serious effect on the constitution of a sick man like myself, so I looked away and went on: "I'm a pretty fair mechanic and I've a bit of cash put away. There's a very nice flourishing little garage down in Kent that I can take over any time I want. And Archie MacDonald there is an outstanding mechanic. We'd make a pretty fair team, I think."

"Have you asked him yet?"

"What chance have I had?" I said irritably. "I've only just thought about it."

"You're pretty good friends, aren't you?"

"Good enough. What's that got to do with anything?"

"Nothing, just nothing. Funny, that's all. There's the bo'sun—he'll never walk properly again; nobody will want him at sea any more; he's probably got no qualifications for any decent job on land—especially with that leg—and all of a sudden Chief Officer Carter gets tired of the sea and decides—"

"It's not that way at all," I interrupted. "You've got it all wrong."

"Probably, probably," she agreed. "I'm not very clever. But you don't have to worry about him, anyway. Daddy told me this afternoon that he's got a job for him."

"Oh?" I took a chance and looked at her eyes again. "What kind of job?"

"A storeman."

"A storeman." I know I sounded disappointed, but I'd have sounded ten times as disappointed if I had been able to take all this seriously, if I'd been able to share her belief that there was a future. "Well, it's kind of him. Nothing wrong with a storeman, but I just don't see Archie Mac-Donald as one, that's all. Especially not in America."

"Will you listen?" she asked sweetly. A touch of the Miss Beresford that was.

"I'm listening."

"You've heard that Daddy's building a big refinery in

the West of Scotland? Storage tanks, own port to take
goodness knows how many tankers?"

"I've heard."

"Well, that's the place. Stores for the oil port and the
refinery—millions and millions of dollars of stores, Daddy
says, with goodness knows how many men to look after
them. And your friend in charge—with a dream house attached."

"That is a very different proposition altogether. I think
it sounds wonderful, Susan, just wonderful. It's terribly
kind of you."

"Not me!" she protested. "Daddy."

"Look at me. Say that without blushing."

She looked at me. She blushed. With those green eyes
the effect was devastating. I thought about my constitution again and looked away, and then I heard her saying:
"Daddy wants you to be the manager of the new oil port.
So then you and the bo'sun would be in business together
after all. Wouldn't you?"

I turned slowly and stared at her. I said slowly, "Was
that the job he meant when he asked me if I'd like to work
for him?"

"Of course. And you didn't give him a chance to tell
you. Do you think he'd given up? He hadn't really started.
You don't know my father. And you can't claim *I'd* anything to do with it either."

I didn't believe her. I said, "I can't tell you how—well,
how grateful I am. It's a terrific chance, I know and admit.
If you see your father again this evening thank him very
much indeed from me."

Her eyes were shining. I'd never seen a girl's eyes shining for me before. Not in this way.

"Then you'll—then you'll—"

"And tell him no."

"And tell him—"

"It's a foolish thing to have pride, perhaps, but I've still
got a little left." I hadn't meant my voice to sound so
harsh; it just came out that way. "Whatever job I'll get,
I'll get the one I found for myself, not one bought for me
by a girl." As a thumbs-down on a genuine and generous

offer, I reflected bitterly, the refusal could have been more graciously phrased.

She looked at me, her face suddenly very still, said, "Oh, Johnny," in a curiously muffled voice, turned and buried her face half on the pillow, half on the sheets, her shoulders heaving, sobbing as if her heart would break.

I didn't feel good at all. I could have walked under a five-barred gate without opening it. I reached and touched her head awkwardly and said, "I'm terribly sorry, Susan. But just because I turn down—"

"It's not that, it's not that." She shook her head in the pillow, voice more muffled than ever. "It was all make-believe. No, not that, everything I said was true, but just for a few moments we—well, we weren't here. We—we were away from the *Campari;* it was something that had nothing to do with the *Campari.* You—you understand."

I stroked her hair. "Yes, Susan, I understand." I didn't know what she was talking about.

"It was like a dream." I didn't see where she came into the dream. "In the future. Away—away from this dreadful ship. And then you burst the dream and we're back on the *Campari.* And no one knows what the end's to be, except us—Mummy, Daddy, all of them, Carreras has them believing their lives will be spared." She sobbed again, then said between sobs, "Oh, my dear. We're just kidding ourselves. It's all over. Everything's over. Forty armed men and they're prowling all over the ship. I saw them. Double guards everywhere—there are two outside this door. And every door locked. There's no hope, there's no hope. Mummy, Daddy, you, me, all of us—this time tomorrow it will all be over. Miracles don't happen any more."

"It's not all over, Susan." I'd never make a salesman, I thought drearily; if I met a man dying of thirst in the Sahara I couldn't have convinced him that water was good for him. "It's *never* all over." But that didn't sound any better than my first attempt.

I heard the creak of springs and saw MacDonald propped up on one elbow, thick black eyebrows raised in puzzlement and concern. The sound of her crying must have wakened him.

"It's all right, Archie," I said. "Just a bit upset, that's all."

"I'm sorry." She straightened herself and turned her tear-stained face in the bo'sun's direction. Her breath was coming in the quick, short, indrawn gasps that are the aftermath of crying. "I'm terribly sorry. I woke you up. But there *is* no hope is there, Mr. MacDonald?"

" 'Archie' will do for me," the bo'sun said gravely.

"Well, Archie." She tried to smile at him through her tears. "I'm just a terrible coward."

"And you spending all day with your parents and never once being able to tell them what you know? What kind of cowardice do you call that, miss?" MacDonald said reproachfully.

"You're not answering me," she said in tearful accusation.

"I am a West Highlander, Miss Beresford," MacDonald said slowly. "I have the gift of my ancestors, a black gift at times that I'd rather be without, but I have it. I can see what comes tomorrow or the day after tomorrow, not often, but at times I can. You cannot will the second sight to come, but come it does. I have seen what is to come many times in the past few years, and Mr. Carter there will tell you that I have never once been wrong." This was the first I had ever heard of it; he was as fluent a liar as myself. "Everything is going to turn out well."

"Do you think so, do you really think so?" There was hope in her voice now, hope in her eyes; that slow, measured speech of MacDonald's, the rocklike steadiness of the dark blue eyes in the sun-weathered face, bespoke a confidence, a certainty, an unshakeable belief that was most impressive. There now, I thought, was a man who would have made a great salesman.

"I don't think, Miss Beresford." Again the grave smile. "I know. Our troubles are almost at their end. Do what I do—put your last cent on Mr. Carter here."

He even had me convinced. I, too, knew that everything was going to turn out just fine, until I remembered who he was depending on. Me. I gave Susan a handkerchief and said, "Go and tell Archie about that job."

"You're not going to trust your life to *that* thing?" There was horror in Susan's face, panic in her voice as she watched me tie a bowline round my waist. "Why, it's no thicker than my little finger." I could hardly blame her: that thin three-stranded rope, no bigger than an ordinary clothesline, was hardly calculated to inspire confidence in anyone. It didn't inspire much in me, even although I did know its properties.

"It's nylon, miss," MacDonald explained soothingly. "The very rope mountaineers use in the Himalayas—and you don't think they'd trust their lives to anything they weren't dead sure of? You could hang a big motorcar on the end of this and it still wouldn't break." Susan gave him her it's-all-right-for-you-to-talk-it's-not-your-life-that's-depending-on-it look, bit her lip, and said nothing.

The time was exactly midnight. If I'd read the clock dial settings on the Twister properly, six hours was the maximum delayed action that could be obtained. Assuming Carreras rendezvoused exactly on time at 5 A.M., it would be at least another hour before he could get clear; so the Twister wouldn't be armed until after midnight.

Everything was ready. The sick-bay door had been cautiously locked on the inside with the key I'd taken from Tony Carreras so that neither of the two guards could burst in unexpectedly in the middle of things. And even if they did get suspicious and force an entrance, MacDonald had a gun.

MacDonald himself was now sitting at the top of my bed, beside the window. Marston and I had half carried him there from his own bed. His left leg was quite useless —like myself, he'd been given an injection by Doc Marston to deaden the pain, mine being twice as powerful as the previous night's dose—but then MacDonald was not going to be called upon to use his leg that night, only his arms and shoulders, and there was nothing wrong with MacDonald's arms and shoulders. They were the strongest on the *Campari*. I had the feeling I was going to need all their strength. Only MacDonald knew the purpose I had in mind. Only MacDonald knew that I intended returning the way I went. The others believed in my suicidal plan for an attack on the bridge, believed if I were successful I would be returning via the sick-bay door. But they didn't believe I would return at all. The atmosphere was less than festive.

Bullen was awake now, lying flat on his back, his face silent and grim.

I was dressed in the same dinner suit as I'd worn the previous night. It was still damp, still crusted with blood. I'd no shoes on. The clasp knife was in one pocket, oil-skin-wrapped torch in the other, the mask round my face, hood over my head. My leg ached, I felt as a man feels after a long bout of flu, and the fever still burned in my blood, but I was as ready as I was ever going to be.

"Lights," I said to Marston.

A switch clicked and the sick bay was as dark as the tomb. I drew back the curtains, pulled open the window, and secured it on the latch. I stuck my head outside.

It was raining steadily, heavily, a cold driving rain out of the northwest, slanting straight in through the window on to the bed. The sky was black with no star above. The *Campari* still pitched a little, rolled a little, but it was nothing compared to the previous night. She was doing about twelve knots. I twisted my neck and peered upwards. No one there. I leaned out as far as possible and looked fore and aft. If there was a light showing on the *Campari* that night, I couldn't see it.

I came inside, stooped, picked up a coil of nylon rope, checked that it was the one secured to the iron bedstead, and flung it out into the rain and the darkness. I made a last check of the rope knotted round my waist—this was the one the bo'sun held in his hands—and said, "I'm off." As a farewell speech it could perhaps have been improved upon, but it was all I could think of at the time.

Captain Bullen said, "Good luck, my boy." He'd have said an awful lot more if he knew what I really had in mind. Marston said something I couldn't catch. Susan said nothing at all. I wriggled my way through the window, favouring my wounded leg, and then was fully outside, suspended from the sill by my elbows. I could sense rather than see the bo'sun by the window, ready to pay out the rope round my waist.

"Archie," I said softly, "give me that spiel again. The one about how everything is going to turn out all right."

"You'll be here again before we know you're gone," he said cheerfully. "See and bring my knife back."

I felt for the rope attached to the bed, got it in both hands, eased my elbows off the sill, and dropped quickly, hand over hand, as MacDonald payed out my life line. Five seconds later I was in the water.

The water was dark and cold and it took my breath away. After the warmth of the sick bay the shock of the almost immediate transition, the abrupt drop in temperature, was literally paralysing. Momentarily, involuntarily, I lost my grip on the rope, panicked when I realised what had happened, floundered about desperately, and caught it again. The bo'sun was doing a good job above: the sudden increase in weight as I'd lost my life line must have had him halfway out of the window.

But the cold wasn't the worst. If you can survive the initial shock you can tolerate the cold to a limited degree, accustomed but not reconciled; what you can't tolerate, what you can't become accustomed to is the involuntary swallowing of large mouthfuls of salt water every few seconds. And that was what was happening to me.

I had known that being towed alongside a ship doing twelve knots wasn't going to be any too pleasant, but I had never thought it was going to be as bad as this. The factor I hadn't taken into the reckoning was the waves. One moment I was being towed, face down and planing, up the side of a wave; the next, as the wave swept by under me, I was almost completely out of the water, then falling forwards and downwards to smash into the rising shoulder of the next wave with a jarring violence that knocked all the breath from my body. And when all the breath has been driven from you the body's demands that you immediately gulp in air are insistent, imperative, and not to be denied. But with my face buried in the sea I wasn't gulping in air, I was gulping down large quantities of salt water. It was like having water under high pressure forced down my throat by a hose. I was floundering, porpoising, twisting and spinning exactly like a hooked fish being pulled in on the surface through the wake of a fast-trolling motorboat. Slowly, but very surely, I was drowning.

I was beaten before I started. I knew I had to get back, and at once. I was gasping and choking on sea water; my nostrils were on fire with it; my stomach was full of it; my throat burned with it, and I knew that at least some of it had already reached my lungs.

A system of signals had been arranged, and now I began to tug frantically on the rope round my waist, hanging on to the other rope with my left hand. I tugged half a dozen times, slowly, in some sort of order at first, then, as no response came, frantically, despairingly. I was porpoising up and down so violently that all MacDonald could be feeling anyway was a constant and irregular series of alternate tightenings and slackenings of the line; he had no means of distinguishing between one type of tug and another.

I tried to pull myself back on my own line, but against the onrushing pressure of the water as the *Campari* ploughed through that stormy sea it was quite impossible. When the tension came off the line round my waist, it needed all the strength of both my hands just to hang on to the life line without being swept away. With all the strength and desperation that was in me I tried to edge forward an inch. But I couldn't even make that inch. And I knew I couldn't hang on much longer.

Salvation came by sheer chance, no credit to me. One particularly heavy wave had twisted me round till I was on my back, and in this position I fell into the next trough and hit the following wave with back and shoulders. Followed the inevitable explosive release of air from my lungs, the just as inevitable sucking in of fresh air—and this time I found I could breathe! Air rushed into my lungs, not water: I could breathe! Lying on my back like this, half lifted out of the water by my grip on the life line, and with my head bent forward almost to my chest between my overhead arms, my face remained clear of the water and I could breathe.

I wasted no time but went hand over hand down the life line as fast as MacDonald paid out the rope about my waist. I was still swallowing some water but not enough to matter.

After about fifteen seconds I took my left hand off the life line and started scraping it along the side of the ship, feeling for the rope I'd left dangling over the side of the afterdeck last night. The life line was now sliding through my right hand and, wet though it was, it was burning the skin of my palm. But I hardly noticed it. I *had* to find that manilla I'd left tied to the guardrail stanchion; if I didn't, then it was curtains. Not only would the hopes of my carrying out my plan be at an end; it would be the end for me also. MacDonald and I had *had* to act on the assumption that the rope would be there and no attempt would be made to pull me back until he got the clear prearranged signal that it was time to begin just that. And to make any such clear signal while in the water, I had discovered, was impossible. If the manilla wasn't there I'd just be towed along at the end of that nylon rope until I was drowned. Nor would that take long. The salt water I'd swallowed, the violent buffeting of the waves, the blows I'd suffered from being flung a score of times against the iron walls of the *Campari,* the loss of blood and my injured leg—all those had taken their frightening toll and I was dangerously weak. It would not be long.

My left hand brushed against the manilla: I grabbed it, a drowning man seizing the last straw in the wide, endless expanse of the ocean.

Tucking the life line through the rope round my waist, I overarmed myself up the manilla till I was all but clear of the water, wrapped my one good leg round the rope and hung there, gasping like an exhausted dog, shivering and then being violently sick as I brought up all the sea water that had collected in my stomach. After that I felt better but weaker than ever. I started to climb.

I hadn't far to go, twenty feet and I'd be there, but I

hadn't gone two feet before I was bitterly regretting the fact that I hadn't followed my impulse of the previous night and knotted the manilla. The manilla was soaking wet and slippery and I had to clasp tight with all the strength of my hands to get any purchase at all. And there was little enough strength left in my hands, my aching forearm muscles were exhausted from clinging so long and so desperately to the life line, my shoulders were just as far gone; even when I could get a good purchase, even when my weakening hands didn't slide down the rope when I put all my weight on them, I could still pull myself up only two or three inches at a time. Three inches, no more: that was all I could manage at one time.

I couldn't make it; reasons, instinct, logic, common sense all told me that I couldn't make it, but I made it. The last few feet of the climb was something out of a dark nightmare, hauling myself up two inches, slipping back an inch, hauling myself up again and always creeping nearer the top. Three feet from the top I stopped: I knew I was only that distance away from safety, but to climb another inch on that rope was something I knew I could never do. Arms shaking aguelike from the strain, shoulders on fire with agony, I hauled my body up until my eyes were level with knotted hands: even in that almost pitchy darkness I could see the faint white blur of my gleaming knuckles. For a second I hung there, then flung my right hand desperately upwards. If I missed the coaming of the scuppers . . . but I couldn't miss it. I had no more strength in me, I could never make such an effort again.

I didn't miss it. The top joint of my middle finger hooked over the coaming and locked there, then my other hand was beside it, I was scrabbling desperately for the lowermost bar in the guardrails; I had to get it over, and over at once, or I'd fall back into the sea. I found the bar, had both hands on it, swung my body convulsively to the right till my sound foot caught the coaming, reached up to the next bar, reached the teak rail, half dragged, half slid my body over the top, and fell heavily on the deck on the other side.

How long I lay there, trembling violently in every

weary muscle in my body, whooping hoarsely for the breath my tortured lungs were craving, gritting my teeth against the fire in my shoulders and arms, and trying not to let the red mist before my eyes envelop me completely, I do not know. It may have been two minutes, it may have been ten. Somewhere during that time I was violently ill again. And then slowly, ever so slowly, the pain eased a little, my breathing slowed, and the mists before my eyes cleared away, but I still couldn't stop trembling. It was well for me that no five-year-old happened along the deck that night: he could have had me over the side without taking his hands out of his pockets.

I untied the ropes from my waist with numbed and fumbling and all but useless hands, tied them both to the stanchion just above the manilla, pulled the life line till it was almost taut, then gave three sharp, deliberate tugs. A couple of minutes passed, then came three clearly defined answering tugs. They knew now I had made it. I hoped they felt better about it than I did. Not that that would be hard.

I sat there for at least another five minutes till some measure of strength came back to me, rose shakily to my feet, and padded across the deck to number four hold. The tarpaulin on the starboard for'ard corner was still secured. That meant there was no one down below. But I really hadn't expected them to be there yet.

I straightened, looked all around me, then stood very still, the driving rain streaming down my sodden mask and soaking clothes. Not fifteen yards away from me, right aft, I had seen a red glow come and vanish in the darkness. Ten seconds passed, then the glow again. I'd heard of waterproof cigarettes, but not all that waterproof. But someone *was* smoking a cigarette, no question about that.

Like falling thistledown, only quieter, I drifted down in the direction of the glow. I was still trembling, but you can't hear trembling. Twice I stopped to line up direction and distance by that glowing cigarette and finally stopped less than ten feet away from it. My mind was hardly working at all or I'd never have dared to do it: a careless flick of a torch beam, say, and it would have been all over. But no one flicked a torch.

The red glow came again and I could now just make out that the smoker wasn't standing in the rain. He was in the V-shaped entrance of a tarpaulin, a big tarpaulin draped over some big object. The gun, of course, the gun that Carreras had mounted on the afterdeck, with the tarpaulin serving the dual purpose of protecting the mechanism from the rain and concealing it from any other vessel they might have passed during the day.

I heard the murmur of voices. Not the smoker, but another two crouched somewhere inside the shelter of the tarpaulin. That meant three people there. Three people guarding the gun. Carreras was certainly taking no chances with that gun. But why so many as three? You didn't need three. Then I had it. Carreras hadn't just been talking idly when he'd spoken of the possibility of foul play in connection with the death of his son. He did suspect it, but his cold, logical mind had told him that neither crew nor passengers of the *Campari* could have been responsible. *If* his son had met death by violence, then death could only have come from one of his own men. The renegade who had killed his son might strike again, might attempt to ruin his plans. And so three men on guard together. They could watch each other.

I left, skirted the hatch, and made my way to the bo'sun's store. I fumbled round in the darkness, found what I wanted, a heavy marlinespike, and then was on my way, marlinespike in one hand, MacDonald's knife in the other.

Dr. Caroline's cabin was in darkness. I was pretty sure that the windows were uncurtained, but I left my torch where it was. Susan had said that Carreras' men were prowling round the decks that night: the chance wasn't worth it. And if Dr. Caroline wasn't already in number four hold, then the chances were high indeed that he would only be in one other place—in his bed, and bound to it hand and foot.

I climbed up to the next deck and padded along to the wireless office. My breathing and pulse were almost back to normal now; the shaking had eased, and I could feel the strength slowly flooding back into my arms and shoulders. Apart from the constant dull ache in my neck where the sandbag merchant and Tony Carreras had been at work, the only pain I felt was a sharp burning in my left thigh where the salt water had got into the open wounds. Without the anaesthetic I'd have been doing a war dance. On one leg, of course.

The wireless office was in darkness. I leaned my ear against the door, straining to hear the slightest sound from inside, and was just reaching out a delicate hand for the doorknob when I just about had a heart attack. A telephone bell had gone off with a shatteringly metallic loudness not six inches from the ear I'd so hard pressed against the door. It jarred me rigid; for all of five seconds Lot's wife couldn't even have hoped to compete with me, then I pussyfooted silently across the deck into the shelter of one of the life boats.

I heard the vague murmur of someone talking on the telephone, saw the light come on in the wireless office, the door open, a man come out. Before he switched off the light I saw two things: I saw him bring a key from his right-hand trouser pocket, and I saw who it was, the artist with the machine gun who had killed Tommy Wilson and cut down all the rest of us. If I had to settle any more accounts that night, I hoped bleakly it would be with this man.

He closed the door, locked it, and went down the ladder to "A" deck below. I followed him to the top of the ladder and stayed there. There was another man at the foot of the ladder, lit torch in hand, just outside Dr. Caroline's cabin, and in the backwash of light from the cabin bulkhead I could see who it was. Carreras himself. There were two other men close by, and I could distinguish neither of them, but I was certain that one of them would be Dr. Caroline. They were joined by the radio operator and the four men moved off aft. I never thought of going after them. I knew where they were going.

Ten minutes. That was the detail the news broadcast about the disappearance of the Twister had mentioned.

There were only one or two men who could arm the Twister, and it couldn't be done in less than ten minutes. I wondered vaguely if Caroline knew he had only ten minutes to live. And that was all the time I had to do what I had to do. It wasn't long.

I was coming down the ladder while Carreras' swinging torch was still in sight. Three quarters of the way down, three steps from the bottom, I froze into immobility. Two men—in that driving rain their black blurred shapes were barely distinguishable, but I knew it was two men because of the low murmur of voices—were approaching the foot of the ladder. Armed men—they were bound to be armed, almost certainly with the ubiquitous Tommy gun which seemed the standard weapon among the generalissimo's henchmen.

They were at the foot of the ladder now. I could feel the ache in my hands from the tension of my grip round marlinespike and opened clasp knife. Then suddenly they went veering off to the right, round the side of the ladder. I could have reached out and touched them both. I could see them almost clearly now, clearly enough to see that both had beards, and had I not been wearing the black hood and mask they would have been bound to see the white glimmer of my face. How they didn't even see my shape standing there on the third bottom step was beyond me: the only reason I could think of was that they both had their heads lowered against the driving rain.

Seconds later I was inside the central passageway of "A" accommodation. I hadn't poked my head round the outside passage door to see if the land was clear; after that escape I'd felt that nothing mattered; I'd just walked straight inside. The passageway was empty.

The first door on the right, the one opposite Caroline's, was the entrance to Carreras' suite. I tried the door. Locked. I walked down the passage to where Benson, the dead chief steward, had had his cubicle, hoping that the luxurious carpet underfoot was absorbent enough to soak up the water that was almost cascading off me. White, Benson's successor, would have had a blue fit if he could have seen the damage I was doing.

The master key to the passengers' suites was in its secret little cubbyhole. I removed it, went back to Carreras' cabin, unlocked the door, and went inside, locking it behind me.

The lights were on throughout the suite. Carreras probably hadn't bothered to switch them off when he'd left—he wasn't paying for the electricity. I went through the cabins, sending each door in turn flying open with the sole of my stockinged foot. Nothing? No one. I had one bad moment when I entered Carreras' own sleeping cabin and saw this desperate hooded, crouched figure, dripping water, hands clenched round weapons, with wide, staring eyes and blood dripping down beside the left eye. Myself in a looking glass. I had seen prettier sights. I hadn't been aware that I'd been cut; I supposed it must have been the result of one of the many knocks I'd had against the side of the *Campari,* opening up the wound in my head.

Carreras had boasted that he had a complete loading plan of the *Fort Ticonderoga* in his cabin. Nine minutes now, maybe even less. Where in the name of God would he keep the plan? I went through dressing tables, wardrobes, lockers, cupboards, beside tables. Nothing. Nothing. Seven minutes.

Where, *where* would he keep it? Think, Carter, for heaven's sake, *think.* Maybe Caroline was getting on with the arming of the Twister faster than anyone had thought possible. How did anyone *know,* as the broadcast had said, that it took all of ten minutes to arm it? If the Twister was such a secret—and until it had been stolen it had been such a top-priority hush-hush secret that no member of the public had known of its existence—how did anyone know it took ten minutes to arm it? How *could* anyone know? Maybe all it required was a twist here, a turn there. Maybe—maybe he was finished already . . . Maybe . . .

I put those thoughts to one side, drove them out of my mind, crushed them ruthlessly. That way lay panic and defeat. I stood stock-still and forced myself to think, calmly, dispassionately. I had been looking in all the most obvious places. But should I have been looking in the obvious places? After all, I'd gone through this cabin once before, looking for a radio; I'd gone through it pretty thoroughly, and I hadn't seen any signs. He would have it hidden; of course he would have it hidden. He wouldn't have taken a chance on anyone finding it, such as the steward whose daily duty it was to clean out his cabin, before his men had taken over the ship. No stewards on duty now, of course, but then he probably hadn't bothered to shift it since the take-over. Where would he have hidden it where a steward wouldn't stumble across it?

That ruled out all the furniture fittings, all the places I'd wasted time in searching. It also ruled out bed, blankets, mattresses—but not the carpet! The ideal hiding place for a sheet of paper.

I almost threw myself at the carpet in his sleeping cabin. The carpets in the *Campari*'s accommodation were secured by press-button studs for ease of quick removal. I caught the corner of the carpet by the door, ripped free a dozen studs, and there it was right away, six inches in from the edge. A large sheet of canvas paper, folded in four, with "T.E.S. *Fort Ticonderoga*. Most Secret" printed in one corner. Five minutes to go.

I stared at the paper until I had memorised its exact position relative to the carpet, picked it up, and smoothed it out. Diagrams of the *Ticonderoga* with complete stowage plans of the cargo. But all I was interested in was the deck cargo. The plan showed crates stacked on both fore and aft decks, and twenty of those on the foredeck were marked with a heavy red cross. Red for gold.

In a small careful hand Carreras had written on the side: "All deck cargo crates identical in size. Gold in waterproof, kapok-filled welded steel boxes to float free in event of damage or sinking. Each crate equipped with yellow water stain." I supposed this was some chemical which, when it came into contact with salt water, would stain the sea for a wide area around. I read on: "Gold crates indistinguishable from general cargo. All crates stamped 'Harmsworth & Holden Electrical Engineering Company.' Stated contents generators and turbines. For'ard-deck cargo consigned to Nashville, Tennessee, exclusively turbines; afterdeck cargo consigned to Oak

Ridge, Tennessee, exclusively generators. So marked. For'ard twenty crates on for'ard deck gold."

I didn't hurry. Time was desperately short, but I didn't hurry. I studied the plan, which corresponded exactly to Carreras' observations, and I studied the observations themselves until I knew I would never forget a word of them. I folded and replaced the plan exactly as I had found it, pressed the carpet snap studs back into place, went swiftly through the cabins on a last check to ensure that I had left no trace of my passing: there were none that I could see. I locked the door and left.

The cold, driving rain was falling more heavily than ever now, slanting in across the port side, drumming metallically against the bulkheads, rebounding ankle-high off the polished wooden decks. On the likely enough theory that Carreras' patrolling men would keep to the sheltered starboard side of the acommodation, I kept to the opposite side as I hurried aft: in my stockinged soles and wearing that black suit and mask no one could have heard or seen me at a distance of more than a few feet. No one heard or saw me; I heard or saw no one. I made no attempt to look, listen, or exercise any caution at all. I reached number four hold within two minutes of leaving Carreras' cabin.

I needn't have hurried. Carreras had made no attempt to replace the tarpaulin he'd had to pull back in order to remove the battens, and I could see straight down into the bottom of the hold. Four men down there, two holding powerful electric lanterns, Carreras with a gun hanging by his side, the lanky stooped form of Dr. Slingsby Caroline, still wearing that ridiculous white wig askew on his head, bent over the Twister. I couldn't see what he was doing.

It was like a nineteenth-century print of grave robbers at work. The tomblike depths of the hold, the coffins, the lanterns, the feeling of apprehension and hurry and absorbed concentration that lent an evilly conspiratorial air to the scene—all the elements were there. And especially the element of tension, an electric tension you could almost feel pulsating through the darkness of the night. But a tension that came not from the fear of discovery but from the possibility that at any second something might go finally and cataclysmically wrong. If it took ten minutes to arm the Twister, and obviously it took even longer than that, then it must be a very tricky and complicated procedure altogether. Dr. Caroline's mind, it was a fair guess, would be in no fit state to cope with tricky and complicated procedures: he'd be nervous, probably badly scared; his hands would be unsteady; he was working, probably with inadequate tools, on an unstable platform by the light of unsteady torches, and even though he might not be desperate enough or fool enough to jinx it deliberately, there seemed to me, as there obviously seemed to the men down in the hold, that there was an excellent chance that his hand would slip. Instinctively I moved back a couple of feet until the opening of the hatch came between me and the scene below. I couldn't see the Twister any more, so that made me quite safe if it blew up.

I rose to my feet and made a couple of cautious circuits of the hatch, the first close in, the second further out. But Carreras had no prowlers there: apart from the guards on the gun, the afterdeck appeared to be completely deserted. I returned to the port for'ard corner of the hatch and settled down to wait.

I hoped I wouldn't have to wait too long. The sea water had been cold; the heavy rain was cold; the wind was cold; I was soaked to the skin and was recurringly and increasingly subject to violent bouts of shivering, shivering I could do nothing to control. The fever ran fiercely in my blood. Maybe the thought of Dr. Caroline's hand slipping had something to do with the shivering: whatever the reason, I'd be lucky to get off with no more than pneumonia.

Another five minutes, and I took a second cautious peek down into the hold. Still at it. I rose, stretched, and began to pace softly up and down to ward off the stiffness and cramp that was settling down on my body, especially on the legs. If things went the way I hoped I couldn't afford to have stiffness anywhere.

If things went the way I hoped. I peered down a third time into the hold and this time stayed in that stooped position, unmoving. Dr. Caroline had finished. Under the watchful eye and gun of the radio operator, he was screwing the brass-topped lid back on the coffin while Carreras and the other man had the lid already off the next coffin and were bent over it, presumably fusing the conventional explosive inside; probably it was intended as a stand-by in case of the malfunction of the Twister or, even more probably, in the event of the failure of the Twister's timing mechanism, it was designed to set it off by sympathetic detonation. I didn't know, I couldn't guess. And for the moment I was not in the slightest worried. The crucial moment had come.

The crucial moment for Dr. Caroline. I knew—as he was bound to know—that they couldn't afford to let him live. He'd done all they required of him. He was of no further use to them. He could die any moment now. If they chose to put a gun to his head and murder him where he stood, there was nothing in the world I could do about it, nothing I would even try to do about it. I would just have to stand there silently, without movement or protest, and watch him die. For if I let Dr. Caroline die without making any move to save him, then only he would die; but if I tried to save him and failed—and with only a knife and marlinespike against two submachine guns and pistols the chances of failure were 100 per cent—then not only Caroline but every member of the passengers and crew of the *Campari* would die also. The greatest good of the greatest number . . . Would they shoot him where he stood or would they do it on the upper deck?

Logic said they would do it on the upper deck. Carreras would be using the *Campari* for a few days yet; he wouldn't be wanting a dead man lying in the hold, and there would be no point in shooting him down there and then carrying him up above when he could make the climb under his own steam and be disposed of on the upper deck. If I were Carreras, that is what I would have figured.

And that was how he did figure. Caroline tightened the last screw, laid down the screw driver, and straightened. I caught a glimpse of his face, white, strained, one eye twitching uncontrollably. The radio operator said, "Señor Carreras?"

Carreras straightened, turned, looked at him, then at Caroline, and nodded.

"Take him to his cabin, Carlos. Report here afterwards."

I moved back swiftly as a torch shone vertically upwards from the hold. Carlos was already climbing the ladder. "Report here afterwards." God, I'd never thought of so obvious a possibility! For a moment I panicked, hands clenched on my pitiful weapons, irresolute, paralysed in thought and action. Without any justification whatsoever I'd had the picture firmly in mind of being able to dispose of Caroline's appointed executioner without arousing suspicion. Had Carlos, the radio operator, been under instructions to knock off the unsuspecting Caroline on the way for'ard, then carry on himself to his wireless office, then I might have disposed of him, and hours might have passed before Carreras got suspicious. But now he was in effect saying, "Take him up top, shove him over the side, and come back and tell me as soon as you have done so."

I could see the heavy rain slanting whitely through the wavering torch beam as Carlos climbed swiftly up the ladder. By the time he reached the top I was round the other side of the hatch coaming, lying flat on the deck.

Cautiously I hitched an eye over the top of the coaming. Carlos was standing upright on the deck now, his torch shining downwards into the hold. I saw Dr. Caroline's white head appear, saw Carlos move back a couple of steps, and then Caroline, too, was over the top, a tall, hunched figure, pulling high his collar against the cold lash of the rain. I heard, but failed to understand, a quick, sharp command, and then they were moving off diagonally, Caroline leading, Carlos with his torch on him from behind, in the direction of the companionway leading up to "B" deck.

I rose to my feet, remained immobile. Was Carlos taking him back to his cabin after all? Had I been mistaken? Could it be—

I never finished the thought. I was running after them as quickly, as lightly, as silently as the stiffness in my left leg would permit. Of course Carlos was taking him in the direction of the companionway; had he marched him straight towards the rail Caroline would have known at once what awaited him, would have turned and hurled himself against Carlos with all the frantic savagery of a man who knows he is about to die.

Five seconds, only five seconds elapsed from the time I started running until I caught up with them. Five seconds, far too short a time to think of the suicidal dangers involved; far too short to think what would happen if Carlos should swing his torch round, if any of the three guards at the gun should happen to be watching this little procession, if either Carreras or his assistant in the hold should choose to look over the coaming to see how the problem of disposal was being attended to, far too little time to figure out what I was going to do when I caught up with Carlos.

And I was given no time to figure. I was only three or four feet away-when, in the backwash of light from the torch, I saw Carlos reverse his grip on his Tommy gun, catch it by the barrel, swing it up high over his head. It had reached its highest point and was just started on the downswing when the bast of the heavy marlinespike caught him on the back of the neck with all my weight and fury behind it. I heard something crack, caught the Tommy gun out of his suddenly nerveless hand before it could crash to the deck, and made a grab for the torch. I missed. The torch struck the deck with a muffled thud—it must have been a ship's rubber-composition issue—rolled over a couple of times, and came to rest, its beam shining straight out over the edge of the ship. Carlos himself pitched heavily forward, struck Dr. Caroline, and the two of them fell against the lower steps of the companionway.

"Keep quiet!" I whispered urgently. "Keep quiet if you want to live!" I dived for the torch, fumbled desperately for the switch, couldn't find it, stuck the glass face against my jacket to kill the beam, finally located the switch and turned it off.

"What in heaven's name—"

"Keep *quiet!*" I found the trigger on the automatic pistol and stood there stock-still, staring aft into the darkness, in the direction of both the hold and the gun, striving to pierce the darkness, listening as if my life depended on it. Which it did. Ten seconds I waited. I had to move, I couldn't afford to wait another ten seconds. Thirty seconds would have been enough and more for Carlos to dispose of Dr. Caroline: a few seconds after that and Carreras would start wondering what had happened to his trusty henchman.

I thrust gun and torch towards Caroline, found his hands in the darkness. "Hold these," I said softly.

"What—what *is* this?" An agonised whisper in the dark.

"He was going to smash your head in. Now shut up. You can still die. I'm Carter, the chief officer." I'd pulled Carlos clear of the companionway where he'd held Caroline pinned by the legs and was going through his pockets as quickly as I could in the darkness. The key. The key to the wireless office. I'd seen him take it from his right-hand trouser pocket, but it wasn't there any more. The left-hand one. Not there either. The seconds were rushing by. Desperately I tore at the patch pockets of his army-type blouse, and I found it in the second pocket. But I'd lost at least twenty seconds.

"Is—is he dead?" Caroline whispered.

"Are you worried? Stay here." I shoved the key into a safe inner pocket, caught the guard by his collar, and started to drag him across the wet deck. It was less than ten feet to the ship's rail. I dropped him, located the hinged section of the teak rail, fumbled for the catch, released it, swung the rail through 180 degrees, and snapped it back in its open position. I caught the guard by his shoulders, eased the upper part of his body over the second rail, then tipped the legs high. The splash he made couldn't have been heard thirty feet away. Certainly no one in number four hold or under the gun tarpaulin could possibly have heard anything.

I ran back to where Dr. Caroline was sitting on the lower steps of the companionway. Maybe he was just obeying the order I'd given him, but probably he was just too dazed to move anyway. I said, "Quick, give me your wig."

"What? What?" My second guess had been right. He *was* dazed.

"Your *wig!*" It's no easy feat to shout in a whisper, but I almost made it.

"My wig? But—but it's glued on."

I leaned forward, twisted my fingers in the temporary thatch, and tugged. It was glued on all right. The gasp of pain and the resistance offered to my hand showed he hadn't been kidding: that wig felt as if it was riveted to his skull. It was no night for half measures. I clamped my left hand over his mouth and pulled savagely with my right. A limpet the size of a soup plate couldn't have offered more resistance, but it did come off. I don't know how much pain there was in it for him, but it certainly cost me plenty: his teeth almost met through the heel of my palm.

The machine gun was still in his hand. I snatched it away, whirled, and stopped, motionless. For the second time in a minute I could see rain slanting whitely through the vertical beam of a torch. That meant only one thing: someone was climbing up the ladder from the bottom of the hold.

I reached the ship's side in three long steps, placed the wig in the scuppers, laid the gun on top of it, raced back to the companionway, jerked Dr. Caroline to his feet, and dragged him towards the bo'sun's store, less than ten feet inboard from the companionway. The door was still less than halfway shut when Carreras appeared over the coaming, but his torch wasn't pointing in our direction. I closed the door silently until only a crack remained.

Carreras was closely followed by another man, also with a torch. Both of them headed for the ship's side. I saw the beam of Carreras' torch suddenly steady on the opened rail, then heard the sharp exclamation as he bent forward and peered in the scuppers. A moment later he was erect again, examining the gun and the wig he held in his hand. I heard him say something short and staccato, repeated several times. Then he started talking rapidly to his companion, but it was in Spanish and I couldn't get it. He then examined the inside of the wig, indicated something with the torch beam, shook his head in what might have been sorrow but was more probably exasperated anger, flung the wig over the side, and returned to the hold, taking the Tommy gun with him. His companion followed.

"Our friend didn't seem too happy," I murmured.

"He's a devil, a devil!" Dr. Caroline's voice was shaking; only now was he beginning to realise the narrowness of his escape, how closely death had brushed him by. "You heard him. One of his own men dead and all he could call him was a crazy fool, and he just laughed when the other man suggested they turn the ship to look for him."

"You understand Spanish?"

"Pretty well. He said something like: 'Just like that sadistic so-and-so to force Caroline to open the rail so that he could see what was coming to him.' He thinks I turned on the guard, grabbed his gun, and that in the fight, before we both went overboard, my wig was torn off. There was a handful of my hair sticking to the underside of the wig, he says."

"Sorry about that, Dr. Caroline."

"Good God, sorry! You saved both our lives. Mine anyway. Sorry!" Dr. Caroline, I thought, was a pretty strong-nerved person; he was recovering fast from the shock. I hoped his nerves were *very* strong indeed; he was going to need them all to survive the ordeal of the next few hours. "It was that handful of hair that really convinced him."

I said nothing, and he went on: "Please tell me exactly what is going on."

For the next five minutes, while I kept watch through that crack in the doorway, Dr. Caroline plied me with questions and I answered them as quickly and briefly as I could. He had a highly intelligent, incisive mind, which I found vaguely surprising, which in turn was a stupid reaction on my part: you don't pick a dim-wit as the chief of development for a new atomic weapon. I supposed his rather comical-sounding name and the brief glimpse I'd had of him the previous night—a man bound hand and foot to a four-poster and looking into a torch beam with wide and staring eyes looks something less than his best —had unconsciously given me the wrong impression entirely. At the end of the five minutes he knew as much about the past developments as I did myself; what he didn't know was what was to come, for I hadn't the heart to tell him. He was giving me some details of his kidnap when Carreras and his companion appeared.

They replaced battens, tied the tarpaulins, and went for'ard without any delay. That meant, I supposed, that the fusing of the auxiliary time bombs in the other two coffins was complete. I unwrapped the torch from its oilskin covering, looked round the store, picked up a few tools, and switched off the light.

"Right," I said to Caroline. "Come on."

"Where?" He wasn't keen to go anywhere, and after what he'd been through I didn't blame him.

"Back down that hold. Hurry. We may have little enough time."

Two minutes later, with the battens and tarpaulin pulled back into place as well as possible above us, we were on the floor of the hold. I needn't have bothered bringing any tools; Carreras had left his behind him, scattered carelessly round. Understandably he hadn't bothered to remove them: he would never be using those tools again.

I gave Caroline the torch to hold, selected a screw driver, and started on the lid of the brass-plaqued coffin.

"What are you going to do?" Caroline asked nervously.

"You can see what I'm doing."

"For pity's sake be careful! That weapon is armed!"

"So it's armed. It's not due to go until when?"

"Seven o'clock. But it's unsafe, highly unsafe. It's as unstable as hell. Good God, Carter, I know. I know!" His unsteady hand was on my arm, his face contorted with anxiety. "The development on this missile wasn't fully completed when it was stolen. The fuse mechanism was

only in an untried experimental state, and tests showed
that the retaining spring on a trembler switch is far too
weak. The Twister is dead safe normally, but this trembler
switch is brought into circuit as soon as it is armed."

"And?"

"A jar, a knock, the slightest fall—anything could overcome the tension of the spring and short-circuit the firing
mechanism. Fifteen seconds later the bomb goes up."

I hadn't noticed until then, but it was much warmer
down in that hold than it had been on deck. I raised a
soaking sleeve in a half-witted attempt to wipe some sweat
off my forehead.

"Have you told Carreras this?" The warmth was also
affecting my voice, bringing it out as a harsh, strained
croak.

"I told him. He won't listen. I think—I think Carreras
is a little mad. More than a little. He seems perfectly prepared to take a chance. And he has the Twister tightly
packed in cotton wool and blankets to eliminate the possibility of a jar."

I gazed at him for a long moment without really seeing
him, then got on with the next screw. It seemed much
stiffer than the last one, but it was just possible that I
wasn't applying so much pressure as I had been before.
For all that I had all the screws undone inside three minutes. Gently I slid off the lid, placed it to one side, slowly
peeled back a couple of blankets, and there lay the
Twister. It looked more evil than ever.

I stood up, took the torch from Caroline, and said,
"Armed, eh?"

"Of course."

"There are your tools. Disarm the bloody thing."

He stared at me, his face suddenly empty of expression.
"That's why we're here?"

"Why else? Surely it was obvious? Get on with it."

"It can't be done."

"It can't be done?" I caught him by the arm, not gently.
"Look friend, you armed the damned thing. Just reverse
the process, that's all."

"Impossible." Finality in the voice. "When it's armed, the mechanism is locked in position. With a key. The key is in Carreras' pocket."

Chapter 11

THE WEAKNESS in my left leg, a near-paralysing weakness, hit me all of a sudden and I had to sit down on the baffle and hang on to the ladder for support. I gazed down at the Twister. For a long time I gazed down at it, with bitter eyes, then I stirred and looked at Dr. Caroline.

"Would you mind repeating that?"

He repeated it. "I'm terribly sorry, Carter, but there you have it. The Twister can't be rendered safe without the key. And Carreras has the key."

I thought of all the impossible solutions to this one and recognised them at once for what they were—impossible. I knew what had to be done now, the only thing that could be done. I said, tiredly, "Do you know, Dr. Caroline, that you've just condemned forty people to certain death?"

"I have done that?"

"Well, Carreras. When he put that key in his pocket he was condemning himself and all his men to death just as surely as the man who pulls the switch for the electric chair. And what am I worrying about, anyway? Death's the only certain and permanent cure for scourges like Carreras and the people who associate with him. As for Lord

235

Dexter, he's rolling in the stuff. He can always build another *Campari*."

"What are you talking about, Mr. Carter?" There was apprehension in his voice as he looked at me; more than apprehension, fear. "Are you feeling all right, Carter?"

"Of course I'm all right," I said irritably. "Everybody's always asking the same stupid question." I stooped, picked up the rope grommet and Haltrac midget hoist I'd taken from the bo'sun's store, then rose wearily to my feet. "Come on, Doctor, give me a hand with this."

"Give you a hand with what?" He knew damned well what I meant but the fear in his mind wouldn't let him believe it.

"The Twister, of course," I said impatiently. "I want to get it over to the port side, hidden in the tarpaulins behind the baffle."

"Are you crazy?" he whispered. "Are you quite crazy? Did you hear what I said? You're going to lift it out of its coffin with—with that? One little slip, the tiniest jar—"

"Are you going to help me?"

He shook his head, shuddered, and turned away. I hooked the hoist on to a head-high rung of the ladder, pulled the lower block until it hung just above the Twister, picked up the grommet, and moved round to the tail of the weapon. I was stooping low over it when I heard a quick footstep behind me and a pair of arms locked themselves round my body, arms informed with all the strength of fear and desperation. I struggled briefly to free myself but I might as well have tried to shrug off the tentacles of a squid. I tried to stamp on his instep but all I did was hurt my heel: I'd forgotten that I wasn't wearing shoes.

"Let go!" I said savagely. "What the hell do you think you're doing?"

"I'm not going to let you do it! I'm not going to let you do it!" He was panting, his voice low and hoarse and desperate. "I'm not going to let you kill us all!"

There are certain people in certain situations with whom there is no arguing. This was such a situation and Caroline such a person. I half turned, thrust backwards with all the power of my good leg, and heard him gasp as his back struck heavily against the ship's side. A momentary loosening of his grip, a wrench, and I was free. I picked up the big marlinespike and showed it to him in the light of the torch.

"I don't want to use this," I said quietly. "Next time I will. My promise. Can't you stop shaking long enough to realise that I'm trying to save all our lives, not throw them away? Don't you realise that anyone might pass by up top any moment, see the loose tarpaulin, and investigate?"

He stood there, hunched against the metal, staring down at the floor. He said nothing. I turned, took the torch in my teeth, placed the grommet on the edge of the coffin, and bent down to lift the tail of the Twister. Or to try to lift it. It weighed a ton. To me it did, anyway; what with one thing and another I wasn't as fit as I had been. I'd managed to lift it perhaps three inches and didn't see how I was going to hold it there for even a couple of seconds, when I heard a footstep and a kind of moan behind me. I tensed, braced myself for the next assault, then relaxed slowly as Dr. Caroline stepped past me, bent down, and slid the grommet round the tail of the Twister. Together we managed to move the grommet up to approximately the mid-point of the missile. Neither of us said anything.

I hauled on the Haltrac pulley until it became taut. Dr. Caroline said hoarsely, "It'll never take it. That thin cord—"

"It's tested to a thousand pounds." I hauled some more and the tail began to lift. The grommet wasn't central. I lowered it again, the grommet was adjusted, and next time I hauled the Twister came clear along its entire length. When it was about three inches above its cotton-wool and blanket bed, I set the autolock. I mopped my forehead again. It was warmer than ever down in that hold.

"How are you going to get it across to the other side?" Caroline's voice had lost its shake now; it was flat and without inflection, the voice of a man resigned to the dark inevitability of a nightmare.

"We'll carry it across. Between us we should manage it."

"Carry it across?" he said dully. "It weighs two hundred and seventy-five pounds."

"I know what it weighs," I said irritably.

"You have a bad leg." He hadn't heard me. "My heart's not good. The ship's rolling; you can see that that polished aluminium is as slippery as glass. One of us would stumble, lose his grip. Maybe both of us. It would be bound to fall."

"Wait here," I said. I took the torch, crossed to the port side, picked up a couple of tarpaulins from behind the baffle, and dragged them across the floor. "We'll place it on these and pull it across."

"Pull it across the floor? *Bump* it across the floor?" He wasn't as resigned to the nightmare as I had thought. He looked at me, then at the Twister, then at me again, and said with unshakeable conviction, "You're mad."

"Oh, for God's sake, can't you think of anything else to say?" I grabbed the pulley again, released the lock, hauled and kept on hauling. Caroline wrapped both arms round the Twister as it came clear of the coffin, struggling to make sure that the nose of the missile didn't collide with the baffle.

"Step over the baffle and take it with you," I said. "Keep your back to the ladder as you turn."

He nodded silently, his face strained and set in the pale beam of the torch. He put his back to the ladder, tightened his grip on the Twister, an arm on each side of the grommet, lifted his leg to clear the baffle, then staggered as a sudden roll of the ship threw the weight of the missile against him. His foot caught the top of the baffle; the combined forces of the Twister and the ship's roll carried him beyond his centre of gravity; he cried out and overbalanced heavily across the baffle to the floor of the hold.

I'd seen it coming—or, rather, I'd seen the last second of it happening. I swept my hand up blindly, hit the autolock, and jumped for the swinging missile, throwing myself between it and the ladder, dropping my torch as I reached out with both hands to prevent the nose from crashing into the ladder. In the sudden impenetrable darkness I missed the Twister—but it didn't miss me. It struck me just below the breastbone with a force that brought an agonised gasp from me; then I'd both arms wrapped round that polished aluminium shell as if I were going to crush it in half.

"The torch," I yelled. Somehow in that moment it didn't seem in any way important that I should keep down my voice. "Get the torch!"

"My ankle—"

"The hell with your ankle! Get the torch!"

I heard him give a half-supressed moan, then sensed that he was clambering over the baffle. I heard him again, his hands scuffing over the steel floor. Then silence.

"Have you found it?" The *Campari* had started on its return roll and I was fighting to keep my balance.

"I've found it."

"Then switch it on, you fool!"

"I can't." A pause. "It's broken."

That helped a lot. I said quickly, "Catch hold of the end of this damned thing. I'm slipping."

He did, and the strain eased. He said, "Have you any matches?"

"Matches!" Carter showing inhuman restraint; if it hadn't been for the Twister it would have been funny. "Matches! After being towed through the water for five minutes alongside the *Campari?*"

"I hadn't thought of that," he said gravely. A few moments' silence, then he offered, "I have a lighter."

"God help America," I said fervently. "If all her scientists—light it, man, light it!"

A wheel scraped on flint and a flickering pool of pale yellow light did its pitiful best to illuminate that one tiny corner of the dark hold.

"The block and tackle. Quickly." I waited until he had reached it. "Take the strain on the free end, knock off the lock, and lower gently. I'll guide it on to the tarpaulins."

I moved out half a step from the baffle, taking much of the weight of the missile with me. I was barely a couple of feet away from the tarpaulins when I heard the click of the autolock coming off and suddenly my back was breaking. The pulley had gone completely slack; the entire two hundred and seventy-five pounds of the Twister was in my arms; the *Campari* was rolling away from me; I couldn't hold it, I knew I couldn't hold it, my back *was* breaking. I staggered and lurched forward, and the Twister, with myself above and still slinging desperately to it, crashed heavily on to the tarpaulins with a shock that seemed to shake the entire floor of the hold.

I freed my arms and climbed shakily to my feet. Dr. Caroline, the flickering flame held just at the level of his eyes, was staring down at the gleaming missile like a man held in thrall, his face a frozen mask of all the terrible emotions he'd ever known. Then the spell broke.

"Fifteen seconds!" he shouted hoarsely. "Fifteen seconds to go!" He flung himself at the ladder but got no further than the second step when I locked arms round both himself and the ladder. He struggled violently, frantically, briefly, then relaxed.

"How far do you think you're going to get in fifteen seconds?" I said. I don't know why I said it, I was barely aware that I had said it. I had eyes and mind only for the missile lying there; my face probably showed all the emotions that Dr. Caroline's had been registering. And he was staring too. It was a senseless thing to do, but for the moment we were both senseless men. Staring at the Twister to see what was going to happen, as if we would ever see anything; neither eyes nor ears nor mind would have the slightest chance in the world of registering anything before that blinding nuclear flash annihilated us, vaporised us, blew the *Campari* out of existence.

Ten seconds passed. Twelve. Fifteen. Twenty. Half a minute. I eased my aching lungs—I hadn't drawn breath in all that time—and my grip round Caroline and the ladder. "Well," I said, "how far *would* you have got?"

Dr. Caroline climbed slowly down the two steps to the floor of the hold, dragged his gaze away from the missile, looked at me for a long moment with uncomprehending eyes, then smiled. "Do you know, Mr. Carter, the thought never even occurred to me." His voice was quite steady and his smile wasn't the smile of a crazy man. Dr. Caroline had *known* that he was going to die and then he hadn't died and nothing would ever be quite so bad again. He had found that the valley of fear does not keep on going down forever: somewhere there is a bottom, then a man starts climbing again.

"You grab the trailing rope first and *then* release the autolock," I said reproachfully. If I was lightheaded, who was to blame me? "Not the other way round. You might remember next time."

There are some things for which to make an apology is impossible, so he didn't even try. He said regretfully, "I'm afraid I'll never make a sailorman. But at least we know now that the retaining spring on the trembler switch is not as weak as we had feared." He smiled wanly. "Mr. Carter, I think I'll have a cigarette."

"I think I'll join you," I said.

After that it was easy—well, relatively easy. We still treated the Twister with the greatest respect—had it struck at some other angle it might indeed have detonated—but not with respect exaggerated to the extent of tiptoeing terror. We dragged it on its tarpaulin across to the other side of the hold, transferred the Haltrac hoist to the corresponding ladder on the port side, arranged a couple of spare tarpaulins and blankets from the coffin to make a cushioned bed for the Twister between baffle and ship's side, hoisted the missile across the baffle without any of the acrobatics that had accompanied the last transfer, lowered it into position, pulled over the blankets, and covered it completely with the tarpaulins on which we had dragged it across the floor.

"It'll be safe here?" Dr. Caroline enquired. He seemed almost back to what I should have imagined his normal self to be, except for the hurried breathing, the cold sweat on his brow and face.

"They'll never see it. They'll never even think to look here. Why should they?"

"What do you propose to do now?"

"Leave with all possible speed. I've played my luck far enough. But first the coffin—must weight it to compensate for the absence of the Twister, then batten down the lid again."

"And then where do we go?"

"You're not going anywhere. You're staying here." I explained to him just why he had to stay there, and he didn't like it one little bit. I explained to him some more, pointed out carefully, so that he couldn't fail to understand, that his only chance of life depended on his staying there, and he still didn't like it any more. But he saw that it had to be done, and the fear of certain death eventually outweighed the very understandable and almost hysterical panic my suggestion had caused him. And after that fifteen-second lifetime when we had waited for the Twister to detonate, nothing could ever seem so terrifying again.

Five minutes later I battened down the coffin lid for the last time, thrust the screw driver in my pocket, and left the hold.

The wind, I thought, had eased a little; the rain, beyond question, was heavier by far; even in the pitchy darkness of that night I could see the blur of whiteness round my stockinged feet as the heavy, wind-driven drops spattered on the iron decks and rebounded ankle-high.

I took my time making my way for'ard. There was no hurry any more, and now that the worst was behind I had no mind to destroy it all or destroy us all by undue haste. I was a black shadow, at one with the blackness of the night, and no ghost was ever half so quiet. Once two patrolling guards passed me by, going aft; once I passed a couple huddled miserably in the lee of "A" accommodation deck, seeking what little shelter they could from that cold rain. Neither pair saw me, neither even suspected my presence, which was just as it should have been. The dog never catches the hare, for lunch is less important than life.

I had no means of telling the time, but at least twenty minutes must have passed before I once more found myself outside the wireless office. Every major event in the past three days, right from the very first, had in some way or other stemmed from that wireless office: it seemed only fitting that it should also be the scene of the playing of the last card left in my hand.

The padlock was through the hasp and it was locked. That meant there was no one inside. I retreated to the shelter of the nearest boat and settled down to wait. The fact that there was no one in there didn't mean that there wasn't going to be someone there very soon. Tony Carreras had mentioned that their stooges on the *Ticonderoga* reported course and position every hour. Carlos, the man I'd killed, must have been waiting for just such a message, and if there was another report due through then it was a certainty that Carreras would have his other operator up to intercept it. At this penultimate state of the game he would be leaving nothing at all to chance. And, in the same state of the game, neither was I: the radio operator bursting in and finding me sitting in front of his transmitter was the last thing I could afford to have happen.

The rain drummed pitilessly on my bent back. I couldn't get any wetter than I was, but I could get colder. I got colder, very cold indeed, and within fifteen minutes I was shivering constantly. Twice guards padded softly by—Carreras was certainly taking no chances that night—and twice I made sure—was certain that they must find me, so violent was my shivering that I had to clamp my sleeve between my teeth to prevent the chattering from betraying me. But on both occasions the guards passed by, oblivious. The shivering became even worse. Would that damned radio operator never come? Or had I outsmarted myself, had I double-guessed and double-guessed wrongly? Perhaps the radio operator wasn't going to come at all?

I had been sitting on a coiled lifeboat fall and now I rose to my feet, irresolute. How long would I have to wait there before I would be convinced that he wasn't going to come? Or maybe he wasn't due for another hour yet, or more? Wherein lay the greater danger—risking going into the wireless office now with the ever-present possibility of being discovered and trapped in there, or waiting an hour, maybe two hours, before making my move, by which time it would almost certainly be too late anyway? Better a chance of failure, I thought, than the near certainty of it, and now that I'd left number four hold the only life which would be lost through my mistakes would be my own.

Now, I thought, I'll do it now. I took three silent steps, then no more. The radio operator had arrived. I took three silent steps back.

The click of a key turning in the padlock, the faint creak of the door, the metallic sound of it shutting, a faint gleam of light behind the curtained window. Our friend preparing to receive, I thought. He wouldn't stay long, that was a safe enough guess, just long enough to take down the latest details of course and speed of the *Ticonderoga*—unless the weather was radically different to the northeast it was most unlikely that the *Ticonderoga* could have fixed its position that night—and take it up to Carreras on the bridge. I presumed that Carreras would still be there; it would be entirely out of keeping with the man if, in those last few crucial hours, he didn't remain on the bridge and take personal charge of the entire operation as he had done throughout. I could just see him accepting the sheet of figures with the latest details of the *Ticonderoga*'s progress, smiling his smile of cold satisfaction, making his calculations on the chart . . .

My thoughts stopped dead right there. I felt as if someone had turned a master switch inside me and everything had seized up, heart, breathing, mind, and every organ of sensation; I felt as I had felt during those dreadful fifteen seconds while Dr. Caroline and I had waited for the Twister to blow up. I felt that way because there had abruptly, paralysingly flashed on me the realisation that would have come to me half an hour ago if I hadn't been so busy commiserating with myself on the misery I was suffering. Whatever else Carreras had not established himself as—and there were many things—he had established himself as a consistent, prudent, and methodical man, and he'd never yet worked out any chart problems on figures supplied him without coming to have a check made by his trusty navigator, Chief Officer John Carter.

My mind churned into low gear again, but it didn't make any difference. True, he'd sometimes waited some hours before having his check made, but he wouldn't be waiting some hours tonight because by then it would be far too late. We couldn't be more than three hours now from our rendezvous with the *Ticonderoga,* and he'd want a check made immediately. Waking up a sick man in the middle of the night would hardly be a consideration to worry Carreras. Nothing was surer than that within ten or fifteen minutes of that message coming through he'd be calling at the sick bay. To find his navigator gone. To find the door locked from the inside. To find MacDonald waiting with a gun in his hand. MacDonald had only one automatic; Carreras could call on forty men with submachine guns. There could only be one ending to any battle in the sick bay, and the end would be swift and certain and final. In my mind's eye I could just see stammering machine guns spraying the sick bay, could see MacDonald and Susan, Bullen and Marston—I crushed down the thought, forced it from my mind. That way lay defeat.

When the radio operator left the office, *if* I got inside unseen, *if* I was left undisturbed to send off the message, how long would that leave me to get back to the sick bay? Ten minutes, not any more than ten minutes, say seven or eight minutes to make my way undetected right aft to the port side where I had left the three ropes tied to the guardrail stanchion, secure one to myself, grab the life line, give the signal to the bo'sun, lower myself into the water, and then make the long half-drowning trip back to the sick bay. Ten minutes? Eight? I knew I could never do it in double that time; if my trip from the sick bay to the afterdeck through that water had been any criterion, the trip back, against instead of with the current, would be at least twice as bad, and the first trip had been near enough the end of me. Eight minutes? The chances were high I'd never get back there at all.

Or the radio operator? I could kill the radio operator as he left the office. I was desperate enough to try anything and frantic enough to have a fair chance of success. Even with patrolling guards round. That way Carreras would never get the message. But he would be waiting for it; oh yes, he would be waiting for it. He would be very anxious indeed to have that last check, and if it didn't come within minutes he was going to send someone to investigate, and when that someone found the operator was dead or missing, the balloon would be up with a vengeance. Guards running here, guards running there, lights on all over the ship, every possible source of trouble investigated —and that still included the sick bay. And MacDonald would still be there. With his gun.

There was a way. It was a way that gave little enough hope of success, with the added drawback that I would be forced to leave those three incriminating ropes attached to the guardrail aft; but at least it didn't carry with it an outright guarantee of failure.

I stooped, felt for the coiled fall rope, cut it with my clasp knife. One end of the rope I secured to my waist with a bowline; the rest of it, about sixty feet, I wrapped round my waist, tucking the end in. I fumbled for and found the radio office key that I'd taken off the dead Carlos. I stood in the rain and the darkness and waited.

A minute elapsed, no more, then the radio operator appeared, locked the door behind him, and made for the companionway leading up to the bridge. Thirty seconds later I was sitting in the seat he'd just vacated, looking up the call sign of the *Fort Ticonderoga*.

I made no attempt to hide my presence there by leaving the light off. That would only have aroused the suspicions, and quickly, too, of any passing guards hearing the stutter of transmitted Morse coming from a darkened wireless office.

Twice I tapped out the call sign of the *Ticonderoga* and on the second occasion I got an acknowledgement. One of Carreras' radio operator stooges aboard the *Ticonderoga* was certainly keeping a pretty sharp watch. I should have expected nothing else.

It was a brief message, speeded on its way by the introductory words: HIGHEST PRIORITY URGENT IMMEDIATE REPEAT IMMEDIATE ATTENTION MASTER FORT TICONDEROGA. I sent the message and took the liberty of signing it: FROM THE OFFICE OF THE MINISTER OF TRANSPORT BY THE HAND OF VICE-ADMIRAL RICHARD HODSON DIRECTOR NAVAL OPERATIONS. I switched off the light, opened the door, and peered out cautiously. No curious listeners, no one at all in sight. I came all the way out, locked the padlock, and threw the key over the side.

Thirty seconds later I was on the port side of the boat deck, carefully gauging, as best I could in that darkness and driving rain, the distance from where I stood to the break in the fo'c'sle. About thirty feet, I finally estimated, and the distance from the fo'c'sle break aft to the window above my bed was, I guessed, about the same. If I was right, I should be almost directly above that window now; the sick bay was three decks below. If I wasn't right—well, I'd better be right.

I checked the knot round my waist, passed the other end of the rope round a convenient arm of a davit, and let it hang down loosely over the side. I was just about to start lowering myself when the rope below me smacked wetly against the ship's side and went taut. Someone had caught that rope and hauled it tight.

Panic touched me, but the instinct for self-preservation still operated independently of my mind. I flung an arm round the davit and locked on to the wrist of the other hand. Anyone wanting to pull me over the side would have to pull that davit and lifeboat along with me. But as long as that pressure remained on the rope I couldn't escape, couldn't free a hand to untie the bowline or get at my clasp knife.

The pressure eased. I fumbled for the knot, then stopped as the pressure came on again. But the pressure was only momentary, no pull but a tug. Four tugs, in rapid succession. If I wasn't feeling weak enough already, I'd have felt that way with relief. Four tugs. The prearranged signal with MacDonald to show I was on my way back. I might have known Archie MacDonald would have been keeping watch every second of the time I was away. He must have seen or heard or even felt the rope snaking down past the window and guessed that it could only be myself. I went down that rope like a man reborn, checked suddenly as a strong hand caught me by the ankle, and five seconds later was on terra firma inside the sick bay.

"The ropes!" I said to MacDonald. I was already untying the one round my own waist. "The two ropes on the

bedstead. Off with them. Throw them out the window."
Moments later the last of the three ropes had vanished, I
was closing the window, pulling the curtains, and calling
softly for lights.

The lights came on. MacDonald and Bullen were as I
had left them, both eyeing me with expressionless faces:
MacDonald, because he knew my safe return meant at
least possible success and did not want to betray his
knowledge; Bullen, because I had told him that I intended
to take over the bridge by force, and he was convinced that
my method of return meant failure and didn't want to em-
barrass me. Susan and Marston were by the dispensary
door, both fully dressed, neither making any attempt to
conceal disappointment. No time for greetings.

"Susan, on with the heaters! Full on. This place feels
like a frig after this window being open so long. Carreras
will be here any minute and it's the first thing he will
notice. After that, towels for me. Doc, a hand to get Mac-
Donald back to his own bed. Move, man, move! And why
aren't you and Susan dressed for bed? If Carreras sees
you—"

"We were expecting the gentleman to come calling with
a gun," MacDonald reminded me. "You're frozen stiff,
Mr. Carter, blue with cold. And shivering like you were in
an icebox."

"I feel like it." We dumped MacDonald, none too
gently, on his bed, pulled up sheets and blankets, then I
tore off my clothes and started to towel myself dry. No
matter how I towelled, I couldn't stop the shivering.

"The key," MacDonald said sharply. "The key in the
sickbay door."

"God, yes!" I'd forgotten all about it. "Susan, will you?
Unlock it. And then to bed. Quickly! And you, Doctor."
I took the key from her, opened the window behind the
curtain, and flung the key out; the suit I had been wearing,
the socks, the wet towels followed in short order, but not
before I had remembered to remove the screw driver and
MacDonald's clasp knife from the jacket. I dried and
combed my hair into some sort of order—as orderly as
anyone could expect it to be after a few hours' sleeping in

bed—and helped Doc Marston as he swiftly changed the plaster on my head and wrapped splints and fresh bandages round the still soaking ones covering the wounds in my leg. Then the lights clicked off and the sick bay was once more in darkness.

"Have I forgotten anything, anybody?" I asked. "Anything that might show I've been out of here?"

"Nothing, I don't think there's anything." The bo'sun speaking. "I'm sure."

"The heaters?" I asked. "Are they on? It's freezing in here."

"It's not that cold, my boy," Bullen said in his husky whisper. "*You're* freezing, that's what. Marston, haven't you—"

"Hot-water bags," Marston said briskly. "Two of them. Here they are." He thrust them into my hands in the dark. "Had them all prepared for you; we suspected all that sea water and rain wouldn't do that fever of yours any good. And here's a glass to show your friend Carreras a few drops of brandy in the bottom to convince him how far through you are."

"You might have filled it," I complained.

"I did."

I emptied it. No question but that that neat brandy had a heating effect; it seemed to burn a hole through me all the way down to my stomach, but the only over-all effect it had was to make the rest of me seem colder than ever.

Then MacDonald's voice, quick and quiet: "Someone coming."

I'd time to fumble the empty glass on to the bedside table but time for nothing more, not even time to slide down to a lying position under the blankets. The door opened, the overhead lights clicked on, and Carreras, the inevitable chart under his arm, advanced across the sick bay towards my bed. As usual, he had his expressions and emotions under complete control: anxiety, tension, anticipation, all those must have been in his mind, and behind everything the memory of his lost son, but no trace showed.

He stopped a yard away and stared down at me, eyes speculative and narrowed and cold.

"Not asleep, Carter, eh?" he said slowly. "Not even lying down." He picked up the glass from the bedside table, sniffed it, and set it down again. "Brandy. And you're shivering, Carter. Shivering all the time. Why? Answer me!"

"I'm frightened," I said sourly. "Every time I see you I get terrified."

"Mr. Carreras!" Doc Marston had just appeared through the dispensary doorway, a blanket wrapped round him, his magnificent mane of white hair tousled in spendid disorder, rubbing the sleep from his eyes. "This is outrageous, completely outrageous. Disturbing this very sick boy—and at this hour. I must ask you to leave sir. And at once!"

Carreras looked him over from head to toe and back again, then said quietly and coldly, "Be quiet."

"I will *not* be quiet!" Doc Marston shouted. M.G.M. would have given him a life contract any day. "I'm a doctor; I've my duty as a doctor and, by God, I'm going to have my say as a doctor!" There was unfortunately no table at hand, otherwise he would have crashed down his fist on it, but even without the table banging it was a pretty impressive performance and Carreras was obviously taken aback by Marston's professional ire and outrage.

"Chief Officer Carter is a very sick man," Marston thundered on. "I haven't the facilities here to treat a compound fracture of the femur and the result was inevitable. Pneumonia, sir, pneumonia! In both lungs, so much fluid gathered already that he can't lie down, he can hardly breathe. Temperature 104, pulse 130, high fever, constant shivering. I've packed him with hot-water bottles, fed him drugs, aspirin, brandy, all to no effect. Fever just won't go down. One moment burning hot, the next soaking wet." He was right about the soaking wet bit anyway; I could feel the sea water from the sodden bandages seeping through to the mattress below. "For God's sake, Carreras, can't you *see* he's a sick man? Leave him be."

"I'll only keep him a moment, Doctor," Carreras said soothingly. Whatever faint stirrings of suspicion he might have had had been completely laid to rest by Marston's Oscar-winning performance. "I can see that Mr. Carter is unwell. But this will give him no trouble at all."

I was reaching for the chart and pencil even before he handed it to me. What with the constant shivering and the numbness that seemed to be spreading from my injured leg over my entire body the calculations took longer than usual, but they weren't difficult. I looked at the sick-bay clock and said, "You should be in position shortly before four A.M."

"We can't miss him, you would say, Mr. Carter?" He wasn't as confident and unworried as he looked. "Even in the dark?"

"With the radar going I don't see how you can." I wheezed some more so that he wouldn't forget to remember how sick I was and went on: "How do you propose to make the *Ticonderoga* stop?" I was as anxious as he was that contact should be established and transfers accomplished as quickly and smoothly as possible. The Twister in the hold was due to blow up at 7 A.M. I'd just as soon be a long distance away by that time.

"A shell across the bow and a signal to stop. If that doesn't work," he added reflectively, "a shell through the fo'c'sle."

"You really do surprise me, Carreras," I said slowly.

"Surprise you?" A barely perceptible lift of the left eyebrow, for Carreras a perfect riot of expression. "How so?"

"A man who has taken such infinite pains and, I must admit, shown such superb planning throughout—to throw it all away by such careless, haphazard action at the end." He made to speak, but I held up my hand and carried on: "I'm just as interested as you are in seeing that the *Fort Ticonderoga* is stopped. I don't give a tuppenny damn about the gold. I do know it's essential that Captain Bullen, the bo'sun, and I get to a first-class hospital immediately. I do want to see all the passengers and crew transferred to safety. I don't want to see any members of the *Ticonderoga*'s crew killed by gunfire. And, finally—"

"Get on with it," he interrupted coldly.

"Right. You intercept at five. In the present weather

conditions it'll be half light then—light enough to let the master of the *Fort Ticonderoga* see you approaching. When he sees another vessel closing in on him—with the whole width of the Atlantic to use to pass him by—he'll become immediately suspicious. After all, he *knows* he's carrying a fortune in gold. He'll turn and run for it. In the half-light, with poor visibility, falling rain, pitching decks, and a gun crew almost certainly untrained in naval gunnery, your chances of registering a hit on the small target presented by a target running away from you are pretty small. Not that that popgun I'm told you've mounted on the fo'c'sle will achieve very much anyway."

"No one could call the gun I've mounted on the after-deck a popgun, Mr. Carter." But for all the untroubled smoothness of the face, he was thinking plenty. "It's almost the equivalent of a 3.7."

"So what? You'll have to turn broadside on to bring that one to bear, and while you're turning, the *Ticonderoga* will be getting even further away from you. For the reasons already given, you'll almost certainly miss anyway. After the second shot those deck plates will probably be buckled to hell and gone. *Then* how do you propose to stop him? You can't make a fourteen-thousand-ton cargo ship stop just by waving a few Tommy guns at it."

"It will not come to that. There is an element of uncertainty in everything. But we shall not fail."

"There's no need for any element of uncertainty, Carreras."

"Indeed? How would you propose it should be done?"

"I think that's enough!" It was Captain Bullen who broke in, his husky voice heavy with all the weight and authority of the Commodore of the Blue Mail. "Doing chart work under pressure is one thing; voluntarily scheming to further this criminal's plans is another. I have been listening to all of this. Haven't you gone far enough, Mister?"

"Hell, no," I said. "I won't have gone far enough till all of us have gone all the way to the Navy Hospital in Hampton Roads. The thing's dead simple, Carreras. When he comes within a few miles on the radarscope, start firing off distress signals. At the same time—you'd better arrange this now—have your stooges on the *Ticonderoga* take a message to the master saying they've just picked up SOS signals from the *Campari*. When he comes nearer, send an Aldis message that you sprung engine-room plates coming through the hurricane, which he's bound to have heard of, that the *Campari*'s pumps can't cope, that you're beginning to sink, and that you want crew and passengers taken off." I smiled my wan smile. "The last part is true, anyway. When he's stopped alongside and you whip the tarpaulins off your guns—well, you have him. He can't and won't try to get away."

He stared at me without seeing me, then gave a small nod.

"I suppose it's out of the question to persuade you to become my—ah—lieutenant, Carter?"

"Just see me safe aboard the *Ticonderoga*, Carreras. That's all the thanks I want."

"That shall be done." He glanced at his watch. "In under three hours six of your crew will be here with stretchers to transfer Captain Bullen, the bo'sun, and yourself to the *Ticonderoga*."

He left. I looked round the sick bay; they were all there, Bullen and MacDonald in their beds, Susan and Marston by the dispensary door, both shawled in blankets. They were all looking at me and the expressions on their faces were very peculiar indeed, to say the least of it.

The silence went on and on for what seemed like a quite unnecessarily long time, then Bullen spoke, his voice slow and hard.

"Carreras has committed one act of piracy; he is about to commit another. By doing so he declares himself an enemy of Queen and country. You will be charged with giving aid and comfort to the enemy, with being directly responsible for the loss of a hundred and fifty million dollars in gold bullion. I shall take statements from witnesses present as soon as we get aboard the *Ticonderoga*." I couldn't blame the old man; he still believed in Carreras' promise as to our future safety. In his eyes I was just making things too damned easy for Carreras. But now wasn't the time to enlighten him.

"Oh, here," I said, "that's a bit hard, isn't it? Aiding, abetting, accessorying, if you like, but all this treason stuff—"

"Why did you do it?" Susan Beresford shook her head wonderingly. "Oh, why did you do it, helping him like that just to save your own neck?" And now wasn't the time to enlighten her either: neither she nor Bullen were actor enough to carry off their parts in the morning if they knew the whole truth.

"That's a bit hard, too," I protested. "Only a few hours ago there was no one keener than yourself to get away from the *Campari*. And now that—"

"I didn't want it done this way! I didn't know until now that there was a chance that the *Ticonderoga* could escape."

"I wouldn't have believed it, John," Dr. Marston said heavily. "I just wouldn't have believed it."

"It's all right for you to talk," I said. "You've all got families. I've only got myself. Can you blame me for wanting to look after all I have?"

No one took me up on this masterpiece of logical reasoning. I looked round them one by one, and they turned away one by one, Susan, Marston, and Bullen, not bothering to hide their expressions. And then MacDonald, too, turned away, but not before his left eyelid had dropped in a long, slow wink.

I eased myself down in bed and made up my mind for sleep. No one asked me how I got on that night.

Chapter 12

[Saturday 6 A.M.–7 A.M.]

WHEN I awoke I was stiff and sore and still shivering. But it wasn't the pain or the cold or the fever that had brought me up from the murky depths of that troubled sleep. It was noise, a series of grinding, creaking metallic crashes that echoed and shuddered throughout the entire length of the *Campari* as if she were smashing into an iceberg with every roll she took. I could tell from the slow, sluggish, lifeless roll that the stabilisers weren't working: the *Campari* was stopped, dead in the water.

"Well, Mister." Bullen's voice was a harsh grate. "Your plan worked, damn you. Congratulations. The *Ticonderoga*'s alongside."

"Alongside?"

"Right alongside," MacDonald confirmed. "Lashed alongside."

"In this weather?" I winced as the two ships rolled heavily together in the trough of a deep swell, and I heard the harsh tearing scream of sound as topsides metal buckled and rended under the staggering weight of the impact. "It'll ruin the paint work. The man's mad."

"He's in a hurry," MacDonald said. "I can hear the

jumbo winch aft. He's started transshiping cargo already."

"Aft?" I couldn't keep the note of excitement out of my voice, and everybody suddenly looked at me, curiosity in their eyes. "Aft? Are you sure?"

"I'm sure, sir."

"Are we tied bow to bow and stern to stern, or are we facing in opposite directions?"

"No idea." Both he and Bullen were giving me very close looks, but there was a difference in the quality of the closeness. "Does it matter, Mr. Carter?" He knew damned well it did.

"It doesn't matter," I said indifferently. Not much it didn't matter: only 150 million dollars, that was all it mattered.

"Where's Miss Beresford?" I asked Marston.

"With her folks," he said shortly. "Packing clothes. Your kind friend Carreras is allowing the passengers to take one suitcase apiece with them. He says they'll get the rest of their stuff back in due course—if anyone manages to pick up the *Campari* after he has abandoned it, that is."

It was typical, I thought, of the man's extraordinary thoroughness in all he did: by letting them pack some clothes and promising the eventual safe return of the remainder, he would eliminate from even the most suspicious minds the unworthy thought that perhaps his intentions towards the crew and passengers weren't of the highest and the noblest.

The phone rang. Marston picked it up, listened briefly, then hung up.

"Stretcher party in five minutes," he announced.

"Help me dress, please," I said. "My white uniform shorts and white shirt."

"You—you're not getting up?" Marston was aghast. "What if—"

"I'm getting up, dressing, and getting back to bed again," I said shortly. "Do you think I'm daft? What's Carreras going to think if he sees a man with a compound fracture of the thigh hopping briskly over the rail of the *Ticonderoga?*"

I dressed, stuck the screw driver under the splints on my

left leg, and got back to bed again. I was no sooner there than the stretcher party appeared and all three of us, still blanket-wrapped, were lowered gently on to the stretchers. The six bearers stooped, caught the handles, and we were on our way.

We were carried straight aft along the main deck passage to the afterdeck. I saw the end of the passage approaching, the grey, cold dawn light replacing the warm electric glow of the passageway, and I could feel my muscles tense involuntarily. The *Ticonderoga* would be in sight in a few seconds along our starboard side, and I wondered if I would dare to look. Would we be tied bow to bow or bow to stern? Would I have won or lost? We came out on the afterdeck. I forced myself to look.

I'd won. Bow to bow and stern to stern. From my low elevation on the stretcher I couldn't see much, but that I could see—bow to bow, stern to stern. That meant that the *Campari*'s after jumbo was unloading from *Ticonderoga*'s afterdeck. I looked again and checked again and there was no mistake. Bow to bow, stern to stern. I felt like a million dollars. A hundred million dollars.

The *Ticonderoga*, a big cargo vessel, dark blue with a red funnel, was almost the same size as the *Campari*. More important, their afterdecks were almost the same height above the water, which made for ease of transfer of both cargo and human beings. I could count eight crates already aboard the afterdeck of the *Campari:* a dozen still to come.

The transfer of human livestock had gone even further: all of the passengers, as far as I could judge, and at least half of the *Campari*'s crew were already standing on the afterdeck of the *Ticonderoga*, making no move, except to brace themselves against the rolling of the ship; their stillness was encouraged by a couple of hard-faced characters in green jungle uniform, each with a machine pistol cocked. A third gunman covered two *Ticonderoga* seamen who were stationed at lowered guardrails to catch and steady men as they stepped or jumped from the afterdeck of the *Campari* to that of the *Ticonderoga* as the two ships rolled together. Two more supervised *Ticonderoga* crew members fitting slings to the crates still to be transferred. From where I lay I could see four other armed men—there were probably many more—patrolling the decks of the *Ticonderoga* and four others on the afterdeck of the *Campari*. Despite the fact that most of them were dressed in a quasi uniform of jungle green, they didn't look like soldiers to me: they just looked like what they were, hardened criminals with guns in their hands, cold-eyed men with their history written in their faces by the lines of brutality and depravity. Although he was maybe a bit short on the side of aesthetic appreciation, there was no doubt but that Carreras picked his killers well.

The sky was low with grey tattered cloud stretching away to the grey indistinctness of a tumbled horizon; the wind, westerly now, was still strong, but the rain had almost stopped, no more than a thin cold smirr of a drizzle, felt rather than seen. Visibility was poor, but it would be good enough to let Carreras see that there were no other ships in the vicinity, and the radarscope, of course, would be working all the time. But apparently the visibility hadn't been good enough to let Carreras see three ropes still attached to the base of the guardrail stanchion on the port side. From where I lay I could see them clearly. To me they looked about the size of the cables supporting the Brooklyn Bridge. I hastily averted my eyes.

But Carreras, I could now see, had no time to look round him anyway. He himself had taken charge of the transshipment of the crates, hurrying on both his own men and the crew of the *Ticonderoga,* shouting at them, encouraging them, driving them on with an unflagging, unrelenting energy and urgency which seemed strangely at variance with his normally calm, dispassionate bearing. He would, of course, be understandably anxious to have the transfer completed before any curious third ship might heave in sight over the horizon, but even so . . . And then I knew what accounted for all the nearly desperate haste: I looked at my watch.

It was already ten minutes past six. Ten past six! From what I'd gathered of Carreras' proposed schedule for the transfer and from the lack of light in the sky I'd have put the time at no more than half-past five. I checked again, but no mistake. Six-ten. Carreras would want to be over the horizon when the Twister went up—he would be safe enough from blast and radioactive fallout, but heaven alone knew what kind of tidal wave would be pushed up by the explosion of such an underwater nuclear device— and the Twister was due to go up in fifty minutes. His haste was understandable. I wondered what had held him up. Perhaps the late arrival of the *Ticonderoga* or the lapse of a longer period of time than he had expected in luring it alongside. Not that it mattered now.

A signal from Carreras and it was time for the stretcher cases to be transferred. I was the first to go. I didn't much fancy the prospect of the brief trip; I'd just be a reddish stain spread over a couple of hundred square feet of metal if one of the bearers slipped as the two big ships rolled together, but the nimble-footed seamen probably had the same thought in mind for themselves, for they made no mistake. A minute later and both other stretchers had been brought across.

We were set down near the for'ard break of the after-deck, beside our passengers and crew. In a group slightly to one side, with a guard all to themselves, stood a few officers and maybe a dozen men of the *Ticonderoga*'s crew. One of them, a tall, lean, angry-eyed man in his early fifties with the four gold rings of a captain on his sleeves and carrying a telegraph form in his hand, was talking to McIlroy, our chief engineer, and Cummings. McIlroy, ignoring the sudden lift of the guard's gun, brought him across to where we'd been set down.

"Thank God you all survived," McIlroy said quietly. "Last time I saw you three I wouldn't have given a bent penny for any of your chances. This is Captain Brace of the *Ticonderoga*. Captain Brace, Captain Bullen, Chief Officer Carter."

"Glad to make your acquaintance, sir," Bullen whispered huskily. "But not in these damnable circumstances." No question about it, the old man was on the way to recovery. "We'll leave Mr. Carter out of it, Mr. McIlroy. I intend to prefer charges against him for giving undue and unwarranted aid to that damned monster Carreras." Considering I'd saved his life by refusing to let Doc Marston operate on him, I did think he might have shown a little more gratitude.

"Johnny Carter?" McIlroy looked his open disbelief. "It's impossible!"

"You'll have your proof," Bullen said grimly. He looked up at Captain Brace. "Knowing that you knew what cargo you were carrying, I should have expected you to make a run for it when intercepted, naval guns or no naval guns. But you didn't, did you? You answered an SOS, isn't that it? Distress rockets, claims that plates had been sprung in the hurricane, sinking, come and take us off? Right, Captain?"

"I could have outrun or outmanoeuvred him," Brace said tightly. Then, in sudden curiosity, "How did you know that?"

"Because I heard our first mate here advising him that it was the best way to do it. Part of your answer already, eh, McIlroy?" He looked at me without admiration, then back at McIlroy. "Have a couple of men move me nearer that bulkhead. I don't feel too comfortable here."

I gave him an injured glance but it bounced right off him. His stretcher was shifted and I was left more or less alone in front of the group. I lay there for about three minutes, watching the cargo transfer. A crate a minute, and this despite the fact that the manilla holding the after ends of the two vessels together snapped and had to be replaced. Ten minutes at the most and he should be all through.

A hand touched my shoulder and I looked round. Julius Beresford was squatting by my side.

"Never thought I'd see you again, Mr. Carter," he said candidly. "How do you feel?"

"Better than I look," I said untruthfully.

"And why left all alone here?" he asked curiously.

"This," I explained, "is what is known as being sent to Coventry. Captain Bullen is convinced that I gave unwarranted help or aid, or some such legal phrase, to Carreras. He's not pleased with me."

"Rubbish!" he snorted.

"He heard me doing it."

"Don't care what he heard," Beresford said flatly.
"Whatever he heard, he didn't hear what he thought he
did. I make as many mistakes as the next man, maybe
more than most, but I never make a mistake about men.
. . . Which reminds me, my boy, which reminds me. I
can't tell you how pleased I am—and how delighted.
Hardly the time and place for it, but nevertheless my very
heartiest congratulations. My wife feels exactly the same
way about it, I assure you."

It was taking me all my time to pay attention to him.
One of the crates was swinging dangerously in its slings,
and if one of those crates dropped, fell on the deck, and
burst open to reveal its contents, I didn't see that there
was going to be much future for any of us. It wasn't a
thought I liked to dwell on; it would be better to turn my
mind to something else, like concentrating on what Julius
Beresford was saying.

"I beg your pardon," I said.

"The job at my Scottish oil port." He was half impatient, half smiling. "You know. Delighted that you are
going to accept. But not half as delighted as we are about
you and Susan. All her life she's been pursued, as you can
guess, by hordes of gold-digging dead beats, but I always
told her that when the day came that she met a man who
didn't give a damn for her money, even though he was a
hobo, I wouldn't stand in her way. Well, she's found him.
And you're no hobo."

"The oil port? Susan—and me?" I blinked at him.
"Look, sir—"

"I might have known it, I might have known it!" The
laugh was pretty close to a guffaw. "That's my daughter.
Never even got round to telling you yet. Wait till my wife
hears this!"

"When did she tell you?" I asked politely. When I'd
last seen her about two-fifteen that morning I would have
thought it the last thing in her mind.

"Yesterday afternoon." That was even before she had
made the job proposal to me. "But she'll get round to it,
my boy, she'll get round to it."

"I *won't* get round to it!" I didn't know how long she had been standing there, but she was there now, a stormy voice to match stormy eyes. "I'll *never* get round to it. I must have been mad. I'm ashamed of myself for even thinking. I heard him, Daddy. I was there last night with the others in the sick bay when he was telling Carreras that the best way of stopping the *Ticonderoga* was—"

A long piercing blast on a whistle brought the tale of Carter's cowardice to a merciful end. Immediately green-shirted armed men began to appear from other parts of the *Ticonderoga,* from the bridge and engine room where they'd been on guard during the transshipment, which was now finished except for one last crate. Two of the men with guns, I noticed, were dressed in blue Merchant Navy uniforms: those would be the radio officers Carreras had introduced aboard the *Ticonderoga.* I looked at my watch. Six twenty-five. Carreras was cutting it fine enough.

And now Carreras himself had jumped across to the afterdeck of the *Ticonderoga.* He said something to Captain Brace. I couldn't hear what it was, but I could see Brace, his face hard and grim, nodding reluctantly. Carreras arranging for the transfer of the coffins. On his way back to the rail he stopped beside me.

"You see that Miguel Carreras keeps his word. Everybody safely transferred." He glanced at his watch. "I still need a lieutenant."

"Good-bye, Carreras."

He nodded, turned on his heel and left as his men brought the coffins on to the afterdeck of the *Ticonderoga.* They handled them very reverently indeed, with a tender delicacy that showed they were only too aware of their contents. The coffins were not immediately recognisable as such: in the final gesture of the consummate actor paying the minutest attention to the last detail in his role, he had draped them with three Stars and Stripes. Knowing Carreras, I was pretty sure that he'd brought them all the way from the Carribbean.

Captain Brace stooped, lifted a corner of the flag on the coffin nearest to him, and looked down at the brass plaque with the name of Senator Hoskins on it. I heard a quick indrawing of breath, saw that Susan Beresford, hand to her parted lips, was staring down wide-eyed at it, too, remembered that she must be still under the impression that the Twister was inside, reached out, and grabbed her ankle. I grabbed it hard.

"Be quiet!" I muttered fiercely. "For heaven's sake shut up!"

She heard me. She kept quiet. Her old man heard me, but he kept quiet also, which must have taken quite a bit of doing on his part when he saw me with my hand round his daughter's ankle. But the ability to keep expressions and emotions buttoned up must be among the most elementary training for an aspiring multimillionaire.

The last of Carreras' men were gone, Carreras with them. He didn't waste any time wishing us "bon voyage" or anything of the kind; he just ordered ropes cast off and disappeared at speed for the bridge. A minute later the *Campari* was under way and, her afterdeck haphazardly packed with crates, was slewing round and heading away towards the east.

"Well," Bullen said into the heavy silence, "there he goes, the murderer. With my ship, damn his soul!"

"He won't have it for long," I said. "Not even half an hour. Captain Brace, I advise you—"

"We'll dispense with your advice, Mister." Captain Bullen's voice was a series of rattraps snapping shut, the blue eyes very frosty indeed.

"This is urgent, sir. It's imperative that Captain Brace—"

"I gave you a direct order, Mr. Carter. You will obey—"

"Will you please be quiet, Captain Bullen?" Respectful exasperation, but more exasperation than respect.

"I think you'd better be listening to him, sir," the bo'sun put in, gravely unhappy. "Mr. Carter was not idle last night, unless I'm much mistaken."

"Thanks, bo'sun." I turned to Captain Brace again. "Phone the officer of the watch. Due west 180 degrees from the *Campari* and full speed. No, emergency power. *Now,* Captain Brace."

The urgency in my voice got through. For a person who had just lost one hundred and fifty million dollars in gold Brace reacted surprisingly quickly and well to the man who had just caused him to lose it. He gave a few quick words of instruction to a junior officer, then turned a coldly speculative gaze on me.

"Your reasons, sir?"

"In number four hold of the *Campari* Carreras is carrying an armed atomic bomb with the time fuse running out, the Twister, the new missile stolen from the Americans a week or so ago." A glance round the strained, incredulous faces of the listeners showed that they knew what I was talking about all right; it showed clearly that they couldn't believe it. "The Twister—"

"Atomic bomb?" Brace's voice was harsh and too loud. "What damned rubbish—"

"Will you listen? Miss Beresford, am I telling the truth?"

"You're telling the truth." Her voice was unsteady, her green eyes jumpy and still on that coffin. "I saw it, Captain. But—"

"So," I said. "The bomb. Armed. Due to go off in"—I glanced at my watch—"less than twenty-five minutes. Carreras knows it's due to go off then. That's why he's in such a tearing hurry to get away: he imagines the Twister is aboard here. And that's why I'm in such a tearing hurry to go in the opposite direction: I know it's not."

"But it *is* here," said Susan violently. "It is, you know it is! That coffin! There!"

"You're wrong, Miss Beresford." The *Ticonderoga* was picking up speed now, the rumbling thrust of her propellor shaft vibrating through the deck plates. I wouldn't have put it past Carreras to have had his glasses trained on our afterdeck as long as he possibly could, so I lay quietly where I was for the next ten or fifteen seconds while about forty pairs of frankly terrified eyes stared at the flag-shrouded coffins. Then the poop of the *Ticonderoga* had swung round to the east, the *Campari* was blocked from sight, and I was out of my blankets, ripping off the outside blankets and splints and fishing out the concealed screw driver before getting stiffly to my feet. The effect upon

passengers and crew, who had believed implicitly that
Chief Officer Carter had a compound fracture of the thigh,
was startling, to say the least. But I had no time to consider
effects. I hobbled to the nearest coffin and pulled the flag
clear.

"Mr. Carter"—Captain Brace was by my side—"what
on earth are you doing? Criminal though Carreras may be,
he told me Senator Hoskins—"

"Ha!" I said. With the handle of the screw driver I
rapped out three sharp double knocks on the lid of the
coffin: three knocks came in reply. I glanced round the
ever-closing ring of watchers; a cameraman should have
been there, recording those expressions for posterity.

"Remarkable recuperative powers, those American sen-
ators," I said to Captain Brace. "You just can't keep
them down. You'll see."

I'd the lid off that coffin in two minutes flat: in coffin-lid
removing, as in everything else, practice makes perfect.

Dr. Slingsby Caroline was as pale as any corpse I'd
ever seen. He looked as if he had been frightened to death.
I didn't blame him: there must be lots of harrowing ex-
periences calculated to drive a man round the bend, but
I think being screwed down in a coffin for about five hours
must beat the lot. Dr. Caroline wasn't yet round the bend,
but he'd been aproaching it pretty fast, with the throttle
wide open, by the time I got to him. He was shaking like
a broken bedspring, his eyes wide with fear, and he could
hardly speak; that knock of mine must have been the sweet-
est music he'd ever heard.

I left the ministrations to other hands and headed for
the next coffin. The lid on this one was either pretty stiff
or I was pretty weak, and I wasn't making much progress
when a burly seaman from the *Ticonderoga*'s crew took
the driver from my hand. I wasn't sorry to let it go. I
looked at my watch. Seventeen minutes to seven.

"And this time, Mr. Carter?" It was Captain Brace
once more at my elbow, a man whose expression clearly
showed that his mind had given up trying to cope. It was
understandable enough.

"Conventional explosive with a time setting. I think it's

meant to blow up the Twister in sympathetic detonation if the Twister's own time mechanism doesn't work. Frankly, I don't know. The thing is that even this could sink the *Ticonderoga*."

"Couldn't we—couldn't we just heave it over the side?" he asked nervously.

"Not safe, sir. About due to go off and the jar of its hitting the water might be just enough to trigger off the clock. It would blow a hole the size of a barn through the side of your ship. . . . You might get someone to unscrew the third lid too."

I looked at my watch again. Fifteen minutes to seven. The *Campari* was already hardly more than a dark smudge far down on the lightening horizon to the east, six, perhaps seven miles away. A fair distance off, but not far enough.

The lid was clear of the second coffin. I pulled back the covering blankets, located the primer and the two slender leads to the inset detonator, and gingerly sliced through these, one at a time, with a knife. Just to be on the safe side, I threw detonator and primer over the side. Two minutes later I'd rendered the time bomb in the third coffin equally harmless. I looked round the afterdeck; if those people had any sense, the place should have been deserted by now. No one seemed to have stirred an inch.

"Mr. Carter," Bullen said slowly. He'd stopped glaring at me. "I think perhaps you owe us a little explanation. This business of Dr. Caroline, the coffins, the—the substitutions . . ."

So I gave it to him, highly condensed, while everybody crowded round, and at the end he said, "And I think maybe I might owe you a small apology." Contrite, but not going overboard about it. "But I can't get the thought of the Twister out of my head—the Twister and the *Campari*. She was a good ship, Mister. Damn it, I know Carreras is a villain, a monster, a man surrounded by cutthroats. But did you *have* to do it this way? To condemn them all to death? Forty lives on your hands?"

"Better than a hundred and fifty lives on Carreras' hands," Julius Beresford said sombrely. "Which is what it would have been but for our friend here."

"Couldn't be done, sir," I said to Bullen. "The Twister was armed and locked in position. Carreras has the key. The only way to render that bomb safe would be to tell Carreras and let him unlock it. If we'd told him before he'd left here, sure, he'd have disarmed it, then he would have killed every man and woman on the *Ticonderoga*. You can bet what you like that the generalissimo's last instruction was: 'No one must live to talk about this.' "

"It's still not too late," Bullen said insistently. He wasn't giving a damn about Carreras, but he loved the *Campari*. "Once we're under way there's no chance of his being able to board us again and kill us, even assuming he comes after us. We can dodge whatever shells—"

"One moment, sir," I interrupted. "How do we warn him?"

"By radio, man, by radio! There's still six minutes. Get a message—"

"The *Ticonderoga*'s transmitters are useless," I said wearily. "They're smashed beyond repair."

"What?" Brace caught my arm. "What? Smashed? How do *you* know?"

"Use your head," I said irritably. "Those two bogus wireless operators were under orders to wreck the transmitters before they left. Do you think Carreras wanted you sending out SOSs all over the Atlantic the moment he took off?"

"The thought hadn't even occurred to me." Brace shook his head and spoke to a young officer. "On the phone. You heard. Check."

He checked and was back in thirty seconds, his face grave. "He's right, sir. Completely smashed."

"Our friend Carreras," I murmured. "His own executioner."

Two seconds later and five minutes ahead of schedule the *Campari* blew itself out of existence. She must have been at least thirteen miles away; she was well hull-down over the horizon, and the high square bulk of the *Ticonderoga*'s raised poop lay in our direct line of sight, but, for all that, the searing blue-white glare that was the heart of the exploding bomb struck at our cringing wounded eyes with all the strength of a dozen noonday suns while it momentarily highlit the *Ticonderoga* in blinding white and shadows blacker than night, as if some giant searchlight had been switched on only yards away. The intense whiteness, the murderous dazzlement, lasted no more than the fraction of a second—although its imprint on the eye's retina lasted many times longer—and was replaced by a single bar-straight column of glowing red fire that streaked up into the dawn until it pierced the cloud above; and, following that, a great column of boiling seething-white water surged up slowly from the surface of the sea, incredibly slowly, seemed to reach halfway up to the clouds, then as slowly began to fall again. What little was left of the shattered and vaporised *Campari* would have been in that gigantic waterspout. The *Campari* and Carreras.

From birth to death that waterspout must have taken a full minute, and it was only seconds after it had vanished and the eastern horizon became clear again that the single flat thunderclap of sound followed by the deep, menacing rumble of the after-explosion and accompanying shock waves came at us over the surface of the sea. Then all was silence, profound and deathly.

"Well, Dr. Caroline," I said conversationally, "at least you have the satisfaction of knowing that the damned thing works."

He didn't take me up on my conversational gambit. No one took me up on it. They were all waiting for the tidal wave, but no tidal wave came. After a minute or two a long, low, very fast-moving swell bore down on us from the east, passed under the *Ticonderoga,* made her pitch heavily perhaps half a dozen times, and then was gone. It was Captain Brace who was the first of all of them to find his voice.

"That's it, then, Captain Bullen. All gone up in smoke. Your ship and my one hundred and fifty million dollars in gold."

"Just the ship, Captain Brace," I said. "Just the ship. As for the twenty vaporised generators, I'm sure the United States Government will gladly recompense the

Harmsworth and Holden Electrical Engineering Company."

He smiled fraintly; heaven knows he couldn't have felt like smiling.

"There were no generators in those crates, Mr. Carter. Gold bullion for Fort Knox. How that devil Carreras—"

"You *knew* there was gold in those crates?" I asked.

"Of course I did. Rather, I knew we had it on board. But there had been a mistake in marking the crates. So much damned secrecy, I suppose, that one hand didn't know what the other hand was doing. According to my manifest, the crates of gold were the for'ard twenty on the upper deck, but an Admiralty message last night informed me of the mistake that had been made. Rather it informed those damned renegades of radio operators. Never showed it to me, of course. They must have radioed the news to Carreras, and the first thing they did when they tied up alongside was to give him the written message itself as confirmation. He gave it to me as a souvenir," he added bitterly. He held out his hand with the form in it. "Want to see it?"

"No need." I shook my head. "I can tell you word for word what's in that cable. 'HIGHEST PRIORITY URGENT IMMEDIATE REPEAT IMMEDIATE ATTENTION MASTER FORT TICONDEROGA: GRAVE ERROR IN LOADING MANIFEST: SPECIAL CARGO NOT REPEAT NOT IN FOR'ARD TWENTY CRATES FOR'ARD DECK MARKED TURBINES NASHVILLE TENNESSEE BUT REPEAT BUT IN FOR'ARD TWENTY CRATES AFTERDECK MARKED GENERATORS OAK RIDGE TENNESSEE: INDICATIONS YOU MAY BE RUNNING INTO HURRICANE ESSENTIAL SECURE AFTERDECK CARGO EARLIEST: FROM THE OFFICE OF THE MINISTER OF TRANSPORT BY HAND OF VICE-ADMIRAL RICHARD HODSON DIRECTOR NAVAL OPERATIONS.' "

Captain Brace stared at me.

"How in the name of—"

"Miguel Carreras also had a manifest in his cabin," I said. "Marked—and correctly—exactly the same as yours. I saw it. That radio message never came from London. It came from me. I sent it from the wireless office of the *Campari* at two o'clock this morning."

It was a long silence indeed that followed; predictably enough, it was Susan Beresford who finally broke it. She moved across to Bullen's stretcher, looked down at him, and said, "Captain Bullen, I think you and I both owe Mr. Carter a very great apology."

"I think we do, Miss Beresford. I think we do indeed." He tried to scowl, but it didn't quite come off. "But he told me to shut up, mind you. Me. His captain. You heard him?"

"That's nothing," she said in dismissal. "You're only his captain. He told me to shut up, too, and *I'm* his fiancée. We're getting married next month."

"His fiancée? Getting—getting married next month?" In spite of the pain Captain Bullen propped himself up on one elbow, stared uncomprehendingly at each one of us in turn, then lay back heavily on his stretcher. "Well, I'll be damned! This is the first I've heard of this."

"It's the first Mr. Carter has heard of it, too," she admitted. "But he's hearing it now."

ABOUT THE AUTHOR

ALISTAIR MacLEAN was born in Scotland. He served with the Royal Navy during World War II and was a school teacher until 1955—the year his first novel, *H.M.S. ULYSSES* was published. His other bestsellers include *BEAR ISLAND, CARAVAN TO VACCARES, PUPPET ON A CHAIN, FORCE 10 FROM NAVARONE*, and *THE WAY TO DUSTY DEATH*. As well as being highly successful novels, *ICE STATION ZEBRA, THE GUNS OF NAVARONE, WHERE EAGLES DARE, BREAK-HEART PASS*, and *PUPPET ON A CHAIN* were also made into motion pictures.